PRINCESS
OF
PEACE

ANTHONY J. RANKINE

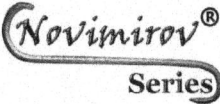

The Family Novimirov® Series
Princess of Peace™
Copyright 2015, Anthony J. Rankine.
All rights and trademarks reserved.

SUGGESTED CATALOGING DATA
Rankine, Anthony J. The Family Novimirov: Princess of Peace

Summary: Novel, Fiction. Romance, Thriller, Religion, Espionage, Terror.

Novimirov® Series
www.novimirov.com

DIOXINOMICS®
www.dioxinomics.com

Tony Rankine
www.ajrankine.com

www.PenorSword.com

Cover Acknowledgements: iStockPhoto, Wiki Commons.
Book Design and Production: Studio Kazinski, Helsinki, Finland.
Trademarks: Novimirov®, Dioxinomics®, Princess of Peace™

ISBN: 978-0-9797320-5-8 (trade paper)
Published by Penors Word Press.
in the United States of America.

PRINCESS

OF

PEACE

Romance in the Gothic Tradition.
Politics in the Stalinist Mold.
Truth is an Inquisition.
History unfolds like the Book of Revelation.

Moscow, Dawn
September 12, 2005

Standing 'cargo in hand,' and snarled within the crowded 3-Day-Visa line at Passport Control, Alfredo's thumping heart slowed as he focused his thoughts on the legitimate side of his visit — How the prospect of a romantic lunch with Natalia might unfold.

The broad-shouldered passenger ahead of him moved off. The rag-shaved guard nursing an AK-49 gave him an affirmative nod, and Alfredo stepped across the yellow tape and came face-to-glass with the immigration control officer. Apprehension eased as he laid eyes on the platinum blonde fleshing out what was an otherwise drab olive-gray, Soviet-starched dress shirt. Behind the glass partition, Miss Blondinka[1] opened a welcoming palm and beckoned Alfredo for his entry papers. He ducked his passport and arrival forms through the meager cavity below the bulletproof glass before taking ownership of his arrival by striking the classic pose of Italian *sprezzatura*.[2]

Blondinka eyed him up and down, flipped open the passport and inspected the photo-ID page. Without looking up, she pointed to a rectangular fingerprint scanner mounted flush with the counter and instructed 'Mr. Borges' to place his right thumb over its aqua-blue surface.

The Tuscan in Alfredo reacted on instinct.

"I'm not American. I'm Italian. *I-tal-ian-ski.*"

---

1 Miss Blondie (Russian)
2 Well-mannered but artful nonchalance (Italian)

All pretense at amiability vanished in a blink. Blondinka raised her head, pursed her lips but kept the tone official.

"New rules for all you aliens. Press your thumb, here."

And, she gestured from the other side of the glass.

Alfredo made an indignant swipe across the scanner.

Blondinka rapped the glass with her knuckle and raised her voice.

"*Nyet!*[1] Hold your thumb still. Three seconds."

Militsia Officer Rag-Shave stood his station but glared over. Alfredo noticed and taking measured breaths, he repeated the process without delay.

One and Two and Three.

"*Da.* Good," Blondinka confirmed, fiddling with a computer mouse.

Alfredo shifted his weight to his right side, but the back of his shoulders remained clenched in dread. Under the identity of 'Umberto Julio Borges', his false passport was an old-style Italian one without any biometric identification data. But, now, this unwelcome kink at passport control had attached his thumbprint to his face and his face to a dummy passport. And, worse, all this evidence was being compiled and locked away in a secret Russian database while he stood naked before the Stalin-era laws of border control.

Before he realized it, she slammed a stamp into his passport, thrust it back and waved him through. Without making eye contact with Blondinka or Rag-Shave, and taking possession of his rights, Alfredo deposited his travel documents into the inner-breast pocket of his business suit, plucked his travel bag off the linoleum, turned and left. Having no checked luggage, he cut a hard right for the customs hall. Uppermost in his thoughts — Clear the airport and vanish into the enormity of faceless Moscow without delay.

Five paces down the concourse, a growling German Shepherd blocked his path. No sooner had Alfredo lock eyes on the mongrel than two arms looped under both his armpits and yoked down hard on the back of his neck. The two officers clasped his belt with their free hands and bundled him through a signless security door. It closed behind the dragging tips of his eel-skin Guccis[2] with a metal on metal crack. Arms, once more free to move, Alfredo caught his first real breath, and a half sense of composure returned.

"*Dokument*," came the bark.

As his eyes adjusted focus, Alfredo stared into the underside of a cheek, stubbled with salt-n-peppered hairs barbed like velcro.

"*Dokument*," came a second bark, followed by a poke to his chest.

Alfredo snapped to attention and flushed his passport from his suit. But, before he could tender it, Velcro snatched it from his grasp and flipped it open. The other komrade, a man short in stature and endowed with a pug-eyed face on a tree trunk for a neck, had already unzipped Alfredo's bag and started laying its contents along an examination bench.

---

1 *Nyet* - No. *Da* - Yes. *Dokument* - Passport (Rus).
2 Upscale brand of Italian shoes.

"Jackpot," he blared, removing what appeared to be a Turkish looking Martini shaker and held out the polished bronze trophy at arms-length.

To regain some initiative, Alfredo asked.

"Do you speak Italian or English?"

Breath reeking of Baltic-salted herring, Velcro snapped.

"English. So, no games. Who are you smuggling drugs for?"

"Sir, that funeral urn contains the cremated remains of a dead man."

And, Alfredo removed a letter from his suit and proffered it.

"Please, read this. It's from the Italian Foreign Minister's Office."

Velcro took the letter and scanned it. Composed in formal Russian, it referred to the ashes of one 'Viktor Magufinski' and appeared to explain the matter. But, Klik,[1] their drug dog, never erred, so on reflex the officer persisted with the usual procedure.

"Denis, put the urn aside and get Klik to work. Borges, take a seat."

And, Velcro pointed to the *stool* — a cast-iron, skillet-black monstrosity bolted to the floor. Alfredo made for its butt-molded seat and brushed aside the half-handcuffs riveted to its sides. Velcro flashed a half-smile as the steel rims of the handcuffs clanged against the chair's angle-iron legs.

Atop an ocean-clam coldness that chilled his buttocks and lapped against the undersides of his testicles like a cast-iron bike seat, Alfredo's torso hardened with affront. Because all his personal luggage was monogrammed with the Ursini family crest, he'd borrowed a bag from his knock-about friend, Monsamori. Now, this crap threatened everything. To quell his rising anger, he stared long and hard into the future. He imagined a time when Sergio, his father-in-law to be, would be restored to his domains as the Tsar of All the Russias, and where grim instruments of torment, such as 'The Stool,' would be reserved for political malcontents.

Pug-Eye returned with Klik. Knowing the drill, the dog first sniffed the length of the bench. Next, standing rigid like a hunting hound, the animal's nose compassed the air. In a single bound, Klik pounced on the empty bag that Pug-Eye had tossed to one corner. The dog yelped and pawed. Pug-Eye tugged him back and ordered him to sit. And, then, he stooped over and rechecked the bag for any hint of a concealed compartment. Finding none, he muttered something as he handed the bag off to his komrade. Velcro swiveled hard about. Arm extended, bag in hand, he faced down Alfredo Ursini.

"Borges, show me the secret compartments."

"It's a normal bag, sir. Please. Please, hava dog sniff it thoroughly."

Velcro dropped the bag and gave Pug-Eye further instructions. Once again, Klik ploughed his nose over the bag, corner to corner. The interior was clean, yet somehow a felonious scent suffused from its sailcloth fabric. Undaunted, Velcro continued his hunt to ferret out a crime, at least a bribable one.

"Borges, on your feet. Take off your jacket. Turn out your pockets."

1 Fang (Rus)

Smelling felony, the dog twisted its nose against Alfredo's knee.

Sensing victory, Velcro snarled — "Off with those pants."

Pug-Eye reined Klik back, and the pants fell free. Pug-Eye slackened his grip and, as if in search of truffles, Klik snuffled his slobbering jowls over the trousers. The dog remained mute, not a yip. Pug-Eye ordered the dog to sit, and Velcro picked up the slag-wet cloth. He pulled each of Alfredo's trouser legs inside-out and then back out again. No concealed drugs. Just cloth, polluted with the residue of a mystery narcotic.

Noticing a shadow of finality dawn across the officer's face, Alfredo ventured — "Sir, I'd say the exterior of my bag was contaminated in the overhead luggage compartment, then rubbed against my suit."

Velcro tossed Alfredo's trousers on the examination bench.

"Yes, Borges. So it seems. *So it seems.*"

But, Velcro, a man who could smell the green scent of moola in a rotting pile of rain gutter leaves was not so easily flimflammed by drug scum. He paused to consider his next move, and then abruptly turned to his associate.

"Denis. Have Klik check that urn more thoroughly."

Pug-Eye held the lid of the urn very close to Klik's nose and rotated it. Alfredo remained speechless. The dog puffed intently. Its breath frosted the metal. Alfredo swore he could see an odor dance its malicious way into that wretched creature's charcoal-black nostrils. Yet, Klik raised no alarm. Nothing amiss. Alfredo relaxed, but Velcro refused to relinquish his quest for a payday.

"Borges, the Italian Foreign Ministry letter explains things. However, you have no diplomatic passport. Nor is that bag or urn under diplomatic seal. We've searched and excluded your bag and clothes. How you really became contaminated, still leaves me wondering."

Eyeing the urn intently, Velcro monitored Alfredo's face.

"You need to open that urn."

Unconsciously, Alfredo broadcast his alarm.

Velcro caught it in a flash.

"Definitely. Letter or not, that urn will be opened."

To allay hostility, Velcro softened his tone, "Out of respect, you may do it."

Alfredo thought about showing the Rooskie his business papers but quickly dismissed the idea. It might suggest side-track and heighten suspicion.

"Alright, sir. Please. Please, hold the urn on the bench. Grip it very tightly. I don't want that dog to disturb the ashes of the deceased." And, Alfredo unscrewed the lid with the tenderness of an explosives expert. Twenty solemn rotations later, he lifted it away to reveal a matte-gray ashen powder. Pug-Eye brought Klik's flexing nostrils two finger-widths shy of the opening. No reaction. Alfredo was relieved but not surprised. The top layer was real ashes, and beneath it, lay a wax seal, and beneath that scent-barrier, lay the real cargo. It was very unlikely Klik would detect or react to it any more than he would to gasoline.

"Put the lid back on. Pants too," Velcro said in resignation.

While Alfredo dressed and repacked his belongings for a hasty exit, Velcro painstakingly filled in an investigative form. He left the room and returned with photocopies of all documents as well as a digital camera.

"Borges, hold the urn close to your face."

Suppressing annoyance, Alfredo complied. Velcro took a photo, and as he studied it, Alfredo snuggled the urn back in his bag between his pajamas and his morning-after underwear.

"Borges, stand still again," and Velcro passed Alfredo the ministry letter.

"Hold it close to your face," and Velcro steadied himself for a clean shot.

Alfredo smiled with diplomatic charity. *Click.*

"Your right thumb," Velcro demanded. And, he quickly rapped it against an ink-pad and plonked it down on the lower-right corner of the photocopy of the foreign ministry letter.

"Here's a towelette, Borges."

No sooner had Alfredo wiped his thumb clean of the worst of the ink than Velcro became rushed and insistent once again.

"Put your signature above your thumbprint."

Alfredo retrieved a pen from his suit and signed — *Umberto Borges.* Now, a fake signature on a document riddled with his real fingerprints was on-file. This unchecked adulteration of his personage in less than ten minutes by some Cossack[1] demeaned his fascist pride beyond measure. The day when Russia would beg Sergio to trouble himself and take up the mantle as tsar could not come soon enough.

Retrieving his passport and the original ministry letter from the bench, Alfredo made haste to put both out of sight. Oblivious to the tremors in his right hand, the papers slid smoothly into the silk-lined pocket of his Loro Piana[2] suit. This small gesture of self-repossession atop the luxurious feel of the cashmere glide against the back of his hand reminded Alfredo that he remained a businessman. Indeed, a high executive.

"Thank you, Mr. Borges. You're now free to leave," Velcro snipped.

Sensing that open and free market boldness would get things back on track, Alfredo splayed his wallet open and removed a business card with a pre-folded fifty Euro banknote discreetly paper-clipped to the back. He handed his offering of *Vzyatka*[3] over to Velcro, and politely asked.

"Would it be possible for one of your men to help get me into Moscow without any further hindrance?"

Velcro noted the card's heft between his fingers. And, when the officer flipped it over for confirmation, Alfredo discerned how the curled-hooks on the Cossack's stubble straightened like a pigtail in orgasm and he seized the moment.

1 Cossack, Bolshevik, Chechen, Tatar — Western pejorative terms for Russians
2 Elite brand of hand-tailored Italian suit.
3 Bribe (Rus)

"I'm happy to pay for your help. Examine my card. I'm an executive with Ursini Beer Brewing. Perhaps, you've tried one of our beers. It's very, very popular in southern Europe."

Velcro was dumbstruck. With its distinctive black bear logo, this upscale European brand was highly thought of in Russia. His awe swiftly shifted to embarrassment, and his tone became almost apologetic.

"Sir, this bag is fine. But, the rest of your luggage must clear Customs."

"I've only this one. Just a short business trip."

"Now, I can help. Denis will drive you. Hotel Metropol — right?"

"Correct. But, there's no need for such a long drive. If Denis could drop me off at the most convenient Metro station, that would be excellent."

"Mr. Borges, Denis would be delighted to drop you at the Metropol."

Drop you — the very idea stank of Baltic herring! The last thing Alfredo wanted was to remain within a hands-grasp of Russian officialdom of any complexion. He wanted underground. He wanted large crowds. He held Velcro in his gaze to confirm his appreciation and replied in his best business voice.

"Thank you for your hospitality. Right now, I'm running behind schedule for an important meeting. I'll be checking-in to my hotel after lunch."

Velcro felt no rebuff. After all, he had the man's money. Prudence now dictated putting the whole strip-search-the-wop episode at arms-length.

"Understood, sir. You need Metro station Rechnoy Vokzal."

And, the officer pocketed the business card and the banknote in one well-practiced motion. He explained to his associate that he could leave early to chauffeur Mr. Borges to Rechnoy Vokzal. And, so it was that Pug-Eye and Alfredo vanished through an airport-personnel exit onto a gated parking lot and drove into the quagmire of traffic engirdling Sheremetyevo Airport.

Metro Vladikino

After much give and take, quibbling and reassurance, from the edge of the backseat of the car, Alfredo perched forward and placed a fifty Euro banknote into a grasping hand hovering over Pug-Eye's right shoulder. Metro Vladikino, on the Gray line was the new destination. This way, if anyone expected 'Mr. Borges' to show up at Metro Rechnoy Vokzal, or anywhere else on the Green Line, no such luck. The downside was that the detour to Vladikino would take an additional ten minutes. But, Alfredo figured it would be an easy thirty minutes before any intelligence system, even remotely eager enough, would track down Velcro and thereafter hail Pug-Eye on his mobile phone and discover the change of station.

His mission was now reduced to absolutes. Drop off the 'Cargo.' Collect the diamonds. Have a romantic afternoon with Natalia. And, despite the information furnished on his entry card about a three-day stay at the

Hotel Metropol, 'Mr. Umberto Julio Borges' would be flying the hell out of Moscow tonight.

With time on his hands, he dialed Natalia. As expected, she was blindsided by his call. After apologizing for his unannounced arrival, their conversation turned to meeting for lunch. To his delight, she was free for the whole day.

"So, you're sure about using our Metro?" Natalia said.

"It's no problem," he returned swimming in the lightness of her voice.

"Metro Komsomolskaya, then. Remember, the stairs in the center of the platform. We'll meet at the bottom, on the left side. *Poka*."[1]

And, she hung up.

That Bitch Can Pay the Price

As soon as she was off the phone, Natalia thought about calling Tatiana. She felt flustered because Alfredo had given her no real warning via email. Now came his early morning call, an hour before she would leave for her normal work. Time was short — very short. So she decided the call to Tats could wait until she began the brisk eight-minute march to Metro Ryazanski Prospekt.

There was no time to shower, so in accord with the prime directive of the Veronikas,[2] Russia's amateur espionage corps, she dressed to impress and dabbed a special pheromone-laced perfume around her neck. Fluffing her hair in place in front of the entry-room mirror, she noticed the clock's second hand was about to complete the minute. She launched herself out the door, down six flights of stairs, out the battered steel exit door and bustled her way along the ice-heaved pedestrian slabs of Moscow as fast as her stilettos could take her. She was on approach to Nevkova's blini kiosk, where a morning line jostled for service amid the fragrance of fresh-baked bread, when she realized — she had yet to call FSB[3] Major Tatiana Gratski, her mentor at the Federal Security Bureau. She retrieved her phone from her purse, swept to the left of the throng and hit [SPEED-DIAL#3].

The phone rang and rang. *Damn it! Tats, pick up.*

On reaching the corner of Ulitsa Krasnova, she swerved right. The phone kept ringing and her sense of unease returned. She would have expected headquarters to alert her the moment Ursini had touched down at Sheremetyevo. But, no. He had ambushed her. So it seemed that only she knew Alfredo Ursini was in Moscow. After a second attempt to raise Tatiana failed, she hit [SPEED-DIAL#1] followed by an unlock-code. This routed the call directly to the Lubyanka, the Moscow headquarters of the FSB. After one second of encryption synchronization, the call went through.

"*Privyet*,"[4] said the operator.

1 Bye (Rus)
2 Russia's Amateur Spy Corps. In honor of Veronika Lewintsova, captured by 'Capitalist Pigs' in 1998.
3 FSB - Federalnaya Sluzhba Bezopastnoty- Russia's FBI+CIA all in one.
4 *Privyet* - Hello (Rus).

Natalia wasted no time.

"*Privyet.*[1] *Ya* Veronika 8-5-3. *Nomer* 8-5-3, do you understand?"

Once the operator confirmed number with phone-ID, Natalia continued.

"Good. Please contact Trainer 0-2-3. *Nomer* 0-2-3. Understand?"

Natalia paused to compose herself.

"My message is urgent. Ursini phoned me. He's in Moscow. I am meeting him at the center staircase at Metro Komsomolskaya, thirty to forty minutes from now. Call back with instructions. Should I proceed with the meeting? Call me back to countermand this action. Did you get that operator? The target's name — Alfredo Ursini. Now, please repeat back to me."

Natalia maintained a marching stride. Phone to ear, she glanced at a Fall Fashions poster and side-stepped a crowd congregating around Zhinski's magazine stand. Once clear, the Metro came into view on her far left.

"*Da.* I repeat this is very urgent. *Poka.*"

Natalia snapped her phone closed and resumed a half-jogging pace. Exploiting a break in traffic, six dress swishes put her across the road. Haste was essential because, in twenty minutes, vast hordes would descend on every Metro station, and the system would become overrun with Moscovites from every walk of life. Shuffling along the footpath for forty meters she turned left and navigated a muddy gravel-filled shortcut to reach the south-western entry of Metro Ryazanski Prospekt, the second-most outlying station south on the Purple line. Hearing an inbound train jarring to a halt, she dashed the last ten meters down the escalator, squirmed her way through an exiting group of students and vaulted into the third to rear-most carriage just as the Doors-Are-Closing announcement was concluding. Spying a shimmer of a vacancy between two babushkas, she inquired in customary Russian — "*Mozhna?*"[2] They wiggled aside, and she wedged her sculpted hips between two ungainly buttocks. Only now did she sit back and take stock of the situation in a more personal light.

Her greatest wish was at hand.

Ursini would be her first and last assignment. In the deepest, most tender recesses of her heart stirred anew that magnificent ache — to reunite with Derek Mitchell and enjoy the symphony of love they had before. Her good friend and Veronika trainer, Tatiana Gratski, who had disparaged her interest in Mitchell from the get-go, had made her a promise. And, today, at long last, after Ursini was taken captive, she would hold Tatiana to her word.

She closed her eyes to imagine Derek's lips pressed to hers. But, her daydream did not last long. The train's entry into Metro Proletarskaya mimicked all its prior station entrances — tenacious braking, jolting to a rust-peeling halt, then a gaggle of passengers shuffling out, followed by another streaming in. But, above ground at Proletarskaya, her mobile phone rang, and she answered in protocol.

"Mother, how are you?"

Tatiana meticulously restated the telephone report provided her.

Greatly relieved, Natalia confirmed — "*Da*. That's the situation."

Tatiana had understood her dilemma and was assembling a surveillance squad to tail Ursini. When Tatiana asked for particulars about the rendezvous location, Natalia replied.

"It's the Ring-line. *Eta normalna. Ya—*"[1]

Tatiana cut her off with a censure, and Natalia grasped the problem.

"An alien! Damn, I was rushed. I should've been more precise."

Tatiana issued a brisk set of remedial instructions.

"I'll be there twenty minutes from now," Natalia responded.

Tatiana issued another directive.

"Wait," and Natalia started tapping the keys of her phone.

"Did you receive Ursini's mobile number?" she asked. "Good," and a pause ensued while Tatiana clarified a few things. Natalia wound up the call.

"*Da*, Tatiana. I'll keep things delayed as best I can. *Poka*."[2]

The line went dead.

Her body squirmed with vexation because two new frustrations lay before her. It seemed Ursini was not destined to be captured, at least not immediately. And, more pressing, Metro Komsomolskaya had two platforms, one for the Ring-line and one for the Red-line, which went into the heart of Moscow. It was customary to meet at the base of the central stairs of the Ring-line, not the Red-line, but it was doubtful that Ursini knew this. For now, Tatiana had told her to stand off to one side of the platform and observe him if he showed up. The ambiguous meeting location would give Tatiana the time needed to put together a proper surveillance posse. Until a team was on-site, tailing one man in the subway system with one or two agents was fraught with too great a chance of failure.

Natalia changed trains at Metro Taganskaya. She boarded the rear-most carriage, so that when she alighted at Metro Komsomolskaya, she could conceal herself in the shadowy rear of the platform. Twelve minutes later, she stood in readiness as her train slammed to a halt. Being the last to exit, she weaved her nimble physique through a large crush of people determined to board the train, knowing that mired within a crowd, she could not have been more effectively hidden.

As people dispersed about the platform, she took up position under the archway closest to its rear and scrutinized the top of the central staircase. With her senses on full alert now, behind her ears, the electrified train, which had borne her in, groaned, lurched and zipped out of the station. Another half-minute passed before the platform thinned to a pedestrian trickle, and she had an unobstructed view of the base of the central staircase.

No Alfredo.

1 *Eta normalna. Ya* — This is normal. I (Rus)
2 *Poka* - Bye (Rus)

But, she reckoned that even discounting the possibility he was waiting at the Red-line staircase, she was early. At the far end of the stairway, she noticed a militsia[1] officer with dog roaming the platform. Her focus sharpened, the lights brightened, and she felt less anxious being the lone wolf.

For the third time, another inbound train exited, and the platform petered out to near emptiness. Still no sign of Alfredo. Manageable so far — but with rush hour relentlessly chugging its way to full-steam, this facile wait-and-see strategy would soon become impractical.

The fifth train now exited.

Still no call from Tatiana, and her sense of uncertainty mounted. After the sixth train departed, even her compromised view of the central stairway did not last more than half a minute before an incoming throng replaced the outgoing. She pulled back behind the column. Waiting for Tatiana and the surveillance crew to show, she resumed gazing at the many faces coming down the escalator from Ulitsa Krasnoprudnaya. Her heart shuddered.

There was Derek and *that bitch*, Ludmila.

They're hugging each other! — Her face flushed hot with despair as she obsequiously cowered her head to avoid detection. Her espionage adrenaline was running higher than ever. She closed her eyes and balled her hands under her armpits and jammed herself hard under the cover of the archway. Pressed against a cold wall of granite, her raging stilled, and she realized how she longed to see Derek's face.

She loved that face. A sunny face.

She softened, glanced around the corner and caught the remains of — *A parting kiss!* Her eyes hammered shut as she clenched herself tight and retreated under the archway again — completely concealed and dead to the world. And, all the while, as she shielded herself, muddled hordes of grim-faced humanity shambled rudely past her. Their contentment and their life force, hemming her in from every quarter, only amplified her pent-up frustration. All she sought was her due, nothing extravagant. A return to normal life — life with Derek. She opened her eyes, and her heart exploded. There. All alone. The bitch was standing a mace-squirt away. And, all the energy she held in check for seducing Alfredo Ursini welled up inside her and burst forth.

"You *suka, suka, sukaaa.*"[2]

And, Natalia let the snarl linger.

Ludmila was taken wholly unawares, thinking at first someone had stepped on someone else's foot. But, the last dramatic — *sukaaa* — indicated a demented woman. Reacting on instinct, Ludmila and the nearby crowd created distance by shuffling away from the archway shadows, closer to the illuminated platform edge. The Metro was full of crazies and drunks. In the dimness of the place, everyone worried a knife blade might soon flash bright with white-hot menace.

1 Beat Cop/Police
2 Bitch, Slut (Rus).

Rebuked by the crowd's overt reaction, Natalia blushed and composed herself. To dampen her anger, she refocused on her mission. She scanned the center of the platform, but it had become too crowded. Surveillance was pointless. Only one thought preoccupied her mind — Somewhere in that morass of humanity, and on his way to catch the Red train, Derek's happy soul was trundling along amid the sullen.

Dry heaves of despair feathered the back of her throat. And, to isolate herself from errant emotions, she looked up at the inbound escalator once again. Still no Tatiana. At her back, drafts emanating from the tunnel became discernible, and the rumble of an inbound train grew audible. Its impending arrival felt like a rap on the shoulder. Mindlessly, she glanced over at the track. Ludmila had her back to her. The air of nonchalance emanating from the slut suffused the air with the malice of boiling gasoline, and her torment over her divided loyalties flashed into fiery rage.

Love is courage — And she marched over to the verge of the platform, wheeled about and confronted her nemesis square in the face.

"You have no business being with Derek."

Ludmila feigned indifference and slanted her head as if to look out for the inbound train. But, Natalia sensed she heard Ludmila's every unspoken thought. Tactful mute was nothing more than insolent pantomime. In less than a heartbeat, Natalia clenched her fists — "Don't ignore me, bitch."

Ludmila remained studiously detached.

Stewing in her wretched responsibilities, Natalia pressed her balled fists hard together, knuckle to knuckle, straining to maintain composure. Ludmila, growing unsettled by Natalia's medusian demeanor, took in a fatal glance and succumbed to the nastiness — "Derek left *you*. Please, Miss, kindly go find happiness with your Italian Internet lover."

Please, Miss, Kindly — sounded like taunt and stoked Natalia's fury. As a Moscovite with proper residency papers, she had anticipated meekness from this country bumpkin. She closed her eyes so tightly she felt as if tears jetted the inside of her nose. Her mind thundered — the platform trembled — the air blasted hot. She was a secret agent of the State. She was on a mission of State. She opened her eyes and she launched her fist.

The impromptu punch had no force, except to put Ludmila in shock and cause Natalia to step back. Natalia relished the priceless look of misery on that *suka*'s face. Madness howled — *That bitch can pay the price!*

A heady maelstrom of rage twisted Natalia's body, and in its great unwinding, and with all her momentum behind it, she drove her arm forward. A young, well-dressed man, who had sensed a second strike, launched himself into the gap, holding his briefcase at chest level.

Wham.

Natalia's fist landed squarely on a valise crammed heavy with auspicious legal briefs and memoranda of law. This and the forward movement of

Ludmila's defender caused all of Natalia's punching force to rebound back into her body. She lost her footing and stepped back from the sting of the impact and the unexpectedness of the recoil. As the fog of the pain of her bare-knuckle blow against the briefcase subsided, she realized her peril.

Descending in protest, the high heel of her left shoe was scrawling out a welt of regret in skidding black rubber against the coarse-grained granite that lined the platform verge. Before she could catch breath, her head had angled over the platform's point of no return. Flexing her anchored right-foot only made her feel further off balance. After a shocked silence, Natalia's hearing returned and with it a delirium of sick inevitability swept over her.

A bystander shrieked, but Natalia heard nothing except the monstrous rumble from behind. Brain on reflex, her eyes looked out to lock onto some horizon. A television flashback danced behind her eyes as if in taunt — *Hit the center of the tracks before the train makes contact.*

How simple! — a wee voice inside her brain peeped.

Her throat squinched as if to laugh out and scream at such a ridiculous notion. But, nothing came. Everything seemed fog-black except for the bronze chandeliers along the tunnel ceiling. And, as her head canted further backwards, she noted how each chandelier beamed upward and spent its allure on the beautiful, cream-veined Stalin marble of the ceiling.

Then came lament.

Then a searing millisecond of regret.

Twenty meters down track, framed between her outstretched left thumb and forefinger stared a solitary face frozen in horror. It shone like a full moon. Enormous eyes. Mouth open in full gasp. There stood, the same militsia officer who had earlier provided her a boost of confidence in her mission. He held his hands chest-high as if reaching out to her. Even his dog jolted in shock. Their eyes locked and remained locked — *To die for love.*

Behind her head and shoulders, halogen lights blazed hot. The air heaved and blasted. And, an engineer behind the controls of an inbound train froze in disbelief. Here, out of nowhere, was every driver's worst nightmare.

A fallen woman.

A lost angel.

A solid bunt against the carmine front fender.

Natalia sensed nothing. The juggernaut still had appreciable speed upon impact. And, her hammered corpse arched through the air blanketed in a foamy sea of electric-white tranquility.

The Uncanny Stench of a Chechen

Pug-Eye not only knew his way around beers, but also around Moscow. Like a charioteer in the Hippodrome of Rome, his street-smart driving exploited every footpath and bike thoroughfare. And, so it was, that Alfredo's decision to enter the Metro at Vladikino to evade detection paid off handsomely.

From Metro Vladikino, Alfredo had an uneventful ride down the Grey-line to Metro Novoslbodskaya. There, he changed trains to the Ring-line. Two stations later, he arrived at Komsomolskaya alighting on the opposite side of the platform. Once there, he located the center staircase of the Ring-line, the rendezvous Natalia had intended. Atop the stairway, he had a clear view over one side of the platform but Natalia was nowhere in sight, so he made for the base, as instructed, expecting the crowds to dissipate.

No sooner had he reached the last step then he made inadvertent eye contact with a militsia officer. The look was chilling. And, worse — *The man had another damn dog!* He averted his gaze. And, seeking to put distance between this new menace, he marched for the platform proper as if intending to catch the next train. The minute ticked by uneventfully as he looked down the track, and imitated the crowd. As the verge of the platform became packed solid, he decided to reposition himself closer to the stairs, where Natalia was expecting to meet him. He turned and went to use his arm to gesture a corridor through the masses when a dog started yelping. Then a growling followed by a tugging at his bag. Alfredo glanced down. A paw was clawing it.

"Stop," a voice barked.

Alfredo looked to his left.

Next came the bite — "*Dokument!*"[1]

Alfredo froze dumb.

"*Dokument*," the militsia officer bellowed again, brows furrowed, suspecting Alfredo carried the uncanny stench of a Chechen about him.

Alfredo reminded himself — *I'm a business executive. Stay calm. Calm.*

"*Italianskii*," Alfredo responded in frenzied Russian. Then he slowed his speech to project authority — "*Ya I-tal-ian-skii biz-niz-man.*"

"*Dokument*," the officer thundered again with martial clarity.

Alfredo put his bag between his legs and reached into his left inside-breast pocket. Shuffling the urn letter back in, he pulled out his passport and opened it at the Photo-ID page. The militsia officer snapped the passport out of Alfredo's hand and scrutinized it. Yipping feverishly, the dog kept clawing away at Alfredo's bag. Heart beating frantically, Alfredo stared down at the mongrel.

"Make room. Make room," the officer snipped.

And, the officer straightened his arms to plough out space. Around the platform, the crowd moved back to open out a semicircular arena, in which Officer Kalugin, his dog Thor, and Alfredo stood hemmed in on three sides.

"Open your bag," snarled Kalugin in perfect Russian.

1 Passport (Rus)

And, rapping Alfredo's bag impatiently with his shoe out rolled his command again — "*Ot-kriv-ai.*"[1]

Alfredo glanced up and stood dumb-faced pretending not to understand, but within the crowd a voice speaking English entered the stand-off.

"Open your bag. The officer wants to inspect it."

"Thank you." And, Kalugin growled at Alfredo — "Open!"

"I understand. Please, read this." And, Alfredo retrieved the ministry letter from his suit. The English-speaking stranger unfolded the letter.

"The officer doesn't understand. Allow me," he said.

"Thank you. It's from the Italian Foreign Ministry."

Kalugin kept his eyes glued to Alfredo and rapped the bag even harder. Alfredo pulled his bag from between his legs, opened it and wasted no time extracting the urn because that would obviously be the focus of attention. Alfredo addressed the helpful stranger because he knew the officer's blatant hostility would only complicate things.

"Please, explain. This funeral urn contains the ashes of a dead man."

The moment Kalugin caught sight of the urn, he pocketed Borges' passport, brushed the loop of the dog-leash up to his elbow and yanked the urn out of Alfredo's hands. He examined it more than suspiciously because Moscow was moving heaven and earth to put an end to the havoc caused by Afghan opium shipments into Russia. Thor's reaction and this Islamic-looking vessel were proof positive that he had cornered a drug smuggler.

The stranger addressed the officer.

"This is an official diplomatic letter certifying that this funeral urn contains the ashes of a Mr. Viktor—"

Kalugin stopped paying attention. A sudden scream triggered him to wrench about to his right and face uptrack. To his horror, he saw a woman at the edge of the platform angled against the lights of an inbound train. Her pitiful gaze shocked him to action. He lurched out on reflex, as if he might catch this poor wretch. Losing all semblence of traction in his hands, the urn slipped from his grasp and began its descent.

Thor smarted with a yelp and jumped up. His master had clobbered him something nasty. Turning to lick its bruised pelt, the eyes of the drug dog tracked the progress of a big ballie thingy wobbling toward the lip of the platform.

Alfredo could not believe it. The moment the urn vanished from sight, he knew he had but one chance. Taking a deep breath, he lunged between the waists of the throng and pushed with all his might.

The urn, not falling at any appreciable speed, bounced off the inner rail. Its base came to rest against the wall. And, its neck lay prone atop the steel track. Unperturbed by the train's blinding halogen lights, Kalugin's gaze remained fixed on that lump of a woman whose body had now been slammed back onto the platform. The locomotive wheels sheared the neck of the urn and wrenched it away from the wall. Whirling like a top, the sundered vessel spewed its ultra-fine powdery contents all over the track. And, the inbound air drafts caused a

1 Open! (Rus).

thick cloud of white to billow up around the sides of the carriages, making it appear the undercarriage was on fire. The semicircle of people around Kalugin lurched backward in panic. Only then did he notice that his drug smuggler had vanished into the mob. He breathed in deep to yell out — Stop that man — but realized crowd control was his new priority.

"Stay calm. It's harmless. Harmless ashes."

And, for the next minute, Kalugin shouted down hysteria.

Kode Krasni

When his eyes flinched on impact, the train driver had no idea what happened to the suicide. Once the train stopped, he opened the doors for the passengers to exit. Almost immediately, Dimitri Polenchenko, the station master, rapped the viewport window to the driver's cabin and entered. He glanced at the nameplate pinned to the driver's shirt, and while raising his badge in his left hand, he wasted no time.

"Engineer Lavrov. It's 'Kode Krasni,'[1] until I give clearance."

And, Polenchenko brought the walkie-talkie in his right hand to his ear.

For the train driver, an eternity passed before the station master muttered.

"Corpse on platform, *harosho*. And, the smoke?"

The train driver went to speak. Badge, still palmed in hand, Polenchenko brought his left finger to his lips. Another moment passed.

"Dust? Huh? *Take* a second look. … Human ashes. OK, resume operations. Also get Prospekt Mira on the horn and rustle up a substitute driver."

As Polenchenko clipped his walkie-talkie to his belt, he addressed Lavrov.

"Komrade, quick, close the doors. We're exiting — Top speed. You'll sub out at Prospekt Mira and give a statement to the militsia, there."

And, the train surged hard out of the stationonly a minute behind schedule and generated a monstrous draft of air that whipsawed and sucked another enormous cloud of white powder off the tracks, thoroughly saturating the station and the tunnel in a deeper smoky haze. Only thirty seconds after Lavrov's train left, did the next incoming train repeat this process. And, so on.

Thus, it was, at 8:21a.m, with the onset of rush hour, did the diffusion of irreversible death over the entire Metro system of Moscow begin.

Okhotni Ryad

Once Alfredo cleared the cordon of people on the platform, he knew he had a handsome chance for safety. He darted up the center staircase to the Red-line crosswalk and made for the connecting station. To blank his mind from the numbness of bewilderment, he repeated but one refrain.

Fumblefingers, Fumblefingers, corrupt commie Fumblefingers.

It grew louder in outrage with his every stride.

1 *Kode Krasni* - Code Red. *Harosho* - Got it (Rus)

Then, to his great relief, Alfredo felt the telltale rumble of an inbound train, so he redoubled his pace. Arriving at the top of the staircase to the platform below, he found his getaway train clattering to a halt. Without pause and before the first exiting crowds would have a chance to ascend, he vaulted down the stairs two by two. Once he hit the platform proper, he took his first gulp of air, revived, muscled through the skelter of people and angled his way through a half-closed door into one of the forward carriages. Once safe inside, Alfredo took a deep and wholesome breath and was greeted by the welcome stench of stale beer.

The train's direction of travel was not important. He needed distance, as far and as fast as possible from this disaster. It wasn't until he reached Metro Lubyanka, the station under the infamous KGB prison, now headquarters to the FSB that he calmed sufficiently to realize that his rackety-rack, sheet-metal train was headed into the heart of Moscow. The best circumstance possible, because an upscale cosmopolitan center is always the safest place for any well-dressed foreigner, especially one who just lost his passport and entry document. 'Mr. Umberto Julio Borges' had entered the country legally but 'Mr. Alfredo Constanzo Leonardo Ursini,' a Western executive from Italy, had inexplicably materialized as if from thin air. Suddenly collecting his full wits, he popped his phone battery — zero signals.

Three minutes later, the train entered Metro Okhotni Ryad. He made a dignified exit. And, staying below ground, he strolled around the vast multi-level subterranean Okhotni Ryad shopping complex just like any café or boutique seeking tourist, except this *tureest*[1] walked as far south as possible.

In the pricey ambiance and plain-sight oasis of an upscale Maison de Café, built under the onetime stables of Tsar Alexander III, adjacent to the concourse serving the West Gate of Kremlin itself, Alfredo located a men's room and washed up. He downed a double-sucre crème-brulé cappuccino to steel himself before texting his father in Florence and Grand Duke Sergio Romanov in Rome. Through Ernesto, Sergio's brother-in-law at the Italian Foreign Ministry, they would have the best and most available means to extricate him from this fumble-fingered mess. Once [SENT] was confirmed, he popped the battery, once again, and left.

Men Maybe Simple Creatures

At Komsomolskaya, station guards converged on the Ring-line platform to help Officer Kalugin re-impose order. All incoming escalators were shut down. All persons were directed to make a quick exit. Another train would be along shortly, and those still on the platform were permitted to board and clear the area.

Derek had been halfway up the staircase to the Red-line when the station went into uproar. He turned, and his heart stopped cold. Clouds of smoke wafted along the platform. He frantically searched for Ludmila. He waved, and she reciprocated. And, he wasted no muscle slicing his way through the roiling throng, until they reunited near the base of the escalator serving Ulitsa Krasnoprudnaya, which they had used to enter the Metro.

1 Tourist (Rus).

Jammed with people, the escalator paddled its way upwards, eventually lifting them above the haze and back to street level. Derek held Ludmila's shivering body close and tight. She sobbed uncontrollably, while blurting out the gist of what had happened.

"Natalia went berserk. Called me a bitch. I walked away. Then she corners me and screams in my face. Then that *suka* punched me." Her voice melted to pitiful. "She punched again. But, a man stepped in, and her fist hit his briefcase and she fell backwards into the incoming train. There was a flash of electricity when she was struck. Oh Derek, it's so horrible."

Derek felt utterly bereft. A fist for Ludmila had once been a hand trustingly placed in his own. Vibrant yet conflicting sentiments towards Natalia gnawed at him still. But, now, in a fit of uncouth temper, the hussy had been ground to death. His thoughts were torn between the sangfroid of finality and the remembrance of the exquisite tenderness and warmth that once had bathed his spirit when he and Natalia locked eyes that first fateful day in his jewelry store. And, he looked mournfully down at the crown of bronze-brown hair atop the scalp of a woman nuzzled in solace against his left breast. And, stroking her hair, he quietly realized that to spirit himself away into Ludmila for comfort of his own was not an option right now.

Heedless of time, walking close, cuddling and silent, the two trundled their way along Ulitsa Myasnitskaya to Derek's apartment. Once settled inside its warmth, Ludmila's tremors remained relentless, so Derek bade her lie on the bed. He swaddled her in a heavy blanket, and lying by her side, he enfolded himself close to her. She eventually drifted into sleep. And, at that moment, the instant of her slumber, Derek's whole being mellowed to unguardedness for the first time in months. Unmindful about how perverse it was that death has the power to slam close one life, and yet for another, uncork fresh happiness, rivulets of inner-peace trickled through every vein in his body. Unlike the drug-scum murder of Marie, his beloved, pregnant wife, Natalia's wretched manner of death put a sudden end to all the duplicity of emotional containment and numbing equivocation he felt over her betrayal with some wop greaseball months before. Men may be simple creatures, he thought, but why not. For if love is the noblest of all human emotions, why should not a man's true and noble heart forthrightly untether love from all foible of mood, snag of vexation and specter of tragedy.

The Odd Sock Here and There

After twenty worrisome and infuriating minutes of telephone silence from Natalia, Major Tatiana Gratski arrived at Metro Komosomolskaya with her surveillance team. By this time, most of the documentary evidence harvested at Sheremetyevo Airport about a 'drug bust that wasn't' had been forwarded to FSB Lubyanka headquarters, and now lay on the desk of FSB General Basil Andreivich Novimirov.[1]

1 Pronunciation: Nov-ee-meer-ov

At the Metro entrance, Tatiana was disturbed to find the place swarming with plainclothes police. After showing her credentials, Senior Inspector Dimitri Ilyavich Druznin introduced himself and informed her of two events. A train collision involving a woman identified as 'Natalia Vladimirovna Bogomolski'[1] and the escape of an Italian suspected of drug trafficking, identified as 'Umberto Julio Borges.'

Druznin explained his focus was on the drug matter. Tatiana became livid when the inspector revealed the woman as well as all other crime-scene evidence were in a forensics van making its way to Moscow Police Central. She immediately phoned General Novimirov and asked him to use his national security powers to interdict the van before others could investigate its significance.

On General Novimirov's tenuous authority, Tatiana ordered the station closed. But, it took a call twelve minutes later from Basil's superior, FSB Director-General Karl G. Besstrashnikov,[2] to put that order into full and practical effect. Trains could pass through the Ring-line station, but that was all. Militsia were posted to prevent passengers on the Red-line trains from exiting to connect to the Ring-line. At Metro Komsomolskaya, the Red-line was street entry or street exit only.

Tatiana's next task was to contain the 'Metro Komsomolskaya Incident.' Absolutely, no press and no names. She had her team interview every militsia officer and station official on duty and sequestered all persons who recognized the name Umberto Borges. These people were then quarantined at an adjoining Militsia station where Druznin's men conducted follow-up interviews to establish who were primary witnesses.

Twenty-five minutes later, Druznin returned and handed Tatiana a box of evidence bags containing clothing heavily dusted with the mysterious human ashes. And, he stated how two primary witnesses, a militsia officer, family name Kalugin and a bystander, family name Gregoriev, who had read the urn declaration letter from the Italian Ministry of Foreign Affairs, had been provided a fresh change of clothes and were on route to FSB headquarters in two separate cars. Tatiana, who set herself the task of interrogating them, thanked Druznin for culling them out of the mob and keeping them separated. On receiving an SMS confirmation, she informed Druznin that a senior FSB colonel would soon relieve her.

Having waited at the door of her car for over two minutes, she was about to hop in when Colonel Sergei Gratski arrived with an FSB forensics squad.

"Excellent timing my love," she said to him in private. "I've brought the scene under control, but a man's authority might get things done with more alacrity and less back-chat."

"I'm sure you've done everything splendidly, Komrade." Sergei's lips rippled with the tender facetiousness of familiarity — "I suspect you've relegated me to being a husband who need only pick up the odd sock here and there."

In winsome giggle, did Tatiana reply to his caricature of her reputation for fastidiousness. "I certainly hope not, dearest. Such sloppiness on my part wouldn't look good on my spotless service record."

1 Pronounciation: Bog-o-mol-ski
2 Pronounciation: Bes-strash-nik-ov

With a parting kiss, both flashed each other the unspoken intentions of newlyweds under the thralldom of desire — *Bye, Sweet Love. Do you later.*

Doves Cooed and Shat

With Ludmila sound asleep at last, Derek left her side to find solitude in the kitchen. Staring at his favorite pattern of chipped and blistering paint on the wall behind the ironing board, something he called *Dali Gone Sovietski*, he pondered the harvest of love and tranquility he might share in a pristine new life with her. While sipping his third cup of black tea, he went to check the time on his phone and suddenly realized his absent-mindedness. He hit [SPEED-DIAL#3]. On answer, he was routed to Sergei's voice mail. The news could not wait. He immediately dialed his Alpha-One priority access number — the first time he had used the feature. The phone rang again. And, to Derek's relief, it was promptly answered.

"Sergei. It's Derek. I'm at my apartment, not work. There was an accident in the Metro. At Komsomol—"

Sergei cut in and popped a question.

"No, I didn't see Tatiana," Derek replied.

And, as Sergei spoke anew, Derek sensed the man's worried mood and chopped back into the conversation — "Sergei. Sergei, listen. Ludmila was attacked. I'm just calling to tell you I might not get to the store today."

After Sergei calmed the waters, Derek unburdened.

"Sergei, there's also terrible news." He hesitated. "Natalia started a fight. She punched Ludmila and then fell back into an oncoming tra—"

Derek stopped short. Voicing the matter proved unexpectedly painful. Sergei sensed distress and picked up the thread to re-instill composure in his good friend. Derek finally calmed and resumed speaking.

"Oh, you know. Yes, definitely. Ludmila saw it all."

Sergei spoke his piece and posed another question.

"A massive electrical strike," Derek answered. And, feeling cold again, he closed his eyes in remembrance. Natalia's soft skin, a living Nordic white instantly electrified into crackling Egyptian rawhide. From what Sergei had stated about a fire under the train, he now realized her smoking body must have permeated the air. Her ghosted skin had literally bathed his lungs in a final caress. He stopped breathing to suppress the rising nausea of feeling 'The Cannibal.' Again, Sergei sensed his friend's unspoken bereavement and coaxed Derek back from the brink of tears. Derek mustered up a reply.

"No. I was on my way to the Red-line. I located Ludmila and brought her back to my apartment. She was in shock but is sleeping now."

At this point, Sergei knew beyond doubt that Derek and Ludmila were major witnesses to what had actually happened at Komsomolskaya. As an undercover foreign operative working for the FSB, Mr. Derek Mitchell knew much about the diamonds-for-heroin side of the operation, and had some idea about a diamond buyer based in Italy, but he was wholly unaware of the involvement of Romanov. Nor was Derek aware of Natalia's mission, just as she was never aware of his. That was something General Novimirov had ordered for their mutual protection, and it was for the General to decide what would be done next. Sergei fielded a tentative proposal, and Derek stared down hard at his watch to regain his bearings and replied.

"Sure, Sergei. 2:00p.m. Room 327 — right?"

Sergei confirmed and reminded Derek to bring his Lubyanka entry-papers.

"My certificate, got it. *Do svidaniya*."[1]

Call over, Derek inched the phone away from his face and delicately placed it on the kitchen table. He shambled over to the balcony and mindlessly gazed out its double-paneled windows. While perusing a pair of nesting doves roosting on the Marinovski's dung-stained parapet, he noticed Dima Sanchestin, a street vendor, trying to peddle his grandmother's *pierogi*[2] to a stocky man carrying a wisp of a girl on his shoulders. The stranger waved his free hand in annoyance. Derek smiled at the thought — *The schmuck-ski just missed tasting the best damn pierogi in Moscow.*

In silence, he watched life roll on. Doves cooed and shat. Human masses waddled like ducks. *DyaDya Dima* made his pitch time after time. Nothing seemed out of place. And, all the while, oblivious to his own circumstances, tears streamed mercilessly down his cheeks.

The Iron Felix

From his second-floor office on the southern flank of the Lubyanka, hands on hips and looking down at the numb of rust-brown granite that had once been the pediment for a seven-meter statute of Felix E. Dzhenzhinsky, 'The Iron Felix,' FSB General Basil Novimirov[3] laid down the law concerning what he considered a run-amok forensics van. His tone could not have been more acerbic.

"Correct. This is an Alpha-One national security matter. Would you like our president to give you a personal call to explain 'Alpha-One'?"

There was a long delay during which Basil was becoming visibly testy.

"Understand this Komrade Analinko. I'm sending FSB officers down to your forensics lab to confirm compliance. If they discover a whiff of a rumor that you have retained a speck of evidence, then your career is through. Clear?"

He waited for Analinko to finish his piece.

"Yes. Please re-route the vehicle to the Lubyanka at once."

As Analinko unloaded about *what-ifs*, Basil strolled back to his desk.

"Komrade, my hands are tied. The analysis will be delayed another hour or so. But, once here, our lab techs will rapidly get the job done and with the most modern equipment. Now assure me again, there have been no reports of ill health from the white soot or ashes that were released. Correct?"

Analinko re-confirmed what the police had already reported.

"Good, Komrade. Now get cracking. *Poka*."

1 *Do svidaniya* - See you later. *DyaDya* - Uncle (Rus).
2 Russian dumpling
3 Pronunciation: Nov-ee-meer-ov

Returned to Lubyanka headquarters, FSB Major Tatiana Gratski had concluded her formal interview of Oleg K. Gregoriev, the witness who had read the urn letter to Officer Igor G. Kalugin. She and a clinician were partway into drugging Kalugin with gamma-hydroxybutyrate for the second phase of his interrogation when a priority call on her mobile interrupted proceedings. She marched into the empty corridor. Sergei was on the line. He informed her that it was conclusively established that her Veronika Operative, Number 853, Natalia Vladimirovna Bogomolski, had started the fight. The target and witness — Ludmila Olenovna Naristikova. To corroborate — Derek Anthony Mitchell.

Tatiana snapped the phone closed and resigned herself to the bitter fact that she could do nothing to keep Natalia's scandalous behavior in the Metro from sullying her exemplary FSB service record. And, to have Mitchell involved in this was just too damn galling. She stormed back into the interrogation room.

"Is Kalugin in an appropriate state now?" she snipped.

"I made adjustments. I'm positive, Komrade Major."

She exhaled hard to cast off her anger. With her onetime operative gone love-crazy, the preservation of her career now fell squarely upon her burly shoulders. She dug deep to soften her heart and enthuse herself to charm. Her lips curled thick and rutty, as if to kiss the high god of vibrators, and she purred.

"Igor. It's me, dear man. Tatiana. Would you repeat your story, please."

At the sound of her sparkling voice, Igor felt giddy with pleasure.

"Tanya. Yes. Where would you like me to start?"

"Leading up to the collision, darling."

"I was holding the urn. Examining the base for Arabic markings. Then a scream. I swiveled around. The train was entering the station. Against its headlights, I saw a woman falling. Beckoning to me. I lunged forward. Next, a ball of light. Her body tossed onto the platform. The train flashed past and halted. Smoke everywhere. Mr. Gregoriev, the man with that letter from the Italian government, told me the urn had fallen under the train, and human ashes were wafting up into the air. I seized up. Tanya, I'm so ashamed."

"Komrade, you did well. After a traumatic shock, you regained control of the situation. I have the testimony of the station guards and Mr. Gregoriev," she went to touch him, but the clinician grasped her hand,

"No, it will break the trance," he whispered.

"Sweet man, please tell me about this Italian man."

"Yes, Tanya. Thor had been nudging his way through the crowd. We found the problem. Drugs. I examined Borges' passport and was surprised to see it was Italian. He looked Chechen. Like a Muslim. Thor does not make errors detecting drugs. Borges obeyed my instructions after Mr. Gregoriev helped me. Borges handed Mr. Gregoriev a letter. Then he produced an Arabic urn from his bag. Mr. Gregoriev was reading while I was studying that urn. Borges looked scared. Thor kept pawing at his bag. I intended to take Borges to the police station and let an inspector unravel the matter. The last thing I did was check the base of the urn for markings, looking for a clue about its origin of manufacture. Then a scream distracted me. In the panic, Borges ran off. Komrade, I'm so sorry for losing him. That wop must be guilty."

"Dearheart, calm down. It's no great catastrophe." And Tatiana continued to soothe him while seeking to unlock hidden details from his subconscious.

Alpha-One Protocol

Stationed in his office, General Basil Novimirov,[1] who had now taken direct command of the hunt for Ursini, snapped up the telephone receiver. FSB Director-General Karl Besstrashnikov[2] was on the horn. He had called a second time because the president now knew about the bungling at Sheremetyevo Airport and most recently at Metro Komosomolskaya. Basil's chief was troubled about their failure to formulate a new plan of action. The only saving grace was that a crack into the larger Romanov *coup d'etat* conspiracy may have opened up. At issue was how to proceed, given that the whole Ursini-Komosomolskaya matter smelt merely of a drug deal gone haywire.

To stay composed, Basil rose to his feet and replied.

"Sir, twenty minutes ago, we intercepted two SMS messages. One he sent his father, Constanzo, and another to Sergio Romanov. He's made request for safe haven at the Italian Embassy. He said he'd lost his fake 'Borges passport.' Nothing about the Metro. So far, no reply. But, it's obvious Ursini expects the Italian government to secure his escape."

At the mention of 'Escape,' an exasperated Director-General recapitulated his assessment of the day's screw-ups. Basil braced himself. When his boss had calmed, Basil laid out the 'Hunt for Ursini' situation before winding up.

"We must presume Ursini pulled his battery or SIM card and left Okhotni Ryad the moment he sent the SMS. Our wop's a very sly fox, sir."

Sly fox was a poor choice. A boss' hectoring ensued. As Director-General Besstrashnikov sounded off, Basil fingered a copy of the airport photo of Ursini holding an urn next to his face. Once the Director-General had finished his piece, Basil explained how he suspected Ursini trusted no one because of the two 'Romanov Trusted' fences he had busted in order to promote Mitchell as the fence of last resort.

"That's why we're still scrambling, sir," Basil concluded.

Director-General Besstrashnikov pressed Basil about plans going forward. After the Director-General had thrown out his last *What-If*, Basil tackled the issues. Men were posted at Mitchell's Diamond Emporium, at the Italian Embassy and Consulate, and at diplomatic residences. The 'Metro Fire' deception was essential to keep Romanov clueless about the true situation, until the government had exercised its authority to decide where the truth lay.

"Zero press means the script is ours to write," Basil finished.

1 Pronunciation: Nov-ee-meer-ov.
2 Pronunciation: Bes-strash-nik-ov.

Basil kneaded the back of his neck as his boss rattled on. Finally, dunned for reassurance, Basil replied — "Sir, it's not radioactive. Nor biological. It's very possible Ursini was doing a 'human ashes' dry run to test Romanov security. Perhaps, it's a deceased jihadi. A good faith gesture toward their Afghan drug lord allies. But, if it's not ashes, our lab will fingerprint it rapidly using infrared spectroscopy."

The Director-General questioned Basil's over-abundance of caution.

"Sir, I still recommend keeping Metro Komsomolskaya closed. All trains on the Ring-line are running except they don't stop at one station. A minor inconvenience considering the larger unknowns."

Another pause, but Basil started to relax. His brows broadcast relief.

"With any new developments? Of course, sir. *Poka*."

No sooner had Basil re-cradled the handset than his secretary, Elena, called over the intercom. The Moscow Police van containing all the crime scene evidence had cleared security, and its contents were being unloaded and inventoried.

"Good Elena. Also, what's the status of witness interrogations?"

"Sir, Gratski's processing the last primary witness as we speak."

"*Harosho.*[1] I need ten minutes of Do-Not-Disturb."

And, Basil disengaged his intercom.

Grabbing a felt-tipped marker pen from his desk draw, Basil fiddled with it between his fingers. Once he felt decompressed, he sauntered over to his white-board and resumed formulating a gambit to fool Ursini into exposing himself. It took less than two quiet minutes for him to pull it all together. He turned his back to the board, poured a cup of tea and spent another silent minute mulling it over. He next talked out the plan, as if giving a mini-lecture to imaginary peers intent on targeting its potential defects and unseen contingencies. Content that his scheme was ready to run by his superior for a decision, he made for his chair, plucked up the telephone receiver and punched [DIRECT-DIAL#2].

"Sir, I've a plan to skunk out Ursini."

And, Basil laid out the details, until Elena broke in on the intercom.

"Sir, Ursini has uploaded an SMS. I'm sending you a translated copy. It should be on your screen," she said.

"Got it, Elena." And, Basil addressed his boss on the phone — "Sir, did you catch that? I'm copying you an instant message."

After a flurry of keystrokes, Basil resumed speaking.

"It seems Ursini's billions have worked their charm. Here's what I suggest. Let the Italian diplomatic vehicle pick up Ursini. Then we hijack the car. This will implicate Italy hands-on aiding and abetting these fascists[2] under diplomatic cover. The wops will have to trade big time to extricate themselves from this. Sir, it's our best means to shoot down their *coup d'état* for good."

A flurry of questions followed before Basil cemented things.

"Absolutely covert, sir. Our Mafia unit can do the car-jacking, chop it for spare parts, make it all appear a totally legit crime."

1 Good (Rus).
2 Generic term for ultra-right, warmongering politics. Nazis, Fascists, Zio-Nazis and Islamofascists

Basil sat high in his chair savouring his boss' approval.

"Exactly, sir. Let the wops complain, fully expose themselves and whine how an important Italian citizen was abducted along with their diplomatic vehicle. More evidentiary sauce for our hammer of justice goose. Now sir, I need your authorization because—"

Basil chuckled as Director-General Besstrashnikov finished his sentence with the well-worn 'above your pay-grade' cliché. While his superior was thinking the plan over, an instant message from the FSB forensics laboratory flashed across Basil's screen. It bore the CWA — Chemical Weapons Alert — insignia.

A shockwave of insanity rippled along the length of Basil's face. He dropped the telephone receiver. It struck his desk and bounced once. Both Basil's hands frantically typed up a taskforce alert. He was finishing the final sentence when he felt obliged to yell out the situation so that it might be audible to his boss, whom Basil assumed was rankled at being cut off for so long without explanation.

"Sir, the pollutant has been identified. I'm sending out a chemical warfare directive. We need a scientific damage assessment. We need to know how much of the Metro will have to be shut down."

Basil hit [SEND] and snapped up the handset from off his desk.

"Sorry to cut you off. Ah, you got the lab report too."

A frenetic exchange of words ensued.

"Yes, in five minutes. Sir, getting back to intercepting the diplomatic car. This makes it imperative. We've been attacked, and the wop government plans to abuse diplomatic conventions to give the perpetrators safe-harbour."

Besstrashnikov ordered Basil to off-load the Metro investigation to a trusted subordinate and devote all his efforts to the hunt for Ursini.

"Will do, sir. See you in five. *Poka.*"

Basil summoned Major Tatiana Gratski to his office. While waiting for her to arrive, Basil phoned Sergei to appoint him Metro investigation commander, and directed him to evacuate Metro Komsomolskaya and return all men to headquarters for decontamination. And, once the station was cleared, he ordered it sealed as air-tight as possible.

When Tatiana entered, Basil hung up on Sergei.

"Major, you're possibly contaminated. Don't touch anything."

And, Basil pulled a pair of latex gloves from a credenza and put them on. He passed her a print-out of the incoming SMS translation with an order for her to double-check it against the Italian original. He next rushed her through an outline of his plan to capture Ursini and the circumstances of the Italian Embassy's involvement. Pressed for time, Basil improvised new particulars and fired them off as best he could. On instinct, Tatiana knew the General was expecting her to sort through his revisions and flesh out the nitty-gritty. She glowed because full exoneration was in sight.

When Basil had finished, she replied.

"Sir, I'll knock out every detail. Expect flawless."

Basil marched across his office — "Major, flawless is irrelevant, anticipate contingencies, expect the unexpected." And, as he reached the door, he stopped abruptly, wheeled around and in a moderate scowl of censure — "One other thing — no more bloody fist fights!"

She winced, and Basil calmed. "Tatiana, if there are open questions, call me. Interrupting any meeting, even with the president, is no problem. Failure on this mission will be the end of all our careers. So don't hesitate to call me."

As Basil barreled through his secretary's office, instructions kept flowing.

"Elena, find out what decontamination is available. Gratski's top priority."

And, once out the door, Basil charged down the corridor to attend a damage assessment meeting shuffling its way into conference.

Target the Bolsheviks

On the second floor of the Intelligence Directorate, located within the heart of the Lubyanka complex sits the Joint Services Conference Room. Metallic copper panels, artfully distressed in hues of textured verdigris resembling green agate cover its interior walls and ceiling. And, all panels seamlessly overlay double-lath plaster, which trebles its purpose. And, from corner to corner across the room, plush Nepalese sound-attenuating carpet conceals more copper-plating, which itself lies atop a slab of double lath-mesh concrete.

Director-General Karl Besstrashnikov and the Metro task force he had hastily assembled were seated, and the meeting was about to start when Basil entered and resealed the cloisonné-on-copper door. A computer controlled emitter-transducer system confirmed Faraday-cage containment was once again restored, and the light above the enameled copper doorframe flashed from red to green. The room reverted to one of complete audio and electronic eavesdropping impregnability.

Director-General Besstrashnikov hit the [LOCKDOWN] button on the conference desk console — *No more intrusions.* As Basil approached his assigned seat, he whispered over Besstrashnikov's right shoulder.

"That operation we discussed is taking shape."

Finger to his lips, indicating they would talk later in private, Besstrashnikov replied — "Good to hear that, General. I've emailed the gist to B. for approval."

Basil sat easier knowing that the president was now in the loop.

The Director-General swiveled about and faced the length of the table.

"Colonel Litvinenko,[1] would you begin, please."

"Director-General, we're faced with a monstrous calamity. The bastard who sabotaged Metro Komsomolskaya released an estimated three kilograms of an exceptionally toxic organic compound called 2,3,7,8 tetrachloro-dibenzo-para-dioxin.[2] Because the dust is the size of pollen, it continues to disseminate rapidly through the Metro's confined air corridors. In short, lethal levels of dioxin are now polluting the length and breadth of the Moscow Metro system."

The room fell completely silent.

Besstrashnikov glared at Litvinenko and growled.

1 Pronunciation: Lit-vin-yenko.
2 Highly toxic, poly-halogenated aromatic hydrocarbon as depicted here.

"*Bolsheviks!*[1] This is an exagger—"

Like a greyhound unleashed upon a lamed rabbit, Litvinenko cut back.

"No, sir. No. No. No. Don't confuse this with some pathetic nerve-gas attack. Here's what we must do without delay. Every train in the Metro system must be brought to a halt. Every person must exit the system, discard all their clothes and scrub down. Every tunnel and opening that vents air into or out of the system must be sealed airtight. No more air movement whatsoever."

Besstrashnikov interjected — "Surely you overstate—"

Litvinenko became trenchant.

"Sir, discussion is over. You or Bushkin must order immediate shut-down."

Bushkin, not President Bushkin. Everyone in the room heard Litvinenko's breach of etiquette. But, it was consistent with his shrill tone of voice and the distress in his face. Besstrashnikov's heart sank. This was a nightmare scenario. He leant over to Basil and directed him to use the room's hard-wired phone to send an alert SMS to Evgenia, the president's secretary, instructing her to get the president in on the conference via the Kremlin video link. Next, Besstrashnikov addressed the assembly.

"Gentlemen, can anyone fault Litvinenko's assessment?"

There was not a whisper of dissent.

Besstrashnikov brought his right fist to his chest as if searching for a heartbeat and slumped. It was an obvious truth that in the tunnels of the Metro wind blasts from oncoming trains were enormous. Dirt-sized grains routinely peppered one's face, and this toxin was as fine as pollen. No great science was involved. No blowhard political opinion needed reconciling.

Head down, and still in the process of tapping out an urgent SMS, Basil vented into the pustulant silence of the room.

"If it's toxic, why no signs of ailment? Damn-well, explain yourself."

Doctor Chernikrov hunched high in his seat and over the table.

"General, I sympathize with your frustration about the narcotics red-herring. Dioxin is more of a carcinogenic pollutant than a homicidal agent. It's not readily absorbed like a nerve gas. Aryl halides take hours to migrate into the human body before physical symptoms show."

The doctor directed his gaze at Besstrashnikov.

"Director-General, we face a silent killer. Chloracne will appear first. A precursor to cancer. And, dioxin readily accumulates in fat. The brain is 95% fat. In adults, expect accelerated dementia. In children, expect autism and retardation. As a weapon, dioxin is about stealth, not flash in the pan extinction. Sir, the long-term carcinogenic toll will be horrendous."

Carcinogenic — clamored hard in the Besstrashnikov's ears. He closed his eyes and covered his face with both hands — *Dioxin. Cancer. Long-term mob violence.* While only an elite knew about Romanov, every patriotic Russian was aware of how Ukrainian President Eunatovski had suffered his own dioxin attack and blamed Moscow. Any commonsense citizen knew this cowardly 'Target the Bolsheviks' outrage on the Metro at rush hour was no innocent happenstance.

1 Holy Crap (Rus).

Lurching hard across the table, another man spoke up.

"Director-General, my name is Captain Ilya Borisovich Botanin, a decontamination specialist. Sir, we can't dither. Think of Polonium-210 milled down to pollen-sized particles or envision the movie *Pu-238*.[1] 2,3,7,8 tetrachloro-dibenzo-para-dioxin is comparable in toxicity to both those deadly radioactive isotopes. Furthermore, dioxin is very stable. In the darkness of the subway system, it has a half-life of 8.7 years. And, each hour that passes, more people inhale this aerated soup of toxic dust the further it disperses. We must stop both exposure and dispersion. And, General Novimirov, its urgent your men return to headquarters so I can begin decontaminating them."

Basil looked up, his face bleak with guilt.

"Already in progress, Captain. Already in progress," and his voice trailed off to nowhere as he swallowed his anger and continued his SMS.

To break the trauma besetting his superior, Litvinenko barked.

"Director-General, please! We need to act, not talk. It's no exaggeration. Every hour prolongs by months the time necessary to clean-up this mess."

The Director-General seized upon this new tidbit.

"What? What! Months. Don't go crazy on me."

Litvinenko stood four-square and faced Besstrashnikov down.

"Sir, we've been nuked. It's no Metro for months," and he slammed his fists on the conference table in time with his words to add unambiguous emphasis.

"Nuked for Months. Sir. Make — the — call."

Besstrashnikov whipped the phone handset from its cradle. And, while speed dialing Evgenia, he snapped out orders.

"Novimirov, stay. Everyone else, outside. Litvinenko, stand by the door. Expect me to call you back in. Botanin and Chernikrov, get to work on decontamination and start scripting a TV segment explaining how the public can decontamin—" He broke off to answer the phone — "Evgenia, Karl Besstrashnikov here. Get Fyedor on the video-conference link. It's a nuclear emergency. Do it, *right* now."

The line stayed open but silent.

Handset at his ear, Besstrashnikov looked at Basil. "Can you believe this shit?"

Basil remained deadpan, bewildered. The door of the conference room clicked shut. The door-jamb light flashed to green. They were alone. When Evgenia returned to the phone, Besstrashnikov issued more instructions.

"Another thing, Evgenia. Phone the Director of the Moscow Metro. Put him on standby to take a call from the president in the next few minutes."

And, Director-General Besstrashnikov hung up.

Basil addressed his friend seeking confirmation of the worst.

"Karl, we're at war. Those fascist fuck-holes hav—"

Basil broke off mid-sentence and lifted his hands to chest level. They were trembling. Besstrashnikov smirked and did likewise. Basil smiled. Besstrashnikov broke the angst with a pat on the back and a quip of camaraderie.

"Novimirov, let's put our hands under the table before the video-screen comes on, and the President decides to fire us both."

1 Pu-238 is the active fissile material in atomic bombs. Highly toxic and radioactive.

The video meeting soon flashed to life. In less than two minutes, President Bushkin assigned each of the three their responsibilities.

He approved Basil's mission — no questions asked and no time for lengthy *what-ifs*. A close friend of the president, Basil was trusted implicitly.

The Director-General was commisioned to organize the cleanup taskforce and given plenary power, short of war, to command the nation's forces in capturing anyone he considered a conspirator or facilitator.

President Bushkin assigned himself three tasks. Organizing the orderly shutdown of the whole Moscow Metro system. Coordinating Russian military forces to gear up and enforce a state of martial law as well as aiding civilian decontamination. And, having the Finance Ministry direct all systemically vital banks to purchase credit default puts as well as call options on all major futures markets in anticipation of wild disruptions in the price of oil and gold once the true state of affairs was disclosed to the public. Bushkin's major focus — Italy — would bear the full brunt of Russia's *Dioxinomic*[1] collapse.

And, all three tasked themselves with keeping faith with the expectations of the Russian elektorate, while doing their utmost to preserve peace in the world.

By Presidential Order

With the presidential videoconference concluded, the Director-General promptly re-convened the meeting, absent Captain Botanin and Doctor Chernikrov. Once all were seated, Besstrashnikov wasted no time.

"Colonel Litvinenko, come here."

Litvinenko was ill at ease because, in the hallway, he had reflected on his harsh outburst and overheard the comments of others. But, as he walked over to face his superior, Director-General Besstrashnikov saluted and wore a proud smile. Pounding his fists — Bushkin had loved it. And, Besstrashnikov's voice brimmed with approval as well.

"By presidential order, Colonel Vadim Olegovich Litvinenko, you're promoted to the rank of General. And, I hereby assign you command of the Moscow Metro decontamination and rejuvenation taskforce."

Tension vanished in an instant, and the whole room erupted into thunderous applause. After quiet returned, Besstrashnikov faced Basil.

"General, you need to get cracking. Use your authority wisely."

"Sir, make decontaminating my men priority." And, Basil scooted out the door.

The verification light reverted to green.

Besstrashnikov pulled out the chair at the head of the table.

"General Litvinenko, please sit here. You're now chairman. I'm merely here to relay the President's decision and take notes."

And, as the Director-General seated himself in Basil's empty chair, he continued issuing instructions — "As General Novimirov has stated, one most pressing issue is getting our men decontaminated. Let's start on that note."

1 1 Portmanteau of Dioxin + (Eco)nomics. See *Dioxinomics* Series. www.dioxinomics.com

A New Hairdo

Back in his office, Basil changed into street clothes. While he did so, he focused his mind on the upcoming operation against Ursini. The phone rang, and Elena patched him through to Sergei. By dint of command, Sergei had remained outside the Metro entrance to ensure that the nosey police complied with the FSB's 'Restricted Area Order.' So, he was the least contaminated. Basil was annoyed with the colonel because he had kept all the men on-site awaiting the return of an ambitious lieutenant bucking for promotion who had gone deep into the tunnels. As soon as the call ended, Sergei ordered every man back to the Lubyanka. And, he personally waited for Lieutenant Krilich to emerge before placing Senior Inspector Druznin in charge with strict orders to keep the Metro doors locked and sealed airtight with wetted cloth. That same hour, Russian special army forces appeared at all Metro stations around Moscow and replicated the provisional containment protocols used at Komsomolskaya.

President Bushkin had made a calculated decision. It was highly unlikely that Romanov would connect the Metro shut-down with Ursini because, lacking an encrypted phone, Ursini had only divulged the 'Borges' passport disaster. The 'Fire in the Metro' story had given Ursini cover, and he had wisely preserved that cover. And, because the whole phone system was now blacked out, Ursini was completely isolated with no way of spilling his guts even if he was stupid enough to do so. By secret presidential decree, until Ursini was captured, continued subterfuge was the quintessential rule of law, public rancor be damned.

Basil was on the verge of leaving his office, when Captain Ilya Botanin knocked and entered. Assigned the task of supervising the decontamination of all FSB personnel, the captain informed Basil that his men needed to report to the rear courtyard. There a de-con crew was in the process of rigging up an oil and detergent scrub-down pavilion. He also appraised Basil about a tunable laser scanner that he was hoping would detect a broad category of chlorinated aryl compounds, including dioxin. While the news heartened Basil, Botanin remained fatalistic.

"General, for now, it's our most effective solution. Keep in mind sir, dioxin dissolves in sebaceous oils on the hair and skin and subsequently penetrates cells like DDT.[1] Breathing or ingesting it is an even bigger disaster because no scrubbing process can reverse the fact that you're poisoned."

Needing a sense of sanity to prevail, Basil became stoic.

"Captain, sounds like you have a firm grip on things."

As Botanin explained the matter, Basil picked up his ringing phone.

"*Bolsheviks*! Captain, let's go." And he marched into his secretary's office and addressed a woman standing by the door.

"You're Natalia Bogomolski — correct?"

"Yes sir. I report to Major Tatiana Gratski."

"My name is General Basil Andreivich Novimirov."

---

1 DDT - Dichlorodiphenyltrichloroethane. (IUPAC 1,1,1-Trichloro-2,2-bis(4-chlorophenyl)ethane.

Basil did not extend a hand in greeting.

"I'm the Major's commander. You will address me as sir or general. We need to talk but right now we're decontaminating all personnel. You most especially. Follow me and touch absolutely nothing."

And, while Natalia confirmed the extent of her contamination in the Metro, the three proceeded along the east corridor, down the north-east stairwell and out into the rear courtyard. In an army-issue hospital tent sealed with duct tape to exclude all light, a prototype infrared scanner was undergoing tests. Using forensic lab samples, a chemical engineer was fine-tuning a laser scanner for the correct wavelength when the door flap cracked open and Basil, Natalia and Botanin sidled their way inside. Due to Natalia's extensive exposure at 'Ground-Zero,' Basil and Botanin considered her little better than a walking corpse. And, because they thought it vital to run tests on a living person, Natalia's oil and detergent scrub-down was forestalled. Ilya Botanin handed Basil a spare set of specially modified night-vision goggles, took control of the laser handset and addressed Natalia.

"Miss, please stand on the glowing 'X' — There." And, Botanin pointed — "Now, close your eyes."

And, he picked up the laser scanner. As if hunting for supermarket price tags, he swept an invisible infrared beam of laser light around her left side. Only those wearing goggles saw the hallmark cherry-red fluorescence of dioxin.

"There, General. You see …" He paused in quandary. "Curious. Her hair and clothes are glowing but nothing on her skin."

After a moment of deliberation, Botanin set aside all ethics.

"Miss, please wipe your hand on your dress. Yes. Now hold it out. See General. Wait, hold on. What? … The contaminants are decaying."

"Is this chemical stable on human skin?" Basil asked.

"No sir. Nor is it speedily absorbed into—"

"*Bolsheviks*! Weaponized dioxin," Basil cut in.

"A good point, sir. But I doubt it. Perhaps, a mistake has been made identifying the compound or we've wrongly assumed the urn was filled—"

Tatiana Gratski's head popped through the entryway of the tent.

"General Novimirov. Are you here? Sir?"

Basil turned and made reply — "*Da*."

"Sir. Are you ready to act on what we spoke about earlier?"

"Have you been decontaminated, Major?"

As Tatiana parted the flap and stepped into the darkness, daylight flooded in and blinded all those wearing goggles. Basil removed his. Once his eyes adjusted, he beheld a woman as bald as a doorknob standing by the flap.

Snapping to attention, Tatiana responded.

"De-con complete. Street clothes and a new hairdo. Ready for duty."

Heartened at her composure in the face of potentially deadly exposure, Basil cracked a warm smile of camaraderie and gestured with an open palm.

"Major, please stand where Miss Bogomolski is."

Staring into the gloom, Tatiana fired back on instinct.

"Natalia Bogomolski? Sir, you're mistaken."

Basil hit the lights and leveled a revolver at Natalia's head.

"No wait, sir. ... Unbelievable!"

Natalia stood shivering and gazed glumly at her friend.

"Tats, it's me. Veronika 853."

"Well, Major?"

"Yes, sir. No doubt. I ... I—"

"Silence, Major."

And, Basil placed his chrome-plated eighteen round Yarygin PYa to his lips. Only a handful of people knew this woman had survived what all evidence indicated was impossible. And, right now, all Basil's thoughts and energies remained tightly focused on the nation's only priority — the capture of the wop from Hell. Waving his pistol hand, Basil motioned for Natalia to move aside, and he ordered Tatiana to stand over the 'X.' As he switched off the lights, he instructed the Major to strip and for Botanin to run tests.

"Anything noteworthy?" Basil asked.

"As you can see there are still visible dioxin patches on Major Gratski. ... Sir, it may be some interaction between skin and the infrared light that causes the decay process. I'll focus on one spot."

Basil stooped low to get a closer look.

"No, nothing yet," said Botanin.

Basil stood upright again and nestled the Yarygin PYa under his chin.

"Still no change. Sir, you now see skin doesn't readily absorb dioxin. Aryl receptors will transport it into a cell's DNA, but only gradually."

And, Botanin proceeded to wipe down all residual contaminants with an acetone wetted rubbing cloth. Once finished, Basil turned on the lights and as Tatiana dressed, mulled over this curiosity. But, not for long, because Bogomolski's survival was an enigma all in itself. And, he had a pending operation to get underway, one that might require her participation.

"Keep running trials. Colonel Gratski's squad should be back soon. Clean them up as best you can. And, Captain — *Spare no effort.*"

Re-holstering his sidearm, Basil made for the exit.

"Major. Miss Bogomolski. Let's go."

Sauntering off to the scrub-down pavilion, Basil appraised them about the basics of a backup plan for Ursini's take-down he was still in the process of formulating. At the entry-way, Basil summoned the woman in charge.

"Miss, this woman needs scrubbing. Wash her hair thoroughly. Repeat as you consider fit, but absolutely no hair on her scalp is to be cut. Clear?"

And, Basil hurried off, leaving Major Gratski to prepare Natalia, his most recent addition to B-team, for a possible face-to-face confrontation with Alfredo Constanzo Leonardo Ursini.

A Flash of Sound Judgement

In the Joint Services Conference Room, each squad captain recited what operations their team would perform in the capture of Alfredo Ursini. Basil knew how adrenaline clouded the mind, and he remained sober throughout. He also understood something vital that these puppies did not. When it came to stealth, a dash of sound judgement was often better than a flash of genius. Once Basil was persuaded that everything was as good as it could be, he gave his men a hearty thumbs-up and waded into his motivational speech.

Basil pulled no punches laying out the gruesome extents of the devastation that Ursini and his fascist allies in Italy had inflicted upon the motherland. He impressed upon his men that they were to arrest every target unharmed, no excuses and no retribution. Because they were going to heist a diplomatic vehicle, Basil emphasized that on pain of a bullet-to-the-head, there could be no breach of cover. Lastly, he reassigned Major Gratski (codename B-1) to lead the B-Team so Natalia (codename B-4) would be under her command. If all else failed, in a moment of desperation, Basil's still evolving backup expedient might need to be thrown into action.

Pimp My Ride

Moscow streets are always congested. But, with the subway abruptly shut down and people stranded at random all over the city, it was now bedlam. D-Team had tailed the Italian diplomatic limousine since it left the embassy. Infrared heat signatures established the car's occupants were driver plus a solitary passenger in back. To ensure the Italians could negotiate the nasty traffic now snarling every major thoroughfare and meet their timetable with Ursini, Basil requisitioned a presidential limousine. To enhance its purpose, he included a full escort — four presidential guards on motorcycle, two in front, two in back. With the aid of all the additional militsia and army units stationed on the choked streets of a city rife with speculation about a *coup d'état*, this motorcade cut through traffic wherever it pleased.

Basil's entourage soon converged with the Italian diplomatic vehicle at the intersection of Ulitsa Novyy Arbat and Novinski Boulevard.

Ever solicitous about maintaining good foreign relations, a courteous guard in the rear pulled his cycle back and extended an invitation for the Italians to join the motorcade as a second car. This thoughtful gesture also created the possibility that the diplomatic chauffeur would be amenable to opening the car door to a trustworthy face if things went awry. Without the Italians knowing, this lucky break from traffic was their nemesis. Thus, it was that one block shy of the not-so-secret rendezvous point on Ulitsa Tverskaya and only eight minutes behind schedule, the presidential entourage parted company with the diplomatic limousine.

A more worrisome aspect remained. C-Team, which had helicoptered in earlier, had still not spotted Ursini. The assumption was he would be stationed near the bus stop, where the diplomatic vehicle was expected to make pick-up.

One hundred yards south of the intersection of Ulitsa Gasheka and Tverskaya, inside a mocked-up television van, bearing RTV's[1] logo, Basil scanned the bustling street through a mast camera. The sidewalk and intersection with Gasheka ahead was a sea of shoulder-to-shoulder motion. He watched the diplomatic limousine pass by his van and pull up at the bus-stop. It's rear door cracked open. Almost immediately, a prostitute with flowing chestnut hair, wearing a bright-green sequin dress, elbowed her way to the curb and approached the door of the vehicle. She tugged it half-open, thrust her left leg in, but got no further.

Basil winced in annoyance.

"Damn it. Some whore is screwing this up. Get in there, B-2."

Another woman exited her seat at the bus pavilion and muscled her head and one arm through the door of the embassy vehicle — "Are you looking for double the fun?" she asked while secreting a magnet into the door jamb.

The Italian chargé d'affaires, already aggravated by the oppressive traffic, was beside himself with yet another unwelcome opportunist.

"Botha you sluts, getta lost! I'ma here on Embassy business."

An exasperated Alfredo stripped off his wig, threw it into the car and spoke in fluent Italian — "Attenzione. Sono Alfredo Ursini. Andiamo."[2]

The chargé d'affaires sat speechless as man dived in to salvage anonymity.

Basil heard every word.

"B-2, magnet in place?" he asked.

"*Da*," she replied.

Adrenaline on overload, she anticipated Basil's next commands.

"B-2, in the car. B-1, activate the GPS jammer. A-Team, you are pimps. One of your girls and a queen are being abducted. Carjack now."

A less than diplomatic hand fended off B-2 and was attempting to shut the door of a vehicle rolling at a crawl, but two A-Teamers in Mafia street garb appeared and yanked the door wide open. They hurled both B-2 and themselves inside. The last man flicked the door-jamb magnet into the gutter, and the heavy, bullet-proof door finally mated with its hasp and cinched to a close.

A-1 made the introductions.

"I see you like our ladies, but we don't like your manners. You must deal through me to get one of these super fine ladies."

The chargé d'affaires, Carlo Rolfino, was aghast.

"I'ma diplomat. Get out and take your sluts with you."

A-1 scrutinized Ursini.

"I see you go for queens, Luigi. That costs extra."

Alfredo snarled — "I'm not a queen. I'm—"

A-1 zapped Alfredo with a stun gun. And, for the chargé d'affaires' benefit, A-1 growled — "I'll set you straight bitch when we get home. You work my corner, you work for me." And for dramatic effect, he zapped Alfredo again.

1 Russia TV (Moscow TV akin to PBS)
2 Attention. I'm ... Let's go (Ital).

A-1 turned his spleen on the chargé d'affaires.

"Luigi, tell your driver to pull over at the next corner, park it and we'll settle this transaction discreetly — biznizman to biznizman."

The car traveled another fifty meters, turned into Ulitsa Gasheka, and drew to a halt on the footpath blocking the apartment complex driveway of *Dom*[1] #17.

Formalities Remained

Basil slid open a hatch to speak to his van's driver, face to face.

"Ivan, park up close to the north corner of Gasheka and Tverskaya. I need a clear shot of the limousine through the mast camera. Oleg, get out and start flagging off any militsia. Ivan, when you're done, join Oleg."

Basil then attended to his head-mic.

"C-team your new task. Interdict all militsia, got it? No militsia. No crap. All others, listen up. A-3, A-4, and B-3 converge on the apartment and keep it locked down. B-1 and B-4, reposition yourselves and stay ready."

Basil looked at the mast camera monitor and focused it on the limousine before issuing additional instructions.

"B-2, glam up Ursini and put his wig back on. A-1, you're going to take a photo of B-2, the diplomat and Ursini in drag. A-2 get the driver to open his door, disarm him and steal all his money. It's Mafia shakedown time."

And, Basil relaxed back in his seat and waited for the fun to resume. On his earpiece, he heard everything and chuckled silently from time to time.

A-1 barked to A-2 — "Boris, get out and get to work."

A-1 pulled out a phone, and B-2 picked up the wig and placed it on Ursini. "Inna, give Luigi a big kiss." — *Click.*

A-1 displayed the phone to the chargé d'affaires.

"Luigi, you three take a fine pic."

"Bastardo," snarled the chargé d'affaires.

"Does a woman in the photo slander your reputation?" And, A-1 laughed before braying out the order of things — "Luigi, here's your salvation. Empty your pockets and you get to push the [DELETE] button. Same goes for your driver. Tell him to obey Boris. No more 'Ima wop ambassadiva' gas-bagging."

The chargé d'affaires was too stunned to respond, so A-1 produced his pistol, a military issue, modified grip nine millimeter Baretta, and twisted its muzzle under the chargé d'affaires' nose.

"Wanna snorta lead snot, Luigi? Or would you prefer hair-trigger upada-ass?"

A-1 grabbed the chargé d'affaires' shirt and brought his unshaven jowl adjacent to the man's cologned cheek.

"Tell the driver *now*, wop." And he released his grip.

The chargé d'affaires engaged the intercom, and the chauffeur exited the car in a flash. A-2 trained a Luger on him and ordered him to empty his pockets.

Basil expanded his directions.

1 Building (Rus).

"A-2, knock the driver out. A brass-knuckle Hollywood punch followed by crack-the-lens Mafioso berserk, got it?" — *Whack*.

Out cold, the chauffeur crumpled to the roadway. While ensuring his back faced the camera at all times, on the hunt for any concealed cash or weapons, A-2 heightened the drama by mindlessly slashing the man's uniform.

Basil's direction continued.

"A-1, get everyone out of the backseat except B-2. Hide your faces but show the faces of the wops. C-1, drop the bag of handcuffs by the passenger side back door of the limo. B-2, retrieve that bag. Closing scene coming up."

Still unconscious, Alfredo was first. Half out of the car, A-1 demanded.

"Luigi, help me drag this queen out."

"He'sa with me. I'll pay. What's your problem?"

A-1 bent in and grabbed the chargé d'affaires' cravat.

"Listen, faggot. Everyone's getting out. I'm taking all your money. I'll pull up his dress, and you'll find his stash. It's obviously in his panties or bra since he has no purse." And A-1 paused to laugh. "I mean purse in the conventional sense, Luigi. I want his money. You're welcome to milk the rest of him dry. Now help me with Senorina Bum-Chum."

Once it dawned on the chargé d'affaires there was light at the end of this tunnel, he followed direction without further evasion. And, thus it was that two on-camera notables and two anonymous pimps scored their allotted fifteen minutes of *Pimp My Ride* fame in classic Warhol tradition. With the loot collected, A-1 showed the chargé d'affaires his phone and, as promised, the 'Deletion' of the threesome photo was confirmed. Or, so it seemed. But, Basil had other plans. This photo would soon end up at the Italian embassy attached to a Mafia demand which, for a modest fee, promised to make the whole unseemly escapade vanish. His goal was to shame the Italians into continued silence for as long as possible by making them think a deal could be struck with the devil.

Basil closed the proceedings.

"Final take, komrades. All wops back in the limo and cuff them. Then keep your backs to the camera and walk into the apartment complex."

While A-2 lifted the semi-conscious chauffeur behind the wheel, A-1 helped the chargé d'affaires bundle the now semi-conscious Ursini back into the car. Next, A-1 played the doorman while a much relieved chargé d'affaires re-entered the car. Without warning, A-1 leant through the door and zapped the chargé d'affaires. Pulling out six pairs of rusty handcuffs, B-2, A-1 and A-2 cuffed all men's hands and feet, followed by a gag over the mouth and a hood over the head. With the car now secured, the three walked off-camera, incognito.

"And, *Il Directore*[1] says cut."

Basil chuckled upon realizing he had just shot the perfect movie for a Russian stag party. But, levity did not linger for long. Formalities remained.

"A-Team back to the car heist business. A-3 get in there and disable the GPS transponder so we can stop jamming. And, get that car rolling to Teatralnyy Ploshad. We have a drag queen to unload on E-Team."

---

1 The Director (Ital).

With the impromptu aspect of the operation concluded, the rest of Basil's operation unfolded according to design. Ursini was dumped at the base of the hulking statue of Karl Marx opposite the Bolshoi Theater complex and captured by FSB dressed as Militsia. Once the E-Team militsia were satisfied he was a legitimate Moscovite, they released the man. All was done before witnesses — some of them westerners from the adjoining Hotel Metropol, which dominates the eastern flank of the square. A kind 'Westerner' even helped Ursini make his way up Teatralnyy Thoroughfare towards the main entrance of the hotel. But, twenty meters shy of the entrance, F-Team emerged from the shadows, and Ursini was bundled into an ambulance. Driven a spare half-kilometer further, Ursini entered the maws of the 'Hotel Lubyanka' and was furnished snug and secure lodgings in the best Honeymoon Suite the basement dungeons afforded.

The Stuff of Riots

During the intervening hours expended in the capture of Alfredo Ursini, Captain Ilya Botanin refined the dioxin detection process and awaited Miss Bogomolski's return so he could run more tests. However, because Major Tatiana Gratski had been exposed at Metro Komsomolskaya, her unmuddled and very motivated mind cut through the sci-brain clutter.

Upon arriving at the Lubyanka, Tatiana convinced Basil to accompany her and Natalia to the decontamination tent. There, she directed Natalia to hold a contaminated shirt under Botanin's infrared scanner and run her hands over the cloth. Wipe by wipe, all speckles of dioxin-red fluorescence vanished. Tatiana proved the simple fact — When spread upon a secondary surface, some force emanating from Natalia's skin neutralized what was supposedly an extremely stable dioxin molecule. With the science more confused than ever, Botanin initiated a short conversation with Basil. While Basil placed a phone call and issued instructions, Botanin sealed the decontaminated cloth into an evidence bag and ordered his assistant to take it to forensics for a full chemical analysis.

Basil hung-up.

"All done, captain. That specimen has Alpha-One priority."

And, Basil signed-off on the bag to ensure no delay would be tolerated.

While these two men were attending to the science of quandaries, Tatiana had been busy removing her uniform. And, once her panties had dropped to the floor, with the aid of the infrared scanner, Tatiana bade Natalia launder the residual dioxin blotches marring her right nipple.

With the nipple cleansed, Natalia repeated the process at all other sites showing residual contamination. As a further precaution, Tatiana then lay on a gurney and had Natalia oil up her hands and give her a complete rub-down in the expectation of cleansing every trace of undetected toxin. Because it was beyond the sensitivity of the infrared scanner, there was no way to prove this process was necessary, but Natalia did as her friend asked on pure faith. And, thus it was that Major Gratski was the first to experience the unearthly physical pleasure radiating out of the hands of Natalia Bogomolski.

Elated at how their nation's fortunes seemed to be on the rise, Basil relegated the task of decontaminating all FSB personnel to Natalia under Captain Botanin's scrutiny. While he strolled to his office, phone at his ear, Basil relayed the good news to Director-General Besstrashnikov. In turn, Besstrashnikov issued a directive ordering all exposed to return to the courtyard for secondary decontamination. Next, an extensive phone conference with President Bushkin.

Initially slow and grudging in coming, compliance accelerated once word got around from first-timers. And, in rapid course, the secondary rub-down process was soon flooded by all comers. No different than Major Tatiana Gratski's residual dioxin blemishes, many others had areas of great tactile sensitivity insufficiently scrubbed clean. So, Natalia found herself rubbing her charmed hands over the most intimate of places.

While all were informed a nurse was cleansing them with a special sponge, everyone who experienced the procedure knew better. And, on pain of a bullet-to-the-head, absolute secrecy remained law because the expectation of horrendous casualties all across Moscow brought with it the specter of horrendous riots should any crazy rumor spread that FSB Lubyanka harboured a miraculous decontamination process.

Natalia was growing more accustomed to handling the naked bodies of strangers, but when it came time to do the hands-on decontamination of Colonel Sergei Gratski, Tatiana's husband, renewed apprehension set in.

"I won't tell Tats, if you don't," Sergei said with a sly wink.

Natalia sighed in resignation and started at Sergei's feet. On reaching his left knee the most surprising thing happened, Sergei felt the rawness melt away.

"Natalia, please hold your hand over my knee. ... That's the spot. Press."

All trace of irritation vanished.

"Botanin, lights please," Sergei directed.

And, he stooped over to verify the outcome.

"Unbelievable. Botanin, look at my left knee."

Sergei noticed Botanin's smirk of curiosity.

"Captain, my right knee, do you see that abrasion?"

Ilya Botanin nodded matter-of-factly.

Determined to prove the miracle, Sergei said — "Natalia. Put your hand over the sore on my right knee and cure it."

Sergei felt the same angelic emanations from her palm, and in less than a second, he knew the scab had vanished.

"Natalia, remove your hand, please. There. Both knees healed."

Ilya Botanin was dumbfounded — "What! No. ... Remarkable!"

Natalia was excited yet subdued — "So, it is true."

The two officers flashed her a look of inquiry.

Natalia addressed Sergei — "When he came to my aid in the Metro, a man told me that my cuts and bruises healed right before his eyes. Apparently, some were very nasty. I told the police about it. But, they just thought I was suffering from concussion. I still felt spaced-out at the time." And as a tear drizzled from her right eye, a shudder borne of the remembrance of her behavior swept the length of her body.

But, Sergei's face shone bright with wonder. Natalia's miraculous survival from bone smashing train impact had a demonstrable explanation, albeit a scientifically absurd one. Her madcap account was probably in some 'Disregard this Loon' file the Militsia forwarded to the FSB, and had yet to be scrutinized. With Ursini snagged, he knew it was imperative to convince General Novimirov to expedite solving this expanding mystery. Nor did Sergei overlook the threat inherent in Natalia's healing powers — *The stuff of riots*. And, he reminded all inside the tent how absolute secrecy concerning Natalia remained the bullet-to-the-head rule of law.

Like in Stalin's Day

Secretary of State Jeffrey Chandler ended his call with Rodney Steele, the US Ambassador to Moscow, and speed-dialed Director of National Intelligence, Lester Coverdale. Deirdre, Lester's secretary, picked up the call, and thirty seconds later Lester came on the line.

"A new tidbit?" he asked as he wiped his salt'n pepper hair off his brow.

"More like confirmation. Rodney's had men in the field for two hours. Skunked out a few contacts. Too much weirdness. All say purge. Your end?"

"Satellite intel shows army tents sprouting like mushrooms in every green space Moscow has. Any info suggesting this is Stalinist cleansing at work?"

"Hard to verify. Many go in, many come out. But, purge is on everyone's lips."

"Got a number on that?" Lester asked.

"50/50."

"Shit." Lester's mobile buzzed on his desk. "Jeff, got to go, it's Norman. Send me a fax report, and keep updating me hourly. Bye."

Lester passed the receiver from right to left hand. As his left cradled the receiver, his right picked up his mobile to take an incoming call from US Vice-President Norman Ousley Weissbrot, the onetime US Ambassador to Russia.

"Norman, I've just hung up on Jeff. His contacts peg this as a purge — 50/50. What's your take?"

"Christ. My contacts report likewise. Worse yet, two insist there's more than meets the eye. Totally under the radar like in Stalin's day."

"Fuck," and Lester's usually unreadable face turned white.

"Yeah," the vice-president replied solemnly. Both men worried how, in the face of pandering to neo-con expectations, President Carter's low-esteem outlook on feminism would compel her to pursue knee-jerk militarism.

"Norman, compile a summary and fax me. Also, Israel is on the march. They want Pollard sprung. This morning, AIPAC did their 'Astroturfing[1] for Yeshu'[2] routine and worked the president over hard. Dues are being squeezed."

---

1 Astroturfing - political sponsors are masked to make something seem a "grassroots" interest.
2 Hebrew pejorative for Jesus.

"Brilliant. Hymies[1] never can time a fuck. How'd Mary-Ann take it?"
"Ginger says badly. Look, I gotta go. Later."

A Virgin's First Kiss

Returned from a twenty-minute 'World Peace' video conference in the Joint Services Conference Room with President Bushkin and Director-General Besstrashnikov, Basil shepherded Major Tatiana Gratski into his office. On the agenda for action was the enigma that was Natalia Bogomolski. During the mission to capture Ursini, she had interrogated Natalia at great length, but secured little that explained how she'd survived. The gist of the matter was known in summary form: A fight, a train collision, and her recovery on the platform. The impact indentation in the steel fender of the train showed beyond a scientific certainty that the collision was definitely bone-breaking if not fatal. Nor did Basil and Tatiana overlook the bruising and lacerations one would expect from a hard landing onto the subway platform. But, they discounted such injuries because the presence of crowds might have cushioned the impact. There came a crisp rap at the door, and they broke conversation. Sergei popped his head through and blurted.
"The news is fabulous."
And, Sergei guided the door to a gentle close and trussed himself against it as if heightened security was in order. Suddenly, his face unleashed the smile of a virgin's first kiss. Basil was taken aback. And, he was not the only one. Sergei's wife was the first to feel the magical pleasure oozing out of Natalia's fingers. Tatiana decidedly did not appreciate the expression rippling across her husband's face, and she threw him a stare that could levitate roof rafters.
Basil broke the growing awkwardness — "Colonel, what's up?"
"Let me show you, sir."
Sergei stooped partway down and started gathering up the fabric of his trouser legs. When the rising cuffs approached his knees, Tatiana shuddered in blush — *Bolsheviks![2] What's this idiot doing showing-off his carpet burns?* But, as the fabric lifted higher, and his knees came into full view, Tatiana's visage changed to one of astonishment.
A leer cracked across Basil's lips.
"Nice legs, Sergei! Is this show for my benefit or your wife's?"
Tatiana pre-empted her oafish husband.
"General, Sergei had work-related injuries on both his knees."
Sergei added — "Cured by Natalia in a single touch."
There was a palpable moment of silence.
Basil's voice quavered with hesitation.
"You're saying she has some healing power?"
Sergei almost cheered — "Yes, sir. And, assuming they did not toss it, we need to hunt down the crazy report about her survival Natalia made to the Militsia."
"Consider it done, Colonel."

1 Pejorative for Jew (American).
2 Crap (Slang).

"And better still, sir. I've a skin-shredding idea how to convince Ursini, to tell us everything we want to know and then some."

Basil lurched forward across his desk and joined in Sergei's jubilation.

"*Bolsheviks*, of course! Splendid. Just splendid. Get back to me with a detailed plan of interrogation. That's your priority, Colonel. Dismissed."

Sergei reopened the door and left.

"Is this power totally out of the blue?" Basil asked Tatiana.

"Sir, unless I saw it … it's incredible. Today, Natalia's a new person. Even her personality. At first, I attributed the transformation to survivor guilt, but," and her voice hardened in frustration. "But, knowing her as my best friend and from my own intuition, Natalia is somehow a very different Natalia."

Looking up from his wrist-watch, Basil nodded his support for her.

"Major, start pulling apart all the police reports. Overlooked details might end this weirdness. I'm past due for my debriefing of Mitchell."

And, as Basil got to his feet and escorted Tatiana to the door, she turned and reminded him of the adversarial situation he might face.

"Sir, it's best to avoid certain issues. Keep in mind, Mitchell despises me because I dumped on him to Natalia. Not just to maintain secrecy, but also as her friend. Personally, she had no business falling in love with a middle-aged Yankee-Doodle,[1] soon destined to leave Moscow."

"Major, I ordered the bust-up for everyone's benefit. Just confirm, Mitchell still has no idea Bogomolski is a Veronika[2] nor that Ursini is a Romanov conspirator. Nor does Bogomolski know Mitchell was working for us. Correct?"

"Definitely, sir. Total cover is still in place. Ursini never told Natalia he had a drop off to make, or where that was. And, Sergei confirmed Mitchell is still clueless about a mystery man who might have shown up at his jewelry store if things hadn't gone awry. In fact, I believe that Mitchell doesn't even—"

Basil cut her off. He needed facts, not suppositions.

"Enough. I'm primed. Police reports for you. Room 327 for me."

As Much About Engineering as Chemistry

As an indispensable 'Romanov Conspiracy' operative with the rank of Honorary FSB Colonel, Derek Mitchell's special entry papers signed months before by Basil himself, had earned him an 'Ask No Questions — See No Faces' escort directly to anywhere he requested. In this way, Derek and Ludmila passed through every FSB checkpoint without the slightest challenge. And, while Derek had showered soon after Ludmila had fallen asleep, and Ludmila shortly after she awoke at 1:30 p.m., at FSB Lubyanka, secrecy was so tight that no one was aware that neither had undergone formal decontamination. And, since Derek and Ludmila had been in no mood to watch television, they were still under the impression that the Komsomolskaya incident was a rush-hour subway fire.

1 American (pejorative): also Y-Doodle, Doodle, Dood and Y-D.
2 Russia's Amateur Spy Corps. In honor of Veronika Lewintsova, captured by 'Capitalist Pigs' in 1998.

Running late for this meeting, Basil collected his thoughts and made pains to project nothing but purposeful optimism throughout his body. Striding up to Honorary Colonel Derek Anthony Mitchell in this mood, Basil extended his hand to an American citizen, whose solidarity it was essential for him to cultivate. And, thus it was outside the entry to Room 327 at 2:14 p.m., Basil became contaminated with the most trace amount of dioxin.

As the first order of greeting, Basil addressed Derek as a fellow officer and apologized for causing him and Ludmila to wait. Basil needed Mitchell to feel at home in the FSB brotherhood as a prelude to addressing the many quandaries he would need to resolve in the days ahead. They left Ludmila seated in the corridor, and took their own inside. Wasting no time, Basil promptly informed Derek that not only had Miss Bogomolski survived, but she had walked away from the accident unscathed. He left any mention of her powers unspoken, hoping Mitchell might fire up some explanation.

Derek was elated.

After listening to a minute and a half of Derek's happy-talk, which shed no light on the mystery, Basil resorted to interviewing Mitchell in earnest. He prodded here and there for insight. But, no luck. Derek restated what Ludmila had told him about the fight in the Metro, and so to Basil, Mitchell's account differed little from those of other witnesses on the platform. Undaunted, Basil diplomatically prompted Derek to re-visit the period when he and Miss Bogomolski were close, and no matter how trivial it might seem, whether he had felt any unusual power in her touch.

Derek laughed to allay his discomfort and talked about the magic of love. Basil lightened to the moment as well. Once he was satisfied that Derek could not have distinguished one power from the other, Basil focused anew on the riddle of how Natalia Bogomolski had walked away from a deadly train collision. Derek gave it more dispassionate thought until it dawned on him — *He hadn't seen any of it personally*. Once Derek explained this oversight, Basil sunk his face into his hands, frustrated by all the crazy talk about 'witnesses' and 'special powers.' *What next*, he thought, *Flying Nuns!*

Then like a home-run-hit to the back of the neck, the obvious washed over Derek. Natalia's first punch must have put Ludmila into a state of shock, which had then caused her to overstate reality. And, Derek fired off his hypothesis.

On that note, what little basis for conversation existed, drew to a lull. Basil's dismay turned into the shared warmth of camaraderie. He had selected Mitchell. Behind all the words in a dossier, he had sensed the noble-heartedness of the man. And, here, this American now sat before him, brimming with the same hope and fortitude Basil felt. However, with forensics on his side, Basil knew, state-of-shock or not, there was no overstatement of reality.

For Derek's part, having endured hours of angst all day, his body flushed warm in quiet rapture glowing hot with endorphins as he began realizing a deeper truth. Ludmila's true and simple heart had expressed itself faultlessly. She loved him so dearly that, in a fit of unconscious innocence, her overwhelmed psyche had snuffed her belligerent rival. Months of cordial intimacy had come to this moment — Love he could forever embrace. The pulse behind his ears beat loud with blood. For him, in this bliss, there was no awkward linger in a conversation now bereft of speech.

But, for Basil, this tragedy was mired in state secrecy.

Months ago, Sergei reported how Mitchell had been taking the break-up with Natalia Bogomolski hard. Ludmila Naristikova was Basil's solution. And, Sergei had slyly inserted her into Mitchell's life because the stakes had been too high. Romanov was coming round to trusting a new go-between, and Mitchell had to be kept mission focused. As an ex-Veronika, Basil had enough history on Ludmila to break what seemed current in Mitchell's life and held the means to reunite Natalia with Derek if appropriate. But, inside, Basil wanted nothing to do with anymore meddling. Once had already been too much. The catastrophe in the Metro was as much about engineering as chemistry.

Seeing no tactful options, Basil broke the silence and tentatively put the matter on the table — Did Mr. Mitchell seek a future with Miss Bogomolski?

Derek sighed in exasperation.

Recognizing sparks of chaffing emotions in Mitchell, Basil backtracked and urged him not to dwell on it. Indeed, Basil did not want to dwell on it. And, to defer consideration of such imponderables, Basil reiterated how putting an end to the Afghan heroin trade and its consequences remained the nation's top priority. And, he emphasized how all private lives were now 'On Hold' as well.

Derek nodded his solidarity.

Deferment was most welcome.

Basil then detailed the forensics proving how the train collision was real and that others had corroborated Ludmila's story. After Basil finished, Derek remained stumped for words. Basil could see Derek was just as mystified as everyone else. And, scanning Mitchell's face for clues, Basil even suspected the Amerikan was contemplating how some Rooskie general was pulling his leg.

The protracted silence spoke of '*Where-to-now?*'

Closing, Basil asked Derek to keep his mind alert and if he recalled anything more, to pass it back to him immediately. Derek agreed and left to fetch and introduce Ludmila to General Novimirov for her interview. He had no idea that Ludmila Naristikova and Basil Novimirov were already very well acquainted.

The Sticky Threesome Situation

Hearing Ludmila recount the fight in the Metro unsettled Basil. The basic details were known from Natalia herself, but the grief in Ludmila's voice rendered her side of the trauma with more emotional force. And, more frustratingly, it confirmed that medically speaking, Natalia should be dead. While Basil inwardly commiserated with her feelings, he remained outwardly dispassionate. And, as distasteful as the matter was, he persisted in cross-examining every weenie detail.

After Basil thanked her for coming in, Ludmila remarked about going back home. Basil smiled and reminded her that both she and Derek would need to remain overnight at the Lubyanka. 'Back Home' did not apply to anyone who'd been contaminated, especially to an apartment to which he would be dispatching a clean-up crew.

"What has happened to the apartment?" Ludmila asked.

All blood left Basil's cheeks for a heart-beat second.

His body froze cold as stone.

Bolsheviks![1] She has hair. He has hair.

Basil's face flushed bright crimson as blood pulsed back into his cheeks. In a day already crammed with minutia upon minutia, he had been so entirely focused on erecting blackouts as a means of snagging Ursini, where failure or the compromise of cover carried the gravest ramifications, small yet catastrophic details went unnoticed. These two were essential witnesses vital to smashing Romanov, Al Guido, and the Afghan heroin trade.

When Derek also confirmed he knew nothing about decontamination, Basil bustled them together and hailed the first man he saw to escort them directly to Captain Botanin in the decontamination center. Trotting to his office, Basil phoned the captain and informed him of Derek's FSB credentials as well as the sticky threesome situation.

A Canine Choker Noosed Hard

While Ludmila was having all her hair removed, Captain Ilya Botanin pulled Derek to one side and succinctly explained the true Komsomolskaya disaster to him including the process of dioxin decontamination. The procedure was shrouded in darkness not only to maximize the detection of dioxin luminescence, but more especially to conceal the miraculous power emanating from Natalia Bogomolski's body. Derek stood dumbfounded because Botanin was confirming what Novimirov had revealed, in half jest he'd thought at the time. Derek grew uneasy because Ludmila was involved. While Botanin went inside to explain the situation to Natalia, Derek briefed Ludmila with only the need-to-know details. In total darkness, a nurse with a special cleansing sponge would neuter every speck of contamination. No sooner had Derek finished then he stripped and two latex-clad nurses expeditiously removed all his hair, from head to toe.

Derek signaled Botanin that they were both ready. With Natalia working in near total darkness and with modified night-vision goggles obscuring her face, the Captain saw little likelihood of a conflict arising. Nonetheless, Derek insisted Ludmila go first so he could stand ready if problems arose.

In complete silence, Natalia ran her hands over Ludmila's body. She felt overjoyed at atoning for her disgraceful assault on Ludmila in the Metro but overjoyed to the point of inducing immodest spasms. Ludmila tried to stifle her

1 Holy crap! (slang).

response to the process, but her body quaked from the symphony of euphoria radiating from Natalia's delicate fingers. When all was done, Botanin escorted a much unsettled Ludmila to the woman's dressing pavilion.

Derek, who had no choice but stew in silence while watching another of Natalia's underhanded assaults on Ludmila, felt like thumping her.

"Damn! Damn you, *suka*. Molesting her is beyond sick. Captain Botanin told me you had the power to cleanse, but hey, let's fuck with it!"

Natalia lifted her goggles and blinked back a tear of despair.

"I meant no … I'll show you."

And, without qualm, she placed her hand against Derek's naked chest over his heart and projected her feelings into him. Derek was transfixed in a flash and a profound ecstasy swept over him. Natalia broke contact.

"Now do you understand? I was so pleased to cleanse Ludmila. To make small amends. I had no intention of violating her modesty."

She hesitated and then made inquiry most delicate.

"Derek, could you not sense my feelings for you?"

"I believe I do. Yes," he sputtered.

Derek felt bedazzled. His mind churned over trying to comprehend an unearthly bliss whose novelty could not be framed in words, except to say hers was an alien power that seemed to rip the very being within him out of his own body. He had known Natalia as his lover for six months, but this feeling was insane in its exquisite, penetrating, annihilating, enthralling beauty. One quaking with the power to deceive Kings and uproot Nations.

His eyes softened to meet her beckoning gaze, and she unleashed a smile into his stare of bewilderment. In the past, she might have exploited his tenderness, but not now. Hers was a life brimming with jubilance. No guile or subtlety was needed to perfect that which she considered preordained.

"Derek, I love you dearly. In three days, you will know everything. All I ask is an open-hearted chance to be with you as before."

Still unaware of Ursini's true involvement, Derek's voice hardened.

"What about your Italian boyfriend, Alfredo, not to mention Tatiana?"

Natalia sighed. The vile past was still putting a wall between them. Annoyance streamed from her lips.

"Tatiana is arrogant. And, that wop has deceived—" Natalia stopped short. Derek was a civilian. She huffed in exasperation and resumed — "Please, Derek. Wait only three days. Don't judge me in your ignorance. I've hurt you. You're innocent and never deserved that. *Daragoi.*[1] Soon, you'll understand that I'm blameless too."

Derek chaffed like a man-poodle straining against his leash.

"After you assaulted Ludmila in the Metro, today, at home, in bed, I looked upon her with an open heart for the first time. *The first!* Natalia, you know me."

Natalia winced inwardly and made reply in a voice breathy with contrition.

"I understand, dearest. All I ask is that you stay open-hearted to me as well. I'm not jealous if Ludmila is your lover. Just remember my feelings."

1 Dearest (man) (Rus).

And, she gently hugged his phallus between her hands. And, as her words reverberated their way along his ear canals, Derek felt pleasure strum the length of his spine and permeate every crevice of his body, turning every chink into a hearth of embers.

"These are my feelings, Derek. This, isn't merely sexual, my love."

And, she broke contact.

"Now, do you understand? I've had to do this to decontaminate total strangers, both men and women. It disturbs me. But, I do it because my power to cleanse these brave souls is a gift I need to share. I wish to show you the depth of my love because you're the only one I yearn to share it with. What you experienced is but a trifling compared to the esteem I hold for the purity of my feelings about my devotion for you ... for us, *Daragoi*."

Derek was overwhelmed. Since hearing the news from Basil, he had tossed up many a fanciful hypothesis to explain how Natalia might have escaped earthly death. But now, he realized that the whole story was far more finely filigreed, the mystery much deeper, and he replied softly and in great earnest.

"Natalia, I promise I'll wait. You and I both deserve to be patient."

"You'll not be disappointed. All I ask is three days, just three. Now please, I must finish my work."

And, she re-set her goggles atop the bridge of her nose and wiped down every precious inch of his body. Then she doubled back over her work until she was satisfied it was perfect. Her final gesture was to kiss him tenderly on the left side of his neck and whisper in his ear.

"Thank you, Derek. I'm so sorry for everything."

Derek took her left hand, raised it to his lips and gave it a gentle kiss. And, holding it against his cheek, he looked down the length of her arm, the way he had all those months ago in his jewelry store.

"Thank you, Natalia. I will be open-hearted. But, when I act, you must accept it nobly without vindictiveness."

"May Satan's curse fall upon me if I do otherwise," she replied.

Derek toddled over to the men's dressing pavilion feeling conflicted about everything. There, he put on fresh clothes before joining Ludmila in the courtyard. She homed in on the sustained redness around his eyelids.

"Your eyes! Did they hurt you, sweetheart?"

"Oh, does it show. I had to get extra treatment. Extremely painful. I definitely don't want that again." *And, what a lie that was*, he thought.

Perching close to his side, Ludmila kissed his upper cheek.

"You saved me again today, my darling. I love you. You act oblivious, but I know that you feel the same way about me." And, putting a finger against his lips, her twinkling eyes delved straight and deep into his orbs, and she whispered.

"Derek, I know you need to be cleansed inside. I know, my sweet man."

Derek's heart stopped, then thumped back hard. He swore a canine choker noosed hard around his glottis was strangulating all sense of sanity from him in a female tug-o'war — *Why am I in the middle of this? Why can't I enjoy pure love without all these female territorial complications?*

Queen of Judgmentalism

Derek and Ludmila proceeded back to General Novimirov's Office. When Derek stepped inside, on seeing Sergei and Tatiana, he stopped short and became unsure about what to divulge.

"General Novimirov, I've new information about that subject. Could we—"

Basil cut in.

"Mr. Mitchell, please close the door. Talk freely, sir."

Derek eyed Tatiana ever so briefly, and his voice came out cold and reserved.

"General, it's as you said. Also, Natalia is altered in character. Altered for the better. She seems..." Derek felt befuddled at putting the matter into words. "This sounds weird, but 'outer worldly' is the only way I can describe it."

Basil sensed the tension in Derek's demeanor and motioned.

"Mr. Mitchell, sitdown, close your eyes and just jabber away about anything that crosses your mind. Please, any frivolity."

Sergei stood, presented Mr. Mitchell with his chair and retrieved another from the back-wall. Derek sat, closed his eyes, tilted his head back and waited. Being separated for so many difficult months, Derek's mental ice-jamb melted and out it all flowed like a backed-up river.

"Natalia has become this woman for all seasons. She is similar to someone twice her age in temperament. She's a saint. Before, she was somewhat narcissistic, vain, pretentious ... I ... I."

He stopped on realizing how much he sounded like Ta-bitch-iana, the Queen of Judgmentalism. And, as Derek resumed speaking his piece, Tatiana sat simmering in tempestuous thought — This *durak*[1] was talking about her best friend, with whom she shared many personality traits. And, Tatiana's mind churned over. What did this foreigner, an arrogant Y-Doodle forty-something male fossil know about the soul of Russia, let alone the soul of a Russian woman or any woman for that matter.

In due course, Derek's recollection slowed, he hesitated then paused.

And, Tatiana pounced on the opening.

"Mr. Mitchell, perhaps you're describing the dejected lover in you."

Basil's glance jetted a stream of raw venom; he expected Tatiana to be professional. One bitch fight in mother Russia today had already been one too many.

"Major, one more squeak and I'll personally hurl you from my office."

Basil turned back to Derek.

"Mr. Mitchell, excuse the flatulence. We're similar in age, and my assessment of Miss Bogomolski parallels yours. However, as her onetime lover, you see her through the eyes of an intimate. A perfect observer of the truth in my estimation. Please, close your eyes again and speak aloud your every thought, no matter how trifling. Just talk."

"Is there any need for Tatiana and Sergei to be here?" Derek replied.

Basil winked at him like a Komrade.

1 Moron (Rus).

"These puppies pride themselves on being my razor strop. They will take what you say as blunt truth and seek to whet it upon their superior strap of FSB experience. Oh yes, a Russian strop, no doubt. And, then they'll lay claim to handing me a sharper razor. For me, it will be entertaining if they confirm what I already know. In their welpish paws, the trick will be not to blunt the razor your disclosures fashion. If they can sharpen the razor anymore, remains to be seen. And, regardless of its entertainment value, I shall know all in spite of them."

Derek laughed in stifled politeness and instantly relaxed.

Sergei stared hard at his wife — *Thanks doobya!*[1]

Tatiana cowered her head.

Basil pricked up his ears again as Derek closed his eyes and resumed speaking. Sometimes, it came out decisively, at other times haltingly, but at all times the spirit of Natalia rang in Derek's choice of words.

"Natalia has always elicited in me a great tenderness for loving her — always. She craves tenderness. But, now it's deeper, fuller, more ravenous, just … just pure enchantment. Natalia has become the woman of my dreams. It scares me. I guess the change in her scares me. Maybe it all scares me."

Flustered, Derek paused to recompose himself.

"I felt like one of those helpless women in the movies, who has fallen madly in love with Count Dracula. Her touch was like his fangs sucking timeless pubescence out of my flesh. I mean … I felt like a teenager."

Such muddle-worded candor before strangers was unlike him. When Derek realized where he was, the trance was broken, and feeling the dweeb, he blurted.

"Please, don't laugh,"

Basil, his face projecting solidarity, leant across his desk.

"Derek, I got the same impression. Please, go on."

Derek smiled — *For the first time, Basil had used his Christian name — General Novimirov could be trusted.* And, as Derek relaxed into the chair again, he had a flash of recall and stiffened bolt upright.

"She said Satan."

Basil sensed breakthrough but remained detached.

"I see. So, Mr. Mitchell, what was the context?"

"She asked me to wait for three days, confident I would love her as before. I promised to hold-off. But, in turn, I insisted that she must accept my choice — be it Ludmila or her — without any further bitterness. And, she promised as well. That's when she swore — 'May Satan's curse fall upon me if I do otherwise.'"

Basil became uneasy. *Satan's Curse* was a two-way pledge that also venerated the Dark Lord. And, Miss Bogomolski's track record of love crazy meant she might put everything at risk to ensure the outcome she craved.

Derek caught the look of consternation on Basil's face and elaborated.

"Basil, here's what's peculiar. Natalia said 'Satan's curse,' and not just curse by itself, like some gypsy curse or some secular thing."

Basil resumed eye contact with Derek.

"It's all insightful, Derek. Please, elaborate."

---

1 Twit (Rus). [Also refers to 'W' the ex-US President elected in 2000 A.D.]

Derek relaxed again, but the more he strived for the words, the less intuitive he became at explaining the strangeness yet familiarness of the situation. Out of frustration, he switched tactics. "Let me ignore what she said and tell you about what I perceived. Natalia projected into me how she was a woman who seemed to understand everything. She was infinitely confident that I would choose her. She said I could be with Ludmila as a lover. She meant this by word and by touch."

Basil grew even more uneasy.

Unaware of this, Derek rambled on.

"There wasn't a hint of jealousy. In fact, when Ludmila later kissed me and told me she loved me, I began to suffer an anxiety attack. I saw myself the object of scandal in a tawdry game of rabid female territorialism. It's very disconcerting."

Derek could not see it, but Basil and Sergei were on the verge of cracking up. As was Tatiana, incensed at this arrogant old fart. She swore that Natalia must be insane if she saw anything good inside this Y-D[1] turd. She had a duty to protect her good friend. Mitchell was no lover. He'd gone from the insult of describing women as existing to be 'a woman of a man's dreams,' to an obnoxious comment about Natalia accepting Ludmila as his lover. But, Mitchell's pretended anguish about one too many harem bitches was beyond contempt!

And, as Derek lay head back, eyes closed, babbling on, Tatiana grew madder and madder. She felt palpable nausea heaving in her stomach, but she kept her silence because her chief seemed to consider Mitchell's disclosures informative. At least, he slyly let his target of interrogation think so.

The Major righted herself when Basil unexpectedly used her name.

"Derek, thanks for your read of Miss Bogomolski's personality. Major Gratski also told me her friend had changed in a way that she could not describe. You've given me a much clearer before and after understanding now."

Tatiana chopped in anxiously.

"Sir, could I be excused for a moment?"

Basil had sensed the Major's rising anxiety. An urgent need to go to the ladies room, he surmised. All the classic signs were there.

"Certainly. But, be back soon, we need to address our guest's interrogation."

Tatiana hurried out, and Basil returned to business.

"Mr. Mitchell, a new focus. Did Miss Bogomolski give you any explanation for surviving a deadly impact with a train? No broken bones. No bruises. No scratches. Your input, please."

Derek raised his head off the back of the chair.

"Interesting? I never asked directly, but I got the distinct impression she considers the whole episode a complete mystery."

"Are you acquainted with *Frankenstein*?" Basil asked.

"The Governor of the US Federal Reserve? Uh no, I—"

Basil interjected.

"No, no. I mean the fictional story. Please, excuse my English. Miss Bogomolski was also massively electrocuted. Ludmila and other witnesses describe seeing a bolt of electricity. Any hunches on that frontier, Derek?"

1 Acronym for Yankee-Doodle. i.e. American. Pronounced: Why-Dee or Why-Tee.

Derek breathed quietly and let the implication sink in.

"So, you're thinking she died on impact with the train. Then jolted back to life but as a different person with some new life force residing inside her body."

"Yes, as strange as that sounds. She is alive. She has an altered personality. She has powers unknown to this world. Literature abounds with such stories. Currently, aliens from outer space inhabiting the bodies of humans are in vogue. It's crazy, but Natalia is reality. Moreover, she can also heal wounds."

Derek fired back.

"There's more?"

"Correct. We're itching to design a medical investigation, but we don't have the science skills to begin asking the right questions let alone hunt down a plausible explanation. But, science can wait. Right now, I need to know if Miss Bogomolski represents a national security threat."

And, Basil studiously waited for Derek's response.

"General, I believe she represents a great gift to national security."

As if addressing an orchestra, Basil put up both his hands.

"Then, what was your *Dracula* description all about?"

"Excuse me. *Dracula* is my personal sense of how I felt overwhelmed when she revealed herself to me in a psychic sort of way. I sensed no satanic agenda. She allowed me to see inside her so I would know she was the woman of my dreams. Of course, such openness ... such seduction must bias my opinion. But, I think I'm being objective."

Since *Helen of Troy* bias was obvious, Basil drilled deeper.

"Did it seem that you were being drained when she used her powers?"

"No. I definitely would have felt that. What I felt was healthy. Empowering. It's more," Derek stuttered — "about God."

Basil squelched a smirk. Americans trotting out God was nothing new.

"You're saying she exudes some regenerative power?" he countered.

"Yes, exactly. Satan and Dracula are metaphors where someone gains, and someone loses. But, not here. It's as you said — regenerative."

And, Derek extended his arm and switched gears.

"Basil, speaking of Satan, what do you know about her insisting that I should wait three days before deciding about her and myself?"

Basil felt ambushed. He had ordered Derek and Natalia's alienation for the sake of their personal security as well as for the larger mission to unmask the Romanov-Al Guido *coup d'état* conspiracy. Despite his best intentions, what had resulted was a three-way slugfest between three passionate souls: all subscribing to true love, all feeling thwarted and all clamoring for resolution. Basil understood the obliterative passions arising from his own divorce all too well. Frustrated people, such as these three, were explosive. After a momentary pause to compose himself, he replied in a manner to openly accept blame and artfully secure maximum dignity for all concerned.

"Mr. Mitchell, I suspect it's my doing. Natalia confided to me her deep love for you. As does Ludmila, I must add. I felt thrust in the middle of something that I ought not be in the middle of. I probably told her to wait a few days."

Basil sighed loud and abundant to make it audible.

"It might be more than three. I don't recall using any specific number."

And, lowering his tone, Basil finished with all the earnestness he could muster.

"Mr. Mitchell, you're now up to speed about the real disaster at Komsomolskaya. Private lives are going to be on hold for some time. Natalia might have the power to take the sting off a massive tragedy. Russia might have to assert a selfish claim to her services for some incalculable number of days. I think she believed that in three days you would come to understand the larger stakes. I ask that you honour her request. We need your help to keep all spirits high."

"Of course. Three days or longer. I understand."

After a cursory knock on the door, Elena's head poked in.

"Sir, I called the Infirmary. Miss Naristikova's coughing—"

Derek leapt up and barreled through the door. Basil, Elena and Sergei scrambled right behind. After Ludmila exhausted herself coughing, Basil hunched down to speak softly to Derek.

"Mr. Mitchell, we've finished. Stay with her in the Infirmary." Basil straightened up — "Elena, this woman is to be treated like my daughter. Make that perfectly clear to Doktor Chernikrov." Basil stooped again and put a comforting hand on Derek's shoulder — "As soon as Miss Bogomolski is free, I'll send her to the Infirmary."

Slash and Burn

Basil returned to his office and placed a short call to Captain Botanin. After he hung up, he jotted down a few notes to preserve his recollections about his meeting with Derek Anthony Mitchell, and then resumed the Ursini interrogation meeting with Colonel Sergei Gratski.

Tatiana remained absent. Gone far too long for a mere bathroom break, her seeming dereliction annoyed Sergei intensely because he considered his wife the perfect lead-inquisitor for the 'Enhanced Interrogation' program he was detailing to the General. Also, absent were her cold-blooded suggestions.

Sergei's credible first attempt impressed Basil. However, after pondering the matter at greater length, Basil inserted several strategic alterations. As a demokrazy,[1] Russia was subject to public scrutiny, so Basil knew Russia's war machine had to be a peace machine. And, no different than a 'Peace Dividend', Russia needed a 'Conversation Dividend', hard truths the people of the world could rally behind. Staged confessions procured by torture would not cut it. And, for these reasons, while on paper Tatiana might have been a compelling first choice, Basil's foresight about the many in-their-own-words terrorist 'Conversations' yet to come, required a warm-blooded, sadistic finesse that would have beguiled Tatiana's all too robotic slash-and-burn personality.

---

1 The political process whereby Russia's elektorate forms its governments.

After Basil explained the gist of his amendments to Sergei, he ordered the Colonel to prepare the embassy chauffeur for a dry run of the techniques involved. And, after that, Carlo Rolfino, the Italian chargé d'affaires, for a full dress rehearsal. It was unlikely that either man knew a lot of details, so they made the best subjects, on whom Basil's revamped process of eliciting conversation could be better perverted. And, the perfection of perversion was essential because, come time to process Ursini, world peace could afford no screw-ups.

Once Sergei left, Basil summoned Lieutenant Olga Nikolaevna Krovsoska, a woman born again into the Russian Orthodox faith.

Shimmering with Estrogen

Basil was appraising Olga about the difficulties of being the lead inquisitor when Elena paged and informed him Miss Bogomolski was waiting in her office. Basil had Olga conceal herself under his desk, before directing Elena to send her in.

Once Natalia was seated, Basil outlined how he needed her assistance in softening-up the Italian monsters they had captured. Initially, she was delighted to help but as Basil explained the process of making the terrorists more open-hearted to conversation and contrition, she became more downcast.

Finally, Basil had Olga introduce herself. Out, from under his desk, Olga straightened, approached Natalia and shook her hand. Because Basil had appraised Olga about Natalia's powers, she was not startled; but in her heart, the electric connection she shared with Natalia felt like a kiss from Almighty. Basil had also appraised Natalia about the need for nudity during the interrogation process, so Olga's nakedness did not startle her. What she found extraordinary was that she had never seen a woman so exquisitely sculpted from head to toe, flaunting a snow-white complexion shimmering with estrogen. Natalia now had greater confidence in the General's plan, and reproved by her misconduct in the Metro, she promised she would play her assigned role.

Once all was understood, Basil ordered Olga to dress and report to Colonel Gratski. And, as he had promised Derek Mitchell, Basil escorted Natalia to the Infirmary so that she might aid or perhaps even cure Ludmila. If nothing else, Basil knew that a supervised encounter with a stricken Ludmila would steel Miss Bogomolski for the softening-up horrors that lay ahead of her.

Choke Me

Covered in a single white sheet of crisply starched cotton, Ludmila lay serene and motionless within the sunset warmth of yellowing Soviet-era flannel pajamas. To reduce the amount of direct sunlight, the room's blinds were shuttered. What light did filter through, cast a series of shadow grey prison stripes that choked the room's sense of space even tighter. Natalia was struck by the way Ludmila's nose shone bright as a shark's fin, riding high against two sombre stripes that ran the length of her body and masked all color in her eyes and cheeks. This narrowing optical effect also made her lips appear incongruous — full-budded and blood-red as if an infant in graceful slumber.

From the other bed, a body moved. Natalia was relieved when Derek rolled his head and looked at her. Basil had already warned her — No sooner had Derek introduced himself to Doctor Chernikrov than he broke into coughing fits. He was now inhaling bottled oxygen to keep his airways open.

Addressing Basil and Natalia, Dr. Chernikrov explained how Derek's and Ludmila's lungs were succumbing to pulmonary edema[1] and how medical science had no means of reversing the inevitable. Natalia clenched the frosted tubular stainless steel bed railings to hold herself steady while digesting the doctor's diagnoses. But, despite her intent to muster stoicism, her temples plumped pink, and her eyes glistened heavy with remorse. Basil's gaze dropped from her face to her toned, white arms and the conspicuous redness in her knuckles, knowing that if there existed any power in Miss Bogomolski to cure this curse, now came the acid test.

Once Natalia recomposed herself, she approached Derek.

"No, I'm fine. Attend to Ludmila first," he protested.

Obeying without hesitation, she made for Ludmila's bed. Grabbing the sheet, she wafted it aloft and floated it down to Ludmila's feet on a puff of air. She gently unbuttoned Ludmila's top and placed her hands against Ludmila's breasts. She knew if she was to heal her internally, it had to come through the same means she used to project her feelings. She introspected to summon her sense of healing from deep within and to project it into Ludmila's body. But, she felt nothing. She repeated this with two hands on Ludmila's left breast alone and focused on a single lung.

Derek cried — "Please try harder. I know you can."

Trembling in self-doubt, Natalia felt the horror that a life laid low by her criminal conduct at Komsomolskaya might slip away through her miraculous fingers. Next, she placed her hands under Ludmila's breast and angled her head like a resolute bull. The effect was immediate. Ludmila flailed about wildly like a taser victim.

Basil took note of everything.

Second after vanishing second, the scene became more macabre. And, watching this spectacle, Derek felt torn asunder with self-reproach. Ludmila had given him everything that was best about her, but he had not. She had loved him unreservedly, but he had not. Her noble life was waning, and he was impotent to even tell her how much he cared for her. And, convinced that Natalia harboured untapped powers, Derek again cried out.

"Do this, I beg you. Treat her like your sister."

Natalia wiped back a bothersome tear and placed one hand under Ludmila's back and one hand over her breast. And, with Ludmila's chest sandwiched between her palms, Natalia tried releasing the gift within. Ludmila's body

1 ARDS - Acute Respiratory Distress Syndrome.

tremored and flinched then, as if possessed by a succubus spirit, it arched solid as marble and every pore of her smooth, almond skin wept beads of inward-lit opalescence.

Derek became distraught.

"If she dies then I too am dead."

And, a coughing fit seized hold of his chest.

Natalia concentrated her mind, her tenacity, her desire to cure; trying her utmost to elicit the mystical force within her body to flash like an arc of electricity between her hands and penetrate deep into Ludmila's body. But, nothing. *Nothing.* She looked over at Derek and spoke through her anguish.

"Let me try it on you. Perhaps my love for you will free the force to cure."

It would take total inspiration — this she respected. With Derek, she was everything that she considered perfect and pure in life. He peeled away the sheet and with a deft twitch of his fingers, buttons released and off came his shirt. She sandwiched the left side of his chest between her palms and focused all her mental energy. Derek's body went into an epileptic seizure suffused with divine pleasure. He could feel all her energy directed at healing him. She focused harder. And, Derek plunged into an opium haze of ecstasy, but still she sensed no healing. Thwarted, she disavowed her own being and unleashed herself in grim determination. Derek went into shock for several seconds before reclaiming enough presence of mind to cry out in short stifled pants.

"No. Don't. Stop — No."

She bore down harder, but Basil darted to the bed and snatched her away.

"Yes, I will. I will," she shrieked in anger and madness.

As she squirmed wildly in Basil's harsh grip, Derek's lucidity returned.

"You must never do that."

Basil erupted, clamped both his hands around Natalia Bogolmolski's throat, shook her ferociously and snarled into her face.

"What's he talking about, *suka*?"[1]

Derek took a frantic breath.

"Basil, stop. Stop! She wanted to save me by trying to release all her life force into my body, even if she died. It was nothing evil. But, she can't."

Derek sucked in another half-breath.

"Basil, her power is limited."

And, overwrought with the knowledge that the beauty of the great purpose of life could not be felt more intensely and yet death be more certain, Derek's eyes cinched shut. Tears beaded from his closed lids and wick'd along his lashes. His mind wandered from the lingering press against his lips of Ludmila's last kiss to a remembrance of his gunned-down wife, Marie. Emerging out of apparition, her body covered in a morgue-white sheet, except for the remains of her face — a bullet shattered jaw twisted up under her right eye. Tears started streaming. His sanity ricocheted between a hurt so devastating it was felt as a dagger in the ear and the promise of eternal oneness, the bliss he felt when Natalia had tried to empty herself of life in order to save his.

1 Bitch (Rus).

Sensing the General's grip on her throat slacken, Natalia clamped her hands over his and pushed them even harder against her neck until her eyes bulged savage — "Choke me. Choke me! I'm cursed with something that's utterly useless."

Basil twisted his hands free, and Natalia melted piteously to the floor in dread-filled wailing. *Vopl* — as the Russians say. She had done this — her fist.

On instinct, Basil stooped over and bundled her limp frame into his arms. As he straightened, he glanced over his shoulder at Dr. Chernikrov and groused.

"Doktor, do whatever you must. I need these two alive."

And, Basil stormed out of the room. His feelings — mixed. Natalia's soft and pliant neck had fit his hands like a glove. The connection was stupendous, beautiful, volcanic with marvel. And, so it was, the trace residue of dioxin on his right hand acquired when he greeted Derek Anthony Mitchell was cleansed.

The Longest and Closest of Friends

Basil carried Natalia into a room reserved for officers and placed her on an empty bed. A nurse hurried in and administered a stiff dose of phenobarbital. Basil hoped it would not degrade under the influence of whatever force or thing inhabited her body. After five minutes of observation, the nurse left. And, he seated himself on the edge of the bed and watched over his patient intently.

With her slumbering in stillness, his subconscious began to introspect.

Beneath all the boil of emotions, when he had placed his hands in anger around her neck, and she placed her hands atop his, the life force within her reached out, around and into him. For the briefest of moments, in the heat of strangulation, their melded beings exchanged the heartache of a nagging dread — if true love was not a fluke, it was a curse.

The minutes rolled lazily by and like an aging king savouring the warmth of a palace-sized log fire in the dead of winter, while watching over a sleeping ward, Basil slowly lost track of the here and now. Natalia's face so tranquil and soft. Her hair, so flaxen, it seemed to shimmer. And, with her every outward breath, the air sparkled with embryosis, and Basil's heart ballooned in his chest and ripened into seasoned youth. And, within his sense of soul, the mesmerizing promise inside of Miss Natalia Vladimirovna Bogomolski gradually became more and more alluring.

After a span of forty minutes, Natalia stirred back to life. For Basil, while the enchantment of solitude was broken, its serene mood persisted. His voice rolled off his lips warm and resonant. It was all '*Koi no Yokan.*'[1]

"I hope you had a good nap."

As Natalia finished blinking her eyes open, her revived consciousness seized upon her last waking thought.

"Oh Basil, it's useless."

And, tears puddled and flowed from eyes that appeared focused on the ceiling but were staring inwardly into the bowels of her deepest misery.

Basil toyed with her welcome informality.

1 To contemplate another and know love is destined. (Japanese)

"Well, Miss, since I'm holding your hand, Basil is fine. You know I had to act. Derek shouted 'Stop.' Please excuse any harshness on my part."

She blinked to recompose and then gazed into his eyes bitter-sweet.

"Basil, I only sought to save my beloved. When he sensed this, he refused the very idea. I felt all his." She stopped.

Her new powers were beginning to awaken her to a depth of emotional insight that now mocked her capricious sense of springtime, her onetime Eden for happiness. She had felt the beauty of how Derek enjoyed a long memory of intense love, starting with Marie, his dead wife and the child she was carrying. It was one thing to know it as a story from the past, shared between lovers, but another to feel the majesty of it course through her body. She turned her head away from Basil and spoke aloud her most searing fear.

"I can do nothing. I can project the force of love into him, but not the force to heal him. … My great love is lost forever."

A heavy numbness overwhelmed Basil. The tone of devastation in her voice sucked the very marrow out of his bones. For Basil suffered a heartache of his own. It was the meat of the tragedy they both shared — love that was true was by that very quality rarely capable of being felt as requited. Whether he was seized by subconscious guilt about ordering the severance of her once budding relationship with Derek or by an intimate knowledge of the pains that racked her, a hurt that he believed they suffered in common, Basil felt compelled to open up to her.

"Natalia, I had the same feelings for my ex-wife, Galena. She was my great love, but she never treasured it. Living in Moscow, she was consumed by pretentiousness. Ever insisting, it was for the advancement of our family."

And, Basil paused to steel himself against a more pressing fear.

"This disaster has worsened because my teenage daughter Anastassia, who grew up in Moscow, now resents living in Ekaterinburg. She's becoming jaded and callous about life. I fear she might start doing heroin."

Basil looked away abruptly. The thought of his children, Anastassia and Ivan, so like him, yet so far away and isolated from the advantages of Moscow, was too raw to contemplate. And, he realized to his horror that while over three years had now passed, he was still not equipped to discuss this personal catastrophe without exposing himself to a complete loss of composure. Tamping back the hardness welling in his throat, Basil let go of Natalia's right hand.

Natalia warmed to and empathized with his grief. And, as she rose to sit beside him, she snaked her left hand up behind his back and placed it gently to the left of his spine, over his heart. The muscular ticks and the spasmodic trembling within the aching chest of this giant of a man touched her deeply. And, so pure had become her new command of the feelings that were all too human in life, she sensed a tender lightness blossom from within him. Its wondrous beauty seemed so perversely out of place that she felt compelled to console him.

"Basil, I'm very sorry for you. I certainly appreciate your hurt. I hope we can help each other." A sudden distraught intruded, she closed down, and her hand slid free — "Please, I don't want to talk about it now. It's all too horrible."

And, silently they sat, coming to grips with the need to refocus their energies and prepare for facing up to the larger catastrophe throughout Moscow that beckoned, if not commanded, their complete allegiance. In a final gesture of release and comfort, Natalia closed her eyes and pressed her hand anew against his back. In this way, Natalia and Basil shared their first intimate communication by entering into that delicate vulnerability of commiseration that one only experiences in times of great tragedy with the longest and closest of friends.

Vopl, Vopl — All About Was Vopl

All over Moscow sporadic gunshots rang out. President Bushkin had decreed — NO SILENCERS. His message: The law was martial and martial the law would be. Having long signed on to the American national security syndrome that 'War is diplomacy waged by other means,' and likewise, being at the mercy of Russia's sloganeering "Sound-Bite" demokrazy, Bushkin knew his elektorate needed a corpse count capable of greasing the homeland security agenda he was formulating with his staff of generals, admirals and air marshals.

Little of the anarchy on the streets was lost on Oleg. While he'd been born as the Soviet-era died, his grandmother had passed on the blood, flesh and tears history of their country. Her dearest husband, Yura, a tank commander felled in combat during Operation Typhoon in the last days of the Soviet exit from Afghanistan, had opened her eyes to the black heart that was the Soviet Military-Industrial complex. And, this, she had impressed upon Oleg, so as to empower him should Russia's fitful demokrazy ever backslide into the survivalist 'National Security' mentality of the *siloviki*.[1]

Having left school as soon as Mrs. Vetrushkin had phoned, all that remained was a one block march eastwards on Ulitsa Zamorenova. Oleg rounded the corner onto Ulitsa Presnenski expecting to find Mrs. Vetrushkin, his second mother, in the children's park of the apartment complex overseeing the toddlers left in her care. But, instead, he confronted a sprawling army tent. The green behemoth swallowed over half of the quarter-acre playground. He panicked and dashed for the entrance to his grandmother's building. A shot rang out from behind him, but he heard it not. At almost the same instant, a soldier stepped into his path.

"Stop," and holding out his rifle, stiff-armed and chest-high, the soldier barked — "Decontaminated residents, only."

"The block captain, Mrs. Vetrushkin, called me. Where is she?" Oleg blurted, oblivious to all menace and more worried than ever about Babayula.

"I know of no Vetrushkin. *Tam*," and the soldier released the grip on his weapon and pointed with his right hand — "Speak to Lieutenant Mirzemlin."

Oleg snapped about, fearing the lieutenant might vanish at the sound of his name. Near the entrance of the army tent, he saw an officer consoling a woman and hurried over. He was midway when the woman lifted her head and brushed back a flurry of locks that matted her wet cheeks.

1 *siloviki* - Strong Man leadership. *Tam* - There. *Harosho* - Good (Rus).

"Mrs. Vetrushkin, are you alright?" he cried out and started sprinting.

The woman looked over at the youth.

"Oleg!" she called and then turned her attention to the Lieutenant — "Sir, this is the boy. Let's get it over with quickly."

"*Harosho*," replied the officer in agreement.

Mrs. Vetrushkin reached out and caught Oleg as he rushed in.

"Listen, Oleg. This is important."

Oleg read her eyes and his ruddy cheeks went white.

"Your grandmother is in a very bad way. Come with us."

With Lieutenant Mirzemlin leading, Mrs. Vetrushkin escorted Oleg into the dim interior of the decontamination tent. The ground was sodden underfoot. And, misted through hissing spray nozzles, the air smelt like a eucalypt rainforest. An attendant wearing a mask over his mouth and hands gloved in latex, pulled aside an entry flap. Before the three crossed over, the Lieutenant addressed Oleg.

"Boy, your grandmother is suffering from laryngeal and pulmonary edema. Put these gloves on. And, obey this rule — You may touch your grandmother's hands, but touch absolutely nothing else. Got it?"

"Yes, sir."

Mirzemlin unhooked a flashlight[1] from a pole by the entryway while Oleg flexed his fingers into the gloves. "Now, follow behind me, Oleg."

The Lieutenant raised his arm, and the flashlight found its mark on a patient in the far-left corner. An orderly was operating a hand bellows feeding air into a tube inserted into the woman's throat. When Mirzemlin reached the stretcher, he extended his arm sideways to stop the boy. While the Lieutenant issued instructions to the orderly to retract the tube and rouse the patient, Mrs. Vetrushkin placed her hand on Oleg's shivering cheek.

"Olegin," she said softly, "Yulia can't speak. I'll explain later. Right now, you must be very strong. Her will to live needs your fortitude, Oleg. Promise me?"

Oleg nodded mournfully.

"Say it, Oleg. Promise me."

"I promise."

Mirzemlin moved to the head of the stretcher and faced Oleg.

"Have faith, boy," he said, "Faith in yourself, too. What I want you to do is whisper in your grandmother's ear. Can I trust in your courage, Oleg?"

The boy nodded resolutely. Mirzemlin laid his right hand on Oleg's shoulder and bade him kneel close to the patient's right ear. Down, he went.

"Babayula. Babayula. It's me, Olegin."

Standing, Mrs. Vetrushkin picked up on a sliver of a smile.

"Oleg, she hears you. Tell her you love her."

"I love you, Babayu. Mrs. Vetrushkin and I will look after you now."

The patient's arm straightened, and Mrs. Vetrushkin bent over and grasped Oleg's right hand and guided it to his grandmother's quivering fist.

"Oleg, she has keys for you. Put your hand under hers. Reassure her that it's you, and get ready to take the keys from her."

1 US English. Avoids 'Torch' ambiguity of British English.

"Babayu, you're safe now. Here, feel my hand?" Oleg intoned, holding back a sob — "Can you feel that big tennis grip of mine, Babayula?"

A massive tear baubled free of the old woman's eye and traced a path down the side of her face before coming to rest at the crinkled lobe of her right ear. The pain inside the woman was unbearable. But, it was an empty pain, because in the blackness, his voice, his humour, his *Sampras* hands caressing hers were everything. She relaxed her fingers, and Oleg received the precious keys.

"I have them, Babayu. Now, promise me. Rest and recover."

Another tear, larger than the first, streamed out. And, bleeding into its companion, the fatted unity fell free of her earlobe.

"When you get bett—," Oleg started.

"Boy," Mirzemlin cut in — "Let her rest. She's in pain and needs air."

The Lieutenant motioned to the orderly, and as the breathing tube touched her lips, the patient gasped out — "*Spasiba*,[1] Lieutenant."

His grandmother's thanks went to this kind officer. Oleg wiped back a tear.

"My thanks as well, sir," he sputtered.

He had no sooner finished speaking then his body started quaking in anguish. Mrs. Vetrushkin held him close until he steadied. Straining to maintain his own composure, Mirzemlin flashed the boy the steely look of camaraderie.

Sensing sublimated emotional turmoil, Mrs. Vetrushkin came to their aid.

"Oleg, I have a note for you. But, outside."

She glanced up and engaged the officer.

"Lieutenant, if you would, please?"

Relieved to be on his way, Mirzemlin directed the flashlight at the entryway flap and led them out. Once through, they stopped so the attendant could remove Oleg's gloves, then the three proceeded across the tent and out into the courtyard.

Wailing was audible from every direction.

Vopl, vopl — all about was *vopl*. The keening of death. It had always been there, but now it registered in Oleg's heart. He felt part of the great crush of grief. Again, he started quaking, and again, Mrs. Vetrushkin held him close. Because, soon, the boy must come to know how terrorism had poisoned his grandmother and thrown their motherland into a global conflagration that might last any span of decades.

While Mrs. Vetrushkin shepherded Oleg toward the building's entry, Lieutenant Mirzemlin marched forward and prepared the soldier on guard. As Mrs. Vetrushkin and Oleg approached the door, the two men snapped to attention and held their hands in fixed salute. The woman and the boy toddled past them and through the doorway the soldier held open. The man released his grip, and the olive-green, steel-plate door swept to a close of its own accord.

Lieutenant Mirzemlin addressed his Komrade, eye to eye.

"Carry on, private."

The Lieutenant wheeled about and strode back inside the tent.

Moments later, a gunshot rang out.

Clean through the head — NO SILENCER.

The third of many duties destined for him that day.

1 *Spasiba* - Thank You. *Vopl* - Graveside Wailing. Keening (Rus)

Issur Davidovich Mirzemlin never forgot.

A grandmother's love. A grandmother's courage.

Her voice, her resolve, her final words — *Spasiba, Lieutenant.*

Chamber of the Undead

In the director's booth outside the notorious Honeymoon Suite, Basil took his seat and inserted an earpiece into his right ear canal. Sergei was setting temperature control dials. He was there to assist and learn the difference between a dress rehearsal and a master performance. To the left of Olga Krovsoska, whose eyes shone with the menace of intent bordering on retribution, stood Natalia Bogomolski. Pincered between stage-fright moods of trepidation and excitement, Natalia's mind was focused on her upcoming performance. And, the more she watched the scene on the high contrast B-MONITOR to Basil's left, the more she took emotional stock of Moscow's most recent fascist monstrosity — Alfredo Constanzo Leonardo Ursini — and the more she reconciled herself to accept what was to come.

Within a room expressly designed to elicit from its occupant a sense of warm-blooded uterine bliss, the naked and hairless barbarian from Italy lay strapped into a dental chair-like apparatus. Outwardly, this harness' spartan form resembled the blocky chalk outline of a crime-scene cadaver. But contoured with a fleshy-foam rubber, it provided its captive the matronly comfort of feeling swaddled like a babe within freshly flayed lambskin.

Despite the fact that Ursini's neck, arms, legs and waist were completely immobilized upon this system of pliant restraint, the 'Hotel Lubyanka' staff had exercised the utmost care to infuse their guest with a sense of quietude. Air blanketed warm against the wide expanses of his flesh deliberately left uncovered. Even Ursini's bodily waste had been taken into consideration. A squirm-proof stub-tube butted tender and tight against and into the cavity of Ursini's seated rectum. Spillage was rendered impossible by a generous application of an electro-gel sealant. A bypass catheter, surgically installed at the base of his scrotum, flanged like a suction cup against the perforated wall of his bladder. Both systems, neat and German-engineered, would attend to the discharge from any excretory ejections in the event Ursini had one or several spontaneous bowel movements over the next half-hour.

Ursini's mouth and upper lip sported a molded guard made of smooth plastic, gummy in texture and fecal brown in color. It suffused a barely perceptible stench of maggoted meat, a level to disquiet rather than nauseate. The mouth-guard functioned to prevent their guest from making tactless comments about hotel management as well as to protect his tongue and lips from involuntary jaw clenches. Based on a stolen CIA design used in America's waterboarding program, it had been accessorized with a plunger held firmly in place by a hydraulic-assist expansion valve. The plunger could be quickly released or locked down whenever anyone decided they did or did not want to hear whatever sounds might emanate from Ursini's face in the course of the proceedings.

Already at post within the room, Doktor Nadya Dimitrovna Soskrova, the physician in attendance, nodded. A brutish door groaned its way open. The place returned to near silence. Alfredo pricked up his ears, but all he could hear were those beastly electric arcs slashing the air, sparking between sets of combs on both his left and right. The chemist in Alfredo well knew why the room smelt as airy fresh as an ancient glade of sylvan ferns rimming the foot of an alpine waterfall. These austere Swiss-quality stainless steel surgical prongs, slender, sharp and clean, generated ozone, de-ionized the air and crackled with the promise of pain yet to be meticulously rendered.

He listened intently. Electricity sizzled. No other sound.

A penetrating fragrance wafting from behind and over his head alerted Alfredo to a presence. It was as if the room had morphed into a Japanese teahouse paneled in raw sandalwood, spruced with jasmine because the emotional atmosphere transformed from bereft to springtime. He was scrying his mind intently trying to put meaning to this novel scent, when in a flash, the light-blue of chiffon floated past his peripheral vision, followed by a flowing brocade of lustrous black hair.

The woman turned her head to reveal an exquisite face framing chatoyant eyes of vibrant green. She glared mercilessly down and took him by surprise. The look was pure — predatory pure. Focusing anywhere to avoid her direct gaze, Alfredo perused her soft yet sculpted nose, her full-blooded lips, but then his attention was drawn to that unmistakable rustle. Ballooning blue fabric was attempting to restrain two massive volcanoes, which had been heaved into rotary motion as they strained to follow the rest of her lithe torso when she had abruptly swiveled about to face him down. As her buxom physique dampened to a more subtle jostling motion, the woman smiled ever so warmly.

"Well Alfredo, your manner of dress had us confused. But, I see that you do indeed like women," Olga paused to establish more delicate connection with a softer gaze and as she drew her finger along the underside of his jaw, she purred.

"I like you, Alfredo." And, Olga stood erect so that her robe slid off her shoulders onto the floor. And, repeating his name with the annealed deliberateness of female menace, she crooned.

"Alfredo, tell me dear man, what do you think it takes to keep this figure of mine in such prime condition?"

And, as if estrogen was the ambrosia of angels, Alfredo's eyes took in the measure of a woman of heart-jolting proportions. She leant closer to him, draping and drawing her left volcano along the naked length of his left side. Alfredo was right-handed and here was this voluptuous *Tatar Titiana* on his left. He felt so entirely vulnerable. And, she knew it.

She hovered closer. Her fragrance was incredible. The ivory fleshed splendor of her right arm coiled like a serpent around the top of his shaved and sensitized head. And, while her right hand began stroking his right earlobe, her left snaked down his waist and teased the tender expanse south of his navel. Sultry exhalations from hot-blooded nostrils danced across his left cheek, wild and exhilarating. Her tongue strummed music and traipsed and rimmed the lobe of his left ear with delicious pleasure. And, once again, the cat mewled soft.

"Alfredo have you ever met a vampire?"

Olga raised her head to scrutinize the look of humoured disbelief she had planted on Ursini's face. She stroked his cheek and grinned ever so knowingly.

"I'm here for my feed, my sweet man."

Lines of smirk corrugated Alfredo's brow.

Olga's tone remained impassive.

"Perhaps my cousin can persuade you. She simply wants your blood."

Fingers danced along Alfredo's right arm, as another woman swept by. She was dressed in a blood-stained white chiffon robe. At last, she turned, and Alfredo recognized her face. Natalia smiled.

"Yes, Alfredo. It's me," her voice breathy and ever so soft.

She paused to take stock of his plaintive gaze. "I was hoping we would meet under different circumstances but I guess fate meant it to be this way. I had dreamt that I'd found my prince, but you chose to disappoint me," she sang — before shrieking like a harpy — "You useless, wop queen!"

Natalia noticed how Alfredo tried to shake his head in denial, and she slapped her left hand down hard on his forehead and snarled raw venom into his ear.

"What were you doing in that dress and with that man today! You have hurt me Alfredo. Hurt, hurt, hurt me. I've been thirsting for a real prince ever since the untimely demise of our dear Dracul."

Olga smarted on hearing Natalia's irreverent words and pounded her nails down hard into Alfredo's chest and hissed loudly.

"Don't mention his great name in this worm queen's presence."

Alfredo heaved in pain.

Olga retracted her nails and took note of the pleasurable happenstance. Bringing her fingertips up to her face, she inhaled the aroma behind the deliciousness, which beckoned. Natalia's lips pouted rutty with expectation as she watched Alfredo's crimson honey bleed to the surface. She breathed deep, craned her sleek white neck across his field of vision and brought her glowing face closer to his wounds. Alfredo felt the warm puffs of Natalia's breathing. Then came soft mewling and finally, as if a week-old kitten, she lapped at the red-blotted punctures ever so gingerly. From a mere return of comfort, Alfredo suddenly basked in rapturous astonishment as a soothing wave of the most tender healing pervaded his flesh and then licked its way across the whole of his upper chest.

Watching his reaction, Olga purred anew.

"Natalia likes your blood, Alfredo."

And, Olga cast a smile — wide as whiskers — before she turned to her left.

"Doktor, cut his arm for her."

Natalia stood aside to give Alfredo the perfect view. The doctor took one step forward and a stainless-steel scalpel went straight to the matter. Before he could even knot his brows to wince, Alfredo's eyes watched the sheen of metal race effortlessly down his immobilized right forearm and stop shy of his wrist.

The blade had flayed open an eight-inch surgical abomination. But, far worse than the overt pain, Alfredo was struck senseless with terror.

They all watched his blood well exuberantly to the surface.

Olga sniffed and expressed her delight.

"What a delicious bouquet! Wait cousin. Me, first."

Olga wiped her finger across the pouting wound and daubed his blood upon each of her jovian yet sensitive nipples. With an accompanying gasp of pleasure, she moaned — "Ah! The blood of first terror is so surreal!"

After licking her finger, Olga addressed Natalia.

"The rest is yours, dear cousin."

Natalia's eyes smoldered with anticipation and flexing the firm fingers of a milk maiden, she squeezed his arm to form a runnel of skin along the length of the cut which allowed the gash to puddle up its full bounty of ruby-red cream. Only when it was about to overflow its trough, did Natalia bend over to slurp and lick. The feeling was magical. In stark contrast to the pain, Alfredo felt a volcanic blast of vampire pleasure pulse pure ecstasy along the length of his forearm. When Natalia had finished, she looked up at Alfredo and into eyes of disbelieving bewilderment. Blood baubled off the edge of her lower lip and down her rounded chin. She gleefully noted his look and again stood aside so he could get a perfect view.

When Alfredo glanced downward, he saw no sign of injury. The heal was complete. Tears welled in his eyes. It wasn't from any residual pain but from the horror that he was not dreaming. This was no fable. The Russians had two vampires. Torture was superfluous. Alfredo realized that he was going to be slowly broken down and gastrointerrogated,[1] corpuscle by corpuscle.

This is my flesh. This is my blood.

Olga smiled and stroked his cheek with the satin-skinned back of her right-hand. Her voice was all throat, sexually charged — "Cousin, he understands. Now, we'll have to sauce up the pain to get a tasty feed."

And, she ended her taunt with a mild rap to his nose.

But, Natalia wasn't listening, she was pawing his phallus.

"Look cousin. He's not circumcised. What do you suggest?"

Alfredo jolted back into the earthly world of terror — *Circumcision!*

Olga looked over her shoulder, and trilling like a chick that has spied its first worm, she made crackling reply — "Something stylish. Let's fashion it into a harlequin's cap fit for a joker, with wedges to create a series of tassels along the sides of his cock."

Natalia remained silent while Olga paused in thought as if seeking a Ralph Lauren moment. And, out popped another idea — "Perhaps a crenellated shape. Yes, like on the battlement walls of the Kremlin."

And, while Olga rattled on, Natalia, as if combing the hair on a Barbie doll, mindlessly stroked their guest's phallus searching her ken for inspiration of her own. As it flexed into its aroused state, Natalia had a 'Hello Kitty' insight.

"Olga, let's cut his foreskin down the center and fashion it into pussy flaps."

1 An Islamic means of obtaining intel.

Olga was appalled. "Cousin, show some piety. We can help this man make a covenant with God. That foreskin needs to be reaped. You know how the taste of foreskin is more sublime than truffles. Perhaps I should chew it off bit by bit then what's left will have a fashionably rugged-male *Banana Republic* rat-eaten look."

"Oh cousin, what style you have! When people ask if our wop is a natural redhead, we can say 'No, he's a Rat Head.'"

And, they bent over, convulsing in fits of laughter. As they stood tall again, their tittering drew to a close, and they noticed how anguish puddled like blood across their dinner's face. Their mouths opened into smile, fangs bared. And, the eyes of vampires that once watered with pure mirth, now dripped with hungered mischief. As time was wasting away, the doctor decided to sober them up.

"Ladies, mastication is not sanitary. I must cut it off."

"Oh no, no. Let us chew it off," they replied, tongues stroking their lips.

The doctor addressed Alfredo.

"Make a choice Ursini. Covenant by scalpel — yes or no?"

"See doktor. He wants us to chow down on his dick," they said in unison.

The doctor confronted him square in the eyes.

"Ursini! If you don't nod yes, I will let them decide."

Alfredo could not believe it. The doctor stepped back to give the vampires clear access, and he nodded furiously. The doctor stepped forward, shooed off the vampires and stooped over. Like a butcher paring gristle off a sheepshank, it took her eight solid cuts to complete the process. The scalpel cut astray of the intended area; not because of any lack of professionalism on the doctor's part but because, by writhing and bucking all over the place, the detainee was refusing to cooperate with a government official. Olga and Natalia faked eating the pieces of skin the doctor threw over his head. They returned to his left and right with blood smears on their lips and were greeted with an artistic achievement even more beguiling than his tender and tasty foreskin.

"Look, Natalia! Look what the doktor has done. It's a big beautiful strawberry lollipop." The relish in Olga's voice ended in swoon.

Natalia bent over. Obscuring Alfredo's view, she licked clean his scored and gashed phallus while squeezing it gently between her hands. For Alfredo, all remembrance of slashing pain was soon swamped in another bout of unearthly pleasure, more rapturous and more horrifying than the last. Once finished, Natalia raised her head and smiled like a gloat. Olga screamed.

"*You pig!* You gorged on all his foreskin blood. It's, it's so precious!"

"Sorry cousin. But, look again."

Between her nimble fingers, she held out his aroused penis for all to inspect.

Olga squealed with glee — "How perfect. We'll have to call it Saint Peter. It reminds me of that ancient triple-crown the Popes used to wear."

Natalia shook her head, offended by Olga's blasphemy.

"I say we call it 'Jughead' because it looks like that hat in the Archie comics. You and I can be Betty and Veronica. What do you say cousin?"

Olga shrieked with maniacal delight.

"Oh cousin, how imaginative you are. I have black hair so I'm Veronica." Throwing it a school-girl kiss — "Hello Jughead!"

Natalia sidled up close to Alfredo's right ear.

"I guess that makes me Betty. If I recall correctly, Jughead doesn't get much action. So I think we have found the right name for it. Yes? Maybe when the Russians permit you to answer questions you can tell them who you like better, Betty or Veronica. Veronica has such huge boobs. Oh, that reminds me," she looked up — "Cousin will I tell him how you maintain your awesome figure?"

"Please do, cousin. I'll help the doktor prepare everything for our feed."

"Jughead, you probably think that gravity has little effect on vampires. But, that's a myth. It affects us almost as much as humans. Do you know how old my cousin is? Well, I'll drop a tactful hint. Over four centuries."

She pointed towards Olga's midriff.

"How can those udders be so hoisted on one so mature?"

Natalia paused again. This time — no hints.

"My sweet Jughead, it's testosterone." Her voice became sententious. "Women need it from their lovers. In that primordial puddle of vaginal semen, while sperm are wiggling upstream, his glorious testosterone is transdermally leaching into her blood. Astute women take after us vampires to stay healthy. But, we four-hundred-year old hags need direct infusions. We must bypass the piddle-man and draw it straight from the source."

With mirth re-ignited, she laughed with glee.

"What delightful puns, do you get it piddle and middle, sauce and source," she snickered anew. Then sudden silence. She pulled away from his ear and rose up high into view. Alfredo saw annoyance burning hot and fierce in her eyes.

"Jughead, your emails stated you had a sense of humour. I guess that was classic cyber-space exaggeration. Well! As far as I'm concerned Veronica can have you lock, stock and barrel. Betty can get by with blood."

Then Natalia calmed — "Time to prepare for my feed. As a man, you probably don't know it but cleaning blood stains is a bitch." She parted her robe and smiled when she noticed Alfredo's gaze of compliment.

"Nice Betty-sized boobs, yes? Pertinaciously fleshy and ripe. Your blood should yield ample testosterone for my physique, especially when you're writhing in pain. You need to ignore that Hollywood foolishness that glamourizes the sensuality of a good vampire feed, my darling Jughead. Frenzied human pain creates a sublime bubbling interplay between the hormones adrenaline, testosterone and cortisol. They spice the blood, giving it an indescribable aroma and flavor. Screamers are the best. The absolute best."

Natalia licked her lips to accentuate the terror and then continued.

"Veronica and I both love a good screamer, my sweet Jughead. As a connoisseur of fine wines, I'm sure you understand. Since you don't have a sense of humour, please do something tasteful tonight and scream for us like you've never screamed for any other woman before."

Wheeling over a video monitor and positioning its sharp rectangular form to the left of her torso, Olga's nakedness exploded back into Alfredo's view. On screen, he noticed the doctor donning latex gloves. Next, his eyes focused on her activities between his parted legs. When the doctor's teeth clenched down upon a scalpel leaving both her hands free to move, the angst on his face presaged a sudden involuntary bowel movement. His third now. Swamped by the bright-white surgical lights of the room, a faint urinator LED flashed red, the near-full warning. But, nobody noticed. Everyone's attention was occupied elsewhere. Olga beamed when she saw the sheen of dread creep further and further over Alfredo's crinkling brow.

"Cousin, he's ignoring my boobs. He's going to be a screamer!"

Considering her cousin far too vain, Natalia replied in spite.

"I think he likes mine better. Yours are too over the top for him."

Olga pushed the monitor to one side.

"Look at these, you dumb wop. Do you have any idea of the depravity I must endure because of these? To keep them amped and plumped so men will find me incomparable amongst mortal women."

"Cousin, stop. Jughead needs to watch. Then he'll understand."

Olga begrudgingly slid the monitor back into Alfredo's view, bent over and whispered a question into his ear — "Jughead. Do you know what formic acid is?"

Being a chemist, Alfredo knew her ridicule was intended.

Suddenly, Olga leapt up giggling and stood behind Alfredo. Next, she jostled until her breasts were thrown into motion and then she pummeled them against Alfredo's shaven pate while tittering in weird amusement.

"Betty. Doktor. Tell me the first thought that comes to mind?"

The doctor glared at Olga, broadcasting her complete exasperation with her childish antics while Natalia screamed with delight.

"Oh, Veronica, I love charades."

And, Natalia mused while Olga kept flailing away. In seconds, Betty started bobbing up and down. It sent her breasts into that marvelous gelatinous swirl, a rotation comparable to that mesmerizing 'Dick Twerking' jig that men do to amuse their girlfriends while biding the time between interludes of intimacy. And, speaking into the mood of whacked-out, Natalia squealed.

"Such witty titties. It's 'Jughead.' See doktor, 'Jughead.'"

Then without warning, mirth deserted Natalia's cheeks. She sighed piteously and tears began to well up in her eyes. Olga ceased her play, bounded over and embraced Natalia close.

"What has happened, sweet cousin?"

"Silly me, I am the sensitive one. Your charade reminded me of our fun times with dear Dracul. The humans call him 'Vlad the Impaler' and in your charade I saw his incomparable wit come back to life. I saw you as 'Olga the Flailer.' Excuse my silliness, dear cousin. Total silliness."

"How sweet you are. I remember too." And she kissed Natalia's forehead with sisterly affection — "Dracul is forever a part of us, my dear one."

The doctor put her foot down.

"Have you children of the night finished playing with your food now. Can we move on to feeding so I can get home for my own supper?"

They both looked down at Alfredo. Their wild eyes betrayed a blend of contempt and hunger. But, Olga mellowed to a thought and waved off the doctor.

"Wait, doktor. I think this will help my cousin's melancholia."

And, beckoning Natalia to join her, she leant close to Alfredo's right ear.

"Jughead, let me tell you the famous Slavic story of the 'Church Bells.' There was once a church where the bells would not toll. All the noblemen and wealthy merchants made large donations to the Church to find favour with God. But, still the bells would not toll. The town's people feared they were cursed. Then out of a cold blizzard, one ghastly winter night, a traveler, a peasant boy on his last legs, dragged himself into the empty church for warmth. Grateful for the shelter, he placed the last money he possessed, two copper farthings, into the donation box. Immediately, the bells started tolling. The priest woke up in amazement and ran into the church. There, he discovered the wretched wayfarer and asked him what he was doing in the church. The boy explained his sad circumstances and his meager donation. The priest examined the donation box and was struck with awe. There, glowing blood-red, were two farthings devouring all the paper money. The bells rang loud and rang long. Soon the whole town rejoiced because now they knew — They had been blessed by God."

The doctor was even more impatient.

"Would you wrap it up. *Right now!*"

Natalia made rebuke — "Doktor! Where is your Russian soul? Reverence and Grace is in order before any meal. This is a beautiful story of spiritual transcendence. Dracul knew how I loved this story. Alfredo is a wop. As his hosts, it behooves us to acquaint him with some feel for our culture before we dine."

"See this gauge," the doctor said indignantly. "You can see he's already shed 1.3 kilos of fecal matter. And, here." Hotly rapping her finger — "0.94 liters of urine. You know they scream loudest and hardest on a full stomach. Through great sacrifice, the people of Russia offered you a banquet tonight. Ursini could've been a fine Bordeaux from the choicest of grapes but with all your tom-foolery don't expect anything more tasty than a cheap wop Chianti with beans."

Natalia retorted in half snarl.

"Doktor, my cousin's story is a noble one. Listen."

The doctor stood silent, but akimbo.

A sense of decorum returned and Olga resumed.

"Well, Alfredo Ursini, tonight you're just a cheap wop chianti with beans. But, let me finish because I think God can undo the curse of the poison you have poured into the subway system and over the length and breadth of Moscow."

Natalia confirmed the mood, her voice vesper-soft.

"Jughead, we are not Godless pagans. We, vampires, are romantic, spiritual beings with a sense of justice and nobility. As Dracul loved and feared God, we love and fear God. Please, embrace salvation. Please, Alfredo."

And, Olga injected an almighty demand.

"You come from a rich family with extensive vineyards and wineries, but to please God you must come up with a penance gift. It should be something comparable to two farthings. All the grapes in all your vineyards will not appease God. You need to donate something more precious than grapes, and not merely blood. Tonight, we aspire to bring you closer to God."

At that moment, Alfredo felt the anal tube butt promiscuously upwards. In response, his buttocks tensed and his thighs flanged and rotated outwards as if he was on the verge of ejaculatory expulsion. Olga stood tall and braced her two hands against Ursini's head to make sure he looked into the monitor. Then she nodded. As the blood liberated from Alfredo's scrotum trickled down into a Pyrex petri dish, the view from the underside camera transitioned into a crimson dissolve shot. The doctor decisively clasped his right testicle and began the slow and delicate process of cutting away the connective ligaments without severing his nerves or blood vessels. The doctor's surgical experience was evident from her technique. Being right handed, she found it easiest to start on the right. Using her healing power on their uncooperative guest, Natalia was quickly able to correct the doctor's occasional errant cut.

For Olga, a screamer aficionado, the procedure unfolding on screen was so mesmerizing that the flexing and contortions of Alfredo's body went unnoticed. However, once his right testicle with its blood vessels, nerves and the spermatic cord was bobbling around on the base of the petri dish, she snapped back to reality and popped Alfredo's gag. The throaty Italian roar was stupendous.

Olga shrieked loud her approval.

"Oh cousin, I knew it. What an animal! He could scream the hair off a werewolf. I cannot wait to feed."

Minutes later, on screen, the blood-filled petri dish was removed, and a bloodied latex glove came into view cradling two kidney-shaped objects. The procedure was put on momentary hold until Alfredo was sufficiently recomposed to watch. Hunched above his whimpering face, Olga laughed maniacally as she noticed horror bloom even deeper within his bulging, blood-swelled eyeballs. Then leaning closer to his ear, she taunted.

"Jughead, did you ever have ants in your pants? Formic acid is the venom of ant bites. It's also a splendid spermicidal agent. This ensures that when I suck your two precious grapes dry, I will get the maximum dose of testosterone. But, before that classic vampire moment, they need to ferment in a beaker of acid to pickle them into the prime condition the discriminating *fangster* craves."

Olga stood up, reclamped her palms around Alfredo's head and, unseen by Alfredo, she made a slight gesture. Alfredo's eyes stayed glued to the screen as he watched a hand gloved in blue latex tilt clockwise. Two testicles rolled free and descended.

Plip, plop, they were taking a bath. A formic acid bath.

In an instant, the comparative rumbling of bleed-out pain from his cleft scrotum burst into a Vesuvian eruption. Engulfed in the volcanic fires of hell with flames that are sensed as scorching but scorch nothing, Alfredo's tongue and tonsils exploded out of his mouth like the back-firing orange-red flame of a jet engine screaming its way to terminal melt-down.

His agony was nirvana for a vampire like Olga. She squealed.

"How splendid. My glands feel a century younger already."

Savouring his precious virgin roar, Olga frolicked about the room. Closing her eyes, she looked heavenward and cupped her hands under her breasts to elongate their roundness. Her distended nipples protruded into the air like the discerning proboscii of two pox-nosed connoisseurs of Cognac greedily seeking to inhale the frenzy of throaty vibrations uncorked from Alfredo's lungs which now energizing the chamber of the undead into a huge organ pipe throbbing in a state of total torment. She made sure he had a perfect view of her joy, then suddenly, she flipped the [GAG-ENGAGE] on his mouth-piece. Like a lobster in a boiling cauldron, an excruciating silence descended over the room. Time to cork all screaming back into the *magnum*[1] for the bubbliest taste of flesh and blood that ever a vampire could ferment. And there, Alfredo lay harnessed, writhing and slithering while his testicles pickled to perfection.

At the director's booth, Basil was monitoring Ursini's vital signs. Everything was within recoverable parameters in the event he expired. His pain levels were almost at their maximum. Excellent news. The only major risk was Ursini suffering a brain embolism or stroke, something impossible to detect or plan for. Compared to Rolfino, the subject in their full dress rehearsal, the young Ursini was using up pain neurotransmitters at a furious rate, so Basil revised his calculations.

Ten minutes later, Basil spoke into his head-mic — "Feeding time."

On this cue, Olga and Natalia took sup between Alfredo's legs. Once finished, they stood straight, revealing their blood-stained cheeks to him. The doctor grasped his emaciated testicles and swapped out the formic acid with a beaker of antibiotic solution. She next sprayed the inside of Alfredo's scrotum with an antibiotic. Natalia picked up each testicle, first the left then the right. Cuddling them within the warmth of her closed palms, she beamed her magic into each. After twin moments of sublime pleasure that sent Alfredo almost into unconsciousness, Dr. Soskrova re-stuffed the man's scrotum with its customary innards, plus one extra widget courtesy of Reverend Woland.

Thus, did three become one.

Olga returned to Alfredo's left and soothed him.

"Well, my dear Jughead, I hope we have helped you come closer to God tonight. My girls, Vesuvius and Etna, thank you for the meal." She jostled with gusto — "I can feel your hormones pulsing through my body already. In case you're clueless, it's estrogen for angels and testosterone for tits. Every sinew in my breasts is coming alive with the tension of a tigress in heat."

Stretching out into yoga's *warrior pose*, and in the graveled voice filled with the overture of a female seeking more than a two-baller tryst, she added.

"You're a scream, my sweet Jughead. We simply *must* dine again tomorrow."

As soon as Dr. Soskrova had completed the final suture, Natalia gently smothered Alfredo's stitched up scrotal tissue in her hand and sent a new pulse of healing pleasure into his body. Alfredo felt full sensitivity return. It was a blessing and a curse. His skull, once flooded with screams of excruciation, now lay puddled with bloody thoughts of extravagantly insane and never-ending purgatory.

1 *Magnum* - Champagne bottle, 1.5 liters.

Savvy to his sense of dread, Olga expressed her compliments.

"Now, Jughead, let me tell you something. My cousin has very discriminating taste. She loves a well-balanced man. Your scrotal blood with its wild blend of hormones was perfect. As for me, my figure craves 'testosterone tartar.' It keeps my metabolism high, and it's great for my abs. As usual, the doctor made the wrong call. Tonight's meal was no cheap Chianti, my sweet wop. You'll be pleased to know we both gave you a Michelin rating of five-stars. Such taste! Such screams! You, my darling Jughead, are definitely where the rubber meets the road."

With everything back to normal, Olga walked around to inspect the job.

"Oh cousin, you're the best at healing wounds."

And, Olga locked eyes with Alfredo.

"Except for your new covenant with God, my sweet Jughead, your fiancée Julia would never know we had a feed."

She wheeled the monitor back into Alfredo's view.

"Have a close look, my dear faithless wop. See for yourself."

Alfredo could not help but look. He focused hard, yearning to confirm that he was mutilated beyond repair and beyond the bounds of further torment. But, he was greeted with a sight that was revulsion incarnate. It was all horribly true. Except for his Raggedy-Anne, foreskin-down-vampire-gullet circumcision, everything appeared pristine. Natalia spoke into the mood.

"Cousin, let's check if Alfredo is becoming more spiritual."

And, without cue, Olga and Natalia asked in unison.

"Alfredo, did you hear the church bells tolling?"

He narrowed his eyes in quiet contempt, but noting Olga's scowl, Alfredo reacted on instinct and nodded his head insistently.

Natalia's face beamed in pure jubilation.

"What a fabulous night of spiritual rebirth it has been! Cousin, you were right about the foreskin covenant. I think God has recognized our ministrations upon this wop barbarian. Farthings be praised. Bells may yet be tolled!"

Olga gushed warm and reverent — "It's good to love God and bring him into the lives of the damned. Through the suffering of Jesus and Jughead, we may yet expiate ourselves of more of our past sins."

They both kissed Alfredo on the cheek, thanked him for their meal, picked up their robes and left the room. The doctor moved all the equipment back to the room's cabinet-lined side-wall on Alfredo's left and returned to his side. She placed her index finger over his jugular vein and broke the silence.

"You fascists turned my grandparents to ashes because they were Slavic. Do you really think two-legged kritters like wops, wogs and ragheads deserve the protection of the laws of war?"

She counted off his pulse beats then removed her hand.

"Perhaps, you've forgotten your dear NATO ally and their infamous decree of February 7, 2002.[1] Have you read it? Humane treatment for detainee kritters is a matter of largesse not a legal right. For eight months, rather than corralling the alleged criminals who crippled their navy vessel in Yemen, the Doodles

---

1 US Presidential Memorandum of Law concerning people in Afghanistan. Section 3 stated detainees have no legal right to humane treatment. Any humane treatment was a calling on grace, not law.

scolded us so-called barbarian Bolsheviks about our restoration of order in Chechnya, part of our own motherland. Then one Sunni September in the year 2001 rolls around, and those hypocrites of convenience throw the laws of war on the ash heap. Apparently, civility would interfere with their fun-time hunting down a bunch of jihadi niggers on foreign shores and stymie their inauguration of a starvation-enforced, child-enslaving regime of chemical weapon exporting druglords. So what prohibits experiments on detainees Ursini? The law of ashes — right?"

Alfredo squirmed in gag-enforced silence.

She glared at him, wheeled about and approached the sink counter. After she had finished washing and wiping down her instruments, she tossed a bloodied towel into a bin. While inspecting each instrument for cleanliness and packing them into a Soviet-era purse-sized leather satchel, from time to time, she glanced over at Alfredo and reminded him of the facts — snippet by snippet.

"No torture here tonight, Ursini. ... Even assuming detainees were human and not kritters. ... Vampires obeying the laws of humanity? That's a joke ... Just ask your fascist superpower ally. Your body is all intact, not one damaged organ, thus as a matter of fascist law — no torture. ... Circumcision is good and proper detainee hygiene. You nodded for me to sanctify your new covenant with God. ... That's Amerikan down-home hospitality right here, y'awl."

And, she buckled her satchel closed. Quiet returned as Dr. Soskrova swapped out the excrement bins and started swabbing the floor. Half-way through, adopting the tone of an elderly mother with two unwed daughters, she propped herself against the mop handle and broached a new subject.

"Did you like meeting Olga and Natalia? They're both single you know. Satan is spoken for, so they're looking for their Prince. Two hotties looking for one greasy prick. Any wop's wildest phantasy."

She broke off, mopped a little more before standing over him.

"And aren't those pair the most darling of vampires? So full of life. I guess you had all those queer Hollywood notions about vampires. But, now you know exactly what those night-loving narcissistic Princesses look for in their Prince. Real vampires have a healing touch. They feed without killing their prey. So respectful of life, don't you think? Feeding without killing, the very definition of humane. Like Olga and Natalia, I have a vegetarian friend who also considers killing animals abhorrent. But, I'm guessing you're a meat-eater, Ursini. Your taste in fashion is a plain giveaway. Frankly, there are things I doubt you male chauvinist dipsticks will ever understand. Only good for providing androgens."[1]

Locked tight in his gag, Alfredo remained mute.

She attributed his silence to her maternal overtures concerning unwed daughters as awkwardness and returned to her mopping. Then stopped again. *Perhaps he would enjoy a more culinary subject of conversation,* she thought.

"How did you find the formic acid? Acetic acid in vinegar is the tarting ingredient used in many salad dressings. But, its more simple chemical cousin, formic acid, now that's the raw venom in fire ants. Perfect tarting for a vampire.

1 Male hormones all categories. (Med).

If ever you see Martha Stewart on TV, remember — vinegar for Black Bean Salad, lemon for Guacamole and formic acid for Testicles-Tartar."

Alfredo remained dazed under a fog of incredulity, not even a flinch or eye-tick. The doctor feigned annoyance at having to carry such a one-way conversation and rapped his gag with her middle and forefinger in tandem.

"Listen up, Ursini. Next time, I might paint urushiol on your testicles before sowing them back into your scrotum. Urushiol is the irritant in poison ivy. It inflames the skin until the itch is unbearable. Bound to your harness, just imagine how testy you would be with the mother of all itches sewn tight inside your scrotum for twenty-four hours."

She smiled in perverse pleasure. Ursini's watering eyes betrayed the fact the wop chauvinist pig was now giving her the undivided attention that was her female due. Her next words curled off her lips to heighten their cruel intent.

"Any normal man would be begging to have his scrotum hacked open, his balls washed in acid and coddled in sweet vampire love. But," and she tapped on his mouthpiece again — "I suspect you're the strong silent type who's into weird stuff. Goes with your fashion sense. Anyway, at Reverend Woland's request, I added a chaperone to your scrotum tonight. The Russians can decide if you're that way or not."

The doctor laughed so maniacally a milky slather drooled out her nose, and highlighted the gloom of an ancient sorrow, which draped the length of her yellowed under-eyes like a valence of nicotine. Alfredo knew she knew more than she was letting on. Without any warning, she produced a syringe in front of his eyes, uncapped it, rapped it with her bony finger and pressing her thumb under his jaw to locate the carotid artery, she injected him in the neck. The sedative coursed through his body like juice divine, and the doctor resumed her sermon.

"Dear boy, vampires can be the light of your life in many ways. Can't you see that those two want to bring you closer to God? They love and fear God. Do you think one day you will love God, Ursini? I tell you this — all your families' grapes can't help you now. You might beg Olga to destroy her source of food and bite off your balls. But, why would God accept such an offering from one so rich when devouring your farthings would be to ruin the gift, which allows his chosen redeemers to prime you for the fires of Hell without end?"

She paused to allow the 24/7 dread to linger in Alfredo's imagination.

"While they're assisting you to better know life after death, Olga and Natalia are convinced that God is slowly expiating their past sins. It's very sweet, sort of like that Catholic *Opus Dei*[1] catharsis I've read about."

She next slowed her speech for effect.

"Of course, there is the option that the morning presents. If you give the Russians satisfaction with whatever they want from you, I doubt we'll be seeing each other for another feeding tomorrow night, Mr. Balls-to-the-Walls Ursini. So think carefully. Have a good nights sleep and be ready for tomorrow."

She looped her satchel over her right shoulder, stooped over his forehead, and like any warm-hearted Italian grandmother, she kissed Alfredo good night

---

1 Literally, 'Work of God.' Orthodox Catholic Papal Order known for its masochistic rites.

before exiting. The door locked closed with a leaden clunk. The lights went out. And, lulled by the crackling white noise of the de-ionization combs as they threw scorching arcs of violet-blue from prong to prong, cleansing the air of all memory of the fragrance of vampire cruelty, Alfredo drifted into slumber.

The Princess of Peace

Swiveling out of the padded aerie of the directors chair, Basil stretched out his legs, and his shoes tapped onto the concrete with the lightness of a dancer. He grabbed the envelope a courier from President Bushkin's office had delivered, took one stride towards Natalia and unleashed his compliments.

"Simply inspiring. We need detailed information out of Ursini as soon as possible. And, by God, you've done it. We might avert world war yet."

Amid a boil of conflicting emotions and in no mood to buy into the syndrome called 'World War III,' Natalia addressed only the greater virtue.

"It was the least I could do to set things right."

And, while the 'Vampire Intercession' subject repulsed Natalia, what truly gnawed at her was even more soul destroying, but she had to ask.

"How are Derek and Ludmila?"

Basil replied as tenderly as he could.

"Miss Bogomolski, they're sleeping for the moment. A nurse is constantly monitoring them." Basil broke off abruptly and faced Olga — "Lieutenant, I'm charging you to be Miss Bogomolski's mentor. Take her to the cafeteria and both of you get a good meal." Basil drew breath to soften his demeanor, turned back to Natalia and placed the ornate envelope into her hands — "Miss Bogomolski, this comes directly from the president's office. It contains your formal commission into our ranks. Keep it with you at all times."

Natalia broke the red and white seal and withdrew a heavy sheet of gilt-edged vellum. Her eyes darted to the flamboyant signature at its base — *President Fyedor Sergeivich Bushkin*. She was taken aback.

Scanning over her right shoulder, Basil read the gist. His heart lightened at the magnificent appellation the president had used to invest Natalia Vladimirovna Bogomolski into leading the greatest crusade imaginable — 'The Princess of Peace.' And, after the moment passed, Basil sought to confirm the great confidence and expectation their nation placed within her hands.

"Special Agent Bogomolski, can I trust you now understand?"

But, locked in awe reading the President's commendation word for word, Natalia heard nothing. Basil's smile deepened in the hope that this sweet lady might now find the calling of a larger duty to mankind as an outlet for her anguish, and so he finished on a note of feigned aplomb.

"My apologies, for this tossed-up memo, Special Agent Bogomolski. I'll organize something more bureaucratic tomorrow."

Natalia still did not respond.

Basil snickered and turned to Sergei.

"Colonel, from this point on, you're taking over vampire direction. Improve it where need be. But, right now, I want you and Major Gratski to start formulating tomorrow's contrition and conversation regimen for our guest. Our target time, nine hours from now. I'll review it in the morning. *Ponyol?*"[1]

"Yes, Sir." And, Sergei snapped to attention.

Basil registered acknowledgement and hastened to his office.

Absolute Power

Elena Michaelovna Nadrenko had a spotless reputation. Once. And, it bothered Basil no end that it had come to this. Before he would sound out his secretary, he decided to get a shortbread into his stomach and slake his thirst. After serving her boss his refreshments, Elena stood contritely erect like a schoolgirl whose brisket was long overdue for a good welting. Basil perused the incident report before him. As he put down his teacup to turn the page, Elena made an utterance. Basil did not look up. He extended his right arm, and then reached again for his cup. He did not know what distressed him most; a head shot into her silky tresses or withering corporal punishment. Elena was a great secretary. Another minute of intense reading went by. Basil slurped down the last of the tea and stared at Elena. His look of exasperation said just one thing — *Well?*

Elena wasted no time apologizing for her presumptuousness in extending authority for His Beatitude, Nikolai Ivanovich Mudretski, the Patriarch of Moscow and Head of the Russian Orthodox Church, to bring his son Teodor to FSB Lubyanka. Because of a passing and speculative discussion about the Second Prophecy of Fatima and Natalia's commission, Basil sensed the president may have been involved. To lower tension, he vented most of his dismay on the fact she had not contacted him before acting.

Elena countered — "Sir, you were in the dungeons with strict Do-Not-Disturb orders. The Patriarch heard about our secret decontamination process. He won't say much but swears he sealed his source to total secrecy."

Basil mused — *Bushkin's hand?*

She watched her boss digest the sincerity in her appeal. Then, sensing a mood of reconciliation might prevail, she explained her reasoning.

"Sir, the Patriarch already knew. By offering our aid, I made good the real security breach. And, did so on condition he and the Church would support our government in mollifying public hysteria."

"Elena, I see you had few options. Who's involved again?"

"His son, Teodor. Apparently, he's in a very bad way."

"I'll do my best to sell it to the Director-General."

"Thank you, sir."

"Then an amnesty from President Bushkin."

Elena flinched in an attempt to restrain a tremble.

---

1 Understood (Rus).

"You owe me big time woman," Basil bellowed, eyeball to eyeball.

Elena understood his thrust and nodded obsequiously.

"Now, let me see the pass you've prepared."

Basil slashed his pen across the signature line. And, while running his eyes down the document, looking to rehash in his mind possible long-term snafus with this impromptu arrangement, Basil instructed Elena on how to proceed.

"Once the Patriarch is sworn to secrecy, let him know about Natalia. She can help the boy and the Patriarch can stay busy ministering to the patients we already have." Basil stopped and looked up in earnest — "I'll meet the Patriarch once I catch up with the President's and Director-General's work. It's DND time again. And, as for you, cross your fingers."

"Thank you, sir. And, I'm certain the Patriarch will cooperate."

"Cooperation is essential. Please dim the lights on your way out."

As she reached the door, Basil added.

"By the way, I have absolute power. No Director-General. No President."

Elena glared back at him.

Basil raised his eyebrows — expressionless.

"Elena — the lights, *pajalsta*."[1]

Basil dropped the DVD containing the Ursini vampire intercession into his computer. After reviewing the accompanying email that Elena had prepared for him, he added his comments, including an approving sidebar about the Patriarch and what the state could expect of this old man given the special circumstances. Basil dispatched the email, video file attached, to both President Bushkin and Director-General Besstrashnikov.

Behind on events, Basil reviewed the televised late-afternoon speech President Bushkin made to the nation. After the Metro was unilaterally shut down at mid-morning, the next four hours was a tumult of public speculation about an impending *coup d'état*. Anger against Bushkin and the military presence in the capital had been on a rising boil — most heated on university campuses. However, the moment Basil's A-Team barged into the Italian embassy limousine on Tverskaya Street, the blackout on reality ended.

Terrorism became the news story.

Woppery remained the state secret.

The more well-connected elements of society, including foreigners, submitted samples of clothes to scientific agencies as well as trusted foreign embassies. At university campuses all over Moscow, students and staff abruptly ended their rallies and clamored before their Chemistry faculties with clothes off their own backs. Terrorism was verifiable. Everyone had a personal stake because nearly everyone's flesh, touched only one time, was contaminated to some degree. The nation went from simmering indignation to riotous outrage. But, first, in accordance with the 'Courtyard Decontamination' instructions being broadcast on all radio and TV channels, it was cold-shower time.

Spare with his words, President Bushkin's emergency address to reassert the supremacy of the Motherland and trust in its authorities, was well written

1 Please (Rus).

and well delivered. In the intervening hours since Bushkin's first public announcement, the legislature had ratified their president's decree of martial law. And, in his follow-up 'Address to the Nation' that evening, Bushkin reminded all citizens that any insolence towards forces keeping public order carried dire consequences. Emphasizing that it was premature to lay blame on Chechen rebels, Ukrainian renegades or Muslim extremists, he also disclosed that the prime culprit was in custody and spilling his beans — FSB style. And, regardless of where accusation might lie as the future unfolded, he pledged the motherland would deploy Russian standards of justice and respond fearlessly and proportionately at a time and using a method of its choosing. He assured his countrymen that no power on Earth would thwart their government from obtaining the maximum retribution possible.

President Bushkin ended his speech with the grim assessment that over the next two to three weeks, some ten thousand citizens of Moscow would be dead. And, in the absence of some medical miracle, within twelve months the catalog of death could reach fifty thousand or greater.

Basil was dumbstruck. He whipped open General Litvinenko's report to determine if the numbers Bushkin had made public were not being conflated for political reasons. Litvinenko's preliminary assessment lacked precise data because the extents of the pollution through the subway system had yet to be fully surveyed. At present, it could only be estimated how many people were exposed and at what concentration levels. However, Litvinenko's Dioxinomic[1] model of human and economic ruination charted how a horrendous tide of death and disfigurement would unfold over weeks, months and years.

Romanov's scheme to incite anarchy was a work in progress.

Exaggeration — *Dioxinomics* was not.

State-Classified Misery

As the ink-black acid of night etched hard into the steel of Moscow's stainless sense of its own humanity and smothered the city in the bleakest of griefs, from the comfort of the FSB cafeteria, Olga and Natalia watched President Bushkin's 'Address to the Nation' for the first time. His appeal for calm was being continuously replayed on all channels along with sporadic reports coming in hourly from the city's many hospitals. The president made no mention of the state secret that Wopland[2] had transformed Russia into Vopland.[3] Nor a peep about how Russia might unveil the salient facts to its citizens as well as the media brainwashed foreigners living in the Western world and still avert world war. That remained firmly in the hands of Basil Novimirov.

Combining the public news with what Basil had told her in his office, Olga understood that vampire intercessions would become the standard model for softening up all upper-echelon detainees. But, Olga's greatest joy was how the

---

1 Portmanteau of Dioxin + (Eco)nomics. See *Dioxinomics* Series. www.dioxinomics.com
2 Name 'Satan' takes in the Mikhael Bulgakov novel, *The Master and Margarita*. Written during Stalin's rule, but banned from publication.
3 Derived from *Vopl* - Death filled wailing (Rus).

Lord of Hosts had entrusted Natalia with the sacred means of ensuring that these irksome procedures did not descend into torture. Striving to beat back all religious conflicts in Natalia's protests, Olga explained the facts of life to her shocked komrade in a tone kindling with patriotism.

"I am religious, Natash. But, think. Not since Hitler and Mussolini have the godless forces of woppery inflicted such misery on the people of Russia. Our vampire intercessions are moral because satanic evil must learn to fear God. By Y-Doodle[1] legal standards, we aren't torturers. No wop has suffered any bodily harm, unless you're doing something underhanded in revenge. Well?"

Olga's accusatory snip took Natalia by surprise.

"Me? No, of course not. But, I'd rather use my powers for redemption."

Olga reached out to her — "Redemption and Justice. Natash, you are."

Natalia tried to chip in — "But Olg—"

This only made Olga more vehement.

"What 'you would like' and what 'we must do' aren't options. Amerika and NATO love mutually assured annihilation. If nukes weren't a joke, do you think woppery would confine itself to its own lands?"

"No, but—" Natalia started to say.

"No buts. We're fighting the most profane evil against God's supreme love for Russia. Not to mention world peace. Those wop pricks have exposed your Derek—"

Olga stopped herself cold because Natalia's eyes distended in pain.

After seconds of silence, Natalia blurted out what she dreaded most.

"I cannot imagine my life now. If Derek dies, I'll go berserk."

"Do you think you're alone!" Olga snapped.

And, as if she'd swallowed her front teeth, Natalia stifled a sob.

Olga tamped back her gaze of contempt. She'd been far too harsh. Placing her hand atop Natalia's to engage her solidarity, she mellowed.

"Show some commiseration. God has blessed you, Natalia Vladimirovna.[2] I can feel it in your body. So can everyone else. As the 'Princess of Peace,' you cannot evade the moral task the Lord has set before you."

Natalia clenched her eyes shut — *Why did I punch Ludmila?*

Sensing Natalia's attitude as indifference, Olga pressed on with her sermon.

"Natash, Russia needs Christianity more than ever. And, it's a stupendous honour to have our president acknowledge the gift and call to service the Almighty has given you. And, look at what our president is doing to quell the hysteria — millions are suffering — millions."

Natalia remained simpering in silence. And, unaware of the facts behind Natalia's outward obliviousness, Olga went full-court with an empathy campaign.

"Natash, think about the other families out there tonight trying to decontaminate at home and watching their loved ones sink into pulmonary edema. And, because of anarchy in the streets and no practical transportation, the vast majority of victims cannot even travel to a medical clinic, let alone a decent hospital."

---

1 Contraction of Yankee-Doodle, American.

2 First and Patronymic middle name. Formal and polite usage.

Saddled with state-classified misery, Natalia nodded in shame. Her attack on Ludmila had caused all this human desolation. Tatiana had spared no effort drilling that point into her during the mission to capture Ursini. But, Olga, currently unaware of this, continued to list Natalia's blessings.

"You're lucky to be alive. You, Natash, have had one great lov—"

On her last words, Olga's jaw clenched in its socket.

Natalia looked over in horror.

"What's wrong?" Then reflected — *Olga's family. Of course!*

Natalia cupped her other hand atop her komrade's. Olga grimaced and recomposed herself, embarrassed how she had caused needless alarm.

"Oh Natash. My private life is so pathetic. I cannot pretend to know how I'd move on if my one great love were to die. I haven't found a man who's attracted to me other than for obvious physical reasons. Inside, I'm such a warm, polished woman. But, when it comes to the chauvinists I work with, I have to put on this alienating game-face exterior. It defiles the real me!"

"Surely, you're exaggerating," Natalia replied in a tone bordering on accusatory.

"Natash, the majority of so-called 'men' don't even have the decency to muzzle their juvenile remarks. I had a joyous and carefree upbringing but by puberty, I found myself becoming more and more socially defined and entombed within this physique. All over Moscow tonight, loved ones will be beside themselves with grief. But, for me, such heartache remains Bystander Anguish." Olga clasped her komrade's hand tighter. The life she led was bereft of intensity — be it love or sorrow. And, like an elderly babushka brandishing 'The Grandchildren Finger,' Olga's sense of self was nagging her harder than ever — "People look at me and think 'Miss Hottie the Blessed.' But Natalia, I'm a woman with soul and I fear I'll never know the true depth of other people's despair. Disenchantment's my bedfellow. That's my great tragedy."

Natalia fired back — "Olga, stop it. Stop it. Life's not a drama fest."

Olga closed her eyes to muster herself, but her wretchedness only showed all the more. Surmising that Olga's problems were caused by the people she socialized with, Natalia went on the offensive.

"Let me say there are noble and valiant men here. Derek's not alone. Look at Captain Botanin. Or better yet, consider General Novimirov."

On the subject of men, Olga went into auto-pilot. She knew little of Botanin, except he was some nerd in the med-science department. However, Novimirov, the ex-Master of the Veronikas,[1] was another matter entirely.

"I wish there were more like the General," she replied. "He's technically single but heading up the Veronika program for the past year. It's said he's a great," she grinned, "lover. It's amazing given that he's pushing forty-eight."

The change of mood was most welcome.

"Well Olga, here's a shocker for you. My Derek is only a few years younger, but you would not know it from his attitude and appearance. I tell you this woman. Life isn't defined by a clock. Man is as reptile does. How many thirty-something nerd-schtick fossilids have you encountered?"

1 Russia's Amateur Spy Corps. In honor of Veronika Lewintsova, captured by 'Capitalist Pigs' in 1998.

Olga giggled knowingly.

"Derek's a highly educated Doodle. I'm sure most Y-Ds have healthy lives."

"Derek told me some do, but many don't. Haven't you seen TV reports? Remember Hurricane Katrina? With all that flab wading around in the water, how could all those Y-Ds drown? How? Fat floats — it's scientific fact."

Olga laughed, and the funk of the day's vampire intercessions and the horrors engulfing Moscow vanished from her thoughts. Only three weeks old, Katrina was but one example amongst many strange news stories about Amerika that CNN broadcast. With emotions off the boil, Natalia seized an opening to propel the mood into the positive.

"Let's go to the Infirmary. I want to see Derek, and he can set you straight."

A reciprocal spirit of conviviality washed over Olga, and feigning a conflict of sexual preference, she quipped — "Hmm ... I think I'm straight. But, if *you* insist, I'm sure Derek won't mind."

Natalia gave her komrade a playful slap. "Let's go, silly."

Yamashita, 327 US 1 (1946)

In the Vice-President's Office, Norman Weissbrot restrained his disgust for Washington's 'Sit on your Hands' culture. He was midway into bringing Army Five-Star General, Harvey L. Kilburn, the Chairman of the Joint Chiefs of Staff, up to speed on how he planned to make inroads into the hearts and minds of Russia.

"That's it, Harv. And, fuck, if I'm not off to Russia by week's end."

"So the president's getting ahead of a situation, for a change."

"*As-if.* She's yet to be appraised of my goodwill visit. We need hard-currency. That's why you must get cracking on poppy eradication in Afghanistan."

"Bushkin's 'Operation Rambo'[1] ultimatum and all off-the-books, too?"

Weissbrot let out an audible sigh because President Carter despised Bushkin. If she knew 'Rambo' was going live, she would scream for Kilburn's head.

"Yes but no, Harv. And, jeez, it's not 'Rambo,' damn-it."

"How about 'Burning Bush?' Something Moses would endorse."

"With AIPAC on the warpath, that'll get you crucified. Let's call it 'Operation 1333,' as in UN Security Council Resolution 1333 of December, 2000."[2]

"The 'Smash Opium' resolution directed at the Afghan government?"

Weissbrot flopped back into his executive chair.

"Boom-chukka-boom. Before we invaded in October, 2001, Robert Charles at State certified the Taliban had hammered opium back to 74 acres. That's the *status quo ante*[3] — 74 acres. Hypocrisy or not, civilized expectation or not, Bushkin takes a poop or not, UN Resolution 1333 hasn't vanished into thin air."

"Nor has *Yamashita.*"

Weissbrot locked Kilburn hard in his gaze.

---

1 Operation President Bushkin proposed in 2002 to eradicate Afghan opium plantations. US and NATO have repeatedly vetoed any such operation proceeding.
2 UN Sec. Council Resolution of December 19, 2000 mandating the eradication of opium plantations.
3 Status Prior to 'Invasion' (Latin).

"Act or hang, general. No more excuses. Karzai is no more a shield for us than Datong Puyi, the last Emperor of China, was for Hirohito and the Imperial Japanese High Command. If MacArthur were alive, he'd skin you."

And, Weissbrot, the hero Admiral of the 1991 Gulf War, laid out the issues facing Commander-in-Chief, President Mary-Ann Carter, as well as General Kilburn if he failed to act. *Yamashita* was a US Supreme Court decision that had elevated into international law the execution of two Japanese generals: General Yamashita and General Homo, after their trials at the end of World War II. Both men stood accused of neglect in the supervision of military forces under their command while those forces were occupying the Philippine Islands. Homo got the bullet. Yamashita, the noose.

Afghanistan was a simple case.

An invading alien army had occupied the country and subverted the *status quo ante* of 74 acres of opium into over 500,000 acres. To be precise, 500,000 acres of food became 500,000 acres of zero-food and promised nothing but starvation to Afghan civilians and the export of narco-death to all mankind.

Yamashita wasn't about episodic murder, rape or pillaging by soldiery, here or there. Nor was it about a derelict ex-Commander-in-Chief of Panama rotting away in a Florida prison. *Yamashita* was about a Christian crusader High Command whose forces dominated Muslim lands and systematically transformed them into exportable evil expressly forbidden in the Qur'an. It wasn't blood on your hands, but rather 'Sitting on your Hands' which was the war crime. Neglect was the heart of the 1946 Supreme Court ruling in *Yamashita*.

'Neglect' was a 'Made in America' death sentence.

Slant-eyed justice or not.

That Beloved Curve

In the Infirmary, the nurse assigned to Derek's care warned Olga and Natalia that both Derek and Ludmila's skin were riddled with chloracne blisters. The toxin had spread from their lungs, the site of irreversible absorption to the rest of their bodies. They approached Derek's bed first. Awash in rancid, puss-weeping sores, Derek's swollen face resembled Ukrainian President Viktor Eunatovski after he had eaten poisoned soup. Natalia's heart sank and she gloved Derek's cheeks in her palms ever so tenderly. Touch after touch, the swelling dissipated.

Olga was wonder-struck.

"Natash, such a gift. His lungs must be horrible. I hope his appear—"

Olga stopped. Her words in the cafeteria about rarified grief and rarified love rained hurt back into her own ears. Her friend was in love. Nothing else mattered. After the last of the blemishes had dissipated, Natalia slid her hands away from Derek's face and she spoke wistfully.

"There, Olga. This is his proper appearance except inflammation in his muscles has distorted his cheeks. Sort of looks more rounded and angelic now."

Natalia felt her heart beat loud and constant. Using her healing power gave her inner-being a deep sense of purpose, and yet moroseness pervaded every joint of her body as if the act of moving threatened to break her bones.

Taking note of the poignancy of the moment, Olga remained speechless. As she contemplated the extraordinary nature of Natalia's divine gift, spent so intently on her beloved, the smile of the 'Witnessing Christian' bloomed across her face. *In her, our world truly has a Koroleva Mira,*[1] she thought.

Dr. Chernikrov, who was paged by the duty nurse when Natalia and Olga first appeared, dashed in. Startled by his hurried entrance, Natalia wheeled about.

"Doktor, what's wrong?"

"Just a routine visit."

"If only everything was routine." Natalia sighed. "Doktor, I'd like to cleanse Derek completely — May I?"

"Anytime. Here, let me help you."

They folded back the bed sheet. Olga shuddered and looked away. Derek was a mass of oozing lesions. Within Natalia, a spirit glowed bright with promise. Tears started flowing, but she remained resolute. Natalia opened her robe, crawled onto the bed and lay over Derek as delicately as she was able. She focused her energy outward bathing his body in healing warmth. Through her right breast, she could feel Derek's heart pulsing with the pleasure of their oneness.

Olga's voice tinkled.

"Natalia, such a smile he has."

Natalia peered over Derek's chin. Upon seeing that beloved curve plump his lips, she wiped her cheek and almost laughed. It had been months since she had been able to lie so close to someone she loved so dearly. She nestled her face into his chest and kissed away those residual areas of skin that were still inflamed. And, after climbing off the bed, she kissed several patches that called for more attention. The doctor and Olga turned Derek over, and Natalia sidled up against his back and repeated the process. Within minutes, her touch had rejuvenated every cubit of Derek's wretched body. She climbed off the bed and re-sashed her robe.

"Doktor, is it alright to wake Derek? Can I speak to him?"

"Natalia, he's on tranquilizers to slow his metabolism. It's very hard for him to get air into his lungs. He will wake up in a few hours. Come back then."

"Will," she hesitated then stared down the doctor — "Will he recover?"

Chernikrov returned her gaze.

"Honestly, I cannot say. But, it would be a miracle if he does."

While Natalia thought she was steeled to hear the worst, she shuddered hard, and her body almost buckled beneath her. In the face of hope, sanity required her to not dwell on the unknown. She looked morosely at the companion bed before toddling her way over — "Would you help me with Ludmila, Doktor."

Once the coverings were removed, Natalia started cleansing Ludmila's body from head to toe. Natalia was tending to Ludmila's back when a soft yet throaty voice from the doorway disturbed their ministrations.

---

1 Queen of Peace (Rus). Allegory from the Bulgakov novel, *The Master and Margarita*, where Satan confers the status of Queen (*Koroleva*) over Vampires and Witches on Margarita for the Spring Ball.

"So it's true. God be praised."

The doctor swiveled on his heels.

"Patriarch. This, you need to watch."

The Patriarch stood silently while Natalia finished cleansing Ludmila. Once Natalia had re-sashed her robe, he approached the bed and helped them turn Ludmila over and back to slumbering repose.

The doctor spoke first — "Do you now understand, Patriarch?"

"No. But, I believe." And the Patriarch addressed the woman whose radiance he had felt from afar — "You must be Miss Bogomolski."

Natalia put out her hand in greeting — "How do you do?"

Inexplicably, she knew it was the Patriarch by touch alone.

"Please, call me Natalia, Patriarch," she said reverently.

"And please, call me Nikolai. Kolya would be perfect."

And, the Patriarch cowered his head — "Natalia, I must ask from you a favour." He looked up, revealing how his eyes were racked with pain. "I apologize for my abruptness, but," and losing composure, the Patriarch let slip a sob-quenched squeak of air — "It's ... it's my son, Teodor."

A jolt of censor streaked through Natalia's body. When the moment subsided, she sensed she'd stood there brooding like a wizen-hearted philosopher for half a lifetime, so she launched into action — "Quick. Where to Doktor?"

Holy Denisovan

On the way to the new final-phase decontamination center, now relocated indoors, Dr. Chernikrov explained the enhanced decontamination process to Natalia. Captain Ilya Botanin was in the dark room busy scrubbing down an unconscious youth under infrared scanning lights. The others stood outside while Natalia donned a pair of night-vision goggles and joined the captain. Once decontamination was complete, Teodor was wheeled out into the full light of the corridor. His puffed, reddened and inflamed body was riddled with macabre handprints, where Natalia had pressed against his flesh to target those locations the scanner had detected dioxin residues. The Patriarch turned away from the sight. And, while Natalia's face went pale with self-reproach, her spirit persisted in its quest to rain hope back into a father's worst nightmare.

"Patriarch, please. I'll heal every part of Teodor's body."

Olga watched as the Patriarch haltingly turned his attention back to the work at hand. During the intermission when Teodor's limp frame was flipped over, so Natalia could heal his back, the weight of stoicism burdening the Patriarch finally overwhelmed the man. He propped himself against the wall and clamped his eyes shut. Tears gushed from every crevice, coating his cheeks in a wet glaze that wicked into his beard, and in the corridor's dim light, made his face shine like wet snow in moonlit hoare-frost on midwinter hay stubble..

Here was the unfettered destitution Olga feared was beyond her comprehension. A tear slowly beaded under her eye. To witness one so mighty, and yet so prostrate before fate. And, her torso stiffened when, as his prayerful mutterings ceased, this grizzled man squelched a sob so pitiful, it caused her to avert her gaze out of respect for the privacy of his misery. And, upon his next gasp, her ears hardened in astonishment as the Patriarch's gratitude rolled from his lips.

"Thanks be to God. And, bless you, Miss Bogomolski."

For a different tragedy gnawed at Olga. In the vaunted fecundity of her prime, the emotions of this stately man swirled around her and seemed to eat her alive. Lovelorn, she felt entirely alien. Olga faced the wall to marshal herself. From behind her, the corridor babbled with commotion, and time rolled mindlessly on.

The Doctor escorted the Patriarch and Teodor, who lay strapped on his gurney, to the Infirmary. And, unaware of her friend's inner-turmoil, Natalia's conversation with Ilya Botanin turned to the present. And, so it was, that Olga caught her name being used as a prelude to formal introduction.

"Ilya, do you know Lieutenant Olga Nikolaevna Krovsoska?"

"Ehh. Yes and no. Only by sight," he replied.

On reflex, as if Natalia had ambushed him to initiate conversation, Ilya spoke to the lady standing face to the wall. He unleashed his standard line for the day — "Lieutenant Krovsoska, have you been exposed?"

Still mired in a lingering mood of melancholia, Olga swiveled about in surprise — "What? ... Me? Not really." She paused to compose herself — "Perhaps, from helping others this afternoon."

A little shy, Ilya countered nonchalantly — "You're probably fine, Lieutenant."

Natalia insisted — "Ilya, please, I'd like to be sure Olga isn't contaminated."

Ilya tuned into Natalia's angst because the Lieutenant's puffed face broadcast a reality beyond denial — "My apologies. Actually, I need to be checked as well."

"So, who'll be my first guinea pig, Olga or you?" Natalia asked.

Olga interposed — "I'm sure I'm fine. Captain, why don't you go first."

Feeling the scapegoat nerd in what he perceived to be Olga's prima-donna reticence, Ilya focused his attention on Natalia, "First, a trial run on me. Next, her."

Ilya politely held aside the flap, and Natalia entered the dark room. After explaining the scanner's enhanced features, Ilya stripped down. On his hands, face and neck glowed small yet distinct patches of contamination. Next, he showed her how to use the hand-held light-wand to make close-up inspections of the more concealed parts of his body. Traces fluoresced, here and there. Finally, for additional practice, he had Natalia run her hands over every tuft, fold and flank of his uniform until it was impeccable. When all was done, Natalia called out from the darkness.

"Lieutenant Olga Nikolaevna Krovsoska, time to report for duty."

Olga was squeamish — "Do you need the Captain there?"

A masculine voice replied — "*Nyet*. I'll let Natalia do the job solo and score it afterwards." Ilya hopped out struggling with a sock. "All yours, Lieutenant."

Olga marched inside, removed her blood-stained robe, and Natalia scanned her komrade from head to toe. Similar to Ilya, minute traces of contamination appeared over her body here and there. Content with her work, Natalia called out.

"Ilya, all done. Cleaned the robe, too."

Ilya re-entered and donned his night-vision goggles. Watching the lieutenant cover herself from his direct scrutiny, his lips curled in quiet amusement. Considering the reputation his male colleagues attributed to her and the fact he'd seen half the FSB personnel naked all afternoon, her physical protestation of modesty came off as refreshing. Taking the light-wand in hand, he let the humour flow — "Lieutenant, don't you know?"

Her face squared up to the male voice in the dark.

"These beer goggles give me X-Ray vision," Ilya finished.

Olga only caught onto the 'X-Ray' part.

"What!" she said and stood akimbo in annoyance.

Ilya pounced — "There, Natalia."

Like a master butcher inspecting a carcass of hung beef for quality, Ilya pointed the light-wand at Olga's upper torso. And, oblivious to any concept of male-female propinquity, he flexed the light-wand against the yielding underside of her meaty left breast and gruffed his displeasure.

"Do you see it now?"

"Huh!" And, Natalia palmed the underside of her friend's breast.

Ilya continued his mini-lecture to hammer the point home.

"Natalia, it's essential that subjects hoist and splay themselves. Otherwise you'll miss seeing a lot of things. Like this."

"Ok. Done," she replied.

Ilya well knew the reason for the problem, but he decided to run Natalia through the checklist of culprits, one by one.

"Lieutenant Krovsoska, please hold out your hands. Splay your fingers."

Natalia was perplexed.

"Her hands! I'm sure I got it all."

"Natalia, if you would please," Ilya snipped

"Ok. It's done," she groused.

Ilya's tone remained professorial — "Natalia, let me show you the problem. It's the long, thick hair. The equipment can't penetrate hair very well. That's why total depilation is essential prior to any decontamination efforts."

Olga protested indignantly.

"My hair's not to be touched. Strict orders from General Novimirov, Captain."

Focused on saving life, Ilya paid no heed to her caterwauling.

"Lieutenant, turn around. Cock your head back so your hair dangles."

And, Ilya whipped the light-wand to and fro amid Olga's jet-black tresses to jostle the strands loose and demonstrate the problem better.

"I see what you mean Ilya. I'll run my hands through her hair."

As Natalia did so, Ilya continued explaining — "Natalia, you must be very thorough. Hair contains sebaceous oils. It's a dioxin magnet. Dioxin particles dissolved in hair oils are constantly contaminating one's neck and hands and everywhere else the subject puts their hands. It's the primary reason adults, children and infants who never went near the Metro today have fallen victim to secondary contamination."

After Natalia made five complete passes aided by Ilya's close inspection with the light-wand, Olga's hair was sanitized, not a fleck of red. Next, Natalia wiped down Olga's back, neck and shoulders, followed by her hands again. Abruptly, as if a temperamental maestro might reproach his orchestra's dereliction with a baton, Ilya sharply rapped the light-wand between Olga's trim legs. The unexpected thwacking caused Olga to part them on reflex. And, the perfectionist in the Captain pounded the quintessential point yet again.

"Look at that. See what I mean?"

Natalia looked down — *Holy Denisovan!*

Ilya continued his lecture — "Natalia, shaving is critical. Truly critical. Regardless of rank, you must enforce the zero-hair mandate. No exceptions. Vanity be damned. You have presidential authority, use it. Remember if hands become contaminated anywhere anyone puts their hands becomes contaminated."

Ilya prodded the right side of Olga's crotch with the light-wand and became goose-step clinical with his protégé.

"There's toxin on that pudendum. Don't be tentative."

And, while hunching low to squat on his knees, Ilya looked up and addressed Olga. Along the svelte of her abdomen and through the cleft of her alpine physique, Olga heard the young Captain's yodel reverberate its way up her midriff. To her, it came across as brutish, ramish, almost a gloat.

"Is this hair also protected by a mission of state, Lieutenant?"

Olga smarted at his impudent question.

"No, Captain-Sir. I'll pull it off with my fingers."

After a trying day of arduous work, Ilya snapped in exasperation.

"Have you *not* listened to my lecture about the perils of hair? Fingers — no. Gloves — yes. Scissors — yes. And, finally a razor, preferably brand-new or better yet bikini cream. You must break the cycle of contamination."

Now stooped lower on his hands, Ilya probed deeper and with the impatience of a school-master whipped her thigh gap with the wand, signaling her to spread even wider. More problems! And, Ilya bade Natalia to crouch low and minister to every patch of cherry-red. With Natalia's every effulgent stroke along the length of her labia pure nirvana, Olga felt her riposte in the cafeteria about being 'straightened out' coming back to haunt her.

From head to toe, Ilya gave Olga another studious bend-flex-and-splay once over. After he'd finished fingering the Black Forest on Olga's crotch, satisfied everything was as pristine as a pine cone, he reassured Natalia.

"Don't fret too much. Just be diligent. Tomorrow everyone should be shaven so it will go much easier. We'll practice more then."

Feeling like a carcass being ignored by two buzzing flies, Olga vented.

"May I get dressed now? P,P,Pa—leez!"

"By all means, Lieutenant." And, Ilya switched on the main light, turned away from Olga and faced Natalia — "Don't forget. Hair is the worst place for contamination. It tracks to hands and then the rest of the body as well as other people." Before turning around, he asked — "Lieutenant, are you decent?"

"Yes," she replied, and Ilya wheeled about.

"Lieutenant, please don't fixate on your appearance."

Feeling belittled by Botanin's paw-the-pubes directness, she fumed — "Who? Me? Me — Fixated! Do I look like a man?" She groped between her legs. "My wang. My wang. My bitchdom for a wang," she squealed.

Ilya looked down, dumbfounded. Olga removed her hand.

"Yes, please do, stare. Ooh! I'm *not* a man." Olga mewled in alto-alto.

The captain in Ilya hammered back.

"Since when are *men* narcissistic? I can order you, Miss Clitsmear, to rip every strand out with your fingers, here and now. Is that clear?"

Natalia interceded.

"*Ilya Borisovich*! General Novimirov needs Olga's hair as part of a special assignment. She's complaining, your colleagues, Ilya, are fixated on *her* appearance."

Ilya blushed — "Excuse my outburst, Lieutenant. I thought—"

"I'm a vain seductress of a woman. A vamp! That's my reputation, right?"

"Please, don't embroil me in gossip. I'm a scientist. Your health matters to me."

Natalia glared sternly at Olga to remind her that she and Ilya were very much *blizki droogi*.[1]

"Oh." And, Olga paused to heed the modesty conveyed in the Captain's last words and his now mellow tone of voice. "Please excuse my impertinence, sir. Most of the jerks here think I work undercover at Hetman Hooters. My bush, opprobrious as it gets sometimes, anchors me. It screams, 'No, the Hell, I do not.'" And with that off her chest, Olga softened her tone. Respect was in order because everyone deserved good health, not good vanity.

"Sir, at least on my head, the hair must stay. What do you suggest?"

"In that case, have the Infirmary issue you a surgical cap. It must provide a good, solid covering. A nurse can show you."

Natalia cranked her head sideways, in the direction of the infirmary and flashed Ilya an engaging half-smile — *Hello, hello, hello.*

In the face of such encouragement, Ilya relaxed.

"Actually Lieutenant, I'm headed to the Infirmary for some shut-eye. Why don't I escort you? We'll get the proper cap, and I'll show you myself."

As they ambled on their way, Ilya explained to Olga and Natalia much of what they could expect over the next few days. Hour by hour, the situation was going ever faster downhill.

To Fight a Spiritual War

After concluding a lengthy telephone conference clarifying the Patriarch issue with President Bushkin and Director-General Besstrashnikov, Basil bounded down to the Infirmary to meet their guest. On the way there, being fluent with the situation in the United States, he made special effort to tamp down his personal misgivings about how any president's 'Speak to God' syndrome had the potential to descend into hamhanded hyperbole.

1 Close and trusted friends (Rus).

He caught up with the Patriarch in Teodor's room. Once the customary Russian introductions had been exchanged, Doctor Chernikrov appraised Basil about Teodor's deteriorating condition. Through unspoken cues, the doctor let Basil know that it was only a matter of time. Teodor's demise was irreversible. A brief conversation then ensued about the greater misery benighting all of Moscow, after which Basil broached the more miraculous element with the Patriarch.

"I guess you now understand that medical science has little to offer at curing this type of contamination. It's very similar to radioactive exposure in its insidious effects." Basil paused to switch topics — "And, you have now seen Miss Bogomolski at work. What do you think the prospects are?"

Heavy at heart, the Patriarch replied as stoically as he was able.

"Her gift is miraculous. But, … It's in God's hands … now."

The Patriarch fizzled to silence. Adrift in torpor, he might discuss anything but this or that or anything at all, but really nothing whatsoever.

Discerning how languidness drowned the man's soul, Basil decided candor might open the door to the sought for Church-State alliance.

"Patriarch, I need to confess that I was unsure about your coming here. It looks like you are getting preferential treatment. But, when I considered it more comprehensively, I realized that once you understood how the best medicine in the world cannot reverse this catastrophe, I had a change of heart. I now believe that you need to see and experience as much as possible, horrible as it is."

"General, I cannot begin to thank you. And, Miss Bogomolski's efforts to comfort Teodor is more than any father could have dreamt for. Just to see it. … Just to see it. … God be praised. God be praised." The Patriarch stifled a sob and his tone became reverent — "Praised whenever he walks amongst us."

Basil was struck how the grieving man's simple words melted all sense of apprehension and he responded to establish closeness through hope in the divine.

"Excuse my abruptness but I must talk to you about a serious matter. It's one where you are the most senior expert in our country and where I'm an utter novice."

His mind still in a puddle, the Patriarch responded on reflex.

"You're having a crisis of faith in God, my son?"

Needing to unburden himself, Basil gently sighed.

"Patriarch, by tomorrow, you'll see millions of Moscow's citizens in crisis. My concerns are trivial compared to the grief over the days and weeks to come. Your country, our …" Basil stuttered with hesitation because he noticed the Patriarch had closed his eyes — "Patriarch, we all need *your* help. We need a spiritual calmness to take hold, to soften the trauma. I want your boy to get the best care right in front of your eyes so you'll better embed into your own heart the misery that awaits so many others as the future unfolds. Others might think that medicine can save them, but the truth is it cannot. Others might even start to hear a rumor about a miraculous healer. But, the truth is she cannot heal any internal injury. There's no Abracadabra. None."

The Patriarch coaxed his eyes open wide and a blush permeated his cheeks.

"The great miracle behind the power she wields is hope, General. It's God's presence. To watch it, to feel it radiate, to waft through space as it does. So real as it is. … It's everything I could ever contemplate as extraordinary." And, the man let out a sigh of resignation — "But it seems God did not intend for her to cure. Simply to comfort."

Basil felt relieved on hearing the Patriarch's sanguine outlook.

"Comfort. Yes, that's her special gift. … Patriarch, excuse my presumptuousness, but comfort is what the government is asking from you and the Church. Surely, I don't have to explain. Aside from the certainty of many direct casualties, there'll also be suicidal grief, suicidal rage and others who'll sink into similar destructive despairs, such as drug use from more of that Amerikan rubbish from Afghanistan." Basil paused to allow his frustration to subside. "Just as our motherland wars against heroin and all manner of biological warfare, we, the Russian nation, are beseeching the Church to fight a spiritual war against despair and suicide."

The Patriarch's heart warmed to the thought of such a mission and he replied with all the augustness he could summon — "General, please call me Kolya. And, understand this, sir — I will rally our clergy to save the souls of all as tenaciously as man is able. *Doubt it not.*"

"Thank you, Kolya. And, please, it's Basil. You and—"

Basil broke conversation because Ilya, Olga and Natalia stepped into the room. While Natalia examined Teodor's face for chloracne lesions, Basil, Olga and Ilya pulled down his bed sheets. There were several new outbreaks on his abdomen. She kissed them on reflex. It was the first time that Basil had experienced her healing aura face-to-face. Her dexterous movements, the deliberate passion underlying her empathy, unstinting as it was, and its sensate effect in his presence, quietly overwhelmed him in a way he would never have suspected. When she finished, Basil gave her a wink of 'Well-Done,' and the Patriarch thanked her. The trio left without further commotion.

Basil and the Patriarch were alone again.

Besotted as a school-boy, Basil stirred first.

"I've seen it on video, but the radiance of it … It's just as you said."

The Patriarch, still tucking in his son's right-side bed-sheet, merely smiled and when he was done, he looked across the bed at Basil.

"So how long has Miss Bogomolski been a state secret?"

"It's not what you think. Today, she should have …." And, Basil explained the story of how Natalia had been struck by a train in Metro Komsomolskaya. Rather than dying or sustaining the slightest injury, she had gained special powers — no explanation. He omitted any mention that Natalia had assaulted Ludmila. And, as Basil discussed the way the discovery of her powers had come about, a new idea intruded and he switched gears.

"Kolya, could I ask you to befriend Miss Bogomolski. Consider it a mission of state. Our president has bestowed on her the designation 'Princess of Peace.'"

Basil noticed the Patriarch's face brighten as if such an appellation was not unexpected. Again, his concerns about presidents who speak with Gods came to the fore — "Patriarch, please don't be colored by Fatima. Just get the facts. We need to find out how she came by these powers and how we might put them to optimal use. Everything you learn is classified. We cannot afford unruly mobs. As I said earlier, Natalia cannot cure anyone. I'm certain of this. She went hysteric—" Basil cut himself off, who was he to criticize her meltdown in light of his own actions.

The Patriarch picked up on the lull.

"Basil Novimirov, say no more. Princess of Peace. Riots. Hysteria. Don't think for a minute I don't understand. God sent us Natalia, and the Church hears and obeys. Helping people through grief is our bread and butter."

Basil's eyes shone with admiration — *It was all about help*. And, he dug deep from a long life filled with his own intense experience of things.

"Let me simply say, Patriarch, 'Great power feels powerful grief.' Miss Bogomolski's beloved, Derek Mitchell, is just like your boy. There's no cure."

The Patriarch closed his eyes to summon courage.

"No cure. Just comfort," he murmured.

Basil reached across the bed and clutched the Patriarch's arm.

"Just comfort, Kolya. And, in comfort, we must find fortitude. Let's go to Mr. Mitchell's room. She'll be there. Once the atmosphere of panic has abated, we can be more public in our policy about the 'Princess of Peace.' But right now, I repeat, everything you see or will come to know about her is classified."

"Agreed, General. Let's go."

Three Become One

The mood in Derek's room was restive somber. Derek lay face down in Ludmila's bed, nestled gently over the full length of her immobile body. In the stippled light of the room, Natalia's face glistened with tears, her countenance was filled with capitulation, yet within her, a spirit worked undaunted. Standing at their bedside with her right hand under Ludmila's back, she had just lowered her other hand onto Derek's back when Basil and the Patriarch entered.

Alarmed by the peculiar atmosphere, Basil went on high alert.

"What's this?"

Dr. Chernikrov nabbed Basil by the arm.

"Hold, General. Ludmila can't speak nor hear. Natalia is channeling the feelings of one to the other. There's no harm."

Natalia pressed her hand against Derek's back. A sublime effulgence bloomed across her face as she transmitted through her gift what Derek wanted Ludmila to feel within her whole body. To know, compared with his past meagerness, the great joy he now felt. And, how he deeply appreciated her forbearance during the few months they had shared together. Most especially, he wanted Ludmila to know of his desire to love her without reservation.

Ludmila could barely draw breath, yet her face radiated an unrestrained pleasure that permeated the spirits of all watching with an unearthly intensity. And, all would have sworn the floor felt organic, fleshy underfoot. And, the air thrummed so lambent with spark and majesty that within a room shadowed in finality, it seemed as if flecks of translucent hope twinkled their way skywards.

From out of nowhere, Ludmila's right arm twitched. Then her hand flexed, and floating with the poise of a ballerina, it came to rest atop Natalia's hand stationed on Derek's back. All three of them surrendered to the closure of this circle of connection. There in darkness, three became one. And, within a brace of seconds, each channeled to the other everything that is speech-worthy in a lifetime infused with warmly remembered days of love conjoined. As time passed, Natalia realized her inclusion had become superfluous. Gracefully extracting her hands, she left Derek and Ludmila melded together in this most serene and intimate embrace.

Ilya and Olga had been present from the very beginning. Quietly standing behind Olga, Ilya remained motionless and sequestered. He was well acquainted with the boundless love Natalia bore for Derek, and unexpectedly, found this spiritual tryst more exacting than he could have imagined.

Olga was not sure what Ilya felt. Only when Ilya brought his hands to rest against her waist, did such thoughts intrude in upon her. Sensing his touch an innocent gesture of closeness in keeping with the ambience of spiritual conjunction, she cupped her hands over his in solidarity. No sooner had she done so then she felt a curious drooling on the base of her neck. She suppressed an urge to flinch and whispered.

"Ilya, what's up?"

"Olga, I feel so overwhelmed. Do you comprehend what we're watching?"

Olga's eyes brimmed wide with empathy and understanding, but she felt flustered, unable to respond. Natalia's genius for affirmative love, grating against Olga's emotional detachment as it did, was becoming a source of inner turmoil and self-examination. And, the surreal mood of the room only exacerbated Olga's anxiety about the burdensomeness of her own emptiness. Her breathing slowed. Her pulse quickened. She stewed in vexation. Stewed in thought. It was when Ludmila reached up to complete the circle of connection that Olga felt another strange tickle, followed by a bothersome dribble. She clutched Ilya's hands more firmly in her own and repeated — "Ilya, are you alright?"

"Olga, have you ever seen anything more remarkable?"

Olga smiled and decided to use the moment to embrace Ilya's welcome proximity. She boldly swiveled about and faced him. Slipping his hands behind her back, she cocked her head to his left and moved closer to his chest, closer to his heartbeat. As if a slow dance. His palms were placed against the sides of her waist; his fingertips hovered just so wonderfully over the inflexion that parted her spine from the dimples in her lithe buttocks. And, like the winds of an Indian Summer, she felt Ilya's breath beat down upon the blush blooming across her left cheek, before the words of his next enchantment registered.

"Olga, she needs our help. She's let Derek go. Did she tell you that she was promised to become pregnant by her greatest love three days from now?"

On any other day, Ilya's utterance might have struck her as the most outrageous 'Pick-up Line' ever contrived. But, immersed in the tenderheartedness of the moment, Olga rebuked herself in quiet. Her instinctual reaction to Ilya's unguarded candor was so frivolous, so accusatory, entirely vain. Ensconced as she was within the world of the 'Pick-up' game that masquerades for courtship in cosmopolitan Moscow, she felt nettled at how the purity of Natalia's desire to be with her dearest Derek mocked the fetidness behind her coquettish presumptuousness. The true soul in Olga, smoldering away like kindling on the brink of flashover, certainly did realize the poignancy of the moment. Her deepest pain was to know that Natalia's grief was beyond her capacity to fathom. It had an extraordinary, selfless beauty, which resonated with Ilya, but to her, cobbled along like a tumbleweed of tragedy. *Perhaps, Ilya is in love with Natalia,* she thought. Then another tickle, followed by a drawling sensation as wetness dribbled toward the hollow of her collar bone.

"What?" She straightened up — "Ilya, let's go somewhere private."

"Not right now."

She untied the sash of her robe, wiped her neck and drew level with Ilya's face.

"Your nose is bleeding." And, she lightly dabbed it. "Natalia has finished. Let's get you out of here before anyone notices."

Ilya saw the bloodied cloth in Olga's hands, and they slunk out together.

Moments after Ilya and Olga left, the mesmerizing enormity of Natalia's hold over the room subsided. Basil regained his presence of mind, walked over and placed himself between the bed and a rune-stone of a lady hammered to shards. He picked Natalia up and carried her back to the room in which she had napped earlier. The Patriarch, whose head was bowed in both awe and contemplation, remained by Derek and Ludmila's sides and he began chanting a gentle prayer.

Perhaps, in a Dream

Basil placed Natalia upon a freshly-made bed. As he retracted his arms, he noted the cool, starch-crisp texture of the sheets and, more perplexingly, how this woman sensitized him to the least of triflings.

"Letting go of your love for Derek must have been very hard," he said

"Until today, I thought—" Natalia's cheeks flushed as she winced out a half-smile, one filled with gnosis — "It's perverse to contemplate, but no. The greatest blessing was being Derek and Ludmila's interlocutor, an angel, in the most sublime intimacy possible between two lovers. And, it's the greatest curse too."

She became still awhile. Taking in the mood, Basil remained silent.

"Basil, there I was, feeling every shared desire, every shared regret between two souls who know for certain how their lives come to an end. But, end together. As if plunging to Earth in a burning aircraft."

And, crushed by the weight of inevitability in her last words now counterpoised against her vile conduct in the Metro, she let out a sob, hard and pitiful. For the first time, she now comprehended the obliterative nature of Olga's pain. Perhaps the same blight, an incompleteness in the depth of love she was well capable of, would haunt her to the grave, and she gave voice to her darkest doubts.

"Basil, there was always this tenacious love between Derek and I. But, now I know how trivial it was compared to the love Derek had with Marie, and which he wanted to share with Ludmila, if only for a single day."

She stopped, and rather than screaming into the pillow, she did the exact opposite. She gazed longingly into Basil's eyes as if to enlist through him the whole of humanity to stand as witness to a great truth locked inside her body.

"Never before have I felt such a manic desire for intensity. What I called 'my great love' was but." She stopped. The emptiness she felt had no name or measure — "I feel totally undone. I'll never have a true great love."

Her voice warbled, but Basil sensed it more as a sigh of capitulation.

"Oh Basil, my life offers nothing but the specter of equivocation compared to what I experienced this night."

The searing plaint in her voice and her words, filled with such luster and promise, warmed Basil to the core. He had exorcised the ghosts of his past months before and now thought more along the lines of a hot pit of passion. Except, he had yet to shear off the habit of clinging to the uninvolved expectations of the lovelorn troubadour. And, sensing the boundless maturity behind her anguish, Basil made reply to re-assure Natalia of the genuine beauty he saw within her.

"Natalia, I can only speculate about what you felt. But, what I sensed confounds description. Right now, I think we all feel like we're thirsting in the desert while Derek and Ludmila enjoy a picnic in Eden. A banquet, you set for them. All I can say, sweet lady, is that to love well is never to forget." And, as if perforce of his own declarations, a yearning for an Eden of his own unexpectedly overwhelmed Basil, and he asked — "Could I lie down beside you? I'm exhausted and need to recharge for tomorrow."

Disquieted, Natalia sat up.

"General, I'm not … not here, like this."

He plucked free her right hand, perched it over his heart and pressed down.

"Does this allay your concerns?"

Her eyes twinkled with empathy.

"Oh, yes. I need the same rest. Please, join me."

After a moment of solidarity, they broke contact. And, down they settled. Both quieted — her hand embalmed in his. And, unbeknownst to her, Basil sensed her waning thoughts and her small prayer to talk to that voice, the inner-voice — *Perhaps, in a dream, it will speak again.*

Thus sheltered from the most draining day each had ever known, before the minute struck zero and the next began, they lay deep in slumber.

No Cut — No Run

Andrei Zinovich Chainikov,[1] a Soviet-era hard-liner known as Alpha-Zero among his friends, was a man reconciled to the bitter fact that Communism remained a grand design that fate had once foolishly squandered on the proles of Russia. But, he did not despair because for Siberian survivalists such as himself, the future always presented exploits. And, the revenge pragmatist in him was ever ready to track, hunt and glut itself on every scrap Western materialism could be suckered into throwing his way. Because, as he saw it, in the game of life the West called 'Survival of the Fittest,' extravagant exploitation was every Russian patriot's new 'All the Doodles You Can Eat' Buffet.

For now, the Kossack in Chainikov was content with the freedom of action his posting as the Vice-President of Russia afforded. As such, he fulfilled his duties as the nominal head of the SVR[2] with vigor and independence. He was also a man who loved to collect newspaper clippings, especially those in the English language. Because the SVR — Russia's civilian-sector foreign intelligence service — was the organization accredited in the foreign press for his nation's glorious assassination record in alien lands.

Within the confines of the crisp air-conditioned SVR Cipher Room, two men nestled themselves into a corner free of cold blusters. Chainikov bent forward and handed Director-General Besstrashnikov type-written proof of the matter, which their secret conference sought to resolve. "The reply from our mutual friend," Chainikov said in his most graveled of voices. "As you see Karl Grigorovich, Voshington[3] is likeminded. The ball to minimize the fallout terrorism has unleashed on our fragile demokrazy is squarely in our court. So, I think we need to run the assassination of Carter by the president again. Are you up to it?"

"Mr. Vice-President, I couldn't agree more. But, the president is still riled about the blow-back from the Beaver assassination."

"Karl, I'm taking the heat on that so you get freedom of action. Use it wisely. Always remind the president of the 30,000 citizens who die every year while 'Operation Rambo'[4] sits idle. That's the '9/11 Clock' chiming ten every year, not some one-off Cuckoo. And, know we have like-minded allies in Voshington."

Besstrashnikov perused the communiqué once more before replying.

"Sir, as soon as the larger mission against woppery comes into focus, I'll anchor it to the president's agenda and make it happen one way or another."

Chainikov nodded his approval and asked.

"We remain likeminded about Weissbrot — right?"

"Definitely."

Once other details were wrapped up, Chainikov held the communiqué over an empty dustbin, struck a lighter and watched the paper curl into ash flakes. He used the flat of his thumb to crush them to dust before putting the bin down.

---

1 Pronunciation: Chai-nik-ov.
2 SVR - Foreign Intelligence Service - *Sluzhba Vneshney Razvedki* (Rus).
3 Washington DC. Another russified word.
4 Operation President Bushkin proposed in 2002 to eradicate Afghan opium plantations. US and NATO have repeatedly vetoed any such operation proceeding.

"Let's go, Director-General."

Walking toward the polished stainless-steel security door, Chainikov noticed his glee-filled face beaming back at him. He stifled a chuckle because things were already long in the works no matter what Bushkin might decide.

The blood of the motherland was konstitutionally blessed under Article 61(2). Article 61(2) enshrined 'Survival of the Fittest.' And, national security trumped every president. National security trampled every law. Russia was a proletarian demokrazy. No alien demokrazy would ever imperil that.

No cut. No run.

Jungle of Lust

General, it's time to get up. Ursini's contrition, sir. Wake up."

Basil rubbed his eyes — "What. Who? Who—"

"Major Gratski, sir. Time to review the contrition process."

Basil smartly propped himself up on his elbows. Noticing Natalia deep in sleep, he took pains to extricate himself as deftly as possible from the bed. Once standing and more revived, he looked down and watched her eyes roll and flex beneath the glassine damask of her beautifully veined eyelids.

He had but one thought — *A vivid dream. Something that might renew this fine lady's resolve to face down a new day of horrors.*

And, when he breathed out and back in to refresh himself further, he realized how much that very thought hurt him. Savouring one last second of the promise her unearthly grace afforded, Basil finally turned his focus upon his own day, one crammed bleak with hardness.

"Major, get your team into my office and we'll hammer it all out."

"Elena's asleep in your office, sir. I suggest the medical conference room."

He recalled how Elena had worked tirelessly into the night, scouring his office clean of potential contamination and he issued his approval — "*Harosho.*"

While Major Gratski went off to muster the 'Preachers,' Basil made directly for the conference room adjacent to the Infirmary. The locked door presented no problem because he possessed a set of master keys to the building — *Click.*

He stepped into a room unexpectedly snug.

On the floor, there they lay, sprawled out naked and sleeping like lambs. He chuckled just short of a chest laugh because he envied them and yet envied them not. But, now was not the time to dilly-dally with probity or protocol.

"Captain Botanin. Botanin! Wake up." He jostled his junior hurriedly.

Ilya Botanin roused second by second. "What the? Who?" His eyes opened wide — "General? *Bolsheviks*! Sir we—"

Basil cut in — "Quick lad, get up. Gratski and her crew will be here any minute. I'll stand outside. Get semi-decent and vamoose."

Basil could not resist taking another peep at Olga spread wide like a dozing cat. And, when Ilya stood, Basil cocked his eyebrows — "Your knees, Captain. I suggest you see Special Agent Bogomolski about those abrasions. Now get cracking, both of you."

And, without looking back, Basil vaulted to the door and took up sentry duty in the hallway. Soon after, Ilya, in his underwear, shepherded a scantily robed Olga down the corridor and past the noise of footfall in the central stairwell. On mounting the topmost stair, the lead 'Preachers' spied their colleagues' scurrying posteriors in the dim corridor light.

"Good morning, Komrades," they hooted.

And, roistering their way down the hallway towards a plum-faced Basil, everyone, except the Major wondered whether the 'Master of the Veronikas' had been a player in what they imagined.

Once seated within the confines of the conference room, deliberations began. However, it was not until everyone had settled into their second cup of coffee that the Jungle-of-Lust bouquet left wafting through the room and through their sybaritic imaginations by a passionate Lieutenant Olga Nikolaevna Krovsoska, ceased in its distraction of their conscious thoughts.

Truth Will Ultimately Prevail

Alfredo's nose twitched, his eyes opened. And, in a room drenched in the alpine-freshness of sizzling electric arcs, overhead lights blazed burning-white like the eye-watering scald of superheated steam. Once his pupils adjusted, Alfredo exhaled in relief. A voice behind his head abruptly intruded.

"Good morning, Ursini. I trust you had a restful night. Time to make some choices. Doktor Soskrova has informed us that it is more likely than not you'll fully cooperate. But, her opinion is academic in light of the fact that you're at complete liberty to decide whose hospitality you prefer."

The voice paused as if Alfredo might need an opportunity to reflect.

"The hospitality of Satan and his enchanting vampires or ours, your fellow flesh and blood humans." The voice cleared its throat — "As you know, by operation of law, we humans are humane. We abide by the laws of humanity. But."

And, the voice let the 'But' linger and spoke no more.

Alfredo felt a clammy hand on his left shoulder. Fingers meandered on his flesh. And, after seven heartbeats had thumped and faded, the face behind the voice moved into his field of view and pierced him with an ominous stare.

"I'm going to release the stopper on your gag, Ursini. Speak freely. Supplicate yourself. Convince me that you're on our side, the side of virtue through redemption. If I sense any prevarication, I'll get the vampires here in a trice."

The stopper came free as a uniformed official found perch atop a stainless steel barstool. Alfredo felt relieved at the first opportunity to make proper conversation since the Mafia pimp zapped him with a stun gun. He swallowed hard to moisten his throat before asking in a hoarse voice.

"Do … do you understand Italian?"

"Italian is fine, English is fine. My name's Major Anatol Soyanovich Shurkin. I normally work in the Ministry of Foreign Affairs. At the Italian desk, actually. But, currently, I'm on special assignment with the FSB." And Shurkin stooped low and snarled — "Don't be fooled into thinking my desk-job camouflages a warm personality, Ursini."

"Anatol, I want to help you if I can."

"Address me as Major or sir. *If-I-can* is not relevant. If you can't then you're useless to us. Believe me, you'll endure weeks of hell before you convince those FSB sadists you really cannot help us. By the way, do you see this?"

And, Shurkin brought a single button remote control into Alfredo's view.

"Doktor Soskrova gave it to me. She said that if I hold it close to your scrotum and push this button — 'Ivy' would come out and play. She claimed to do so would unleash the ménage à trois from Hell. 'Miz Pizduka'[1] was snickering at the time, so I guess you and she are sharing some inside sexual joke at my expense. I'm being played for a candy-ass bureaucrat. — right?"

Shurkin snickered in silence at the horror enveloping Alfredo's face before assuring Ursini about his own more sangfroid assessment.

"Ursini, calm down. Of course, I don't believe her." And, Shurkin's lips grew taut — "Why? Because she said that if I push it, within the hour and for the rest of the day you would be begging me to fetch her so she could return with her vampires and cleave wide your scrotum with a scalpel."

Shurkin paused to let that absurdity run its course.

"*Feminist rubbish!* So Ursini, fess up. What sort of setup is this?"

Shurkin watched in amusement as Alfredo's face crinkled in terror as he strived to find some sane means of explaining the bizarre nature of the matter. Sensing a response was coming, Shurkin pressed his finger against Alfredo's lips and he continued the game. His voice drizzled with derision — "I know your reputation, Mr. Jokester. I saw the television footage of you in that woman's wig and that green sequin dress. Real class act!"

Increasing the pressure on Alfredo's lips, Shurkin bent lower, hovering menacingly over Alfredo's face as if hankering to lick his eyeballs — "But really. A wop begging to have vampires split open his nadsack. That's the height of whacked-out, even for a deviant like you, Ursini."

Shurkin sat erect again but, like a father ferrying a diaper slathered in milk-shit to a waste bin, he kept his arm outstretched clamping Alfredo's lips between thumb and forefinger, before resuming his tirade.

"I think you and those FSB mongrels are mocking me."

Shurkin brought the remote control level with his nose, and using his index finger, he toyed with its prominent copper button — "It doesn't look like a typical stun gun. Hmm. It's a prank — right? I push — I get zapped. That's it? Juvenile idiots! Just let me find my gloves."

He removed his hand from Alfredo's face and started rummaging in the side pocket of his suit.

Sensing a wounded pride, Alfredo hopped to it — "Sir. German pigs killed the doctor's grandparents in World War II. She deludes herself by thinking I'm responsible. I suspect she wants a dupe to poison me. Then, you'll be blamed. I'm useless to you dead. I wouldn't play with that device, sir."

1 Portmanteau of Pizda + Suka meaning Cunt-Bitch (Rus).

Shurkin huffed — "Let's stop wasting time then. I'll put it away."

He hurriedly swiveled off the stool — "*Bolsheviks!*"[1]

Alfredo heard the clatter of plastic on concrete. Only a single thought flooded his mind — *Please no. God no.*

"Silly me. No big one. It landed button side up."

Snickering quietly, Shurkin bent over, retrieved the remote and as he straightened his back and stood up, he tossed it on the side cabinet counter. Bringing his knees to his chest one by one, he stretched his back, before returning to the stool. From eyes to lips was Shurkin's smile. Ursini's face betrayed the most salutatory of outcomes — a shared commitment to the truth. Surviving their first balls-to-the-walls crisis together, the nut-sack duo of 'Shurkin and Ursini' were now forever FET — *fraternitas ex testibus*.[2]

On the monitor, Major Shurkin showed his captive the rudiments of the FSB intelligence file on the Romanovs. Alfredo realized the grim reality facing him. More likely than not, the FSB had the capacity to detect if he was holding out. There was no sanctuary for sanity. No safe choice. On pain of Satan and his vampires, Alfredo knew he was obliged to accede to the Russians every demand, regardless of whatever he thought he knew or thought he knew not.

Confession, voluntary or otherwise, was irrelevant.

Contrition would be whatever Russia dictated contrition to be.

The direct questions were the easy part. But, the essay questions, where Alfredo had to recount everything he claimed he knew or was presumed to know — meaning 'knowledge in the balls' evidentiary facts incapable of being water-boarded into some flight of fancy — those questions gave him the horrors. He tried to convince the Major that what he said could be corroborated. But, time after time, a skeptical Shurkin scowled on hearing Alfredo's hesitations and dubious assertions. Alfredo become distraught when the Major abruptly re-gagged him, pushed the monitor aside, donned his dress hat and marched from the room. Almost simultaneously, Dr. Soskrova entered. The woman's eyes glowered with snark.

When the door creaked open again, Alfredo's nose flared wide. He expected to inhale the morbid yet magnificent scent of a vampire. On hearing footfalls, his heart started racing. To his left a man wearing a cardinal's *galero*[3] and whose face was obscured by a 'Komrade Stalin' mask came to a halt and introduced himself as Reverend Woland. Spare with his manners, Woland wheeled the video monitor to a stand-still on Alfredo's left and switched it on using a remote control clutched within a prosthesis that substituted for his right hand.

"Ursini," he growled. "This is Carlo Rolfino, the chargé d'affaires conspirator from Wopland's fake embassy enjoying the company of our darlings, Olga and Natalia. We're watching the action on fast forward. However, I'm sure the torment flashing by is familiar to you."

When the juicy part began, Woland hit [PLAY].

"Do you recognize the sound of formic acid's spermicidal activity Ursini?"

1 Crap! (Slang).
2 Brotherhood from Testicles. Roman and Baboon rites. See etymology of 'Testify' (Latin).
3 Catholic Cardinal's hat, wide-rimmed.

Every shaved follicle on Alfredo's body itched. Woland hit [STOP] then [FAST FORWARD] until the clock reached [7:13 a.m]. Then he hit [PLAY] again. "Here's Rolfino an hour after 'Miss Ivy' gave him a 'Cartman style' ball-licking."

Under a bright spotlight, Rolfino was squirming. His face glistened. Oral exudates frothed through crevasses in his gag, quivered down his chin like wafts of bubble bath and lay shimmering like rainbows atop his strapped-down shoulders. Woland resumed — "You're now watching contemporary video. I'm here to confirm your compliance regarding your next assignment. Your videotaped conversation."

Woland instructed Dr. Soskrova to hold a tape recorder near Alfredo's mouth. He clutched Alfredo's ear and commanded him to read the script shown on screen. This was repeated three times before Woland re-gagged Alfredo.

Dr. Soskrova left the room.

Alfredo was relieved beyond measure — *No Vampires!* But, as Woland took seat, Alfredo began pondering Woland's precise words, and his heart started racing. *Videotaped conversation? Surely, he's after a confession. Why not a simple confession?*

Woland pointed at the monitor. There — Rolfino remained writhing away, his puffy face ruby-red atop a neck scintillating in lather. Alfredo watched as Soskrova stood before Rolfino and played back the tape of his own voice close to a surveillance microphone. Then, she vanished off-screen.

Woland fiddled with the remote. The monitor went black then flashed to life again. Alfredo watched as a fresh suspect was being prepared for what was certain to be an impending vampire intercession. Soskrova entered and repeated the verification process.

Woland spoke into a microphone built into the remote control.

"Men stand aside. Control room, zoom-in on the face."

Alfredo's eyelids flared wide in disbelief. On screen was Sergio Romanov.

This process was repeated three more times. It proved that 'Operation Glue Factory' had rendered out of Italy all the other major terrorists. After Sergio Romanov came Ernesto Colonna, Sergio's brother-in-law, the official at the Italian Ministry of Foreign Affairs, who had signed the Italian government's declaration of contents letter concerning the ashes in the urn. The next chamber disclosed the capture of Constanzo Ursini, Alfredo's father, shaved from head to toe, ready to go. And, in the final chamber, was a young man about Alfredo's age. A total stranger, yet to Alfredo, he looked familiar.

Smiling at Alfredo's squint of curiosity, for the first time that morning, Woland sweetened his voice as he revealed the identity of the mystery detainee.

"That last wop is Silvio Calamari, son of the Italian Prime Minister. Snatching him from a yacht in the Aegean was the best we could do under the hasty circumstances. Of course, his father, Aurelio, remains our target. Regardless, we expect the boy to spill the beans about the many conversations between him and Daddy concerning Wopland's plans to overthrow the government of Russia. Including, how the 'failed-state' of Wopland has contracts with a syndicate of woppery you wops call 'Al Guido.' Not to mention their fascist 'private contractor of deniability' so-called Grand Duke Sergio Romanov and his contracts to do the dirty work. We already have the gist from Romanov's office records." And, Woland laughed maniacally before resuming — "Soon, all these detainees will socialize with Doktor Soskrova and Satan's darling vampires, Olga and Natalia. You might recall George Washington's famous maxim — '*Truth will ultimately prevail where there are pains to bring it to light*'."

Pretending to misread the look of doom blooming across Alfredo's face, the man in the Stalin mask softened his tone to reconnect with his young captive.

"Dear, dear boy. Don't be such a jealous wop. Natalia was only a cyber-space fling. Nothing more."

To root Alfredo back on task, Woland changed channels, jammed his prosthetic thumb and forefinger under Alfredo's jawline, pincered his throat and directed him to watch the monitor again — very closely.

"Ursini, here's what you'll be saying in a video conversation two hours from now. Read, listen and recite." And Woland leant in close to his detainee's ear. Alfredo felt desert-hot breath whistling from the slit of Stalin's mouth — "It's not a matter for negotiation, Signore Wop. You might recall just as Hitler fabricated so-called proof that Polish terrorists invaded Germany, you wops fabricated bogus documents claiming Niger was shipping uranium to Iraq."

And, Woland snarled in a voice betraying a Mesopotamian accent.

"At no time before the United Nations did Wopland insist the Amerikan delegation stop regurgitating your wop garbage."

And, while Woland stood erect, he clenched his prosthetic hand tighter against Alfredo's glottis and balled his human hand into a fist — "It's clear wops don't give a fuck about world peace."

Woland loosened his grip.

"Today, peace-loving demokrazy is writing the script to cure the shit you unloaded on the motherland. You wops are nothing but actors in our stage-play. What is true and what is crap is irrelevant. Now — read, listen and recite!"

Woland stormed out.

The lights remained on. And, as Alfredo urinated from time to time during the rest of the day, a rudimentary Russian-made video about the global forces of woppery attacking the Moscow Metro repeated and repeated and repeated.

What Washington Needs

All jostling on the US Vice-President's bed came to rest.

Pet-named Uzi on some nights and W'ugg on others, Norman Ousley Weissbrot relaxed the grip of his legs around Ginger's left thigh and propped himself up on his elbow. As he bent his knee to slide out of the 'Sidewinder Pretzel' position, what was left of his erection slipped the confines of the crotch of the Director of National Security, Ms. Ginger Arnold. After a moment of contemplation rubbing his cheek on the crook of her knee, he broke the lull.

"Sidewinder not quite hit the target, Gin'g?"

There was more to it than the buzz-kill that was Russia. Israel was also serving up shit. Something Ginger was tasked to mitigate personally. And, green-eyed Ginger was not a divorcée to suffer fools gladly. Straightening her right arm to reach out to him, she smirked as she felt his warm drizzle crawling its way downward towards her black site.

"It's also, my period, Uzi. Just a day or so away."

And, as she made eye contact, Ginger beckoned him to clasp her hand. He let his left forearm fall to the sheet, and as she toyed with his fingers, she finished.

"Sometimes it's on. Sometimes it's off, sweetie."

"You know what's best?" he chipped.

Sensing he was about to crack a whopper, Ginger cocked her head.

"Between us, Gin'g, it's all — *Je ne sais* fuck, baby."[1]

And, as if acknowledging the end of a finger-licking KFC basket, he wiped the corner of his mouth against the smooth of the drumstick taper of her calf. Ginger laughed and let her head flop to the pillow.

"You're a breath of fresh air, Uzi. Just …" She hesitated. She had no words for this, so she burst into French — "*Moi aussi. Je ne sais* fuck, *amant*." [2]

Feeling his free hand roaming over her leg, taking the temperature of an orgasm that was still-born, she smiled. With her menses days away, surely he knew better — but that's why she adored him — of course, he knew better. His earnestness in intimacy counterpoised against his casual at-home-ness with the great queeving[3] outdoors was why the Vice-President made her feel so liberated.

"Uzi, do whatever you want. It comes, it goes. I like it all. I like this." She squeezed his fingers in hers — "Fucking is overrated."

"Overrated is overrated, Gin'g."

And, Weissbrot emptied his lungs with a laugh and floated his right hand away from her inner thigh and over her bush. In the quiet interlude that followed, he preened her ornamented maidenhair with his thumb and index finger, amused at how it differed from the flowing, raven hair of her scalp. Her tarnished-copper eyebrows, flirting as they were with rutilism[4], was a dead giveaway that sometime into her conservative fifties, he was toying with the pubes of a woman who promised to be a flaming redhead. Time would tell, and he had all the time in the world. Breaking the silence, Ginger addressed the dread they both felt about the full cabinet meeting in the morning.

"Uzi, what's your read on Bushkin's game?"

"Piled onto the hokum he spouted about Italy six months back? Just more crap for Mary-Ann to digest That's what has Lester sweating, you know."

"And?" she replied.

"You know as well as I."

Evading the awkwardness of the subject, he noticed a bauble of white clinging to the tip of Uncle Fester's head. He took his stocky penis in hand and rubbed Fester on the underside of Ginger's outstretched thigh as he resumed.

1 I don't know (French).
2 Me too. I don't know … lover. (French).
3 *Queef, Queeving* - vaginal fart (Eng).
4 *Rutilism* - generic trait of red hair (Med).

"So ... what's your read on Mary-Ann?"

"I've known her since kindie." Ginger propped herself up on her elbows — "The stress of election, on top of years of toil and sleeplessness — It's low-level Alzheimers, Uzi. She's still paranoid over the Etoumbi Ebola outbreak in the Congo back in May. It's in her blood, she insists. And, fuck all this appeasing not-my-kid neo-cons. Not to mention the AIPAC mob and Jews screaming for a pardon for Pollard. Now, Bushkin's bearing his fangs — yet the fuck again."

Seeking to lie face to face with Ginger, he maneuvered her leg over his torso and palmed the sheet of the bed until his burly face drew square with hers.

"Fangs. That's more Chainikov's style. Bushkin's more eel. Zap. Stun. That's what worries me. Mary-Ann is so prone. National security that is."

"D'you think Lester will have firmed up the facts by morning?"

He placed his fingers under her chin, thumb stroking the underside of her lower lip, just north of the cleft that must have been an awesome dimple when once she had the puffy pink-face exuberance of a pre-teen.

"Facts? That's wishful." He deliberately left unstated the worldwide devastation the 'Mallory Wilson Affair'[1] had caused the CIA.

"No intel breakthroughs from Moscow?" she asked.

"Affirmative. And, keep it in perspective, Gin'g. We're talking electric eel jizz when it comes to so-called solid, high-voltage 'Facts' having any relevance in this showdown."

"You're on to confer with Naomi — right?"

"Alarm all set?" he asked.

Ginger rolled over to the bedside table, twisting until she came to rest on her stomach, stretched out her right arm and retrieved a mobile phone. She brought its illuminated face under her propped-up chest close to Weissbrot's gaze. And, as he relieved it from her grasp, she became aware of the coolness of tomcat drizzle lounging against the underside of her clitoral hood. She smiled into the beauty of a discomfort that could not be more exquisite. And, in no mood to break their conversation and hit the bathroom, she parted her athletic legs so open air could dry out her alleyway.

Weissbrot turned onto his left side to deposit the phone back onto the side-table and brought his hulking arm across her shoulders.

"Reset for five."

And, he placed the flat of his right hand against her neck and ran his thumb down the pronounced groove of her yoga-rific spine. Next, bringing his palm against her left buttock, he tweezed it between thumb and all five fingers.

Head canted to her left, Ginger spoke into the bicep of his free arm.

"Is Washington up to spec, Mr. Vice-President?"

It was one of their inside jokes. She had perfect legs molded into the world's most bitable ass. So bitable that, one evening, he had joked to her how if he ever gnawed into her buns of Corbomite, his teeth would shatter, and like America's first president, he'd be reduced to wearing 'Cherry Tree' dentures. He plonked

1 Occurring on July 14, 2003, the 'Mallory Wilson Affair,' put every CIA informant around the globe on notice that the US White House would stab anyone in the back, including their own government personnel. The upshot - the CIA lost informants (human intelligence HUMINT) left, right and center.

his hand onto her other buttock, flexed out his fingers and waxed her cheek in a clockwise motion. Correction was in order.

"This here's Washington," and he kept the menace of his hand swirling as he brought his lips behind her ear — "George is your left." He bent his head and horse-kissed the muscular roundness of her shoulder and kept the swirl in motion before he added — "I'm sure Bushkin would concur."

She giggled — "That Cossack — Concur?"

He brought his hand to rest.

"Washington needs a spanking."

She raised her head to make her delight obvious, and her back arched so that Washington broke contact with the powers inherent in the right hand of the Vice-President. She reigned in her laughter as soon as she noted the enticing state of affairs being offered the public official — *Now, what will he do?*

He smiled — *Tempting, hmm.* But, she was close to bleeding out, so probably more sensitive than usual. He relaxed his arm and kneaded her tush.

"Joining me with Naomi, tomorrow?" he asked.

"No point. Anyway, it's Lester's show. Hope he keeps it all smiley face."

"Check and check. But, like me, Lester acts on his feelings. Doesn't god'damn chit-chat about'em." He feathered the goose-bumps on her ass, before voicing his greatest concern — "I'm not sure Mary-Ann is equipped—"

Ginger chopped in.

"That's my job. Just, you two make sure it's not a Russia-up-the-rectum dump. And, be forewarned, the president's cycle is synched to mine."

"Huh?"

"Menstrual, Uzi. Mens—"

"Fuck a Truck. It's—"

Ginger cut in.

"My job — *My job.* You boys do your thing. Just—"

"Take it softly." Weissbrot fired back as he squeezed hold of Washington.

"Exactly, Uzi. Take it softly when it comes to Mary-Ann. Ever since that Wop-who-would-be-Tsar crap, she despises Bushkin. It's vendetta."

"Double-barreled tampons at twenty paces," he joked.

"Black-rotted, ebola-smeared tampons. Face-shot up Bushkin's nostrils."

There I Was — My Face in Tears

From the doorway of Teodor Mudretski's room in the Infirmary, an inquiring voice intruded upon an old man sitting in half-slumber.

"Patriarch?"

Remaining seated, the Patriarch turned.

"Ah-oh. Good morning."

"May I speak to you in confidence for a moment?"

"Please come in, Miss Bogomolski."

As she entered, the Patriarch rose to greet her more formally.

"And please, it's Natalia, Patriarch."

She glanced at Teodor, and her face melted with compassion. Already feeling tentative, the sight of the youth gave her an excuse to interpose delay.

"Patriarch, let me minister to Teodor first. Would you help, please?"

Natalia wiped her hands over Teodor's face while the Patriarch untucked the bedding. Once the sheets were removed, she discovered a host of new dioxin boils marring his abdomen. She took her time healing them, all the while growing more annoyed about evading what troubled her. She looked up.

"Patriarch, I had a very vivid dream last night. It's not surprising because yesterday was the most traumatic day of my life but—" She stopped to muster courage — *Candor's essential* — "Patriarch, I take no position on religion. None. While I've seen movies featuring Jesus and a television adaptation of *The Master and Margarita*,[1] I don't dwell on such phantasy. It's all two-thousand years old and obviously our modern-day literature is based on presumption, if not speculation about ancient happenings."

As the hearth within the Patriarch's heart flared in recognition of the classic preamble from a skeptic-in-need, a subtle warmth pervaded the man's blizzard-worn cheeks. In a Russia slowly re-discovering its Christian heritage, such conversation openers were not uncommon and the man replied in stride.

"Natalia, your dilemma is religious — right?"

"Yes. … Before I talk about that, let me tell you something you need to know. Yesterday, I should've died from a train collision in the Metro."

"Natalia, General Novimirov told me all about it. Is there more I should know? Something providing a fuller understanding of your problem."

"Patriarch, I've hidden nothing. But, it's still so disturbing. I'm a realist Patriarch, but yesterday I was the recipient of a miracle. It saved my life and has transformed me somehow. It's… It's—"

The Patriarch cut in — "As obvious as all Hell — Perhaps?"

And, he raised his eyebrows to project empathy.

Natalia's relief was so palpable her breathing was held in check — *Such directness from a pious Christian*. She knew the man would open his mind and hear her thoughts rather than hear what it pleased Church dogma to hear.

"Patriarch, it's shameful how it all happened. I was asked to do a top-secret assignment for the Russian government. And, that poisoned the relationship between Derek and me. I saw Ludmila in the Metro and in a fit of jealousy … in my haughtiness … I was suffering in the service of my country and seeing her with the man I loved." She winced — "Patriarch, I slugged Ludmila and in doing so I fell backwards into an inbound train."

The utterance triggered remembrance and with it trauma. She brought her hands to her face to maintain a modicum of composure before resuming.

"And, now look what's happened."

She gulped in a mouthful of air. She screamed into her hands.

"I'm the world's most loathsome bitch."

1 Mikhail Bulgakov's allegorical novel featuring Christ's temptation, betrayal and crucifixion.

For the briefest of moments, a scowl of disbelief transected the Patriarch's face. Here before him stood the Why and the How of a parent's worst nightmare. The rims of his eyes felt plump with tears. But, he blinked it all back. And, over the intervening seconds of silence while Natalia calmed, the Patriarch pondered the matter more thoroughly. Novimirov had neglected to inform him of this fight. Rationally, he could understand why, yet he still felt galled at the purposefulness behind the omission. And, with Natalia, in such pain as a result, not to mention his own, he felt booted from a plane. No parachute.

Natalia noticed the man's look of consternation and realized her folly.

"Oh Patriarch, please excuse my rudeness. I'm so—"

The Patriarch broke in with the grace of a grandparent.

"Hush no. No, child. Just speak your mind. Get it out of you."

Natalia addressed the elder man dolefully in the eyes.

"Patriarch, I should be dead. Smashed to pieces for what I did. But, when I returned to consciousness, I was lying on the platform immersed in a cloud of smoke, without the slightest cut or bruise. In fact, when I walked out of Metro Komsomolskaya, I walked out with supernatural powers."

Needing time to absorb and reflect, the Patriarch patted the air, signaling her to be still. But, after a protracted period of contemplation, he realized he had no proper reply. Endowed with years of optimism about the marvels of life, he decided to trust in experience alone and responded on pure instinct.

"Natalia, let me say this. It's an absolute fact that within *all* people great power is always at their command if they choose to believe and use it. In your case, this power is unique but it merely remains a power greater than human science comprehends. I haven't met any person at the FSB, who says otherwise. I now ask for candor. Natalia, perhaps you *already know* what it is?"

"Well — I think I do."

The Patriarch's eyes brightened. His voice softened.

"Natalia, I understand you're a religious skeptic but you can tell me anything. I'm not some senile scared-of-death croak looking for God. I've been reconciled to Biblical truth for centuries. Just talk, I'll listen."

Centuries — Natalia felt afloat on her feet. The Patriarch was completely disarming. And, the perfect means of opening up to him drifted into her mind. She stood erect at the side of Teodor's bed, and as if swearing an oath on the Bible, she placed her right hand over Teodor's heart. She asked the Patriarch to reach over the bed and put his hand atop hers. As she felt a gloved warmth of closure blanket her knuckles, she closed her eyes and relaxed into the serenity needed to summon the spirit and ease into her story.

"Now let me tell you what I remember about my dream, Patriarch. It was a great tragedy. I saw myself standing at the forefront of a gathering of people." She stopped. Her heart was racing. Her cheeks incandesced. And, overwhelmed by the inrush of bewilderment welling all over her, she blurted.

"There I was — my face in tears. In front of me was my son being crucified. A crown of thorns mutilated his forehead and a sign over his head read — Jesus of

Nazareth, King of the Jews. You might say I've been watching too many movies, but I tell you I could read the Latin, the Greek and the Hebrew. That's what gnaws at my memory because I don't know any of those languages. And, the crowd, they muttered. I cannot recall any specific conversation, but I understood every word and it wasn't Russian. *Not Russian.*"

The Patriarch could feel the conflict of emotion within her.

"I believe you dreamt it. I believe, Natalia. You said, 'my son was being crucified.' Please, just tell me what you remember about that part."

She inhaled and brushed aside her tentativeness.

"Patriarch, it's no dream. It's recall. I was there. My face and my body in ancient robes. I was watching. I wanted to show courage and fortitude, but it was ripping me apart. How could any mother bear watching her child being so cruelly mocked by his own people and murdered by Roman dogs? Those satanic pigs from the temple taunted him, but his last concern was to heal the rift — to make peace between the Israelites they were leading astray and God. It sapped all his energy, he held nothing back for himself. His love for man in stark contrast to the contempt they had for the God of Man was unimaginable … it was beyond."

She stopped to reconnect with the quietude of an inner spirit.

The Patriarch saw Teodor's face twitch. He abruptly lifted his hand from atop Natalia's and cupped both his son's cheeks. The boy was smiling. And, close to the Patriarch's trembling thumbs, formative tears moistened the outer-most recesses of Teodor's eyelids. His dear child was reacting to the same feelings emanating from Natalia that he'd held in check while she spoke. He knew not how long he held fast to Teodor, but at some point he glanced over at Natalia and apologized — "Excuse me for breaking off like that."

She looked into the eyes of a man filled mighty with hope.

"Would you like time alone with Teodor?"

His lips smiled. His eyes smiled. His brow line crinkled with joy. His heart wept. And, re-immersing himself in the miasma of that extraordinary connection that Natalia had ignited between Derek and Ludmila less than twelve hours before, he knew that here before his eyes, it was happening again. Three becoming one.

"No, oh no. Teodor is listening … feeling … Oh God, he knows."

And, the Patriarch did his best to beat back a father's sob.

"Let's continue, please."

He perched his quaking left hand reverently back over hers.

Natalia closed her eyes and focused on summoning up her sense-memory.

"I was there. It's no dream."

She hesitated. To conjure up recall became a struggle.

"I was dressed in a long black robe. The day was very dark. Yes, there was a woman by my side. Roman soldiers. One, two, …"

She rocked her body and took several deep spine-stretching breaths as she searched for the ecstasy of re-immersing herself in her dream.

"Oh Patriarch, this is hopeless. I'm trying to recall what I recall I recalled. My words spill out like an upended bucket now. But, I assure you it's as clear to me as if it happened yesterday. It's not ancient history. It's not some crazy hallucination wrapped in some Bible movie. It *happened* because it *happened to me*."

She stopped but then continued — exasperated.

"I try to pretend to be a skeptic but I confess that from knowing nothing and believing nothing, I know there is a God of Man. Reality is reality. I have been given a truly great power, a gift from God or from Jesus. Something — *Damn it!*" More flustered than ever, she puckered her cheeks, as if she had bitten the inside of her mouth. The Patriarch remained silent, but his eyes beckoned. She sighed and her voice tightened as she vented — "How and why, Patriarch, I don't know. I just know. I don't want to discuss it because it makes no sense. I'm telling you this because you, at least, won't think I'm crazy." And to avoid his gaze completely, she slouched over the bed and set her forehead at rest on the Patriarch's hand.

The Patriarch was tempted to cradle his free hand over her hair to render solace but held back. She rotated her jaw sideways and rested the nub of her left temple on his plump knuckles. And, as tears welled into fullness from every recess behind her eyelids, Natalia let issue her innermost plaint.

"You probably think I'm an arrogant self-aggrandizing boaster but I tell you I'm pathetic. A pathetic bitch, who would gladly surrender all her powers to restore Derek Anthony Mitchell to the merest possibility of life. I guess that also makes me a selfish, pathetic bitch." And she rotated her head, buried her face down atop Teodor's warm belly and wept without restraint.

The Patriarch was at a complete loss about what to do. As her blubbering slowly muted, the elder man began hoping he was finally ready to offer comforting reply. He looked down and froze. His precious son's right hand was nuzzled tenderly amidst the locks of her hair. Joy was the tincture in the air he breathed as he perused, absorbed and marveled over the first real movement he had seen from his child since admission to the FSB Infirmary. It was all the more poignant because Teodor's mother had died giving birth, and he doubted that his eighteen-year old had ever known the rapture of female intimacy.

Along a spine as sturdy as a whipping post, the muscles around the Patriarch's torso quaked with emotions that were impossible to corral. He opened himself to become one with his son, and in doing so, he became one with Natalia's confusion and frustration. He felt superfluous. But, holding close to the love of his faith in the possibility of God's bounty, he softened to the reverie of being — Alive — and thus his words came out as if cut into flesh.

"Natalia, I believe that an extraordinary work will unfold through you. I also believe that you will experience events both joyous and tragic. I believe your dreams are preparing you for the days ahead. It's my privilege to be of service to you."

An unexpected voice intruded.

"Bless you, Father. Bless you."

The Patriarch steadied himself against the bed railing. His spirit felt balanced on a quivering tightrope strung tight between Heaven and Doom. His jaw clenched hard. For here was his virgin son — destined for the grave — leaving this Earth having experienced the best Truth possible in life. And, without further attempt at restraint, the Patriarch's tears flowed without mercy. He brought his fist to his aching heart. He rubbed mercilessly. The absolute best Truth.

The Tartars of Tsarophobia

In Washington DC, over twenty-two hours had now elapsed since President Bushkin had called upon the military to quell the chaos in Moscow. During the intervening period, Vice-President Weissbrot had conferred at length with Director of National Intelligence Lester Covedale and the Metro-Crisis taskforce based at CIA Headquarters, Langley. Based on intel extracted from hormone sniffers CIA had installed in the Oval Office, Lester speculated blood would soon flow. Something, Ginger more or less confirmed.

Up at five o'clock and thirty minutes later, Weissbrot sat face-to-face with Naomi Geraldton, the President's secretary. While they scripted the issues the president needed to grapple with, Naomi confirmed a fuming volcano still lay beneath President Carter's outward demeanor of detachment.

Ever since Russia's madcap accusations before a secret session of the UN Security Council on March 15, 2005, where Bushkin had denounced Italy for harboring some tsarist pretender to the throne of Russia, Carter's doggedness that she was not a president with whom the 'Tartars[1] of Tsarophobia' could trifle had grown worse.

And, the pre-election Neuro-Linguistic Programming and coaching to seduce and win over not-my-kid, neo-con, blue-blood influence peddlers continued to plague matters long after victory. Each day, the Grover Karlson, *Power of Negative Electioneering*,[2] approach to public relations seemed to vandalize her mood and mind. So much so, everyone who knew her swore the neo-con/liberal divide was slowly tearing her in two.

The 'Crisis in Russia' meeting was on the verge of convening, so Weissbrot left to take a roll call of all officers in attendance. And, Naomi marched into the Oval Office and brought President Mary-Ann Sybil Carter up to speed.

Presidents are from Mars
Bureaucrats from Uranus

Within the White House Cabinet Room, the tea-service clatter fell silent and the last cabinet officer scurried to his seat. After satisfying herself that 'His Rotundness of Defense,' Dr. Miles Glorioso, had finally compressed his bouncing-buttocks of a posterior into his assigned chair, President Carter flexed

---

1 Cossack, Bolshevik, Chechen, Tatar — Western pejorative terms for Russians
2 Grover Karlson's tome on how to win elections in the American version of democracy.

her cycle-fit glutes and stood tall. Reading from the opening statement Naomi had prepared, her labored voice betrayed her continuing lack of mental focus.

"Good morning ladies and gentlemen. Excuse the early meeting but—" she stopped and peered at the wristwatch Naomi had strapped to her left arm — "Oh my! It's nearly 2:00 p.m. in Moscow."

She drew in a lung-full before calming. "We've had plenty of time. Yes, indeed."

She froze and dispassionately raised the document she was holding until it drew level with her eyes, and she resumed in a deadpan voice — "It's now time we dissect the Moscow crisis and the martial law decree that President Bushkin has instituted, not only in Moscow, but throughout all of Russ—"

The room's cherry-stained oak Regency-era clock chimed — 6:00 a.m. President Carter stopped reading, put her hands on her hips and looked askance. Her dark mood matched the color of her nail polish — lacquered eggplant.

Something was amiss.

Inaudible groans echoed within the chests of all her senior cabinet members. While several considered the president was proving how she was becoming more dimwitted as the job ground on, the majority still attributed her hyper-vigilance to the pandemonium created by the outgoing Republican administration of J. W. Potusson. Ginger Arnold, the National Security Director, had known Mary-Ann since their cabbage-patch days and suspected her childhood friend was succumbing to some form of low-level Alzheimer's dementia. Part of the toll on a woman having to sport neo-con appeal while running for and being elected president of the world's solitary superpower. But, regardless, because neither woman was a digital-age Google-pedia zombie, Ginger had faith in Carter's nose-to-book astuteness and considered her growing difficulties more embarrassing than crippling.

Carter lofted her eggplant nails skyward.

"Wait-a minute. Just hold on."

President Carter stared down the clock until the prim thought of tardy flashed across her mind and she let issue — "Cabinet, have we had a roll call? I'm sure we haven't. The constitution binds me to verify that no one's goofing off in my administration."

Forearmed and bright as day, Vice-President Weissbrot chipped in.

"Madam President, roll call taken. I certify to you personally that we're all present and ready to serve and execute our oaths of office. Would you please finish reading your statement and command your meeting into order."

Carter squinted at the sheet — *One last line.*

"Lester Coverdale, please start your presentation."

The Director of National Intelligence launched into action.

"Madam President, the last twenty-four hours have provided us a clearer understanding. Our analysis confirms that in his address to the nation President Bushkin did not exaggerate when he stated the human toll would be horrendous. Putting aside the fact that we abhor the martial law now instituted, there is no reason for us to be overly alarmed. At least, not—"

"*Overly alarmed!*" Carter blurted.

Lester patted the air with his hands as he responded.

"Madam President, at least at this stage, we should not be overly alarmed. Right now, the Russians seem to be doing what we would be — gathering intelligence. But, let me be frank, when they have whatever proof they need, they will act. And, I mean *whatever proof,* Madam—"

Carter homed in on — *They will act* — "Lester, Bushkunt boasts he's caught the perpetrators. This isn't 9/11. The silence of suicide doesn't exist. Face reality — Our world is like *Jurassic Park*. War is our nature, and always finds a way. *Always!* So how should my Seals[1] drop Bushkuntosaurus Rex? Which eyeball?"

Lester quietly concurred, but the President's *snark-to-war* mentality could not be allowed to get out of hand. He knew where she was trying to steer the facts, but it was premature. He nodded gently in her direction and re-established warm eye-contact. Her countenance softened, and he aimed to soothe her anxieties.

"Madam President, I agree with you. But, we must remain calm, especially towards the Russians. It's their 9/11. Not since Adolf Hitler launched 'Operation Barbarossa' to invade the USSR, has the mood of their nation been so unified to the single purpose of seeking retribution. I say this very candidly, Madam President, because there's going to be nothing the US can do to avert whatever 'Hell to Pay' response President Bushkin has in the works to placate his electorate."

Carter hammered back — "American presidents are expected to take action. Lester, what *action* do you propose I, *Madama President*, take?"

Lester dreaded this, but it had to be aired and moreover, it had to be accomplished, no matter how unsavory the president might personally find it — "Under the circumstances, be sly, Madam President. World peace needs stealth, before strength. Use your feminine wiles to become friends with Bushkin. Show boundless empathy and seek ways to mollify their anger because—"

"Emote. Emote. Emote," Carter blazed, insulted by the brazenness of the sexploitation expected of her — "That's what sly-dogs who manufacture excuses do, Lester." She paused to dig deep because her ovaries were cheerleading a grinding migraine between her temples. And, because the Sasquatch in Coverdale was characterizing a marionette for a president that whitie-boy might call electable, she let rip — "Just because I've got titties, I'm won't kowtow to Good'ol Boris Bolshevik expectations or stereotypes of any stripe. I repeat, what action do you propose I take?"

"Madam President, our first endeavor must be to placate because—"

"Do I look like Neville fucking Chamberlain?[2] While I'm its duly elected president, the United States won't be doing cock-sucking 'appeasement.' I, Lester, I — that is me — I won't tolerate cock-a-doodle Cossacks fog-horning around the planet on some crazy crusade swatting terrorists and upending governments which gas-bagger Bushkunt claims aids, abets or harbors them. Is that clear?"

Lester girded himself because action first necessitated operative facts. And, it was his duty to deliver those facts no matter how distasteful the president considered them. "Madam President, this isn't about acquiescing. It's about maintaining

1 America's elite naval based commando forces. Famous for assassination, they pride themselves on their markmanship — headshots with bullet through the eyeball pizzazz.

2 British Prime Minister (1937-1940) during the Nazi era. Famous for "Peace in our time" appeasement.

democracy in a redneck neo-con state like Russia, where civilian government currently holds sway over its nuclear-armed Soviet-era military. Their anger needs to be defused because based on President Bushkin's psychological profile, I expect his machinations to impress the Russian electorate will be a lollapalooza. If we try to obstruct Bushkin, not only will we fail and cause pointless acrimony, but we will have created a generation of 150 million Russian citizens who will only remember that America sought to trivialize their 9/11 catastrophe. At the end of the day, goading World War III over this is plain lunacy."

Her eggplant nails ensconced within her fist, Carter slammed the table. Her late-thirties breasts jolted in conformity with the impact.

"Screw World War. Boris Bushkunt's not going to menace the world liberation movement while I'm its duly-elected leader."

She swiveled her chair about, stared down Vice-President Weissbrot and she made demand once again.

"Attention, Lester Coverdale. Russia is only going to be brought to heel when it tastes the unrepentant determination of the United States of America. What damn *action* do you propose I, President Carter, take?"

Weissbrot picked up on her ploy and entered the fray.

"Lester, the president has a constitutional obligation to exercise executive power and veto any Russian notion of going berserk, gallivanting around the planet, setting up puppet governments and hunting down hoodlums in the hope of procuring guilty verdicts before kangaroo-courts of Russian justice."

Carter swiveled her chair about again and cast Lester a *Presidents are from Mars, Bureaucrats are from Uranus* look — "One-sided, secretive, hoped-for guilty verdicts must *never* threaten the peace of the world," she growled — "That, by God, will be my legacy!"

Sensing that he was being made the target of convenience, Lester decided to simplify things, especially for a president he considered dimmer, and as a result, more bellicose each passing day — "Let's skip chasing cowbell. Madam President, focus on 'Whatever Proof' because here's where it's perilous. Say the Russians allege and half prove that flying saucers dispatched from Ukraine attacked Moscow. Russia invades Ukraine. What are we going to do about it?"

"That sounds interesting."

And, Carter contemplated the scenario as if a conventional response was expected from her. Suddenly suspecting Lester was planting an egg, she snarled.

"Am I supposed to take that seriously?"

"Bingo, Madam President. It's irrelevant if you take it seriously. It's irrelevant if you think that the proof the Russians produce fails to meet the White House's subjective satisfaction. The only — *only* — relevant thing is whether your average 'Karl Rove[1] Cossack' thinks it's credible."

President Carter appeared unmoved.

Lester surmised that his reference to flying saucers was to blame. After pondering if he should expound on Hitler's 'Operation Himmler' to illustrate the conundrum, he decided she might better grasp historical facts closer to home.

1 American term denoting extreme Right Wing.

"Madam President, if you recall when a coal bunker explosion crippled the USS Exeter off the Atlantic coast, the Navy diligently investigated and discovered the hazards of coal dust in our warships. Six months after that investigation, a similar coal bunker explosion destroyed the USS Maine, docked in Havana Harbor in the Spanish Colony of Cuba."

Carter tweezed her lower lip, taking it all in.

His voice deadpan, Lester continued.

"Did the US make good the horrendous damage to Spain's harbor? No. Our newspapers went hog-wild, inflaming the American public until Congress declared war on Spain. By disavowing messy details and cultivating fuzzy reality, our own citizens have always embraced the ingenious fervor enabled by mob patriotism inherent to any democratic system of governance. Now a democr—"

Carter cut in.

"Got it, Coverdale. To borrow the thinking of Teddy Roosevelt, our democracy ensures we elect presidents savvy enough to know the difference between moose piss and Cool Aid. What's your real point?"

Lester fired back.

"The Soviet Union is long gone. Fancying herself a democratic pitbull, mother Russia is off-the-leash. Especially because we in the United States have promoted standards of belligerency endorsed by the democratic rule of 'No Cut, No Run' patriotism."

Carter remained locked in thought for several moments before responding.

"So. … So, if the Russian government sits conveniently tight-lipped while some Cossack controlled media heroine, akin to Oprah, crows like a rooster at dawn, and airs the 'Motherland of Liberty' agenda and galvanizes red-behind-the-ears public opinion, Bushkunt can wash his hands and pussy-out by 'Loving, Honoring and Obeying' democratic will. That's your assessment — right?"

The president's words triggered a childhood memory for Ginger Arnold and she banged her fist on the table in jubilation — "Exactly."

Carter stared over the table at Ginger, who then smiled as deep as she could. The connection of friendship was instantaneous. And, Ginger went for an emotional jugular, a place where Alzheimer's had only slight effect.

"Do you remember Reverend Finneas Calhoun Barton, Mary-Ann?"

Carter beamed — "Of course, Ginger. Can Bartie help us?"

The mood under the eggplant brightened ten degrees. Ginger gave her friend a winsome nod and kept the momentum going by deploying an allegory from the Sunday school they both attended as pre-teens.

"Think of Our Lord Jesus. The Jewish lobbyists, who had Pontius Pilate's ear, screamed — 'Crucify him. Crucify him.' That, Mary-Ann, is the Cossack media ranting. Russia's special interest jingoism is the biggest threat to our national security. Once their warmongering media target someone for death, Bushkin can, as you said, wash his hands like Pontius Pilate, play-act the role of 'Ms. Democracy' and lash out at whomever. The Bible informs, Mary-Ann. I think the first item on our agenda is to identify Bushkin's most likely target based on the media 'call to action' paradigm common to most rhinestone democracies."

Carter thanked Ginger for her clear-headedness then made cold demand.

"So Lester, what's the scoop from our intelligence operatives about that Jesus-hating Pontius Pilate in rhinestone Russia?"

Lester made a show of an exhale of exasperation to clear the air, before reconfirming the biggest albatross still plaguing CIA operations.

"To be blunt — Nothing. The fallout from the outing of CIA WMD Chief Mallory Wilson during President Potusson's administration continues. We've only soft contacts who act as pressure relief valves so we don't get overly agitated. But, right now, they're staying absolutely quiet. We threatened to expose one man like Potusson did with Wilson. He just laughed and caved by claiming they'd captured several terrorists and vampires were torturing them. All we have are jokers and tidbits."

Brows furrowed, Carter railed.

"So you're saying these crypto-Cuntsacks[1] intend to taunt me like Potusson taunted the UN with phony MI-6 Niger documents[2] out-sourced from Italy. Not to mention that Curveball crap from Germany. Well?"

Vice-President Weissbrot flashed Lester a dirty look — An order to dial back the cowbell. Now was not the time to confront the President. Her unchecked raging would only cloud debate and could get Lester sacked.

Lester replied in a measured tone to engage her empathy.

"Madam President, calm down. That ham-hawk, Potusson, schemed *with* the British, the Italians and the Germans. We're here to protect you *from* Bushkin's scheming. The Russians don't trust us and we can't trust them. But, if you want 'yes or no' truth from the Kremlin, you'll have to flip a coin because no informant trusts us to keep their identity secret after the 'Mallory Wilson Affair.'"

An aide who had whispered in his boss's ear and left a brief for him to peruse, slunk discreetly back to his assigned seat.

Attorney General David Hicks came to life.

"Good news, Madam President. We have an American inside Russia's FSB. An FBI agent, named Derek Anthony Mitchell. He's working with high-ranking FSB personnel on a covert sting targeting Afghan heroin. But, there's a snaffu. We've lost track of him. Lester, could CIA track him down?"

Lester suppressed his surprise.

"David, I'll make that a priority." Lester reached across the table, snatched up the brief, passed it to his adjutant and gave him an *Immediate-Action* gesture.

In search of actionable intelligence rather than Russian whining that suggested America coddled Afghan druglords, Carter became even more testy.

"Do what you must. Just do it without pestering me. I need to do something presidential, today. So, what of our allies' espionage networks?"

"All quiet there as well, Madam President. No leaks — Period."

Carter closed her eyes in dismay, but Lester refused to relent.

"And that is why our allies are likeminded. When the Russians do respond to this, it's going to be titanic. Here's what bothers me."

1 Derived from Cossacks, the forces the Tsar used in his pogroms and purges.
2 Italy and Germany: Two sources of fabricated evidence about Saddam Hussein's hidden WMD, which was presented before the UN Security Council on February 5, 2003 as America's justification for invading Iraq.

Lester steepled his forearms to dramatize the next unloading.

"The Russians have locked down all evidence of the attack, including the whole Metro system. We've tried to skunk out any witnesses who were at the scene and found no one. All we have are garments that we've tested and have confirmed are predominantly contaminated with 2,3,7,8 tetrachloro-dibenzo-para-dioxin. I've formulated four hypotheses to explain all the hush-hush and to prepare us for what to expect."

Lester balled his left fist and stuck his thumb in the air.

"*One*. This is an internal screw up. Something like Chernobyl."

Next came the index finger.

"*Two*. A catastrophe has been staged to provide Bushkin the means to subvert democracy in Russia."

Then an erect middle finger.

"*Three*. The Kremlin has yet to dummy up news leaks for the mainstream media's consumption pointing the finger at some Barabbas."

And, Lester fisted the air with his right hand, thumb outstretched.

"*Four*. Hush-hush because any premature public disclosures will interfere with a legitimate large-scale raid being planned against a complex terrorist organization." Lester nestled his hands on the table — "If so, expect the Russians to imitate our 'Night and Fog'[1] policy of imprisoning detainees at the old Nazi SD outpost in Szezytno-Szymany[2] and other black sites. And, take note, in all scenarios, a toady Russian media will cook the news to incite mobs to embrace the agenda. As Ginger intimated — 'baying for the blood of Jesus' jingoism exceeds terrorism as the greatest peril to our national security. Media tycoons juic—"

Carter threw Lester a glare that could strip skin off skulls.

"Coons! Coons! Damn it, what next? Spouting off about the Jewnited States's so-called Zio-Nazi warstream press controlled by a handful of King Kikes? May Jesus forgive them any past transgressions because, AIPAC or not, I'll have you know 78% of Jews voted for me, thanks to US press coverage. And, need I add that our scourge-the-traitor media has always kept our catnap electorate from snoozing off."

Lester let his exasperation off the leash.

"President Carter, it's about juicing the news to—"

"Phizz-bit! Jews. Again." Carter burst.

"Juicing, Madam President. Orange juicing the news—"

Carter slammed the table to cut Lester off. Favors were due. Her migraine needed no leavening. Like Frankenstein's bolt through her brain, she felt lobotomized because less than a day before, AIPAC had lectured her on how Jews in Florida had abstained from going Buchanan[3] on her ass, which, in turn, had elevated her into the presidency. The tiresomeness of 'special relationships' anointing presidents for the specific purpose of porking the whole country up the hindquarters had her privately swearing that by year's end what little hair

---

1 'Nacht und Nebel' Decree of Adolf Hitler. Abduct any scum you can't/won't charge with crime.
2 Poland — Latitude: 53° 28' 55" Longitude: 20° 56' 16" (WGS84)
3 In 2000, Jews in Palm Beach, Florida, voted heavily for Patrick Buchanan and thus threw the US presidential election in the favor of the Republican Party candidate. In British jurisdictions, it is called 'the donkey vote.' i.e. Jews riding the Pat Buchanan donkey heralded in an unintended Caesar.

remained on her scalp would be as white as a Pepsodent snowcone. She fixed Lester in her gaze.

"Do you, Mr. Coverdale, envisage our presidential-access news media being Bushkunt's lackey? In essence, you're ridiculing Jews as yerrow-perrow, Orange-Oreo, fifth-column traitors to our country — right?"

"No, of course not. Madam Presid—"

"So, let's have our Jewish media checkmate Bushkunt's Cossack media"

Lester rolled his eyes and blurted.

"And, just why would our media play the stooge?"

"Jingoism, of course. But, we can sweeten the pot by throwing Israel under the hooves of the Cossack horde. That'll get them buzzing like Jubees."[1] And, Carter's black heart lightened has soon as the last word curled off her lips.

"Madam President, it makes for good sound-bite. But, when it comes to neutering warmongering, you can't checkmate a negative with a negative. The media is only a weapon pointed at politicians to corrupt them or pointed at the public to deceive them. The US media can neither corrupt nor stymie the Russian news media's march to war, regardless of incentives."

Ginger chimed in to get things back on track.

"Mary-Ann, if our press try what you suggest it will only add fuel to the fire. We need to focus on seeking that truth prevails, not agendas."

Carter looked at Ginger and then back at Lester.

Lester saw a way through the impasse.

"Madam President, consider this. If the so-called Cossack media point the finger at some Muslim whack-job, at some Saddam, or even some Egyptian goddess of love and then Bushkin jiggers the evidence to play along — Do you think the US media are, to quote your own words, going to 'crow like a rooster at dawn' denying and denouncing 'the story' as a lot of hornswoggle?"

Carter brought her finger-tips to the bridge of her nose.

Ignoring the eggplant, Lester plowed on — "Hardly. Like trumpets at Jericho, they'll thunder about Bushkin being a kindred soul in the great democratic struggle against the Axis of Evil and the Grand Caliph, Lord Voldecamel. And, the foxy sloganeering won't end until every patriotic US citizen bleats the same fantasy masquerading as so-called news story to every twerp on the planet."

Seeking calm, Carter closed her eyes — *Truth must prevail.*

"Lester, if you please, I'm after facts, not media hogwash."

Feeling more exasperated than ever about explaining the irrelevance of facts to the president, Lester enlisted Ginger's metaphor to illustrate the conundrum through something Carter had endorsed earlier — "Madam President, don't project America's trustworthiness onto Russia. Trust what Ginger reminded us about Sunday school. Jesus is a perfect example of the games of manipulation we can expect. The trial of Jesus wasn't about facts. It was democratic choice in the hands of Jews — 'Vote Jesus or vote Barabbas,' 'Caesar is our King' and 'Christians burnt down Nero's Rome.' Today, the US media vendetta targets Islamic neanderthalism and countries seeking to fire up nuclear-powered electric

---

1 Three meanings: Jamaican Girl, Testicles, Jews (Slang).

grids. That's what war-mongering looks like. Flip open any American newspaper and see the media agenda for yourself. We consider 'freedom of the press' a bulwark of democracy — *and so do the Russians!*"

"So, you're saying a 'fact' is whatever Bozo the Bullshevik says is a 'fact,' as long as it appears in print — ink on paper — right?"

"Exactly, Madam President."

While Lester painted a picture that suggested Bushkin was imitating a great democracy, in Carter's opinion, Russia's excuse for democracy was little more than an ape show and she switched gears — "Lester, surely you have some gut feel about Bushkunt's target independent of any trumped-up media agenda. Who do *you* personally think Bushkunt will be fingering for this incident?"

Lester froze; his mind raced for options.

Carter saw nothing but — *Bureaucrat.*

"Who's the god-damn Barabbas?" she thundered.

Chastened by the president's scold, and yet ignoring it, Lester replied evenhandedly because this part of the puzzle was too serious.

"Madam President, for now Bushkin has stated that it was not the doing of Chechen or Muslim extremists, so Ukraine seems a very likely target. Not flying saucers, of course. But, because President Eunatovski was poisoned by dioxin. Eunatovski blamed his attempted assassination on the Russians. And, Eunatovski's assertion makes sense. Hence, it's possible that this 'dioxin event' is the opening for Russia to justify the invasion and re-integration of Ukraine permanently back into Russia. I say 'event' because there's no disproof that Bushkin or some other Russian pan-Slavic extremist did not orchestrate this catastrophe as a ruse. Nor is there any affirmative proof a genuine outside attack occurred. It could very well be the work of Chechen separatists and Bushkin's just lying when he claimed it wasn't because he hankers for Ukraine."

Vexed by all of Lester's *what-ifs*, Carter became flip.

"For that matter, Georgia or Belarus might be targets."

Attorney General Hicks decided to remind the cabinet of his very first assessment of Bushkin regarding Russia's Pre-Emptive Action Notice of March 15, 2005.[1] "If we're strolling down Bolshevik Boulevard, what about Italy? Remember the Tsarnaev report before the UN? You might recall, Romanov was reputedly on the warpath to become the next Tsar of Russia. I was worried that Bushkin had lost his marbles, or was playing a game of Chicken-Kiev. This so-called Metro attack might be priming the money shot in Bushkin's '*The Man Who Would Be Tsar*' deep-throat-to-Lady-Liberty stage-play."

Ginger, Lester and Weissbrot closed their eyes in utter, fucking dismay. The volcano in Carter erupted. But, revolted by her own rising fury, she tamped herself down and nodded her head approvingly in Hick's direction.

"Thank you, Mister Attorney General. Barely two months after my inauguration, I get hit with that insulting notice from Bushkunt about how

---

1 Akin to America's Iraq/WMD report of February 5, 2003, on March 15, 2005, Russia's UN Envoy Tamberlin Tsarnaev presented his nation's 'Pre-Emptive Action Notice' (PAN) before a closed-door session of the UN Security Council. Russia claimed Sergio Romanov and other fascists, Italy was providing safe-harbor, were hatching a plot to overthrow the government of Russia by force or similar unlawful means.

some Italian Romanov was pre-empting his dictartarship[1] by making his own comeback as tsar. Could someone please remind me what has happened since that hairy, Jew-hating Cuntsack thought he could teabag me?"

Weissbrot oozed charm. Agendas needed to be schmoozed over. The matter was too serious for more eggplant-up-the-ass intrusions.

"Madam President, permit me. Five months ago, Ginger and I went to Moscow and met with President Bushkin on several occasions. We successfully secured the release of our citizen, Omar Khalid. The press hailed your plan as brilliant, remember? Ginger and I also established a secret foreign relations protocol between the US and Russia concerning the lesser nations of the world based on the superpower principle of 'Fair-play Balanced with Hypocrisy.' Before and after our trip, your whole cabinet agreed that the Russian pre-emptive action notice regarding the Romanovs and Italy was a test to ascertain your leadership *cojones*.[2] A test that you passed with flying colors, Madam President. Wouldn't you agree, Ginger?"

Grateful for his level-headedness, Ginger eagerly backed up the vice-president's spin and threw in a white-house-lie for good measure.

"In fact, several Russian contacts later confirmed you were being tested and you grand slammed the test. We know Bushkin respects and fears you, Mary-Ann. Please, stay calm—"

Carter chopped in.

"You bet Bushkunt respects me! I wham-damned him, thank you!"

With the president's sense of liberality returning, Secretary of State Jeffrey Chandler loosened his arrow-head bolo tie and waded in — "Madam President, ignore the Romanov hokum. I assure you that relations between Russia and Italy are as strong as can be. I have an update on that missing Italian diplomat. Russian television is broadcasting eyewitness mobile phone video. It squares with Russian police statements from others about how the car stopped at a bus stop in search of prostitutes and ended up being hijacked by two pimps. The car and diplomat remain missing, but the kidnappers later dumped one prostitute near the park opposite the Bolshoi Theater and into the hands of the police. Because Moscow is in a state of chaos, the police considered the prostitute a victim, got his address and released him."

"Jeff, what's this got to do with Bushkunt's tsar crap?" Carter injected.

"Madam President, it's more about Italy and the rule of law. The Russians are genuinely gung-ho on good relations with Italy and have promised to give top priority to searching for the diplomat and executing everyone involved in the kidnapping. The hijack broadcasts on TV are proof of their resolve."

Smelling a turd in the tamale, Weissbrot wasn't biting.

"Sounds confused, Jeff. Convenient how police let that faggot go."

"Not so, Norman. The prostitute left the police in the dark about the hijacking. Fake name and address. They had no reason to hold him. He wanted to go home and clean up. I emphasize there was an original scare created because several witnesses reported a car in a Russian presidential motorcade had been

1 Play on 'Tatar' (a Muslim Russian ethnic group from the Crimea) and Dictator.
2 Balls, testicles (Spanish/Mex).

hijacked. These witnesses came forward as they thought it was another part of the terrorist attack. Of course, the Russians were scratching their heads. Also, the Italians have confirmed that they did not contact the FSB when they saw their car's GPS tracking signal vanish off their scopes. Only after the televised story broke, did the Italians come forward. And, only then did the mystery of the 'Russian presidential limousine hijack that wasn't' get cleared up. If anything the Italians held back to conceal a scandal about one of their homosexual diplomats."

Chandler looked down his aquiline nose to engage Weissbrot.

"You were in Moscow a year ago. You know the Italians personally. So please, tell me, what's the score on the fag frontier?"

Recalling a certain remembrance, Weissbrot chuckled.

"Jeff, finito. We can swap tales later. But, yep, I'm sold."

With the speculative theories now aired and dismissed, Lester proceeded to analyze realistic scenarios. The meeting ended by concluding that Bushkin's master-plan was to subvert democracy in Russia and invade one of the former Soviet republics. In all likelihood, Ukraine was Bushkin's target. Less than a month after September 11, 2001, every Russian was well aware of Ukraine's weeks of deceit behind the shoot-down of Flight 1812 by what was proven to be a Ukrainian S-200 naval missile. Russians would readily embrace the proposition that Moscow had suffered a retaliatory counter-strike because Ukrainian President Eunatovski accused Russia of using dioxin to poison him as part of a failed attempt to sabotage Ukraine's 2004 election.

Just as Scotland might be a great strategic take-back for England, 'Novo-Russiya,'[1] the former USSR Republic of Ukraine, would be a great strategic take-back for Russia. Almost one in seven of its citizens were ethnic Russians. Under a scheme the CIA labeled 'Russian Spring,' it was feared they might agitate to rejoin their true-blood motherland. And, Ukraine also had many unexploited oil and gas resources, not to mention many military assets. Those in Crimea included the Sevastopol naval yards and the ten-megaton nuke-proof submarine port tunneled one-kilometer into the side of a mountain off the Balaclava inlet with its adjoining and currently empty Soviet-era nuclear missile vault.

'Anschluss — 2005' seemed Bushkin's agenda.

Turning Ukraine into Russia's 'West Bank' would be Carter's.

Her eyes' twinkled with glee. *Game of Tsars! Payback!*

Wipe Away the Tears

Perched forward in the directors chair outside Undead Chamber No. 6, Colonel Sergei Gratski spoke nonchalantly into the control mic.

"Vamps, time to wrap it up."

The Silvio Calamari session had brought to a close the last of the day's five vampire intercessions. Four minutes later, Olga, as Veronica, and Natalia, as Betty, left their last sweet Jughead to Doctor Soskrova's tender care and returned to the dank, moldering dimness of the subterranean passageway.

---

1 Tsarist term. Region in eastern Ukraine populated by many ethnic Russians.

An admiring Major Tatiana Gratski greeted them.

"Olga and Natalia, I've heard about these vampire intercessions. Watching the tail-end, I must say your work is pure inspiration."

Every joint below Natalia's neck went rigid as mortar.

"Inspiration! It reeks of sadism."

In no mood for protest, Tatiana fired back.

"Natalia Vladimirovna Bogomolski, we aren't tweaking the tit of a Tatar here. Like a ticking time bomb, Amerika stands ready to sabotage the motherland's capacity to maintain peace in our world. Speed is vital. We had Ursini watch today's sessions when his wop arrogance needed reminding that he's not alone when it comes to spilling the beans."

Olga stationed herself between the two women — "Natash, see yourself as a vampire for Jesus. I do. Let your dreams of Golgotha inform you. Wops are godless, blood-sucking, Christ-killing fascists. They converted our Metro system into their most recent version of their gas-chamber and have once again brought mass death into the lives of the Slavic nation of Russia." And, sensing a need for closeness, Olga cupped Natalia's chin — "By inflicting and curing tribulation, we provide these monsters a level of divine enlightenment that Dante never dreamt of. They'll know the discomforts of Hell much better before the hour appointed for their execution."

Natalia closed her eyes, and Olga wondered if she was trying to recall something, perhaps from her dream. After a prolonged silence, Olga prompted — "Do you remember how that patsy of Caesar, Herod the Great, went berserk murdering every firstborn male in Judea in the hope of killing Jesus?"

She waited. But, Natalia said nothing.

"Mother of God, Natalia! That's what these bloody wops have done to us."

Natalia opened her eyes as if alerted to something but remained mute.

Tatiana piggy-backed on Olga outburst.

"Natalia, please, listen to Olga. The current child death toll is 4,724, and over eighteen, 12,466 are dead." And, Tatiana bellowed to prevent Natalia from interjecting — "These are dead citizens, Natalia. Not dead fish in the Dead Sea. So skip the lordy-lordy routine and show me your damn compassion."

As intended, Tatiana's words boxed Natalia into taking ownership of her guilt in this grotesque tragedy. Discerning a need for a salutary atmosphere to take hold, Tatiana softened her tone and explained how six unfortunates under Dr. Chernikrov's care needed her healing touch.

Natalia roused and addressed Tatiana square on — "Let's go. *Bistro.*"[1]

Two steps a stride, the trio climbed the stairwell to ground level, where Olga parted company for the cafeteria to catch up on the day's events. On the way through the Infirmary, Tatiana decided a brief diversion to check-in on Mr. Mitchell might be the perfect means to re-focus Natalia on the mission of world peace.

Natalia's delight at seeing Derek talking with animation into a video camera evaporated when she noticed Ludmila's bed was empty. Her hate-filled thoughts

1 Quick (Rus).

— *Please, Miss, Kindly* — moments before punching Ludmila, thundered across her skull. She had done this to Ludmila. Dead-Fish #17,191. A vertebrae crunching cramp racked the length of her torso, followed by a sense of doom, then a spasm of impending nausea fluttered like a feather made of fish-hooks against the grain of her gut.

But, there would be no puke.

A shimmering vortex, like the wrath of angels spinning white-hot, held erect her spine and kept her on her feet. Suddenly, all the brilliant colours of the earthly world exploded back into Natalia's eyeballs more vivid than ever and, as if a beggar cured of blindness, she had no choice but look and take it all it.

Basil stopped recording the moment she had entered, and he walked over to Derek's bed. When Natalia regained her composure, all she knew was Basil and Derek were quietly conferring. As she righted herself from her inadvertent slouch against Tatiana, Basil approached the doorway.

"Natalia, Derek's a fighter. He's helping to make sense of this disaster. Our work is vital, so I must ask you to return after he's taken a nap."

And, Basil used the broad sides of his thumbs to wipe away the tears on her puffed cheeks and rendered a gentle kiss upon her forehead.

"From us both, my sweet lady." He winked — "Now, off with you."

She nodded to Basil obediently. Then shot Derek a glance. His face burst warm in a smile so magnificent the luster of it bathed her body in a salving glow. After taking a prolonged breath to dally a moment longer, she left without protest.

What Would Jesus Do

On the way to the special-patients room, Tatiana paged Dr. Chernikrov. The doctor met them in a heavily-guarded corridor just outside the doorway and explained how six women were suffering an allergic reaction from the process of decontamination. All six had been fully sedated, both their faces and bodies concealed under full-length sheets.

They entered. A guard re-bolted the door behind them.

The doctor and a nurse peeled back the bed-sheets and revealed a curiosity. While all six women were a little disheveled and roughed up from what appeared overzealous decontamination scrubbing, nothing seemed amiss. The doctor laid out the means for curing the problem and initiated the healing process with the most serious case.

"Natalia, her first, please. I think you can get your hand in there."

Natalia felt repulsed. But, she accommodated the doctor's request when he informed her how Julia's injuries were sustained in patriotic work restoring order to the nation. Natalia knew that it was the least she could do. She steeled herself and imagined it was Ludmila's life she was saving. The next woman was Sofia. Being older and obviously a mother, the job went much easier.

The third woman caused Natalia to become tentative again.

"Doktor, what does she do?"

When the doctor hesitated, Tatiana spoke up.

"Doktor! Natalia! These patriots don't deserve such gossip. Their work is arduous and classified. And, please, think of their modesty."

Natalia blushed at her impertinence — *What would Jesus do!*

Maintaining a respectful silence, Natalia focused her energy on curing the tears, sores and calluses lining the vaginas of the four remaining patients.

After performing endoscopic examinations, the doctor certified all six patients were cured, so Tatiana and Natalia left for the cafeteria to join Olga. Only Tatiana knew that after the doctor had finished reviving them, their Kremlin Honour Guard would escort Julia, Sofia, Roberta, Alfetta, Confetta, and would be Tsarina, Ariana Romanov back to the Kremlin Palace. And, there, under the stewardship of Imperial courtiers, these six would-be Russian aristocrats would be strapped down like bordello mullet and resume their duties at raising Russian troop morale for another twenty-four hours.

The Heart of a Marathon Runner

Tatiana and Natalia caught up with Olga in the steel-on-porcelain clatter of the FSB cafeteria. After Olga informed them that the news on the television remained very bleak, their conversation shifted to matters personal. Without a second thought, Tatiana proceeded to tease her junior officer — "During our meeting this morning, we all smelt that unmistakable fragrance of yours. So Lieutenant, I guess you fancy Captain Botanin?"

Olga blushed at her superior's crude ambush. Also feeling stung by Tatiana's intrusion, as well as the nasty snip in her voice, Natalia put her foot down.

"Olga is a very respectable lady, Tatiana. Stop listening to snide gossip. And, as for Ilya Botanin, he's a close friend." And, beaming her solidarity into Olga's eyes — "It's no surprise that Olga and Ilya find great joy in each other."

All remained tranquil for a moment as Olga returned Natalia's affirmation. But, when she noticed Tatiana's stare of stiletto-snark, she collected herself.

"Major Gratski, I am not going to discuss private matters with anyone. I assure you, Ilya is a very honourable man. Any woman who knew him as I do would fall in love with him in a heartbeat. If we erred on the side of passion, let the blame fall on me. After all that's my so-called hot-to-trot reputation — right?"

Her rebuke concluded, Olga immersed herself in a daydream about how her dearest Ilya would have made precisely the same statement to exonerate her, excepting that from his sweet lips, the oafs he called colleagues would have considered it a boast.

But, Tatiana saw only facetiousness in Olga's airy countenance.

"Lieutenant, it doesn't advance your career, for General Novimirov and others to sit in a passion pit that Ilya and—"

Olga smarted and let fly.

"Stop right there! I told you I seduced him. I needed love, tenderness and a release for my ardor. I'd endured a long day with blood all over my naked body, culminating in a depraved vampire session seducing a piece of wop carrion into thinking I craved his foreskin and testicular juices. I'm sure a Veronika[1] wag possessing your quaint charms can wrap her head around that."

Natalia giggled all too knowingly and interceded.

"Tatiana, please. This is Olga's private life. She's my close friend too. And, a very loving, soulful person she is. One who understands many things you do not."

Natalia knew a diversion was called for.

"Now, both of you listen. This info comes from Ilya. Are either of you aware that dioxin is a teratogen?[2] That means you had better think of becoming pregnant as soon as possible because even if you're contaminated only once, it's most likely you'll never have babies in the future. *Never.*"

On hearing these words, Olga's demeanor crashed. This morning, after they had salvaged their privacy and were dressing, she had been flip with Ilya. He'd remarked that dioxin had congenital effects and so time might be limited for becoming pregnant. At the time, it stuck out like a sweet Nerdy-Von-Nerd line. And, still afloat in her 'Miss Hottie' snow-globe of a brain, she had dismissed his comment as the awkwardness of a man unaccustomed to making love to fabulously beautiful women — *But, Ilya was serious!*

Olga closed her eyes to beat back the urge to weep. She had but one thought — *I want love, not pretense.* And, further recalling Ilya's good grace and deliberative manner of speaking meant solely to address her good health, she felt the spine splitting dread that the vain and frivolous reflexes of her 'Moscow Girl' personality might never bleed out of her. How dearly she wanted to exorcise all her alienating mannerisms and cast off all vile and pointless negativity. But, it seemed impossible. Tamping down a sense of nausea, she looked deep into her soul and vowed to purge herself of all her nonsense. With him, she needed to become pure. Energized by primal passions and spiced by hormones, she pledged herself to make love constantly and ferociously until all conceit was burnt away and she was bathed in the purity of a life she had always dreamt of, but had been denied. When a snippy remark intruded, the far bigger picture rolled over Olga. Sundering her friends' babble, she interjected.

"So this wop-puke amounts to chemical castration?"

Breaking off with Tatiana, Natalia replied.

"Definitely. For both men and women. Ilya told me that many future fetuses will malform and spontaneously abort," and Natalia bedded the pads of her fingers in the knuckle grooves of her friend — "Olga, if you two are an item, you both have some critical decisions to make. You need to stop fooling about and start procreating or you may *never* have healthy children."

Feeling the blast of Natalia's love affirming manners ripple up her arm, Olga closed her eyes to choke back her worst fear — Stalemate — a penchant to emotionally hedge. She had to say it aloud. Make it a wish fulfilled today.

1 Russia's Amateur Spy Corps. In honor of Veronika Lewintsova, captured by 'Capitalist Pigs' in 1998.
2 Agent capable of causing mutation of ova and death to a fetus in the womb.

"Natalia, I love Ilya. I might feign nonchalance, but I tell you I do."

And, she flipped her hand open and grasped Natalia's left hand to make a show of her desire for solidarity. Natalia understood and unleashed her empathy down into the marrow of every bone in Olga's body — "Be valiant woman. Under the circumstances, I doubt Ilya would be shocked to hear that but he might suspect you're playing a game with him. Does he know the real you?"

As her temples and brow reddened in dread, Olga's eyes started to water. And, she squinched them half-closed to regain a modicum of composure. While professing her love for Ilya was an awkward matter, professing the foibles she saw in herself she did with complete ease — "Oh Natalia, you talk about the 'real me,'" she slobbered. "The 'real me' is a piece of kitty fluff. I love Ilya and would do everything to protect—" She stopped to take in a breath of fortitude, and in a voice brimming with defiance, she made oath — "Him, I could *never* hurt."

Olga's distraught countenance and the unspoken fears behind it shocked Tatiana. Her jawline clenched hard, giving her granny neck, as she realized how others might point the finger and say the fall of the dominoes of woppery started with her scorn for Derek. Then a wholly needless hurt for Natalia. Then, the Metro. And, now this. Tatiana felt driven to make amends.

"Oh God. Olga, please forgive me. Don't waste time. I'll do everything to vouchsafe your reputations. Do it with my blessing, *just do it.*"

Olga opened her plump red eyes — "Thanks, Tatiana. I would love to have a great married life like you and Sergei. I guess you'll tell Sergei about this catastrophe tonight so that—"

Tatiana let out the school-girl squeal of a pinched bottom.

"Oh, I don't think I'd get the chance to open my mouth. From what I saw of your naked vampire performance, I can't imagine Sergei being anything but hog-wild crazy with me all month. And, to be honest, even if Sergei was a four-hundred-year old vampire, I'm in the mood to get crazy on him myself."

The zestiness in Tatiana's words hatched a ricochet of pixy glances around the table. This wasn't from any vampire performance that sucked the zestosterone out of the zesticles of six wop terrorists, but from hormones surging inside all three. Indeed, Tatiana's extended bathroom break, after she had hastily exited General Novimirov follow-up interrogation of Derek Mitchell, had included genuine nausea. She relished the thought of Dr. Chernikrov confirming her pregnancy and then telling Sergei the wonderful news. Her libido was juiced into overdrive and if she was not already pregnant, the fleshy ventricle between her legs that seemed to pump like the heart of a marathon runner was exploding to become so.

Olga grinned at Tatiana — "That's you and I. Now, we need to help Natalia."

Tatiana chirped — "She's immune — Has all the time in the world."

The lobes of Natalia's ears blanched as she recalled the inner-voice. It had lulled her into overlooking the obvious, and she blurted her disbelief.

"I might. But, *he* doesn't. Oh God!"

Tatiana's face flushed with guilt.

"Oh Natash, I'm such a useless bitch. This tragedy might have been averted if you and Derek had remained in love. I was only trying to spare your—" Tatiana stopped herself. Her orders to alienate Natalia from Derek remained top secret. They had been proper and reasonable. All fault lay in her — her malice had been calculated to be hurtful. Tatiana took breath to reset herself before voicing an all too familiar theme.

"Natash, it seemed so improbable with some past-his-prime Doodle."

Gored at the reminder, Natalia clamped her hands over her ears, slammed her head down hard on the table and howled.

"I already know your opinion of Derek the Dowdy Doodle."

Tatiana's heart felt crushed. And, prepared to come to grips with her denial, her offhandedness, she gently pried Natalia's hand away from her left ear and whispered her plea — "Natash, please forgive me. Please!" Her eyes watered — "That fight is as much my doing. My dear friend, please. Please, forgive me."

A charming insight flashed over Olga. Without betraying what Ilya had confided to her in the marvel of that moment when his nose had bled on the hollow of her shoulder, she spoke aloud bold words of comfort.

"Natalia Vladimirovna Bogomolski, listen to your fairy godmother."

And, waving a desert spoon, Olga laid it firmly on Natalia's left shoulder. Natalia sat up again and flashed Olga a quizzed look. Olga raised the spoon high above her head and pointed it like a lightening rod before bringing the bowl of it down close to her lips to speak into the implement like a microphone.

"As the guardian of your love life, I declare that your wish is granted and within three days you shall become pregnant by the greatest love of your dreams."

Natalia laughed. Her reddened eyes shone blue. And, having privately fretted for hours now about whether she was transforming into an alien unto herself, she realized how Olga shared her own confident and radiant spirit. They were kindreds endowed with the same sunny-new, life-loving personalities. Natalia grabbed both her friends' hands.

"I feel a thousand times better. I know the right man will come into my life. I'll look hard, listen closely, feel the mood, and pounce on the poor bastard myself."

Tatiana buttressed her feeling of relief with an oath to champion her cause.

"And may God strike me down, if I ever do anything to interfere with your desire to enjoy the greatest love imaginable, my dearest friend."

Boundless Optimism

After finishing their lunch on an upbeat note, Olga and Natalia joined Dr. Nadya Soskrova in Undead Chamber No. 2. Although the gagged Italian chargé d'affaires Carlo Rolfino might have reckoned it had been over one hour, since Olga and Natalia popped their sunny faces through the door, the doctor was only in the sixth minute of washing down his urushiol inflamed testicles in a beaker of formic acid.

While the gagged silence of the room would have made it appear that conversation with Rolfino would have been uncomplicated, it was unlikely that such was possible. The man was writhing in torment, his face, a livid scarlet, and his bloated throat distended crimson and wattling in rage like a male South Pacific frigate bird[1] shrilling hard, declaiming its ire at how some two-legged lab-coat monkey was pawing with two eggs absconded from its rookery.

The situation counseled caution.

Why remove his gag and embarrass the wop with an attempt at humourous converse, Olga thought. After all the man possessed the rank of a diplomat and was entitled to some semblance of deference. So, in this fire-ant nest of gelded silence, she did in mime that which could not be spoken.

Rolfino might have thought that the sparkle in her eyes, the warmth in her cheeks, the ruby sheen of her engorged lips, the fluid rhythm and scented spring in her body was some vampiric delight upon seeing, smelling and sensing his agony. But, he would've been mistaken. When she toyed with him to distract him from the godly ministrations of Natalia and the doctor, the only thing she imagined was her darling Ilya, writhing above, under and everywhere over her body. Ilya was her inspiration and if that pure preternatural inspiration scared the hell out of this godless wop, she considered it nothing more than God's pleasure talking.

Attuned to her friend's boundless optimism, Natalia saw and sensed everything that Rolfino did. And, it ignited a longing to find someone who would fulminate in her the same boundless delight that was coursing through her friend's body. By circumstance, the chargé d'affaires became the beneficiary of Natalia's heartfelt thoughts, because mindless of their medicinal purpose, she projected her hot-blooded desire for love into her healing powers and into Rolfino's body. Swaddling his emaciated testicles within palms she felt as puffed and glowing, the spirit of love within her radiated its unearthly tenderness and revived each organ to a beautiful, virgin luster. After Natalia used her nimble fingers to decontaminate his scrotal cavity of all trace of urushiol inflammation, the doctor expeditiously sewed the whole unit together, including a fresh ménage-à-trois companion courtesy of Reverend Woland.

Three became one — again.

With a final healing touch along the rim of the doctor's makeshift sutures, Natalia gave something Rolfino would not have expected, the exquisite pleasure of a scrotal colonic.

Fancying Rolfino was now open to attribute divine purpose to his prolonged suffering and his subsequent healing, both miraculous of itself and miraculous in its instantaneous effect, the ever intuitive, Olga spoke to the sublime expression of relief that transected the man's face — "My darling Jughead, I hope you're coming to your senses. God empowers us vampires to afflict and salve mortal men until they know his might and his mercy are beyond the realm of human reason. Only from him can spiritual salvation come. Only from him!"

---

1 Fregata minor. Males have a huge red glandular throat sac.

While Olga stayed at post in the FSB dungeon corridors, ready to remind their guests about what awaited them if they chose to prevaricate about their videotaped conversations, Natalia returned to the FSB Infirmary to check-in on patients. Derek, most especially. A new patient of some high rank now occupied what had once been Ludmila's bed. Doctor Chernikrov greeted Natalia and explained how Derek was barely able to talk. While the doctor applied a mild electric current to the platysma muscle on the underside of Derek's jaw, Natalia snaked her fingers into his distended mouth and swabbed the anterior of his throat to revive his larynx. After she was sure she had done her utmost, she signaled the doctor to stop. She gloved Derek's left thumb in her right hand and gazed deep into his eyes to project the unity of the love they shared into his whole being.

"Thanks," he croaked. "Seen my videotape?"

Natalia's spirit lightened at the determination in his voice.

"No, dearheart. Is it important?"

"My work. There's no need for secrecy now."

Upon mention of secrecy, Derek noticed a wince of grief mar her face. And, out there, somewhere below his heavily reduced range of vision, his thumb was held captive in the bliss radiating from her grip. To heighten their connection, he pressed its flat more firmly against her right palm and savored the yielding of lover's flesh as never a thumb felt pleasure before.

"*Maya Daragaya—*" he started.

But, he stopped, overwrought by the fact he would never use those two words again in his life. *Maya Daragaya — My Dearest —* it hurt. To recompose himself, he looked intently into her eyes and sealed in his heart the beauty of watching how her irises dilated in response to the most trifling pleasantries his lips might sputter. And, after the moment passed, he resumed.

"Basil has told me about your work—"

"All this secrecy, it's for idiots," she let fly.

Derek shook his head in disagreement.

"Basil showed me proof, *Daragaya*. My government considers the Romanov conspiracy a gambit President Bushkin concocted to subvert democracy in Russia. And, because the Potusson White House sabotaged meaningful US espionage when they outed CIA WMD-Chief Mallory Wilson, Basil decided to ring-fence us. His reasons for secrecy make total sense. Trust me. In fact, just hours ago, Basil told me the White House did a 'Mallory Wilson' replay and got an intelligence coup about Russian vampires."

Through his nostrils, air puffed in snicker at the thought of how an 'intelligence break' about Rooskie blood-suckers would play out in Washington. He took a fulsome, painful breath and continued.

"With both our lives on the line, neither of us could be told."

He paused — *Her eyes* — Those magnificent eyes shimmered back into his with such courage. He relaxed his gaze and resumed — "I wish I'd known about your mission to seduce Ursini. I apologize for the hurtful way I reacted. It must have been agony for you these long months."

He labored to draw breath.

"Would you move our hands up to my face, please."

As Derek held the back of her hand against his cheek, he closed his purulent eyes. Tears welled along their perimeter. His lips moved, at last.

"Natash. I haven't much longer to live."

Natalia shuddered like a corpse electrified back from the dead. He felt her self-sanction — *Beautiful and quiet* — as well as her attempt to marshal the appearance of stoicism in the face of the inevitable — *Dauntless and heart-wrenching*. And, he opened his eyes.

"I want to thank you for connecting with me and sharing that connection with Ludmila." He noticed her smile — a half-smile — but it was everything to him now — "I think that was the most intimate thing we've ever done. You and I. She and me. I know that probably sounds very bizarre, my sweet Natash," finishing with a graveled twinkle in his tone.

A faint laugh blubbed its way through Natalia's throat.

"Nothing like bizarre," she said. "It couldn't have been more sublime. Bizarre, my sweet man, is what happens in the dungeons below."

"I hope it isn't too oppressive. Those conversations allowed me to explain things much better. See my videotape. What will happen in the weeks ahead will change the world. There's no reason that retribution should not be proportionate and in accordance with American 'Preservation of Peace' norms."

Heartened at hearing how the vampire intercessions were empowering Derek's last wishes for peace and justice, Natalia wanted him to know, alive or dead, she would always champion his cause.

"Derek, you know I despise narco-terrorism as much as you. My government will carve out whatever it considers proportionate. But, I'm also convinced that Y-D[1] will stick its meddlesome snout into our affairs."

The patriot within him flushed — *War on Terror*.

Feeling renewed warmth pervade his fingers, Natalia continued — "No Russian will ever forget Amerika's previous president and that spastic Negro professor from Yale, who thought she was an expert on Russia. During the eight months that proceeded September 11, 2001, they ignored the warnings of Richard Clarke[2] as well as the record of militarism by Bin Laden, Al Qaeda and Muslim jihadists in Kenya, Mozambique, Saudi Arabia and Yemen. Instead, that Negroid bitch publicly lectured the world about Russia's so-called war crimes in Muslim dominated Chechnya. Nor do we forget how, for almost four years now, opium and heroin have swamped the motherland."

He nodded his approval — *Lives were at stake*.

Natalia beamed her solidarity into his affirmation then resumed — "As proclaimed in the Amerikan government's spare-no-expense Superbowl XXXVI ads — 'Drugs Empower Terror.' Terror murders over 30,000 of my fellow citizens each year. Ten times so-called 9/11. Nor will any Russian or Muslim forget how

---

1 Russian slang for American. Noun and adjective usage.
2 Adjutant to US Director of National Security whose warnings about failure to act on the assassination order against Osama bin Laden were ignored by the incoming president in 2001 A.D.

the thousands of tons produced on vast US-NATO protected opium plantations is only possible on the backs of Afghan child slavery. 'Operation Enduring Freedom,' it's called. Winston Smith[1] would be proud. And, because occupied Afghanistan has become a zero-food agriculture country, 'Enduring Freedom' is enforced under the shackles of starvation."

Out of exasperation, she calmed and re-established their common cause.

"My dearest, look how drugs have destroyed your everything."

The icy-hot memory of Marie, his pregnant wife, gunned down in San Diego during a drug turf war swept over him. The mere thought of her name always conjured that horrid specter in his head. And, his eyes dried as they always did, whenever he displaced the grotesque with the smile on her face the day he lifted her veil and — he beheld — Mrs. Marie Daphne Mitchell. If ever a man knew agony in any sense of disembowelment, it was in this. Among the spray of bullets, a stray had shattered Marie's mandible and twisted the right half of the bone back into her eye-socket. In his grief and cherished memory of her and their unborn, he had joined the FBI to do her incorruptible justice. And, now, that open wound of love lost was about to swallow him whole. But, railing against the hard injustice that had chewed up his life, he flashed Natalia a defiant look.

"Natash, I will always fight. Marie and Ludmila are gone. You, my lady, are here. I only hope we succeed. We must." His mind steadied, and he warmed to a smile — "We will."

He coughed, wheezed out and breathed in. And, knowing how the good fight was now four-square in her hands, he turned to the real news.

"Do you know I'm going to be buried next to Ludmila? Actually did you know that the Patriarch married us, an hour after you left?"

Remaining stoic, Natalia looked deep into eyes of mesmerizing brown, beamed her approval through every part of his body and made reply.

"How perfect that must have been."

He beamed back — *Grace streams out of her.*

"Perfection is what came before, dear lady. But, I know Ludmila died in peace knowing that we'd lie together. Forever. The Patriarch explained we would have to be married in order to be buried at Novodevichy Cemetery."

And, Natalia smirked for the first time that day.

"Mr. Mitchell, it seems you still have the strength to twist arms. I hope the Patriarch survived that experience. It's quite an honour for a foreigner, you know."

He glowed — *The luxuriance in her voice.*

"Yes, I know. Basil did most of the arm-twisting. Do you know, it may seem like hours to you, but being away from Ludmila seems like a whole lifetime to me. I shall find comfort and tranquility only when I'm laid to final rest."

He felt her hand flinch. Again, he pressed his thumb firmly into the flesh of her palm and made contact with her glimmering eyes.

"Also as a result of my conversations with Basil, I had him make three promises." He stopped to fix her in his gaze — "I hope they bear fruit."

She sensed unguence behind his words.

1 Main character in the novel *1984* by G. Orwell — *Freedom is Slavery* is one of its four tenets.

"Oh, that sounds very, very mysterious. I think you're pretending to not tell me something," she teased, as she jostled his enclosed thumb in her left hand and used the fingernails of her right to strum the length of his upper arm with tender, glancing motions.

Derek snorted his joy through his nose. But, feeling himself on the verge of suffocation, he gulped down a quick breath of air and relaxed again — "Do you know Basil is just as lost a man as I was, after I lost Marie? He wanted to know a few things. I think I helped. The world shouldn't be complicated. I had him make three promises to ensure I hadn't been presumptuous. After all, I only gave him my opinion and I'm just a Doodle in so many ways." And, he restrained a giggle.

Her lips teased out a smile as broad as the rings of Saturn.

"Derek, I know you. I'm sure you gave him the best advice possible. Even the wisest Russian political strategist could never understand the politics of Lady Liberty the way you do?"

He laughed outright. It was one of their inside jokes. He went to make snappy reply, but the coughing fits started. On reflex, Natalia bent close to his face and put her right hand against the side of his neck, hoping to evoke some analgesic response in his airways. After Derek regained his composure, he playfully nudged Natalia away with his free arm.

"Hey, hey. I'm a married man now."

She closed her eyes, so deep was her grin of communion.

And, Derek spoke into that communion.

"Understanding Lady Liberty? I'm not that certifiable."

Natalia smirked for a second time that day. She opened her eyes.

And, Derek spoke into those eyes.

"We will always be one, you know."

She nodded — *Absolutna.*[1]

The man in Ludmila's old bed stirred.

Derek decided — *An end to banter.* And, he switched gears.

"Before I forget. Baldo has a note for me. It's on his bedside table. Could you get it for me, sweetheart?"

And, she walked over and retrieved a small scrap of paper.

"Here. Would you like me to read it? It's just numbers."

"That won't be necessary."

And, she passed him the note.

Derek elaborated on the mystery.

"Baldo is of gypsy extraction. Fascists murdered his ancestors. He says these numbers will help me ward off evil spirits. I'm just humoring a dying man," he stopped momentarily — "Natash, let's talk about …"

And, for the next twenty minutes, they remained locked in a quiet conversation about the good times they had shared. And, they discovered how they often remembered things very differently when they spoke about what they thought they remembered about times past. He did this to revive in her a return for the longing for that which he perceived mattered most for her in life. They talked and talked until fatigue caused Derek to drift into slumber.

1 Absolutely (Rus).

Natalia sat still for silent long, searching out the innermost sanctum of humility in her being — her hope-chest of eternal remembrance. Then, she kissed him, took a final look, sealed the feeling in her heart and slipped out of the room, dreading how she might never hear his voice again, dreading that tomorrow she might return to a room with another empty bed.

Kill One Mad Cow or Risk a Stampede

During a telephone update from Director of National Intelligence, Lester Coverdale, about the situation in Russia, Vice-President Norman Weissbrot decided that privacy was indispensable, so he entreated Lester to heed the call to honor the fallen by visiting their 'Dear friend Yancy.'

Within the hour, at a secluded grove in Arlington National Cemetery, Lester and Weissbrot paid homage to all slain patriots in America's wars by making a symbolic visit to the grave of Lt. James Yancy Bateman. Bateman's name was #257 on an auspicious list of 365 chronologically selected souls, who had all made the ultimate sacrifice for their country. Today marked the anniversary of the lieutenant's untimely death some six decades before.

After Lester and Norman concluded their perfunctory blessings to their patriot-of-convenience, they kneeled. And, as if to stroke its eggshell white marble surface, they leaned in close to Yancy's headstone and commenced the real business of their meeting in hushed voices. Lester opened.

"Are you prepared to assassinate on such short notice?"

"Buzzard guts, Lester. No more tap-dancing. National security makes it imperative we bring 'Operation Mad Cow' to finality."

"No argument here. But, acting in haste, you'll become personally exposed to a high risk of detection."

"Don't forget we have the 'Ginger Option,' our deniability safety-net."

Stung about how cheap that sounded, Weissbrot quickly followed up.

"But I'm willing to face the consequences of any blow-back. Our country doesn't need to relive the madness of the Potusson-Bin Laden years because our attempt to assassinate Bin Laden on the fly in 1996 with a Mad Cow prion[1] prototype backfired and turned him into a raving looney."

"Rest assured the new stuff is better, faster. My boys in Cuba have tested it — CDA — Camp Delta[2] Approved. There'll be no Bin Laden blow-back."

"Good. I want cadavers. No more fucking finessing. And, Glorioso?"

"The good doctor is coming around. Bitty steps, for now."

"I'll leave that to your charms. So, we done?" Weissbrot asked.

"Like a Chihuahua, compadre."

Weissbrot and Lester placed two red roses ceremoniously on Lt. Bateman's headstone. This solemn and auspicious gesture marked a handshake in another guise. With solidarity thus acknowledged, they parted, each to his separate car, confident that their country and its constitutional governance would be preserved.

---

1 Creutzfeld- Jakob disease is the human form of Mad Cow disease (bovine spongiform encephalitis).
2 Essentially a 'frontal lobotomy,' the prion pathogen was finally perfected in Cuba at 'Camp Delta.'

Fill Your Mind with the Breathings of your Heart

Toward day's end, intending to rejoin her friends, Natalia returned to the hearty bustle and distraction of the FSB cafeteria. Once there, she noticed Sergei and Tatiana communing over a private meal. In the back corner, Ilya and Olga were doing likewise. Feeling even more alone in the world, she was on the verge of leaving to check-in again on Derek when a familiar voice intruded from behind.

"Miss Bogomolski, would you care to join me for dinner?"

The heaviness in her chest flashed into promise. She wheeled about.

"General, I'd love to. Perhaps, you can tell me what you and Derek were doing today. I spoke to him earlier and he said I should see his videotape."

"Certainly. Is after dinner good for you?"

"Perfect."

They shuffled into the queue and placed their orders. As their meals were being set before them, a wine steward presented Basil with a bottle of Georgian late season Burgundy from the FSB subterranean wine cellar compliments of President Bushkin. And, sitting within the secluded confines of the Officer's Dining Hall, they ate, drank and chatted about the events of this — the second day.

Eking out what remained of the evening's daylight, they ventured onto the streets for a constitutional. Linked arm in arm, meandering around the precincts of the Lubyanka, the crisp air of autumn's dying days refreshed their spirits and reinvigorated their conversation.

From time to time, Natalia warmed when Basil's fingertips meandered over her ivory-skinned knuckles. Inquiring to her hands, she sensed his desire for connection. But, from his lips, she encountered his reserve — a disarming distance that sounded cool-handed in her ears. Only when the sun was shuddering deep into the clouds, firing volleys of striating pinks reddening into a convulsion of crimsons, did she feel the reawakening of her private yearning to seek out and take romantic action.

On returning together to his office, Basil remained the gracious host and served up a pot of scalding hot jasmine tea with heavy-on-the-sugar Greek shortbread, fresh from Nigras[1] Patisserie on the grounds of the Kremlin. They sat, nestled close and watched Derek's video. Towards the end, the world-peace skeptic in Natalia capitulated, almost to the point of panic. There were many things she half understood from Derek. Now, she reached out to Basil for clarification.

"Basil, Derek's certain his government will meddle."

"As am I. It's well known that when any head of state farts Y-Doodle insists on sniffing like a love-starved orangutan. We're fortunate that every government on the planet doesn't imitate their 'National Security' syndrome. However, in the wop assault on our country, we intend to fully embrace Amerikan policy as confirmed by their elektorate. Derek's help has been inestimable in this."

"But I doubt Derek has any real power with the Y-D government."

Basil almost succumbed to an indiscreet laugh.

---

1 In May, 1863, Constantin Nigras from Thessalonika, Greece, emigrated to Russia and under the royal patronage of Tsar Alexander II, established his family's world renowned bakery inside the Kremlin.

"Power is beside the point. Reality and the shaping of public perception gives us peace. Derek's video will showcase reality to people all over the world. For the government of Russia, our peace-preserving duty is to shape people's perceptions. When we act, the Doods need to realize that Russia is not some dancing bear sideshow under Ringling Brother's Big Top. I'm sure I don't have to remind you about their two-faced, Geneva Conventions carping concerning Chechnya hurled at 'Neanderthal' Russia prior to September, 2001."

Natalia threw Basil a look of anguish. He softened his tone.

"Natash, in these anarchic times, the curse of Russian exceptionalism dictates a policy of 'Fair-play Balanced with Hypokrizy.' US Vice-President Weissbrot, who visited months back, as well as many patriotic Doods, like Derek, know this is *realpolitik* talking. Woppery doesn't have a schedule. It's an agenda, not a timetable. 'Cut and Run' is not an option for maintaining world peace in our demokrazy because, just like Amerika, we Russians must adhere to the reality woppery has served-up on our motherland — Y-Doodling hypocrisy be damned."

Doodling — Hypocrisy — Reality — Woppery! she thought. Behind all of it was Afghan heroin traded for diamonds, and now dioxin. Misery gnawed at her like it had with Derek, six fateful years ago. She had basked in the resurrection of a man, who felt his life crushed to nothing. Inside, Derek had died the day Marie and his unborn had. But, in her motherland, in the most unexpected way, he had returned to life. And, through him, she had experienced love, filled with the unique tenderness of a widower on the cusp of indifference about life and death. Their bond was the greatest gift each could have given the other. A bond others might call unstoppably manic.

But, now, it was Derek's demise that seemed unstoppable.

She felt nothing but annihilation and swore the flavor curdling around her tongue was the exact same she tasted when her eyes reached out to the militsia officer just moments before she expected a decisive end to her own life in Metro Komsomolskaya. The taste of Kremlin shortbread — sweet in the mouth, sour in the belly. And, keenly aware how she was going insane toiling to reconcile it all, she turned to Basil and vented.

"You're certainly right about doodling hypocrisy. How can anyone forget that Amerika invaded Panama because of drug smuggling. I cannot imagine Y-D tolerating opium and heroin poisoning their society from a country Russian military forces might invade and occupy en-masse."

She stopped cold on recalling how months earlier, before the Ursini mess skewered their love life, Derek had wanted to show her the movie — *The Panama Deception*. That Academy Award-winning film dealt with Panama after the US government removed Manuel Noriega by military force and installed a corrupt red, white and blue narco-puppet. The murder of Derek's pregnant wife had a Washington face. And, now, another facet of woppery had felled him, along with tens of thousands of her countrymen. Yet, despite all this horror, Derek's noble life remained consumed with purpose, even in the shadow of death. Her whole body felt shattered merely contemplating how she might say — *Goodbye.*

But, just as Derek had parted with Marie, and most recently with Ludmila, she must do the same no matter how much it hurt.

Tears of fortitude welled up in her eyes.

"Thank you for showing me Derek's videotape, Basil. It's very touching for me to discover how a true friend of our nation was working to combat all the carnage flooding in from US-NATO occupied Afghanistan."

She put her palm atop Basil's fingers.

Basil murmured — "Please unburden, Natash. You need closure."

She shook her head resolutely to head off a sob.

"It's cruel, Basil. The drug trade has scorch-earthed Derek's whole life. He showed me a report from the US General Accounting Office, titled *The War on Drugs: Narcotics Control Efforts in Panama*. After their invasion of Panama, the quantity of drugs funneling into Amerika exploded and killed his family."

On her last words, Natalia drew as still as the desert. Pathos shimmered off her flush cheeks as sultry winds might waft off hot sands. Basil smiled deep in his heart because her eyes were an oasis in flood — betraying proof of the soul behind the woman. And, he knew exactly what she meant. He had not chosen Derek Anthony Mitchell at random. He had fully scrutinized the man's past. And, today, Derek confided to him the whole, untold story. The sniper rifle purchased days after Marie's death. A solitary box of bullets to hone his marksmanship. And, that final 'retribution' bullet, the last in the box, which he expended, before he sawed that instrument of vengeance into short sections and dumped the lot into San Diego Bay one moonless night.

Derek had faced down his own — *Let God Decide* — moment.

And, now, here in Moscow, another such moment. Natalia's attack on Ludmila. Her fight for the love of love had felled Derek. Basil alone knew just how stupendous the irony and justice behind all these events were. Matters, all the more heart-wrenching because of the extraordinary attraction that existed between Derek and Natalia. A bond, that if he had known of its tempestuous consequences months earlier, he would have handled entirely differently. And, in this light, Basil sought solace of his own.

"Natash, I'm very sorry we couldn't tell Derek about you. The 'Mallory Wilson Affair', let alone Panama, Afghanistan and Iraq, proved that his own government couldn't be trusted to not make a political football of anything or anyone. If a whiff of a rumor was leaked that you or Derek were connected to our efforts to crack the Romanov *coup d'état* conspiracy or the US-NATO protected Afghan slave and narcotics trade, then our work would've collapsed and one or both of you could have been murdered. Secrecy was vital."

That word — *Romanov* — made her sick. She had to know.

"Drugs I understand, but what's the point of dioxin? What?"

Her wet eyes glistened like fire-opals that sought to put the firmament to shame. And, Basil took pains to explain as delicately as possible.

"That's still not entirely clear. There's a media rumor that suggests that Ursini's dioxin attack on Moscow was to send Ukraine running into the arms of the EU and Amerika."

Basil stopped to let Natalia voice what she might know on that score.

Natalia shot him a quizzed look, expecting him to elaborate.

Basil pondered momentarily before deciding to stick to script.

"Here's what we know for certain. Some drug ring based in Afghanistan planned to purchase the Ursini urn. Payment to Romanov would be in raw diamonds derived from the US-NATO protected Afghan heroin trade. It's frustrating because we were getting close to exposing this woppery. But, their attack on the Metro made everything obsolete in a flash."

Natalia caught the idiosyncrasy — "Attack doesn't make sense. Why would these monsters want to annihilate one of their biggest heroin markets?"

By order of the Kremlin, 'attack' was never to be confused with 'accident.' That was the law of the land, secret as it was. And, given the operative facts, well known to both of them, Basil made uneasy reply.

"It's very doubtful they did. Romanov would never cripple the country where heroin sales put diamonds in his hands. As for the Afghanis, they probably intended to bite the Satan that feeds them — or I should say, makes them narco-zombies. So Amerika seems their likely target. No Y-D would dispute that."

Basil stopped in quandary about how to say what needed explaining. Sometime soon, the 'Princess of Peace' policy would be made public. Words that she might utter could have devastating consequences — no equivocation could be tolerated.

"Miss Bogomolski, this is very important. You must never refer to this attack on the Metro as an accident. *Never!* Burn that into your head."

Hearing the consternation in his tone and knowing how the attack was really an accident, wholly unintended, Natalia balled her hands under her throat in anguish — "So I *did* cause this. Don't pretend."

Basil felt overwhelmed with guilt. Reluctant as he had been, it was he who ordered Derek and she alienated, and this had driven her over the edge.

"Natash, you can't think like that. Customs officials thoroughly searched Ursini. Nobody knew the wop was carrying dioxin and nobody can say with certainty how that dioxin was going to be used. You could have focused on your mission and refrained from assaulting Ludmila. But, you did not. You should have died. But, you did not."

And the words just spilled out of Basil's mouth — "Evil was transported into our country and God decided what was and was not going to happen in the Metro. Science explains heroin and dioxin, but no science explains you. Your assault on Ludmila Naristikova was a crime. You can *not* deny it. And, the consequences — huge. Now, we *all* must face up to our new responsibilities. You most especially. You're a soldier of state now. By your own hot-tempered fist, you have forfeited life as you once knew it."

And, when Basil's scold of words ended on *By your own hot-tempered fist, you have forfeited life*, Natalia began to shiver uncontrollably. Burdened by mutual guilt, Basil's heart sank, and he enfolded her in his arms. He felt none of her special power. It was all her suffering this truth.

And, to minimize her sense of guilt and the ubiquitous nature of the evil the Russian nation faced, Basil rocked her to and fro and repeated the most damnable facts over and over. Fascist atrocities, US-NATO drug facilitation, starvation enforced poppy-ninny slavery in Afghanistan, the anti-Crusader jihad, Y-D's WMD boondoggle in Iraq, and like armament industry elitists in all fascist powers — Romanov sought his cut of depravity. After quieting down, Natalia renewed her quest — there was more to this and she knew Basil knew more.

"First heroin, now dioxin. What's the point of all this pollution? What!"

Basil sensed that she might knuckle down to the larger mission of world peace that President Bushkin had chartered for her if she knew the full Romanov conspiracy, where the facts were beyond doubt, so he evaded no more.

"Natalia, you must never repeat this. Got that?"

"Of course," she replied.

"We got wind of Romanov's ambitions months ago. Our envoy at the United Nations, Tamerlin Tsarnaev, called to order a secret session of the Security Council and made report of our investigations at that—"

Natalia injected hotly — "So how ... Why were we attacked?"

Basil unleashed his frustrations as well.

"Natash, in short, Amerika lead the charge in ridiculing the Tsarnaev report. Please, put all that aside. Thanks to your vampire intercessions, here's the gist of the Why. So-called Grand Duke Sergio Romanov sought to become tsar by fulminating anarchy based on the Potusson-Bin Laden model of neo-fascism. Romanov considered it prudent to do trial runs on the further destabilization of the United States, before deciding on a course of action to upend our government."

Given the tension, Basil could not help but laugh.

"What is it, Basil?"

He inhaled audibly to reset the mood.

"A perfect example in hypocrisy where the destabilization chickens came home to roost, just floated across my mind. Please, excuse me."

"More misery?"

Her glance was filled with fret.

Basil returned her a pained look — "It's not funny, Natash. Just ironic. The governments of Britain and Saudi Arabia setup a slush-fund financed to the tune of $100 billion. The fund was generated on the backs of British motorists when Saudi Arabia sold discounted oil to Britain. Under the trusteeship of MI-6 and Saudi Intelligence, the Al-Yamamah slush-fund was designed to destabilize governments. Exactly the thing Romanov wanted to do to Russia. Sick, isn't it?"

Natalia recoiled — "Utterly. So where's the humour?"

Basil wet his lower lip and cranked his left eyebrow skyward.

"Within such a vast pile of money designed to do evil, $300,000 is a few minutes of interest at the bank. Natash, history's most famous $300,000 came out of Her Britannic-Saudi Majesty's Al Yamamah slush-fund. Have a guess?"

"Any other day, Basil. I'm just, just—"

"Of course, my apologies." And, he focused on a quick finale — "The French have a famous saying — 'Honi Soit Qui Mal Y Pense.' It means — 'Misfortune befalls those who think evil.' The most famous $300,000 in history paid for flight training in Arizona and Florida, as well as all other expenses of fifteen Saudi citizens, two Yemeni citizens, one from Lebanon and another from Egypt, who then committed suicide by aircraft. Destabilizing governments is what MI-6 and Saudi Arabia had in mind, and that is what history's most famous $300,000 funded."

She sat up rigid — "You mean 9/11?"

He gazed into her beautiful, vibrant eyes — "Yes, Natash."

And, she snapped out the obvious.

"Slush-fund, means 9/11 terrorists are MI-6 paid operatives."

"Exactly," he rejoined. "Nothing to do with Afghanistan or Afghanistan's excuse for an extradition process. Rather, everything to do with destabilizing governments, Romanov-style. Have you heard the other 9/11 scuttlebutt?"

"No — huh? What?"

"More like conspiracy theory, really. Something Vice-President Chainikov publicly endorses. How the IRA[1] were armed and funded from Amerika. Chicago and Boston, principally. And, how Amerika refused to extradite these financiers of terrorism to Great Britain. Then the second cousin to the Queen, Earl Mountbatten, out with several of his family in a fishing boat were dynamited to death. And, eighteen soldiers as well. All in a single day. And, still Amerika refuses to extradite these monsters. So, the scuttlebutt is the so-called accidental financing of 9/11 through the Al-Yamamah slush-fund was a score being settled by a very senior MI-6 official or a relative of Earl Mountbatten. This is the true reason why all information about the real financing of 9/11 is top secret."

"So woppery has a stiff upper-lip pedigree," she bleated. Then Natalia tapped her left fist against the bridge of her nose — "Why all this woppery? *Why*?"

"All subversion needs scapegoats. The history of the West's exclusion of Russia speaks volumes about their evil agenda. In 1954 and thereafter, time after time, the West rebuffed our country's every request for admittance into NATO. If Russia were a NATO member, would 'The Heroin Holocaust' exist today? No."

Natalia flinched.

Basil put his hand on her shoulder before continuing.

"And, never forget the night of October 28, 1956, a week before we were compelled to bolster Hungary and the unity of the Warsaw Pact against NATO threats to European stability and hence world peace. On that night, the Israelis piloted a Meteor NF-13, delivered by the British just days beforehand for this exact mission. 200 kilometers south of Cyprus, they shot down an Ilyushin Il-14 carrying Egyptian officials and journalists, murdering all aboard. Of course, the victims were all wogs as far as the Israelis, British and French were concerned. Or if you prefer that charming Nazi and Zio-Nazi euphemism, *Untermench*—"[2]

She interjected — "Why are you telling me this. Why?"

"It's about the 'Fraud on Peace,' Natash. Please, hear me out."

---

1 Irish Republican Army

2 Subhuman (German and Yiddish). See also Goy (Hebrew).

Basil rocked her for several seconds before continuing to enlighten her — "These particular murders were part of a larger profanity against the peace of the world which the British refer to as 'Operation Musketeer.'"

"Operation Mousketeer?" she interposed.

Basil clamped his eyes shut, fighting back the urge to explode into laughter. "No, Natash. No. Mouseketeer is propaganda designed for children in the West to blind them to realities, such as starvation enforced child slavery and the Western fraud of moral exceptionalism." Then from nowhere Basil sung — "M-I-C — poppy-ninny slavery. K-E-Y — I'm starving. That's why. M-O-U—"

Catching onto his weirdness, Natalia pulled away.

"Natash, it's zombie-ganda for kiddies. I'll explain later. Just keep in mind Abraham Lincoln's golden rule — 'Those who deny freedom to poppy-ninnies and mouseketeers, deserve it not for themselves.' As for Britain, France and Israel, their evil is pronounced 'Musketeer' like in the Dumas novel, *The Three Musketeers*. And, don't let the French pronunciation 'mousketair' throw you off either."

Basil paused to recompose and snuggled up to her again.

"On October 24, 1956, the three musketeers, Britain, France and Israel, signed a pact to wage war against Egypt. Known to history as the 'Protocol of Sevres,' the script they composed for their Class-A war crime, a war of aggression, was no different than the script Nazi Germany and the Soviet Union composed for the invasion of Poland in 1939. The 'Protocol of Sevres' was supposed to be secret, but came to light weeks later. On the night of the twenty-eighth, the Three Musketeers murdered their first wogs of Egyptian descent. The plane was south of Cyprus over the Mediterranean Sea the night before their large-scale invasion of Egypt."

Natalia injected her outrage.

"So it's Amerika, Britain, France and Israel as well as those satanic wops."

Basil smiled — *Thank God. She's starting to understand* — and he nodded.

"Furthermore, Britain and France exercised their veto power in the Security Council to shut down the gimmick that calls itself the 'United Nations.' And, never forget, an Amerikan and British 'suppression of 9/11 truth' alliance invaded Iraq screaming WMD and linkage to Al Qaeda. Again, telling the United Nations to rot in hell. Without Russia's membership in NATO, here's what the West's consistent, historical 'Fraud on Peace' looks like, my princess."

Natalia sat up straight and stiff. To her, this 'Princess of Peace' soubriquet reeked of political farce. Basil read the annoyance on her face.

"Natash, trust me. Trust the power within you. Trust the purpose of our vampire intercessions. The Soviet system had many faults. But, like canaries in God's coal mine, Koba[1] taught us well. We know the enemy. We know what satanic evil looks like. We know the deceptions Satan deploys. It's a tragedy so many Russians still continue to buy into the western crap how their motherland has little better to do than orchestrate anti-Western propaganda."

She pulled away to get some space and looked Basil in the eyes.

He responded by fixing his gaze on hers and lowed.

---

1 Nickname for Joseph Stalin, Head of the Soviet Union (1922-1953).

"As a true-hearted patriot Natash, I tell you this — You're a God-send with a unique, special, beautiful role to play. To me, you're part of the Almighty's comeback plan for empowering the human race to snuff out satanic evil forever."

He stopped so he could scrutinize her reaction.

Still feeling bewildered, Natalia took her time to respond.

"I do trust. Trust you, Basil. Evil," she stopped.

Basil picked up on the heartache behind her silence.

"Sweet lady, evil is what it is. Selfish, warmongering, murderous, child-hating. As they say in France — 'Honi Soit Qui Mal Y Pense.' You would think the scum in the West, as well as their prole elektorates, would take stock of their evil schemes. CIA and Al Yamamah slush-funds are pure dynamite. The means for evil to finance false flag attacks as a ruse to declare war. In the West in 1939, 'Operation Himmler' blew up a German radio tower. Hitler proclaimed 'Enough coddling, time to invade and put an end to Judeo-Bolshevism exported from Poland into the German fatherland.' Of course, every Doodle knows about Hitler, just as every Dood knows about CIA slush-fund terrorism as well as Al Yamamah and its most famous $300,000 investment in destabilizing governments."

Natalia sprang to life and growled.

"*Hypocritski Amerikanski svinyi.*"

"Natash, I'm being facetious. And, be more studious about your cursing. You can't be called hypocrite-swine unless you have a moral heart. Most Y-Ds are zombies. They grow up like zombies and live like zombies. Every patriotic Russian knows this. To quote that great Doodle, Alexander Hamilton — '*An electorate that stands for nothing will fall for anything.*' Afghanistan and Iraq prove the fact. Give us a Fuhrer, point the finger, and Y-D's zombie army is on the march. And, zombies are a banker's pride and joy because they're clueless about what a national debt of $6 trillion and counting really means. Ask any Y-D about debt, about who financed 9/11. And, ask him about the Al Yamamah slush-fund or any CIA slush-fund for that matter. All you'll get are dumb-looks, the pretense of moral ignorance about their own evil-hearted demo'n'cracy."

Basil paused to pick up a Nigras shortbread and proffering it close to her mouth, he indicated for her to bite. As she did so, he resumed.

"The Al Yamamah slush-fund was designed to finance the destruction of other governments and manufacture so-called ungovernable wastelands, peopled by cretins, where the unsung slogan 'Freedom is Slavery'[1] means you live like a dog, rather than die like a martyr. It's no different than if Chernobyl was retooled to create nuclear weapons and then exploded. But, don't expect any Dood to admit slush-fund pollution and Chernobyl pollution are one and the same."

And, as she chewed, Basil twiddled with the stub of leftover shortbread.

"Hence, so-called 9/11 is Amerika's own Ukrainian Chernobyl come home to roost. But, don't expect any doodle-hearted Doodle to admit that either."

He scoffed down the shortbread and suddenly choked.

Natalia slapped him hard on the back — "Basil?"

He shook his head to clear his airways.

---

1 One of four government slogans from the George Orwell novel, *1984*

"I'm okay, thanks. Have you heard of the '911 Truther' movement?" he asked.

"Those conspiracy nutcases? Derek says they're kooks."

Basil hunched over trying to hold his chuckling in check. He waved his head.

"More like spooks. It's another CIA scam."

"More Doodle shit?"

"Natash, calm. The CIA cooked up a whole series of videos and half-baked facts to pin 9/11 on Mossad, amongst others, including a gold heist, followed up with several thermite sabotage and controlled demolition conspiracies." He put his finger on her lips to bade her be still — "Why? Because a command decision to dynamite the interior of the World Trade Center was made once it was clear the buildings were doomed. And, I'm not just talking about WTC Building #7 here, either. The interiors of all skyscrapers are super strong because they hold up half the vertical load and then some. Once the point of no-return had been reached, the cores had to be blown out so the wreckage would fall to Earth vertically and as cleanly as possible."

"But, it would anyway. … Where's this coming from?"

"Natash, it's straight-up structural mechanics. One plane wiped out the eightieth floor. A few floors below was a single-storey skylobby and a treble-storey floor housing heavy-duty elevator, electrical and HVAC plant. These four levels were bonded together within a supertruss system, making them equivalent to a solid fifty foot band of steel and concrete. It's a super-rigid cap that limits side-sway due to bending. If you look at exterior photos of the towers, these supertruss caps appear like dark bands. No windows. Without controlled demolition of the core, the monolithic upper sections of both towers would have slumped down against these supertruss capping systems and careened sideways off the tower in an unpredictable manner. Then these intact upper sections would've shattered other buildings hundreds of feet away. The World Trade Center was designed to take a 767 aircraft collision. And, in the event of a catastrophic failure, the rigid core of the building was dutifully engineered for controlled demolition so the bulk of the upper level debris would cascade down-ward semi-encased within the exterior walls, which act like a funnel and tube. Both towers collapsed vertically and very cleanly. *Both*. You can even hear the demolition charges on audio. It's no fluke. Nor villainy. To protect other build-ings, a 1,300 foot progressive collapse, including any fatalities, is practical design aimed at public safety. Not cross your fingers, Hail Mary and say your prayers."

"So, they aren't kooks."

Basil smiled — "Spooks, sweet lady. Spooks. The CIA is all about manipulating public sentiments. Salt facts in with a healthy dose of whacked to muddy reality so proles can't go sniffing out the truth. Their Majesties of Britain and Saudi Arabia supplied both funds and manpower. Why else would you think 9/11 is a fraud? A three thousand body-count handsomely greases the Y-D crusader agenda. In penance, Britain was only too happy to paint Saddam Hussein as an Al Qaeda sympathizer and invade Iraq. UN be damned. Yet again, spooks engineer kooks to distract proles. The financing of 9/11, the manpower behind

9/11 and how the twin towers were demolished in a controlled manner are only questions kooks, traitors and anti-Amerikans ask. And, when their slush-funds to do evil unto others blew up in their jolly faces, the Y-D government re-purposed the boomeranging of their own satanic intentions into an excuse to blame their intended target 'Afghanistan' for the outcome. Just like Hitler and Poland. Never forget your French, Natash — '*Honi Soit Qui Mal Y Pense*.'"

Bristling hot with anger at the thought of demolished lives, she blurted.

"Remember that fifteen-year old Canadian teenager who tossed back an Amerikan grenade that had been hurled at him? Then the Doodles accused the child of being a combatant because an unarmed-by-choice civilian declined to be demolished into dust at the hands of Y-D soldiers."

He snuffed a laugh. There was nothing funny about Y-D hypocrisy.

"Not to mention the Amerikans videotaping Tariq Abu Zaedah a fifteen-year old being sodomized at Abu Ghraib as part of their 'enhanced' how to 'Terrorize Muslim Mothers' to confess campaign." Basil chipped back.

"Child anal rape, too?"

"Natash, let's focus on the big picture. Woppery has an agenda and a plan. The attack on our Metro is no accident. Woppery's first tactic requires public deception. Ignore Tariq. Ignore Omar Khadr, the Canadian. Consider Y-D's Afghanistan scam. Neither the country nor any citizen of Afghanistan had anything to do with 9/11. All the while Doodle-land plays more 'Patty-Cake' with Britain for harbouring terror—"

"More joint CIA-MI-6 sabotage?" she interrupted.

"Be still, woman. In 1998, the Doodles fingered several British subjects who've never set foot in the United States. Seven years into their accusations, the Doods are still lobbying for the peaceable extradition of these naughty Noddies."

"So … I mean," she waved her head, feeling lost.

"Natash, the point is Afghanis are wogs, Brits are not. Doodle action in Afghanistan isn't about values. It's about scoring points with a self-loathing Y-D electorate. Never confuse chest-thumping political correctness with the quiet valour of a high-plains hero whose only compass for decency lies in the eyes of a child. Reducing Afghan children to a state of poppy-ninny starvation slavery informs every moral-hearted human about what woppery looks like. More so, because the illegal product of such slavery kills off 30,000 Russian addicts each year. And, don't forget, 'death exported out of Drugistan' heroin is ramping up to kill over 2,000 Y-Ds each month."

Natalia cut in, hurt — "Derek's unborn. Don't toy with this."

Somewhat exasperated, Basil inhaled deeply.

"Natash, this is no joke. There are between 300,000 to 500,000 addicts in Amerika, all hooked on the nirvana of poppy-ninny slavery. On average, they die 13.6 years into their addiction. Do the math. That's 22,000 minimum each year. But, if you ever tap any Dood on the shoulder and ask for official records about 'death exported out of Afghanistan' and how many thousands of Y-D zombies expire from heroin every month, expect more dumb-looks of disbelief from that zombie nation."

"Please excuse my outburst." And, she sighed.

He raised her left hand to his lips and pecked it.

"Natash, never forget in the eyes of every Joe-cock-a-Doodle out there, we, Rooskies, are Anteye-Amerikan gas-baggers. But, here's reality. While Amerika's fascist media love to crow about the death of movie-star addicts and how 100 deaths per month are 'patriotic military zombies sacrificing for their nation,' this same red-white-and-bullshit media conceal the fact that 660 Y-D military veterans, disgusted by their pathetic amoral lives, blow their brains out from suicide each and every month. Oh yeah — spatchcock my gizzards, y'all — rink'n, stink'n Soviet propaganda."

"What!" she shrieked.

He placed his thumb under her lower lip.

"It's all true. Doods in uniform walk past the fences of poppy-ninny Auschwitz with noses stuck high in the air, pretending not to see or smell the plain obvious. Later, these zombies blow their brains out. Nor do zombie-media blowhards trumpet aloud the worldwide death toll exacted by 'The Heroin Holocaust.' In short, Satan has enslaved children in a game of hunger. They're God's canaries. All one need do is listen for *Vopl* — the wailing of children. There be Satan."

Suddenly, a spirit blinded Natalia's sight. She closed her eyes and when she reopened them, just as if it was yesterday, a single, prophetic thought hovered in her mind. It was about an idea for a vile novel and movie series fascists were hatching in the West. Tentatively titled, *Hunger Games*, children in this literary phantasy were compelled to live on the brink of starvation and those aged twelve to eighteen had to face-off in gladiatorial combat. The *Hunger Games* franchise was designed to indoctrinate the hearts and minds of zombie kids growing up in affluent countries so that the ridicule, the misery and the suffering Satanists inflicted upon Muslim children was 'New Millennium' — Freedom is Slavery — normal. Its spirit-of-life message — *White child-heroes rebel. Darkies are terrorists.*

Natalia felt nauseous. Moments ago, she had chided Basil for what she suspected was hyperbole, and now all she had was this crazy vision of the future with a phantastical idea about woppery scheming to unleash a novel on the world. Tamping back her reluctance to share such inanity, she squeezed Basil's wrist and made ready to tell him, but he firmed his finger over her lips.

"Shhhh, Natash. Let me get back to woppery and Romanov's designs to destabilize our country. Romanov and Al Guido sought to arm anti-Satan jihadists with dioxin so they could foment chaos in countries on the verge of toppling into one-way, voter-endorsed totalitarianism."

"Amerika," she muttered.

Basil drew his finger away and nodded.

"Furthermore, Romanov knew that if the so-called flower of democracy were pushed deeper into its Potusson-Bin Laden totalitarian model then it would be much easier for woppery to upend the government of Russia and proclaim it Liberty, Amerikan-style. To quote Adolf Hitler — '*One great benefit of the totalitarian state is that it forces other nations to imitate us.'* Amerika's fascist militarism outstrips the combined military budgets of the next ten biggest nations because it's designed to put fear into Amerikan citizens and radicalize the whole world into imitating them. 'Democracy' is the scam name these fascists use for their satanic agenda. Demo'n'cracy is reality. Hunger. Hunger—"

Basil suddenly parked his anger. He smirked at what he could only ascribe to a mental hiccup, because sensing the wonder of life behind Natalia's eyes, he reckoned this charming hiccup was the closeness he felt for her and she for him. Recomposing himself to resume his tirade against a world descending into the clutches of woppery, he recalled something Derek had only mentioned in passing, but which now struck him as a phenomenal insight.

He cleared his throat and softened his tone.

"Natash, pretend you're a kid. Not in fascist Italy, Germany or Amerika, but a kid in US-NATO-occupied Drughistan. Each morning you wake up. You look north, east, south and west. All about you is starvation. Unless you're a four-legged goat, there's not a speck of food growing anywhere. It's all poppies. You might as well be living in a Nazi concentration camp, surrounded by barbed-wire because you can't eat barbed-wire either. Elie Wiesel made it abundantly clear in his memoir, *And the World Remained Silent*, that starvation doesn't require fences. Working those poppy plantations gets you food. Because, just like Gaza, across the fascist world, Zio-Nazi banks, subsidized by demo'n'cracy, operate to provide funds for the purchase of food that supplies 'Concentration Camp Drughistan.' And, the product of starvation enforced Muslim child slavery is heroin. That's 'Western Free Market Economics.' Lazy Zio-Nazi scum that feed off slavery and subsidization. 'Democracy' is just a Western excuse to abdicate morality. Like a German peering through the barbed-wire into the heart of Auschwitz, 'The Heroin Holocaust' and starvation enforced child slavery is right before your eyes. As Wiesel said, *And the World Remained*—"

"But Basil—" Natalia cut in.

He pressed his finger to her lips again and softened his gaze.

"Natash, do you truly wish for closure?"

"Yes. Oh, yes," she replied. "Truly."

Just looking into her frantic eyes, Basil's heart melted with love.

"Natash, this comes from Derek as much as me. Conjure in your heart Moses freeing his people from bondage. I call upon you to use your power to reach out to all poppy-ninnies. Incorporate their suffering into your bones, the same way their mangy bodies become infused with narcotic residues and start putrefying."

He firmed his fingertips against the underside of her chin.

"Natash, I pray to God that you are the 'Princess of Peace.' Please, be this and more. Make love a force of nature and commune with the love Derek had for the infant in the belly of his wife that never drew breath. I'm certain if you love these children, you'll find your deepest, most personal prayers fulfilled."

And, as the fingers of Basil's left hand shifted and nestled against the warmth of her right cheek, he stooped low and kissed the knuckles of her left hand. It was a kiss of true love. Neither of them felt a quantum of ardour, but rather a dazzling meekness, which trundled the length of their beings and filled their minds with the breathings of their hearts. And, as if an inner sense of truth within her had altered the future somehow, all notion of some crazy novel titled *Hunger Games*, vanished from Natalia's memory and recollection.

After a long period of quiet vigil passed, Basil refocused on their mission — "Heroin and dioxin are death by pollution. This, US-NATO woppery has unleashed upon our motherland. Some die quickly, but most wither away over years. Fast or slow, it's genocidal murder."

"Genocide!" she squealed.

Her cheeks reddened, chagrined by her outburst.

Basil squinched back a grin that made the under-quarters of his nose flatten, and he flashed her a valiant look — "No more Boris Bolshevik baby-kissing, dearheart. By the power of Django, we, courageous Kossacks, are going to go Abraham Lincoln, Vampire Slayer, on evil."

Amid the bleak, his whacked-out humour was so apt.

She discovered — Her lungs were drawing air after all.

He leant in close, kissed her forehead and cupped her cheeks in his palms — "Seriously, Natash, we're going to smash evil. Smash it like Stalin and Eisenhower smashed fascism. And, the world needs your help, Miss Vampira."

He gave her a playful tweak on the nose.

"Our first task is to prevent Amerika going totalitarian, at least past the point of no return. You know sweet lady, Derek Mitchell is the greatest patriot the Doodles will probably never know."

Natalia's eyes glowed, as did Basil's.

He could not help but nuzzle his lips against her philtrum.

Then he drew back — "Natash, remember, this is all top-secret."

She nodded, and he refocused on the Romanov-Al Guido plot.

"The great aim of Romanov and his fascist allies was to reinstate a tsardom in Russia resembling the British Westminster system with a King and Parliament. However, the British model was only their foot-in-the-door ploy. Ultimately, these wops intended to subvert it further to produce a tsarist government where spurious elections are media orchestrated jokes."

Fascist — Tsarist. The words gnawed at her. *Tsar* was derived from *Caesar. Fascist* from *fasces,* the Roman insignia of power. The pair glorified the tyranny of woppery. She had emailed Alfredo Ursini for months and was well acquainted with his bluster as a romantic prince.

"This attack is the same as their attack on us in 1941," she said.

Inside, Basil warmed — *Attack* — her mind was squaring up to the official evil of the matter. And, he responded in an even tone of voice.

"Welcome to 'Attacks' of the new millennium, Special Agent Bogomolski." He felt her face flinch in his fingers as she clenched her eyes shut. He stroked a lock of hair over her left ear before sitting back — "Don't fret, brave Princess. Six months ago, we told Italy and their fascist allies what would happen if this crazy Italian scheme saw some wop Prince emerge out of the mists of Reaganism to slay dragons in the so-called Evil Empire."

Wop Prince — Evil Empire. The horror of it all throbbed behind Natalia's eyeballs like a migraine poised to swallow her brain. Her head was there, throbbing between anger and despair. Her hips and legs were there, wanting to feel the gentle majesty of Basil's hands at play. But, nothing else. If she had a torso, she did not feel it. There was no space in-between for the devastation she felt. She made a wish to die and resurrect in any era except this one. But, within her being, an angel smiled at such caprice. It knew better. And, pulsing into life, it pressed close and kissed her on the interior surface of her lips.

Basil spoke into the worrisome silence.

"Natash, are you okay?"

And, he leant in, cupped her cheek and felt the incandescence of a woman reining back unsought pleasure. The paradox left him confused. Natalia opened her eyes, beamed into the welcome proximity of his gaze and vented.

"Oh, Basil. I want a great love, not a damn prince."

"Natash, let's not talk about woppery anymore. You now know everything that Derek knows, as well as the far larger stakes for us all."

And, Basil stilled himself, so she could ponder in silence.

Natalia's mind buzzed with contradiction and guilt. There was so much to reconcile. But, with all discussion of decades of evil burnt away, a tincture of grace now rippled down her spine and revived her innermost cravings. And, in this mood for life renewed, she spoke to vanquish all her inhibitions.

"Basil, I feel lost. Derek has Ludmila. And, my friends are great people. But, when I see how giddy in love they are, I feel more empty than ever."

Basil heard the call of desire behind her plaint, but biding the secret promise he had given Derek, he reluctantly remained steadfast in his silence.

To her mind, Basil came across as dispassionate. And, not artfully so. By touch alone, she knew he harboured strong feelings for her. His taciturn mood confounded her, almost to exasperation. But, drenched in prodigious forces pulsing hard inside her, re-action dictated she honour her own promise — action.

"Basil, I'm a young woman. In me, lives the spirit of love. You couldn't imagine the type of juices that I'm stewing in. The divine deliverance we provide those wop detainees is tame by comparison."

Basil laughed defensively, perhaps evasively. But, in reality, his whole body smoldered and his hands felt plump with the yearning to hold her flesh within his warmth. How easy it would be to pounce. But, no. The Paradise he sought to manifest with her was not about the juvenile. There would be no surrender of his true-hearted self to a crumble pie of sexual sabotage because his promise to Derek had a magnificent purpose. And, he parried her sudden broadside with his first unguarded thought — impromptu humour. It came out clumsy.

"I guess we should share the dungeon videos with everyone and let them vote on which agony is worse: vampire intercession or love in a state of suspension."

She was momentarily bewildered by his offhandedness, almost to the point of bursting into tears. Vampire by night, Angel by day, ministering to living men, women and especially the children, nearly all of whom were destined for cremation, ripped her apart. A relentless, ball-suckling virulence between her legs felt like screaming, and be purged of anguish, but then she softened. Amidst all the misery, she knew it was time for true connection. And, seeking to pierce his defensiveness, she mimicked his humour with a good-natured retort.

"General Novimirov, I think you're teasing me now."

The mood of standoff eased in an instant. Basil realized how parlour games harboured nothing but insincerity, and might be perceived as insolence under the hot-blooded circumstances. She deserved some form of honourable explanation for this impasse and he spoke to enlist her understanding.

"Sweet lady, according to Derek, it might be a good thing for you to stew in your juices for twenty-four hours. After all, a day without love is but the briefest of seasons."

Natalia replied swiftly and without exaggeration.

"Brief or not, I feel like my whole life is being held in check."

Searching for the genuineness he intended, Basil softened his heart. By interposing the shield of forbearance, he felt she might think he was evading her earnestness with smarm. This had to stop. Circumspection rolled off his lips.

"Natash, please hear me out. I spoke to Derek about you. And, about me. He gave me 'Marching Orders' in this. I trust his judgement — don't you?"

She had sensed his tender reticence ever since dinner. Their walk together. His caring at odds with his distance. And, most discernibly, the melody of quandary in a lustrous masculine voice that to her remained deep and august. And, now, it made sense. And, how perfect it was. Her words in clarion reply rang out as if from nowhere, and yet they boomed in upon them both, as if from every point of the compass.

"You're talking about us, aren't you?"

Basil loosed the rosiness blush of a soul saturated in enormity.

"Yes, Natash. Exactly. I fancy to think of an 'us.' Even so, I promised Derek to keep my distance this one night because I need to reconcile myself to being in love with you. I'm concerned I'm being improvidently seduced by forces emanating from you. Forces, I've never felt before."

She teased but not coquettishly — "I think my real force is that I'm a normal, spunky, young woman." She felt trite the instant her lips came to rest.

Basil's eyes twinkled at her unguarded levity, as well as the prospect of spunky. Yet, Basil was a man, as if marching off to war, and he maintained an air of deliberative standoff to keep his true desires properly composed.

"I don't want a 'Veronika.'[1] You're trifling with words to arouse affections that you shall not enjoy until I know that you can be with me as my beloved."

Her heart stopped at his words. And, leavened with the beauty of moral heartedness, something that for her was now as vital as food and air, she made reply — "It's so frustrating. I've no idea what power has overtaken me. But, this I do know — it's God given. And, I sense the same spirit flows in your veins, Basil. You have a young soul and I adore your sense of grandeur about life. Please know how the power of your own allure is no less intoxicating to me."

1 Russia's Amateur Spy Corps. In honor of Veronika Lewintsova, captured by 'Capitalist Pigs' in 1998.

His voice rang with insistence.

"Natash, please stop trying to seduce me and listen. I made a promise to Derek. He told me to stay this course because when he opened his heart to Ludmila it healed him totally. You were there. Take stock of what you told me about Derek's love for Marie and then Ludmila. I'm a man cut from the same cloth. Love is about boundless grace, not captivation, nor the polity of a 'good match' or societal expectation. Do you not crave that delirious integration from one you would love and who would love you eternally? Perhaps I'm a pig, but if others have it, I want it too. Don't you?"

Her whole body pulsed with the beauty of prospect.

"More than anything. More than any special power," she ended in whisper.

"Well, think of it like this. Love is the Great Luck. Be it ill-fated or not, only those who completely abandon themselves to it have the most auspicious of lives. Here lies the simple magic I seek, Natash."

He closed his eyes momentarily to summon the stillness he needed to invoke the great truth — *The Fireball Heart* — he sought to conjure from thin air, levitate in his palm and cast into her being to bind them.

"On day one, I opened my heart to being in love with love. On day two, that's today, I opened my heart to being in love with a love for you. I'm only asking the same from you on this our day two. On day three, if we share the mutual desire of being in love with loving each other then words become superfluous." He smirked because there was no holding back — "And … And, we make our own Great Luck … our own Great Love."

Her face blushed crimson and gold.

"If you had spoken to me like this three days ago, before Ursini ever showed, I would have been perplexed. Don't ask me why but it makes perfect sense. My life has become pure enchantment."

Softening to her radiance, Basil let the charm flow.

"Dear lady, it must be marvelous seeing life through your eyes."

"You have such a beautiful mouth, sweet man. I cannot imagine what marvels I would see if I viewed life through your eyes. But, I'd love to."

"Then I make this solemn promise to you," and he leant over to murmur — "You are very precious to me. I would never pretend otherwise."

Basil's face blazed like the interior of an ancient stone-hearth and Natalia's cheeks basked in the heat. And, as Basil spoke anew, he conjured into being his call upon the imaginary power of telepathy so as to impress upon her the deliberateness behind his every word so that before each syllable had sprung from his lips, she would know how very true it all was. For what he sought was what Derek promised it could be — Both their eyes would open, and their thoughts would be at one with their hearts.

"Natash, I want you. I want us to share the majesty of life together. Derek assured me that if I honoured the promise I made him then you would know everything. No hesitation. No evasion. Everything."

The plum rush of hearing such words of determination, so flush with his brilliance and so lambent with his feelings, had floored her, but the augustness behind his candor had touched her to an even greater degree and reduced her to tremors. How could she not embrace the perpetuity of his desires? And Derek's wisdom, beyond trustworthy! Reply gushed from fevered lips.

"With all my heart I shall wait, Basil. I have only this to say. I've known you so briefly, yet, I know I could love you forever. When you feel I'm ready, that moment shall be the start of our lives — you and me."

Basil's whole body quivered. Eyeball to eyeball, sultry with silence, all the magnificence of intensity of a shared *fait-accompli* was there, but none of the tension. Impetuousness would not prevail. With all well done, now was the proper hour to say farewell. He walked her to her room in the Infirmary. At the doorway, as she made to enter, from nowhere a thought intruded upon him.

"Natalia, may I have your hand?"

She placed it into his beckoning palm.

He looked down, turned it over and using the full range of his fingers, he stroked it once. He flipped it over and stroked the back of it once then brought his lips down and kissed, raised his head and brought her palm up to his lips and kissed it again. And, while blanketing her hand against his glowing cheek, he gave words to the aura within — "I have made this wish — this solemn prayer. Natash, I ask that you mold yourself in the way of beauty so exquisite in women because I want to fit you like the perfect glove."

Insane with half-swoon delight, she felt stumped for words. So, her mind drifted back to that first wonderful day when Derek had trifled with her and stared down the length of her arm and into her eyes. She directed her gaze to Basil's hand, still cradling her own, and she addressed his hand.

"May I?"

"Please do," came reply from Basil's lips.

And, as Basil noted every movement so as to engrave it into perpetual memory, his right hand placed itself in hers. Upon seeing his open palm in hers, in a flash, Natalia knew that somehow she had already saved Basil's life. She had saved him! How she could not say. But, the power of this truth sent a wave of rapture down her torso. And, in this reverend keep of love, Natalia held Basil's hand, repeated his gestures, closed her eyes and made entreaty.

"And I pray to become she who fits you like a perfect glove."

Basil kissed Natalia on the forehead and they parted company.

Mistress of the Snark

Good morning, sleepy head." Olga stooped over and gave Ilya a lascivious kiss — "That's a small token of the wonderful night I had with you darling."

Roused from the grogginess of deep slumber, Ilya gazed upward and his first undisguised thought took flight.

"You must be an Angel because I certainly slept with one."

Smelling fresh coffee trying to percolate its way through the delightful fragrance of Miss Olga Nikolaevna Krovsoska, he pushed himself to sit upright and addressed her curious lack of response.

"I hope I was not too out of practice for you, *Daragaya*."

"Certainly not!" And feeling dragged from contemplation to snookered, Olga smartly added — "Sweetie, it was superb. I love the way you enfold me so close and do me to kingdom come."

She passed him the cup of coffee and kneading levity with ardor she redirected her focus to one of unwavering intent.

"There's no way that I'm going to let go of you until I hump you into the grave. It's up to the cunt-hunter in you to survive, sweetheart."

Ilya burst into laughter.

"My wicked vampire, what a mouth! Boast not, because I'm going to give you the Ilya Van Helsing treatment and hump the grave out of you."

Giggling with delight, she pirouetted to the kitchen to retrieve her own coffee, popped her head around the corner and taunted.

"Pierce me, darling, but not through the heart."

"What cheek." He kicked off the sheet.

"Come Mistress of the Snark. Meet your doom."

She was prancing toward him, her chiffon robe bobbing from side to side, giving him a flash of cinnamon-nipple-latte here and there when the phone rang. She looked up at the ceiling maddeningly as she swiveled about, scurried to the kitchen and hastened back with Ilya's mobile.

The call was short and urgent. With less than forty minutes to report to work, showering and dressing with dispatch left them fifteen minutes to hoof their way from Derek's apartment down Ulitsa Myasnitskaya to the Lubyanka complex. Ilya went off to his meeting while Olga took time to drop in and thank Derek for the use of his thump'n great bed.

Shuddered to a Standstill

Natalia woke well rested but perturbed by a repeat of the prior night's dream — watching herself witness the crucifixion of her eldest, Jesus of Nazareth. On a placard nailed atop the Roman crucifix, his name and title were clearly declared in three languages, which she understood fluently.

This morning her recollection brought with it more vivid details. In this particular dream, she had tried to intervene and heal her child but Roman soldiers menaced her and barred her way. She tried to wish them away, but she could not. Dreams she could control but recollections she could not. This tragedy was in her and of her.

The most memorable detail was that similar to the defender who had come to Ludmila's aid in the Metro, a man had stepped forward putting his body between her and the soldiers. He held her close, comforted her with soothing words and gradually shuffled her back into the anonymity of the crowd. She recalled everything about the man except his face. He seemed to have none or perhaps she had not looked upon his face. It was a blank. But, everything else was vivid: his tone of voice, his manner of expression, his deportment and demeanor, and his spirit. She knew this man. She was certain. It was Basil.

Listening attentively to her recounting, the Patriarch was taken by surprise when the car jolted to a halt, waiting to turn across traffic. His warm, wrinkled hand lay atop hers and he sensed the despair raging through her body. But, while he was sympathetic, he did his utmost to remain dispassionate. Having heard her out without interruption, he now sought from her niggling specifics that remained unspoken.

"Do you remember what this 'Basil' apparition said to you?"

"No. Well, a vague idea. Not exact words, Patriarch."

The Patriarch had an insight.

"What language did he use?"

"The common tongue," she replied without a second thought. Then she smarted with recognition and elaborated — "It wasn't priestly Hebrew, nor Latin or Greek. It was the common tongue."[1]

"And no one spoke Russian?"

She smiled into his insistence and made emphatic yet polite reply.

"Yes Patriarch. No Russian. I definitely would've noticed that."

The silent impasse did not last long. The car shuddered to a standstill. Before opening the door completely, the chauffeur poked his head inside and reminded Natalia to put on her mask. Twelve burly guards marched the pair through the throng congregated around the entrance to Moscow Central Hospital. Natalia was led to the Phase-III Decontamination Center. The Patriarch, with television crew in tow, was escorted around the hospital, where, room by room, he blessed the ailing and thereby televised spiritual comfort to the city as well as the nation as a whole.

Get More Ruthless

On the phone with Rome, Basil hammered back.

"Get more ruthless. Y-D lives are at stake."

Basil grimaced from time to time, then shot back.

"Colonel Tiranov, in theory, that's a cute idea. But, *absolutely not*. If we do decide to subject ourselves to another dose of being an organ-grinder's monkey and contact Y-Doodle, it will be done from Moscow."

Basil patiently heard out Tiranov before responding.

"We did the honourable thing six months ago at the UN Security Council. Amerika laughed at us. China, Britain, and France are witnesses to our good faith dealings. This wop attack vetoes everything. And, in case you've forgotten, like some plantation mistress, their President Carter likes to wail on Russia to score points with Y-D rednecks. Urn or no urn, there's no way woppery is going

1 Aramaic. See movie, *The Passion of the Christ*, for audio.

to further compromise national security. By all means, try to find that urn. But, know this, maintaining complete secrecy is paramount. Is that *crystal clear*?"

As Tiranov spoke, Basil reclined in his chair, then replied.

"Yes. Rolfino is in transit. His description of our vampire intercessions for any wop who doesn't spill his beans will make your job much easier."

Tiranov voiced skepticism.

Basil let loose a measured laugh.

"Trust me on this, Komrade. Only Amerika resorts to torture. And, never forget the cover story, Rolfino was in Italy while he made contrition, never in Moscow. In Italy, he has no diplomatic status, so no harm — no foul. Got it?"

Heartened, Basil smiled at Tiranov's new suggestion.

"Perfect, colonel. Proceed. And, remember absolute secrecy. *Poka.*"

The Rise of the Bzombies

Captain Ilya Botanin took his seat at the snap meeting Metro Taskforce General Litvinenko[1] had convened in the Joint Divisions Conference Room.

Major Bulekov made the opening presentation. From more refined data, his damage assessment group had distilled better predictions of how the carnage would play out over the coming weeks. His most recent hour-by-hour breakdown of the harvest of death was grim. Dead at midnight last: 24,677. An additional 10,200 dead estimated for midnight tonight. Without pause, Bulekov fired up a series of overhead projector slides. The only good news in the graphs was the daily death rate would fall off rapidly over the next four days. By the end of the eighth week, he expected a total numbering between 75,000 to 80,000. '9/11' times twenty-five. 'The Three Musketeers (1956).' 'Chernobyl (1986).' 'Al-Yamamah (2001).' 'The Heroin Holocaust (2002—).' All of it — Death.

The room darkened into absolute silence.

General Litvinenko stood to re-establish command, for now was the opportune moment to introduce the military ramifications.

"Komrades, today we have a guest. Colonel Dimitri Natrupov is the adjutant for General Tendinov. He's preparing our nation's Bzombie[2] brigades."

Bzombies? — The men flashed bemused looks at each other.

Natrupov stood up while Litvinenko explained.

"Bzombie brigades are being assembled from 'Shock-and-Awe' citizens who aren't expected to live beyond ten weeks. The motherland needs men and women whose last beat of their shattered hearts will be a huge patriotic explosion. From what Major Bulekov has shown us, it appears we easily have some 30,000 able-bodied Bzombie conscripts. I'm ordering Bulekov and all others, who think they could help Colonel Natrupov to confer with him after this meeting."

Natrupov reseated himself, and Litvinenko turned to Bulekov.

---

1 Pronunciation: Lit-vin-yenko.
2 The Ultimate Suicidal Martyrs - Portmanteau of Bombies + Zombies

"Major, I believe the next issue is long-term lethality. Resume, please."

Bulekov stood and directed everyone's attention to his next sequence of slides. The worst cancers would be in organs poisoned by the pollen-sized dioxin dust — the lung, bronchia and throat. Lung cancer was essentially incurable. Assuming a 90% mortality rate for all types of cancer, 120,000 casualties could be expected by the end of the first year. The next year would see 100,000 premature deaths. And, the number would drop 20,000 each year thereafter. The biggest factor subject to actuarial error was the extent of exposure. But, based on two days of data, he confidently projected that by the end of the sixth year, a total of 420,000 people would die as a direct result of inhaling less than a biologically lethal dose of dioxin.

The science clearly supported Bulekov's model.

He had assumed that 98% of the 3,000 grams of dioxin released was still wafting up and down the Metro system, primed to kill. Only 2% of the dioxin had contaminated the masses of people who had used the Metro. He next split the 2% into 1% on people's clothes and 1% breathed in or ingested. Clothing analysis suggested a 1% figure was reasonable. His model showed over 800,000 people were exposed to a total of some 30 grams of dioxin, amounting to 37.5 micrograms per person on average. A single microgram is considered a disastrous dose even though true low dose lethality remained hard to determine. However 37.5 times a disastrous dose was undoubtedly lethal, be it over the short or long term.

On top of the 420,000 direct fatalities, Bulekov expressed his opinion that another 300,000 people would succumb to premature death from other debilitating conditions attributable to an overall decline in vigor. The numbers required more extensive epidemiological studies to quantify with greater precision, but he maintained that his preliminary projections were conservative worst case estimates. Assuming Russia initiated an immediate and massive expansion of medical infrastructure, the best case scenario was 800,000 dead, consisting of 80,000 dead within eight weeks and 720,000 over the next six years.

Hearts thumped in chests, but silence remained.

800,000 dead — *The harvest of woppery.*

Bulekov turned his spleen on the economic implications. The medical costs of attending to the walking dead over six grim years was crushing. But, the truly ruinous was measured in decades because there were vast numbers of people poisoned but not to the point of certain death. Bulekov assumed medical intervention could keep these cot-cases alive for decades. He described them as the 'Walking Undead' because they were economically useless except as the recipients of a lifetime of hospital and sanatorium care. He estimated their number to be some 1.5 million citizens — all lifetime zombies.

The room shared but one thought.

A Wopocalypse created a Bzombie Nation. Time to feed on wops.

Oblivious to the collective mood for revenge, Bulekov stressed that while the numbers were still rough and ready, the horrendous consequences of polluting subway systems were not. All present knew the salient facts. Russia was a nation of 150 million people, and Moscow, the intellectual, political and financial heart of the country, was a city of 20 million, and over half of all Moscovites once relied on the Metro each and every day. Nothing the bureaucrat in Bulekov said came across as exaggerated.

As a scientist, Ilya Botanin felt strangely unmoved. Stalin's genius for rhetoric wafted across his mind — '*One death is a tragedy, one million a statistic.*'

The numbers — *Huge.*

The problems — *Vast.*

The ramifications — *Interesting!*

It all seemed so perverse, so outer-worldly. Science run amok. When would he connect? He just couldn't connect. It gored him to not know why.

Bulekov next presented a synopsis of the fertility issues. Again, it was far too early to make solid predictions because 13 nanograms was only an estimate of the dioxin intake sufficient to cause chromosomal damage in sperm production. This meant a mere 1% of the 3 kilos of dioxin released — 30 grams of dioxin — equated to 2.3 billion damaging doses for the male reproductive system. It was beyond impossible to forecast how many males had received a damaging dose. The only recourse was to immediately store in sperm banks what seed was still fresh and undamaged in each man's ampullae and epididymis.

Despite the fact that his exposure could only have been marginal, this news smacked Ilya like a 2x4 in the crotch. He knew there were hazards, which he had mentioned to Olga, but he had not thought to bank sperm. A bitter coldness crept over him. The man in Ilya was in love. But, what of she? That was not clear at all. His sweet Olga seemed far too serendipitous. Suddenly, anxiety flooded in from every direction. It mattered to him — it all mattered to him. He was in love. And, who was he to accuse Olga of serendipity because she might well say the same thing about him, a haughty nerd who had heedlessly squirted his brains off. Cunt-hunting be damned. They had to meet. She needed to know. He needed to know because he had hopes, and neither, in his estimation, deserved the uncertainty of an irresolute future.

After Major Bulekov fielded all questions concerning his casualty and health report, Major Antipov marched to the lectern and presented his 'Dioxinomic[1] Damage Assessment.' He divided the annihilation of mainstream economics into three categories: Human, Industrial and Fixed Assets.

The attack had created two classes of human carnage. For the first class, age at death was no longer hypothetical. Faster than a speeding bullet, 800,000 people were warped from their calendar age to within six years of their death age. Regardless of their calendar age, another 1.5 million citizens were suddenly bestowed the age of retirement, but not necessarily the short life spans that a nation's pension program expects. With a solitary swing of the fascist axe, woppery had inverted the demography of Russia to one comparable to Japan, where the retiree-to-worker ratio amounted to socio-economic suicide.

Antipov's demographic damage assessment bled into the motherland's next

---

1 Portmanteau of Dioxin + (Eco)nomics. See also *Dioxinomics*® Series. www.dioxinomics.com.

disaster: Industrial Decline. As a world power, Russia faced an enormous labour shortage. Worse because the more highly trained populace of Moscow and the center of finance for the country had taken the blow. Year by year, Antipov's slides dramatized the misery all healthy citizens would endure because of the economic contraction the forces of woppery had unleashed.

Antipov concluded his presentation describing the annihilation of the value of fixed assets. Value is psychological. The Metro system was shut down because, polluted or unpolluted, the place was little better than a fascist gas-chamber to any creature exposed to it, cockroaches included. Since a timetable and budget to decontaminate was still in the works, Antipov focused on the more vexing question — *What's the point?*

"I snap my fingers." He snapped — "The system is now completely spotless. So we announce to everyone, 'Citizens, please start using the Metro and get back to a normal, productive life.' See the problem, komrades? It's a joke, isn't it?"

The room was iceberg still.

First to rouse, Litvinenko's words came slowly.

"Major, your larger point is that the concept of life in a city, Moscow, Saint Petersburg, Volgograd, and any sizeable city is obsolete because on any given day some psycho-wop can covertly trickle cheap as shit pollutants into any place bustling with people. So, decontamination is pointless — right?"

Antipov ducked the question because pointless was not his call to make.

"Sir, woppery's juiciest targets are subways. They used to be a carefree transportation treasure. But, polluted just once, subways become a toxic dumpsite that's super-expensive to decontaminate. And, woppery's Dioxinomic domino effect applies to all cities, sir. New York, London, Paris, Tokyo—"

Litvinenko interjected — "You're talking about worldwide civic collapse!"

Antipov stared blankly at his superior.

"Absolutely. And, economic collapse too. The New York subway is pollution piss. And, this makes the value of all New York real estate equally piss-worthy. I'm compiling a report on the matter called *Dioxinomics: The Myth of Superpower in the Age of Dioxin*. Dioxinomics trumps economics—"

Litvinenko interrupted because thrice now that word had jangled.

"Dioxinomics?"

"Sir, woppery proves 'economic value' is a delusion, a human condition arising from the 'Money Psychosis.' As long as pollution is real, Dioxinomics is real."

Litvinenko squinched his eyes in disbelief.

Antipov saw the need to elaborate.

"A $100,000 mortgage is an economic phantasy. It assumes a thirty-year loan means thirty years of zero-toxicity. Every banker need only ask a no-brainer — 'Is this property's price based on reality or on the fiction that pollution of real estate is impossible?' One is 9/11 real, the other 'Barbie-World.'"

Litvinenko felt sucker punched.

"Please, Major. Leave Barbie and Doodle out of this."

"Impossible. *Every* subway system in *every* city is a dioxin magnet. 'Barbie-World' says 'A nutcase flying a plane into a building to commit suicide? Naah, that'll never happen!' That, sir, is pie-in-the-sky splat-on-the-window talk. Cold, hard, reality says otherwise. Economics is Barbie. Dioxinomics is real—"

Litvinenko interjected.

"Antipov, you sound like a fucking, warmongering Doodle."

"Sir, commiserate with the Metro victims. Dioxinomics is hard-currency fact cut into your skin. Economics is 'Barbie-World' green ink, printed on 'Barbie-World' paper. It's based on a psychological condition — the 'Money Psychosis.' Economics is as laughable as Confederate dollars printed on hot-pink doilies."

"More sick jokes, Major?"

"World-wide civic collapse is my focus. It's no joke. Paper is Barbie. Dioxin is real. Look at the derivatives markets, such as credit default swaps. That fallacy is all premised on the 'Money Psychosis,' not the creation or delivery of real products. And, Central Bank 'cyber-money' is the worst Money Psychosis of all. Do I have to explain this in terms of ex-President, Boris Zeltsin?"

Every Russian had already experienced Zeltsin's form of *Dioxinomics.* Beginning in 1993, Boris Zeltsin had manufactured trillions in 'cyber-money' for his friends. His cronyism polluted the money psychosis and drove the old Soviet rouble[1] into the grave. Litvinenko's prolonged silence at the Zeltsin reference made it clear to Antipov that he had struck a nerve, so Antipov drove home his final point.

"Sir, terrorism was cute for its time but woppery has cracked the mold of civilization. Similarly, the hula-hoop fascism of Mussolini and Hitler's day was a fad in comparison to the Dioxinomic reality we now face. Real estate is no longer gold. It's gelded, worldwide and forever. And, I mean — *forever.*"

After another stunned silence, Litvinenko opened the meeting to debate. Like a winter's first snowflakes, the questions came light and tentative at first, but in time the room descended into a blizzard of conflicting opinions and counter-opinions, which Litvinenko found harder and harder to marshal.

When his gut had endured enough, he stood and barked.

"Silence! Silence, right now."

The room quieted, and Litvinenko re-composed himself.

"Komrades, let's look at hard facts. Here, in a room full of talented scientists, we've descended into what? A rabble, capitalists would call a 'stock market.' You've proved Major Antipov's point about Dioxinomics lording over the 'Money Psychotic' Barbie-World of Economics. From the first proto-cities of Egypt in 8000 B.C. until 2005 A.D., the only true asset the human race ever enjoyed was the capacity for cities to be clean, disease-free environments. Warfare was once an overt and expensive operation that required the resources of whole societies. Now brandishing the cheap, fizzle-proof, covert weapon of pollution, woppery has served up a new doomsday, in which the gold-standard in asset revaluation is 2,3,7,8 tetrachloro-dibenzo-para-dioxin."

Litvinenko next turned to Ilya Botanin and asked if there were any updates about harnessing the powers of the 'Princess of Peace' and put them into broader

1 Russian and Soviet currency unit (Rus). Pronounced: Roo-ble

use. Ilya gave a short summary of his observations and stated that at this time he had no fresh insights or deductions that might supplement those in the written report he had already filed. There was no magic bullet to Dioxinomics.

Heavy hearted, Litvinenko adjourned the meeting and directed that the Metro cleanup committee meet in private and continue its mission, unfettered by any considerations of common sense about economics, Dioxinomics, human nature and the likelihood of future acts of woppery.

The room was left to Colonel Natrupov's use. Major Bulekov and a large body of men, including Ilya, stayed behind to confer with the colonel. Their sole purpose was to build up the largest possible avenging Bzombie force from citizens who had yet to be diagnosed as Russia's walking dead.

The Call to Purge

After a six-minute conference with General Litvinenko, Director-General Besstrashnikov ordered Dr. Chernikrov to set aside space and equipment to bank sperm in the FSB Infirmary. Within the hour, the doctor notified the Director-General everything was in place. Almost immediately, in trickled the first of many bureaucrats. Over time, like caviar and vodka at a party for anorexic Russian supermodels, from mere drips and drabs the sperm started flowing profusely. By day's end, every hot-blooded patriot heeded the call to purge at the many sperm banks the Russian Army setup across Moscow to preserve unpolluted samples of its male citizen's reproductive seed.

A Two-Rouble Whore

Because national security considerations necessitated absolute secrecy, the second Ursini urn targeting America weighed heavily on Basil's mind. To revive his spirits, he closed his eyes and focused on the ridicule the Americans had slung at President Bushkin, when Russia had raised Romanov's scheming before a secret session of the UN Security Council six months earlier. The Americans, joined by the Italians, had privately derided the president's claim as the stuff of spy novels — a juvenile gambit designed to subvert democracy in Russia. As Basil calmed himself for the meeting ahead, the very thought of America's rush-to-derision caused a perverse grin to transect his face. Feeling ready, he opened the door into the visitors lobby, marched through and extended a hearty Russian hand of welcome to his seated guest, the chrome-domed US Ambassador, Rodney Steele. After a perfunctory exchange of pleasantries, he escorted the ambassador directly to the Infirmary and the matter at hand.

Navigating his way to Derek Mitchell's room through a hallway crammed with sexually primed FSB officials and enduring the occasional poke, Ambassador Steele was treated to a side of Russia and its bureaucratic culture he had only heard rumors about. Basil opened the door to Mitchell's room and found the place filled with FSB personnel. All were naked from the waist down, rattling loose change from their piggy banks. Eager to meet Mitchell, Steele peered over Basil's shoulder, and like a two-rouble whore, got an eye full. Anticipating that the men might slacken from their half-finished civic duty, Basil fired off a command.

"Komrades, don't salute. I'm after Mr. Derek Mitchell. Anyone know where the Amerikan patient from this room is now located?"

Without missing a beat, a squat man shuffled his way into view.

"Sir, Mitchell is three doors down on the left."

"Thank you, Lieutenant." Basil closed the door and addressed Steele — "Mr. Ambassador, new room it seems. Please, follow me."

On his way down the corridor, Basil continued exuding jocularity.

"You know it's rare for an Amerikan to catch us with our pants down. Very rare. You've seen a unique side of the FSB today. Some of these men are our nation's finest commandos. Of course, it's secret. So I'll leave it to you to guess who," ending on a note of mystery.

Steele was appalled — *What sort of Infirmary is this!*

Following Basil and striving to avoid the odd buttock graze, Steele slithered past another phalanx of men standing at attention. Basil stopped and opened another door. He entered the single bedroom and found Derek blanched and much weaker than the previous day. However, with the aid of bottled oxygen, Doctor Chernikrov had revived the dying American for a brief visit.

Ignoring Ambassador Steele's objections, Basil and the doctor refused to leave the room. Fatigued by Steele's high-handed quacking, Derek, who had critical information to pass in secret, strained to make himself heard.

"Stop posturing. Come here, Ambassador."

Basil and the doctor stationed themselves by the doorway while Steele moved up close to the bed. Derek pretended to catch his breath and whispered. "Hold my hand." Steele did as asked and felt the folded paper Derek was palming him. And, Derek finished, again in whisper — "God Promises Salvation. G-P-S."

Steele understood. At heart, Mitchell was FBI and had probably overheard a lot of FSB gossip. Closing his fist to conceal the transfer, he made amends.

"I apologize for my rudeness. Please, call me Rodney, Mr. Mitchell."

Derek spoke aloud but hoarsely.

"Understand, Russia is not the enemy." And, he relaxed his head and closed his eyes to focus his energy because matters were too grave to get wrong. America needed clear-headed, operative facts.

Steele assumed the misery racking Derek's face was another message.

"Come back to the embassy, Mr. Mitchell. Our doctors are first class."

Derek opened his eyes and smiled. Steele decoded this seemingly forced gesture to mean Mitchell's next words would state an assertion in the positive. "Rodney, I'm a VIP here. My treatment's state of the art. Basil, the DVD, please."

Basil rolled a video monitor by Derek's bedside and hit [PLAY].

"Rodney, on this, you'll see proof why the Russians want me alive. Have no doubt, Russia isn't the enemy."

Derek started coughing. Shifting his stance, Steele pocketed the note.

As the footage sprung to life, Basil elaborated.

"Ambassador Steele, after watching the DVD, you can ask Mr. Mitchell any reasonable questions to clarify things."

Doctor Chernikrov threw in.

"Try to confine it to yes-no questions, Ambassador."

Derek nodded to Steele — *Simple, please.*

The DVD ran its course and provided most of the information Steele sought. But, he needed to know which disclosures were real and which were fabricated. It was obvious Mitchell had information that the Russians did not want leaked — *Why the note? And why no questions in private?*

"Mr. Mitchell, is there anything else?"

Derek took pains to smile anew. Steele noted it.

Derek pre-empted — "No, nothing. And, yes, the DVD is trustworthy."

Steele asked — "So you know who's responsible for the attack?"

Derek drew deep breath to make answer, and his face flinched from pain. Steele noted it, and Derek finally gave voice to the question.

"Yes. Several people saw him fleeing the Ring-line, including me. I assure you the right man has been captured. That's all I can say for now."

Basil smirked like a cat with cream on its whiskers as he heard Ambassador Steele make the predictable Y-Doodle demand.

"Please tell me more, Mr. Mitchell."

Derek felt exasperated being — *Interrogated* — as if facts weren't clear.

"Rodney, it's a criminal investigation. Please, confer with Novimirov."

Steele was annoyed.

"You're a US citizen, Mr. Mitchell. Who attacked you?"

Fighting back a grin, Basil interposed — "Ambassador Steele, Mr. Mitchell has informed you that he's a material witness in an ongoing FSB investigation concerning a terrorist attack that has caused massive death and destruction. There's certain information, which by law and by the terms of his assignment with us, he's not permitted to discuss with foreign governments until we say so."

Steele shot back.

"An act of terror has struck down a US citizen. That makes it his government's duty to investigate and bring the perpetrators to justice."

Basil's grin deepened. The Ambassador's caterwauling demand to unleash GI-Joe-Justice upon terrorists had come sooner than expected.

"You make an excellent point, Mr. Ambassador. Here's a manifest of US citizens. Undoubtedly, some are secret federal officials. They're being provided health care in various centers around Moscow. I dare say it's up-to-date." Basil handed a manila folder to Steele — "Please make your rounds and interview them all. No different than Mr. Mitchell, they might provide the intel your government seeks in order to mete out justice on whomever you care to finger as terrorists. I'll even organize an escort for your car to speed you on your mission."

Steele stared down at the dark-green folder to conceal his contempt for Novimirov's open-handed smarm, before making a last attempt.

"Any detail at all to help us, Mr. Mitchell?"

Derek looked Steele resolutely in the eyes.

"In my hometown, we have a saying, 'God Promises Salvation.' Act on it."

Steele suppressed a smirk of affirmation. Mitchell had made clear the note would answer much, so Steele decided to leave and report to Washington. He thanked Mitchell and General Novimirov and inquired when it might next be possible to return. Dr. Chernikrov, Derek and Basil agreed a follow up that afternoon was fine, so long as it was no later than 6:00 p.m.

On the way out, Dr. Chernikrov pulled the ambassador to one side and advised him that it was unlikely that Mitchell would be alive tomorrow. If a follow-up visit were urgent, he should return before six. After Steele learned of this, he asked Basil for a motor escort to the US Embassy.

Basil responded very cordially — "Of course, Your Excellency."

Once the diplomatic limousine was in motion, Steele scrutinized the note Mitchell had palmed him. *Pay Dirt*! The escort was the right call. Time was of the essence. He dialed Lester Coverdale's direct line to explain the rudiments of the data in his possession. Elated, Lester confirmed that Steele should anticipate a conference with the president at the embassy.

The Second Prophecy of Fatima

Having already kept the Patriarch waiting for over twenty minutes, no sooner had Basil returned to his office than an incoming call from Colonel Tiranov in Rome compounded the delay. The good news was the government of Italy had bought into the story about the abduction of Silvio Calamari. Overnight, Italy had declared the alliance between Al Guido and Al Qaeda public enemy number one. The bad news remained unchanged — zero leads on the whereabouts of the second urn. Tiranov reminded Basil that, torture or no torture, it might well be on its way to the United States. On that bleak note, the call ended.

Basil re-cradled the handset. He was outwardly calm but inwardly distressed because maintaining the covertness of espionage operations was becoming more problematic, especially in this helter-skelter hunt for the second urn. As an intelligence official savvy to the cynicism and arrogance of the US government, he realized how an 'Urn Attack on Lady Liberty' would smooth the way for all the plans Russia was drafting. But, as a father, he would never wish a Dioxinomic[1] disaster to overpower even his worst foe. Hoping a private lunch with the Patriarch might settle his nerves, he punched the intercom button.

"Elena, please show the Patriarch in. And, bring lunch as you come."

The Patriarch entered first. Basil motioned toward the empty chair by his desk — "Excuse my tardiness, Your Eminence."

The Patriarch sat and reminded Basil.

"General, please, it's Kolya."

Basil doffed his head in acknowledgement.

---

1 Portmanteau of Dioxin + (Eco)nomics. See also *Dioxinomics®* Series. www.dioxinomics.com.

"Of course. And, it's Basil, Kolya."

Once Elena had left, Basil opened.

"So, Kolya, how's your boy doing?"

"As well as can be expected. Only a miracle." The Patriarch clenched his jaw tight. When he noted the alarm on Basil's face, he resumed — "Basil, I've seen so much suffer—" He choked again in momentary pain, and when he calmed he noticed his heart pounding and he set his mind to focus on life's marvels and about how divinity walked amongst men.

"You know Basil, Miss Bogomolski's doing such extraordinary work."

Basil's face brightened at the sound of her name.

"Tell me, do you have some insight into her power, now?"

The Patriarch had much to get off his chest and started with a caution.

"Basil, God is going to come into our discussion. Not because I'm Patriarch, but because, without any earthly explanation, that's what's left — God."

Basil made conscious effort to relax his shoulders. At the presidential level, the 'Fatima angle' with its 'Princess of Peace' dividend had been bandied about for two days now. But, political blather meant little, because the true exploit could only be had from a venerable source. And, to Basil, the time seemed ripe to connect to and start tapping that very source.

"Kolya, I'm open-minded. Yes — I'm not religious. But, I'm no atheist. So, please, voice your opinions. I do trust your sense of judgement."

And, Basil artfully lowered the atmosphere of high expectation by preoccupying himself with serving their meal. While he inverted two cups on two saucers and poured out their tea, the Patriarch opened with the world's most famous Catholic prophecy about Russia.

"I'll start with the second of three prophecies the Virgin Mary made at Fatima in Portugal. Here's the story in a nutshell. On July 13, 1917, during a third visitation, the Virgin Mary spoke of Russia. She said that evil would descend upon Russia and cause other nations to go astray if the Vatican did not consecrate Russia to her immaculate heart. But, more concerned with Vatican doctrines and politics, no papacy has ever orchestrated a genuine consecration."

Basil pointed at the sugar bowl.

"*Sakhar*, Kolya?"[1]

"*Nyet*. But, milk, *pajalsta*."

As he passed the Patriarch his libation, Basil asked.

"So you think the Metro attack is ultimately a Vatican plot?"

"What! Not me. Basil, do you know something?"

Basil fronted his response with grim-face.

"Nothing indicates direct Vatican involvement, so far."

Stealing a moment to recompose himself, the Patriarch reached over and selected an anchovy sandwich. When his fingers made contact, he smirked at the irony — *Loaves and Fishes*. And, as he straightened his back, he made reply.

"Basil, the Vatican's failure to consecrate, is beside the point, because in the Second Prophecy, the Virgin Mary, made humanity a beautiful promise.

1 *Sakhar* — Sugar. *Nyet* — No. *Pajalsta* — Please (Rus).

Regardless of any action by any Pope, she would open her immaculate heart upon Russia and thus upon our world and triumph over evil in the end."

Basil scooped up a herring sandwich and rocked back in his chair.

"Kolya, I don't wish to appear callous but this quaint piece of Catholic folklore sounds like anti-Communist dogma. Why give it any credence?"

"Basil, hold that thought, but first, hear me out. The Fatima Prophecies derive from a series of visitations by the Virgin Mary. The Vatican diligently investigated these visitations and concluded that 'Our Lady of Fatima' was indeed acting as God's Emissary. But, here's the clincher. Weeks before the start of the Bolshevik Revolution, during the last visitation on October 13, 70,000 people witnessed the great 'Miracle of the Sun.' Thousands retold the same story of how the sun danced across the sky, horizon to—"

Basil interjected — "Dance of the Sun? Sounds like—"

The Patriarch squirmed in his seat and cut back.

"Do I look like a stooge for the Vatican?"

"Humble apologies, Patriarch. I'll do the eating, you do the talking."

"Basil, please, this isn't some novel about Jesus stoofing a piece of mullet and the sperm of the Holy Trinity spawns a love-child. Nor are the Fatima Prophecies ginned up tripe designed to drum up pilgrimage tourism. These prophecies started with three children. Children, Basil. The oldest, Lucia, was ten and was punished by her mother for grand-standing. Now, three youngsters from a small country like Portugal suckering 70,000 adults to congregate in a remote paddock is a miracle all in itself. But, ignore that, because this throng, many of them Marxists, atheists and communists, all looking to ridicule 'Catholic crazies,' witnessed the exact same 'Dancing Sun' miracle. Vatican fraud is impossible. *Impossible!*"

And, the Patriarch leant forward to emphasize his point.

"In fact, this miracle caused Portugal to pull back from the brink of socialist anarchy. The Fatima visitations occurred during the reign of Pope Benedict XV. And, according to the 104'th prophecy of Saint Malachy, that pope's legacy is 'Religio Depopulata.'"[1]

Basil raised his free hand — "Saint Machi? Depopulation?"

The Patriarch backtracked.

"Basil, in 1139 A.D., eighty-five years after the schism between the Orthodox church in Byzantium and the Roman Catholic church in Rome, Saint Malachy wrote down a sequence of prophecies about future popes. There are 112 of them. One for each Pope's era. The reign of 104'th pope in the sequence, Benedict XV, saw the rise of totalitarianism along with its atheistic purges and terrors. Not just Russia or Judaism, but traditional Catholic strongholds like Spain, Mexico and Germany."

"Religion Depopulated," murmured Basil.

The Patriarch nodded and ploughed on.

"Historic facts validate prophecy. Spain plunged into civil war, which ended with Generalissimo Franco ruling a fascist state until 1975. But, Spain's neighbor,

1 Religion Depopulated (Latin).

Portugal, turned back to its religious foundations, which kept its republic intact and spared it the fascist ordeals of the twentieth century."

"So what connects all this to Fatima?" Basil asked.

"History unfolds, Basil. Unfolds! After Benedict XV, came Pope Pius XI. His designation in the Malachy prophecies is 'Fides Intrepida' — 'Intrepid Faith.' This pope certified on October 13, 1930 that the Fatima Prophecies had no explanation other than the divine and he pushed back against 'Religio Depopulata.' Fail or succeed, he pushed back against fascism."

Basil let out a gruff huff — "The popes coddled Hitler."

"That's 'Pastor Angelicus,' Pope Pius XII, Basil. Not Pius XI. 'Pastor Angelicus' means Messenger Shepherd. And, while fully endorsing the prophecies of Fatima with a statue also glorifying himself, that Judas, Pius XII, sat on his 'Don't rock the boat' hands and watched the First Prophecy come to fruition. It's known to us as 'The Holocaust.' Three in four victims were slavic. ..."

And, as the Patriarch explained, Basil's mind turned over and over. He was well aware of the Vatican's never-ending game of pedophilic amnesia about the Holocaust. In his book, *Ne Jamais Désespérer*, Gerhard Riegner exposed the most glaring omission in the eleven volume Vatican recitation of supposedly 'all' Holocaust documents in its possession. In Volume Eight of the Vatican's *Actes et Documents du Saint Siege relatifs a la Seconde Geurre Mondiale*,[1] while the lengthy memorandum of March 18, 1942 sent to Rome from the papal nuncio in Berne, Switzerland, was described in summary form, the original document, which detailed on a country by country basis the measures taken by the fascists to exterminate both Slavs and blood-Jews, was and remains inexplicably absent from the Vatican archives to this day. Proof the Vatican Secretariat of State possess the original appears by way of footnote 466n in Volume Eight. And, in the conveniently 'disappeared' Swiss memorandum, so-called blood-Jews murdered included many, who, along with their children, were born-Catholic, and not merely long-standing converts to Christianity.

The betrayal of the Ministry of Saint Peter found its apogee in Nazi-occupied Holland, where the Protestant and Catholic Churches combined forces in protest. To stymie mass insurrection, Hitler's Reich offered to exclude any blood-Jew converted to Christianity predating 1941. The Protestant Churches accepted. But, consistent with its Inquisitions in Spain and subsequent purges in the 1500's, the Vatican embraced the opportunity to Blame-it-on-Hitler and rejected the compromise. As a result, the Nazis rounded up *all* Catholics of Jew-blood and transported them to Poland. And, there, as foretold in the First Prophecy of Fatima, these sheep under the ministry bestowed upon Saint Peter were slain and cremated in — '*a great sea of fire that seemed to be under the earth.*' And, their ashes — '*raised into the air by the flames that issued from within themselves together with great clouds of smoke, now falling back on every side like sparks in a huge fire, without weight or equilibrium, amid shrieks and groans of pain and despair.*'[2]

The Patriarch took a breath and sat back in his chair.

"And, the Bible informs history, too," he added.

1 Acts and Documents of the Holy See relating to the Second World War (French).
2 From the the text of the First Prophecy of Fatima — The Holocaust — come to pass.

Head erect in attention, Basil stopped chewing.

"Twelve is the number of betrayal, Basil. Like Judas Iscariot, the twelfth apostle to Christ, rather than spend thirty pieces of silver to safeguard the flock from pagan wolves, with war raging about him, Pius XII funded a propaganda film titled 'Pastor Angelicus' instead. Hitler's cinematographer, Leni Riefenstahl, would be proud to call it her own. Exalting his faith and his craven papacy, the true message this film provides is the Vatican's endorsement of how the prophecies of Saint Malachy are as puissant as those of Fatima."

Basil felt an urge to break in, but suppressed it because the Patriarch's voice hardened with indignation.

"Meanwhile, as the Messenger Shepherd, 'Pastor Angelicus,' immortalized his so-called piety in a movie about himself, a fascist Holocaust turned the Lord's sheep into ashes, just as the First Prophecy foretold. History unfolds. Portugal was spared the horrors of 'Religio Depopulata,' but not the rest of the world. And, we, in Russia, for whom the Second Prophecy commanded consecration, we endured a fascist holocaust spearheaded out of Europe as well as seven decades of Communism. All of it, godless totalitarianism."

With so much interlocking villainy, Basil felt a little dazed.

Noticing, the Patriarch sat bolt upright and waved his sandwich.

"Basil, heed the lessons history teaches if nothing else."

The FSB General grimaced at the Patriarch's veiled scold. But, also sensing a spirit of exaltation within the man, he decided to pop the burning question.

"So, as the Supreme Head of the Russian Orthodox Church, are you prepared to heed the historical." Appalled at his indelicacy, Basil shifted gears — "Patriarch, what I mean is — the Second Prophecy — are you prepared to certify that 'Our Lady of Fatima' has blessed Miss Natalia Vladimirovna Bogomolski?"

The Patriarch's chest tingled at the prospect — *Anointment.*

"Basil, the blessing from God's Emissary at Fatima has a name and two feet. Miss Bogomolski lives when she should be dead. No broken bones. Not even a bruise. And, her dreams! It's clear a holy spirit known to all believing Christians has interceded and now resides within her body. She can project some of this power to the exterior. Anything she touches is cleansed or healed. She is very meek, very worldly, outerworldly. It's hard to explain. It's … It's—"

Basil concealed a warm inner blush behind a discreet smirk.

"Kolya, I know what you mean. But, please confirm, are her powers consistent with the Fatima legend … I mean, Fatima scenario … I mean."

Basil felt flustered about how to be detached yet respectful.

The Patriarch took the matter in stride.

"Basil, don't feel ill at ease about religious 'crazy-talk.' I'm in the process of coming up to full speed with the Fatima visitations myself. I was shocked to learn yesterday that the Vatican has gone out of their way to create deliberate deceptions, especially about the Third Prophecy."

Basil rolled his eyes — *The Vatican loves inspiring disbelief.*

The Patriarch ignored it and soldiered on.

"By their own canon law, the Vatican allows all Catholics the right to debate Church doctrine and discuss any apparition of the Virgin Mary without any dispensation from a bishop. But, in the special case of Father Alonso, Fatima's long-standing chronicler, the Vatican has banned his twenty-four volume, *History of Fatima*. They continue to make sport of Father Bruner, the head of the Fatima Conference because he insists that the 20-30 line Fatima letter signed by Sister Lucia about what the Virgin told her concerning the Third Prophecy, should be made public. So far, the Vatican has only released four pages torn out of her notebook which describe in the first person what Lucia, Jacinta and Fernando saw with their eyes. Children recalling a perplexing vision and the words of the Virgin herself are two vastly different things."

Clutching a fresh, tail-wagging herring sandwich, Basil put up a hand.

"Wait, Kolya. Documents can easily be forged. The Katyn Massacre, for instance. Is there something hands-on? Someone like Natalia?"

"There used to be. But, Sister Lucia, the last direct witness, died seven months ago, in February. What's noteworthy about the Third Prophecy is the Vatican silenced her under penalty of excommunication. And, lest her mouth evidences the truth, the Vatican even forbade Sister Lucia from declaring in public that the alleged Third Prophecy disclosed by the Vatican on June 26, 2000 was an authentic document. Only the Pope and the Cardinal head of the Congregation for the Defense of the Faith may speak about it. In the face of silence dictated by excommunication, there are too many inconsistencies."

Clearing his throat of a fish gill, Basil piped in.

"Kolya, please. The whole thing sounds like a sick wop soap-opera."

"My son, don't let Vatican skullduggery make you cynical about God. The 'Miracle of the Sun' is no fraud. Thousands of witnesses. Games apply to the Third Prophecy, which is reputedly about the collapse of the Roman Catholic Church. Something long predicted in the prophecies of Saint Malachy. History stands on its own legs. Death cannot silence tru—"

The Patriarch stopped cold.

History and Death — His cousin, Teodor. Across his mind flashed the depredations of Catholic Croats against Orthodox Serbs, Christians the Vatican denigrated as 'Schismatics.' As SS Obergruppenfuhrer Heydrich himself noted at the Wannsee Conference — In fascist-occupied Yugoslavia, predating Hitler's *Final Solution*, Ante Pavelic and his Ustashe massacred over 500,000 Orthodox Christians. All had been deliberately denied the opportunity to convert to Catholicism. Not to mention the 30,000 Jews murdered. These acts of butchery were orchestrated at the Vatican during the reign of Pius XII, the Messenger Shepherd, because Franciscan friars had lead the ethnic cleansing charge in many villages across the Balkans. And, when the war drew to its close, with the Vatican and Italy firmly under the protection of the Allies rather than under the menace of fascism or the cardinalship of Vatican childmolesters, over $80 million of Ustashe loot, most in the form of gold coins, was funneled through the Institute for the Works of Religion, otherwise known as the 'Vatican Bank,' and made landfall in Argentina. Throughout the centuries, the Vatican's contempt for human life, even for the Lambs of Jesus seeking the love of God under the stewardship of the Shepherd, was well recorded in its many *for-profit* Inquisitions, and not merely confined to the reign of Supreme Pontiff, Pius XII, *Hitler's Pope.*

And, the Polish pope, John Paul II, known in prophecy as 'De Labore Solis,' which means 'From the Labour of the Sun,' as it danced from horizon to horizon all those years ago on October 13, 1917 at Fatima, had his role to play. From John Paul II, a portion of the Third Prophecy, disputed as it is, was finally revealed. So the sun's labours were not completely in vain. And, the current pope — 'Gloria Oliuae,' meaning 'Laurels from the Olive,' and thus prophesied that during his reign, he would anoint the next pope — was little different from his predecessors. All his proclamations asserted the Third Prophecy was no real secret, nothing more than a *'summons to penance and conversion.'* But, penance and conversion was satanic deception. On March 3, 1941, the One-True-Faith had denied his cousin Teodor's right of conversion. Rather it labeled him an Orthodox schismatic, and thereupon murdered and looted him like a Jew — *Teodor. My Teodor.*

Basil murmured into the Patriarch's silence.

"Patriarch, you've had a quiet insight? Miss Bogomolski?"

The Patriarch shook his head mournfully.

"A family recollection. Another Teodor. Fascist-occupied Croatia."

"Do you need a moment, Kolya?"

The Patriarch resettled himself into facing the here and now.

"No, Basil. No. Let me refocus on the Second Prophecy and Russia. Now, on several occasions before priests, Sister Lucia declared the consecration of Russia, as called for in the Second Prophecy, never took effect. She was relating the words of the Virgin Mary herself from other visitations. But, the Vatican's games of denial continued. Even unto 1978, when Pope John Paul I, known in prophecy as 'De Medietate Lunae,' meaning 'From Half Moon,' validated the ongoing deficiency and promised in a letter to a colleague to enact the required consecration. But, rather than Soviet Russia being consecrated, this pope, who was inaugurated on August 26, 1978 with the moon in half-phase, was assassinated by poison, another half lunar cycle later. From half moon to half moon, John Paul I lived, but no consecration took place, just anti-Russian sabotage."

Basil frowned. That made perfect sense. Killing off one Pope, and elevating an anti-Commie Polish pope. And, putting aside his anger that American extremists and Vatican radicals preaching how Russia was the 'Evil Empire' had polluted Ursini and incited the Romanov-Al Guido attack upon his nation, Basil addressed the pre-eminent need to fill the world with peace.

"Kolya, you affirmed earlier that God has blessed Natalia. Can I assume the Russian Orthodox Church holds that, through Natalia and the power of the Virgin Mary's immaculate heart, the Russian motherland will uproot evil?"

The Patriarch's back stiffened.

"Ye. Yes, but ... Well—"

Seeing how the elder man felt ambushed, Basil cut in.

"Patriarch, let's leave that to future historians. Right now, are there any new details about Natalia's powers? Perhaps, something related to prophecy?"

The Patriarch relaxed into the welcome shift in focus.

"Damn, how could I forget."

And, he lurched over Basil's desk, as if to whisper.

"Basil, it's premature, but she might have the power to cure the addictive nature of heroin. And, maybe, all narcotic addictions."

Basil's jaw dropped. A tiny fish-head tumbled into his lap.

"*What!*" he said.

"After doing her hospital rounds this morning, three nurses later came up to me and reported that several chronic addicts were becalmed and clear-headed. I told them to expect the Lord to work miracles and swore them to silence. I then telephoned Dr. Chernikrov, who is now handling the matter clinically, including security issues I presume."

A surreal glow swaddled Basil's whole body. Less than fourteen hours ago, he had encouraged Natalia to incorporate the suffering of the poppy-ninnies of Drughistan into herself. Basil hoped she might find personal solace as well as a softer outlet for using her powers in their nation's crusade against the global forces of woppery.

Now this — *Ask and ye shall receive* — he thought.

Nor was it a total surprise.

Most addictions are caused by brain chemistry gone awry. Projecting her unearthly feelings of love and well-being into each patient, why shouldn't the empathy radiating from Natalia's being remold the brain into the healthy organ it was designed to be. And, Basil spoke into the mood of shared elation at how blessings have names and hearts and feet.

"Kolya, I can tell you from personal knowledge, and yes, damn it, *on faith*, those addicts are on the mend. Peace is a Princess, and she walks amongst us."

Basil took breath to tamp down his excitement before resuming.

"Her dreams. Is there anything new on that front?"

"She still describes them as memories recalled from her past. She's had the same one about Golgotha, twice now. More is coming into focus. Dr. Chernikrov is of the opinion that her dreams are survivor guilt trying to resolve itself through the cathartic process of a Biblical story. I guess you know more about the opposite effect — false recollection resulting from sleep deprivation?"

Basil's face attempted an exculpatory façade.

"Yes. I'm sorry to say. It's an unpleasant aspect of my work. So, you're thinking its less of a dream and more a search for reconciliation?"

"Basil, she says that she reads and speaks Hebrew, Latin and ancient Greek. At least, in her dream-state. She says it's second nature to her and also claims to hear no Russian. Furthermore, she cannot command her dream characters to vanish. In short, she asserts everything is direct recollection from her own personal knowledge. Recollections consistent with what the Virgin Mary herself would have observed nearly two thousand years ago."

Basil felt unsure what to ask, but he had to keep the Patriarch talking.

"Please tell me what she's dreaming — ah, recalling about the past?"

The Patriarch sensed the barriers to believing that Basil would face, and so he replied in a measured tone.

"She's at Golgotha. Just outside the walls of ancient Jerusalem. It's the day before Passover, the first week of April, 30 A.D. Surrounded by friends, she's part of a sea of people. They're all watching the crucifixion of a person she calls her firstborn son, Jesus of Nazareth. She tried to approach the Lord's crucifix. But, when Roman legionaries menaced her, a man came to her aid. She didn't see his face, but she's convinced that man is you."

Basil laughed then stopped in embarrassment.

"Please, my humble apologies. I see what Dr. Chernikrov means. Sounds like Natalia's experiencing cathartic dreaming. Let me guess, I spoke Latin."

The Patriarch smiled — Basil's reaction was not unexpected.

"My son, don't feel awkward. It's already in the scriptures. Miss Bogomolski could be dreaming up a phantasy based on her reading of the Bible or biblical novels. But, here's the clincher. She lives and she heals. That's reality. She has these dreams. That's reality. If she were an ordinary person with such dreams, we might say she is having delusions of grandeur. But, every minute of the day, she does what science cannot explain. That's reality."

Basil apologized once again for his prior tone of skepticism. And, during the rest of their meal, the Patriarch took the opportunity to inform Basil about the life of Jesus and his followers, at least as far as 'The Life of the Lord' was selectively abridged in the Church's official records and dogma. By meal's end, they agreed the best policy was to keep Miss Bogomolski in the dark about the Fatima Prophecies because if prophecy had any truth in their nation's future, such ought come from her spontaneously.

The Most Exquisite Things

In the confines of the Lubyanka cafeteria, Ilya and Olga found time for a late lunch together. Olga pressed him to not hold back about the situation.

"Ilya, last night, you were so blasé. But, the horn-dogs jamming the Infirmary today say otherwise."

Ilya felt snookered. He'd underplayed matters to maintain calm.

"Olga, I knew the facts weren't the best. But, last ni—" he stopped and re-focused on the real point — "We can't be together tonight. I'll need to bank what sperm I have so only uncontaminated samples get stored."

"Of course. You're thinking that we—" She hesitated, now the how-to-relate dilemma was hers. In a hushed tone, she pressed on — "Ilya, I have a gut feeling nothing was wasted. Only time will tell."

Ilya dropped his knife in shock.

"You might have mentioned that before—"

Olga interjected to allay any hint of deceptiveness.

"Ilya, I don't want you to feel ambushed. Today, you probably consider me a ravishing beauty but in a few months, I hope you'll know the whole me better."

Ilya mellowed — "Excuse my outburst. It's not like that. I enjoy you immensely. Fabulous as it is, your beauty I overlook. But, my mind is troubled. To me the inner person is," he paused in quandary, "Olga, beauty is icing—"

Flustered, he stopped again. He needed to return to the mood of that rarified hour when she had wiped his bleeding nose. He was trying to frame this delicately, especially when only hours before during the Bzombie and Dioxinomics presentations he had censured himself for his own hypocrisy. Her beauty was ravishing, but that was *not* what made him feel close to her. Yet *she* might have other opinions about her own sense of allure. And, he worried that he might offend the very special something in her life that she treasured above all else.

For Olga, Ilya's lengthy pause caused panic to set in.

"What's troubling you, *Daragoi*?" she whispered.

Ilya looked into himself for resoluteness and then into her beckoning eyes. If they were ever to be an item, he owed her the un-annealed truth.

"Olga, I once had many ambitions. But, this vile attack on our people means my talents will be directed at cleaning up this wop mess, probably for decades. This morning, I discover woppery may forever sabotage my reproductive health. I want a serious woman, Olga. I just abhor the Princess type. I don't want to appear rude, but that is the only thing about your character that worries me. Olga, you're an extraordinary beauty. … I mean … Please, more than any other woman, you need to find someone truly decent?"

That term 'Princess' made Olga balk cold. Then a smile transected the full width of her heart. Ilya's candor was so refreshing. The man was a pure confidant, a genuine soul, no matter what. And, how perfectly he had comprehended her personal dilemma — The most beautiful needs the most decent. For, in her world, decency was hard to come by. And, she trilled without reservation.

"I have Ilya. He's sitting across the table from me."

But, Ilya appeared unmoved.

She quickly shifted her tone and elaborated.

"I say this with absolute sincerity. I could not imagine myself being happy with anyone but you, *Daragoi*. And, please, my true personality is nothing like a Princess. I detest that nonsense. If you knew about," she parked her tongue — that was secret. But, the pause gave her space to recompose herself — "Ilya, I hope beyond hope that we can find favour with each other. I want deep and abiding love."

Ilya had closed his eyes.

To her, he seemed unaffected by the sincerity in her voice.

Olga responded in desperation.

"Ilya, I pray about you. Pray! I can't imagine life without you."

She stopped — What more was there to say.

Now, the pulse-thump behind the eardrums wait.

Halfway through, Ilya had closed his eyes to take in her words, such was their humble-hearted allure. *How is it that women can say the most exquisite things?* he thought. But, now, eyes open, Ilya's ears end-stopped a smile that stretched from lobe to lobe. He reached over and blanketed his hand over hers.

"*Maya Daragaya*, such sentiments. I wish exactly the same. *Exactly*. I'll always endeavor to be the man of your dreams as long as you want a noble soul throughout your life. I want to do spectacular things in my profession. I don't wish to be preoccupied with fame or wealth or have a wife who is."

Olga's eyes blazed wet and wondrous mad.

He saw her joy. And, overwhelmed by a feeling of amazement, Ilya lifted her trembling hand and placed it against his forehead.

"Feel that sweet lady?" He paused to commit to memory her look of bewilderment — "My head feels like a bird that has flown into a plate glass window. That's how knocked out I am."

His crazy fabulous words blew her apart — *A genuine soul no matter what!* And, she could only whisper her determination to prove herself.

"Sweet, sweet Ilya, you'll discover the real me, once I shed my Moscow habits. Then I think that you will have no choice." She smirked, knowing he was hers — *His face betrayed all* — "but to adore me," she jostled mischievously, "utt-dderly."

Ilya laughed in relief, peered deep into her eyes and strummed her crimson, left cheek with the tips of his fingers.

"Olga, Olga, Olga. Keep going like that and the Infirmary maids will have to break out milk buckets to store my cream."

And, they descended into another light-hearted, frisky meal together.

The Battle Hymn of the Republic

In Washington, DC, the clock in the White House Situation Room chimed — 10:00 a.m. — 6:00 p.m. in Moscow. The CIA had sifted through the secret note and DVD Ambassador Steele had been handed. And, following up with supplemental investigations, the agency felt ready to disclose its findings and best guesses. After Vice-President Norman Weissbrot certified he had taken the role call, Director of National Intelligence, Lester Coverdale, pointed a laser stylus at a big-screen monitor and leaped into action.

"What you're viewing, Madam President, are masses of Russia's latest tanks and armored vehicles. Using the coordinates obtained from Ambassador Steele, our satellites found them on the Plains of Karaton. It's the Russian's Smertimolat series being put through coordinated attack exercises 130 kilometers inside their border with Kazakhstan. As you can see, their SM-21 and SM-23 units are very fast and very maneuver—"

Pointing with her nails — Skyblue — President Mary-Ann Carter broke in.

"They're the boxiest and ugliest things I've ever seen. Those Tatar engineers need to come to Detroit and learn—"

To deflect attention from her childhood friend's ongoing weirdness, NSC Director Ginger Arnold interjected with a question she hoped would accentuate the good news that led to this breakthrough.

"Ambassador Steele, we have Russian operatives defecting at last?"

Appearing on a desktop monitor, Steele sprang to life.

"No, Ms. Arnold. The coordinates were secretly slipped to me in a note from an American FBI agent on assignment in Russia. He's gravely ill and remains in the FSB Lubyanka Infirmary. That's how—"

Carter's outburst came swiftly.

"What! First, Bushkunt pillages the Barbies in Mattel's Moscow warehouse, followed by Disney, and now he's captured our operative?"

Steele was already chaffing because he had been instructed to not see Mitchell again until this meeting finalized a plan of action. In essence, postponing a follow-up visit until the next day, and so, probably never. But, now, rather than addressing the menace posed to national security, he felt annoyed at facing a hen-pecking because of two corporate grievances.

"Madam President, I will be speaking to the Russians about the problem with Disney and Mattel. I'm not ignoring your friends, Madam—"

The audio feed died, but Steele's mouth remained moving.

Deducing 'Operation Barbie' was a distraction Russia's FSB mongrels had unleashed to complicate things in Washington, Lester re-asserted control.

"Madam President, please calm. We have an FBI agent named Derek Mitchell. He's not captured. After locating him, Ambassador Steele went to see him to find out what he might know under the table. Mitchell was at Metro Komsomolskaya when the whole incident took place. And, he's testified under oath to several things. All recorded on DVD." And Lester pointed the laser stylus at another monitor displaying Mitchell's diseased face, but which otherwise wasn't running — "Now, while the testimony he gives makes perfect sense and is believable, we have no idea if the information provided is credible. I prepared a summary of the salient portions of his videotaped statements."

Carter shifted in her seat twice until her buttocks were splayed just so, primed to deal with the expected onslaught of bureaucratic obfuscation.

"Why, Lester, should I consider things you say we shouldn't trust?"

"Excellent point, Madam President. I only extracted what we can corroborate independently. Further, by providing us with coordinates, and this drug deal gone wrong, Mitchell's demonstrating he's working on our side and isn't necessarily some patsy slowly dying under the clutches of the FSB."

The situation reeked of convenience, so Ginger waded in.

"Lester, Mitchell's at the Lubyanka. If the DVD could be false, what makes you think the note isn't? And these tank movements, why couldn't they be staged — a freak load of faked-up 'transparency'?"

Lester's gut churned — *More bitch face!*

"First, MizzzArnold, the note contains the handwriting of two authors. The coordinates are written by a Russian and are not consistent with Mitchell's. The seven and zero digits are obvious give-a-ways. Mitchell did write a small explanation, it reads: 'From patient, GRU General Kromenko.' And on the flip side, there's a separate word, 'Dioxinomics.'[1] We're still chasing that clue down. But, let's focus on what we call hard intel. Assume President Bushkin hand wrote and gave us this. He's saying 'Look here.'"

"Booha!" Lester thumped the table — "There are several brigades of Russia's most modern armored units doing offensive warfare exercises along their border with Kazakhstan."

Carter seized upon what she considered blatantly obvious.

"So Bushkunt's quit his jolly whining about how it's America's job to catch his damned dope smugglers and is finally policing his borders — right?"

Ginger Arnold threw her friend a sympathetic glance.

"That might be a side benefit, Madam President. But, he wouldn't use Russia's best armored divisions to chase down smugglers. Lester, what makes you think that this isn't a pretense to throw us off his real plans?"

"Based on a vehicle count, we estimate we're watching 80% to 90% of their nation's Smertimolat forces. Obviously, their most modern offensive forces are not marshaled along the Ukrainian or Georgian borders. That's what this note and our eyes are telling us. As I said, assume Bushkin gave us this note, we're being told where their military intends to attack. And, Mitchell's DVD statements corroborate. The Russians are going to unload on Afghanistan."

Lester's bombshell hammered the room to silence. Unexpectedly, the dullness that pervaded Carter's mind lifted and sheer panic vented.

"We're in Afghanistan. This. … This can't be happening!"

Ginger didn't like where this might be headed.

"Lester, what makes you think Bushkin isn't targeting Kazakhstan, Uzbekistan, Turkmenistan, Tajikistan or Kyrgyzstan as the culprit or a scapegoat, perhaps?"

Lester smirked like a cat toying with a lamed bird.

"Another excellent point. I suspect he is."

And, Lester twiddled with the remote and aimed the laser at the big-screen.

"Bordering the Caspian Sea, the whole western half of Kazakhstan, Uzbekistan and Turkmenistan is loaded with Soviet-era oil and gas fields." Lester hit a button, and a map of Europe and Central Asia dotted with wells and refineries appeared. All interconnected by a network of red lines — "These republics rely on Russian pipelines to export their product into Europe and China. Now that we've done the heavy lifting to pacify jihadi elements in Afghanistan, Bushkin figures he can take back the region's enormous Soviet-era oil and gas resources without a massive Muslim uprising. To back up his gambit, don't be shocked when Bushkin lifts the stage curtains on new millennium reality and fingers Al Qaeda for sabotaging the Metro."

Like a whack on the chops, Carter smarted at the mention of Al Qaeda and more than ever she remained besotted with only the worst about people — "Is Bushkunt going to invade Afghanistan? Just a simple *Yes* or a simple *no*, if you please — *pa'leez*, Lester?"

---

1 Portmanteau of Dioxin + (Eco)nomics. See also *Dioxinomics*® Series. www.dioxinomics.com.

The president's bluntness hammered the room into silence. There was nothing simple about this. The ex-Admiral in Vice-President Norman Weissbrot believed that if it was anybody's duty to exude confidence into this frail woman's life, surely that duty fell upon the Office of Vice-President.

"Permission to sound-off, Madam President."

Tired of Lester's shrilling, Carter nodded into Weissbrot's squared-jaw.

He acknowledged her stormy affirmation and seized the helm.

"Simple only applies to suicide, Madam President. I'd like your permission to fly to Moscow. Today, if possible, ma'am. I know Bushkin, personally — face-to-face." He stopped to allow the cut of his confidence to still Carter's anxieties before resuming — "He's your typical Boris Bolshevik, ma'am. The Russians have a long-running grievance about being inundated with drugs coming from a country under our complete military domination. We've pretended not to notice opium poppy production that has grown from seventy-four US-verified acres to over half a million acres. Nor have we intercepted the convoys that transport refined opium across Afghanistan and then over its borders."

Confirmed only with Lester Coverdale and Norman Weissbrot's endorsements before a dickering Senate five weeks ago, Secretary of Defense Miles Glorioso, the third secretary-designate President Carter had nominated, figured Weissbrot was targeting him, and smartly chipped in.

"Norman, you know I'm working to derail this obscenity."

Weissbrot batted his hands downwards. A call to be still.

"Miles, I'm not criticizing you. The Taliban government complied with UN Security Council Resolution 1333[1] and smashed opium production to seventy-four acres. That's the 9/11 *status quo ante.*[2] What did we do? The exact opposite. We violated Resolution 1333. All up, I'm saying Russia doesn't view anti-drug policy as something that comes and goes at the whim of every American administration. Our last president's NSC Director, an egghead in Russian Studies from Yale, ignored the Al Qaeda attack in Yemen on October 12, 2000. And, in regard to Russia's Chechen Muslim insurrection, she wasted eight months scolding President Bushkin for violating the Geneva Conventions. After 9/11, she authorized torture and shouted down or sacked anyone who mentioned the narco-terror issue to President Potusson."

"And I'll fire anyone who tries to stovepipe me," Carter snipped.

He'd got the opening he'd sought — Weissbrot locked Carter in his gaze.

"Here-here, Madam President. As administration monitor, it's my job to make sure no one treats you like an idiot. Ma'am, look at the situation like any normal Russian citizen. Afghanistan went from a country under Taliban control where drugs were hammered to non-existence and food was abundant, to American control, where zero-food agriculture is pervasive, children live on the brink of starvation and drugs are mass-produced. Those Russians, who believe in true-hearted democracy, resent this because the Afghan drug trade amounts to chemical warfare, enabled by child slavery enforced through systematic starvation."

1 UN Sec. Council Resolution of December 19, 2000 mandating the eradication of opium plantations.
2 Status Prior to 'Invasion' (Latin).

Furtive tears rimmed President Carter's under-eyes.

"Child starvation? Slavery? Oprah … Oprah Spinfrey never told me …."

And, Carter drifted into silence and shot the vice-president the perplexed look of one being made a fool. Weissbrot quietly cursed at his gaff and, engaging Oprah-speak, he switched gears to a matter on the liberal agenda.

"Embrace your sadness, Madam President. Let it empower you. And, never forget heroin addicts spread HIV/AIDS to others. Hard-nosed, not-my-kid neocons and ideologues might call AIDS and the drug-induced death of addicts, especially addicts in Russia, 'red, white and blue' natural selection befitting Commie atheists, but Russia has its own ideologues with their own opinions about what 'red, white and fuck-you' chemical and biological warfare looks like."

Secretary of State Jeffrey Chandler chimed in.

"So, Norman, you're thinking the Russians are going to pull a sneak attack like we did on Panama when Noriega cut the strings from the CIA. And, we conveniently decided he had facilitated drug smuggling — right?"

Weissbrot, Lester and Ginger rolled their eyes at Chandler's bluntness. President Carter picked right up on it.

"Ahem. Excuse me Jeff, but from what I see, it's no sneak attack."

Then her mood brightened.

"The intel Mitchell's provided is paying off. He seems very credible to me."

She nodded in Weissbrot's direction with pride.

"Yes, indeed. Very credible."

Weissbrot wasted no time speaking into her clarity.

"High Five, Madam President. Mitchell's DVD has confirmed my worst fears. They don't show it, but the Russians are furious. They've increased drug patrols. Used dogs, extensively. And, in exchange for diamonds, they're trying to buy up the drugs before they get to the public. And, last of all, whether we believe it or not, Mitchell, the intermediate in all this lunacy, corroborates Bushkin's public statement that three kilograms of dioxin was all it took."

Carter flashed Weissbrot a quizzed look.

"Madam President, three kilo's amounts to 6.6 pounds. Think of Pillsbury doing a 'Martha's Christmas' promotion. Five pound bag of flour with 33% freebie. Now, Madam President, was that dioxin meant for release in Moscow? Hardly! I'd say the United States was the intended targ—"

A sharp chirp distracted everyone.

Weissbrot looked at the source.

"Madam President, the audio feed from Moscow is live again. Perhaps, Ambassador Steele can elaborate? Mr. Ambassador?"

"Madam President, I've been listening. Because of their investigations, the Russians refuse to discuss the dioxin side of the matter beyond what's public. Mitchell told me he knows more but refused to divulge. I don't get the feeling his silence was coerced. More like a law enforcement offic—"

With Panama still fresh in her mind, Carter snapped.

"Did you remind Mr. Mitchell that US citizens have been attacked and, no different than Article 61 in the Cossack Constitution, the US President also has a unilateral right of global sneak attack against any foe that harms our citizens or otherwise allege might do harm?"

Steele stiffened at her harsh rebuke.

"I certainly did, Madam President. But, Mitchell refused—"

Carter slammed her fist on the table.

"Mitchell's just Bushkunt's tampon!"

Weissbrot and Lester both looked at Ginger for guidance. Unlike her inner cabinet, Steele was not aware of the fractious situation in the White House, and his matter-of-fact outlook was inadvertently making things more unmanageable. While Lester whispered to an aide to have the video connection with the embassy severed for good, Ginger reconnected with her good friend.

"Madam President, let's agree without argument that the United States doesn't accept Russia's right to invade Afghanistan. You don't want Bushkin invading Afghanistan. Do you understand me, Mary-Ann?"

Carter looked bemused — "Did I misspeak?"

And, Ginger shoe-stopped the opening.

"It's not your fault, Madam President. I think the Ambassador's gaff gave you a false impression. Look. Our connection to the embassy has faded."

While Carter looked over at the monitor, Ginger resumed — "Madam President, Lester needs to answer this pivotal question — Why shouldn't the United States believe the Moscow Metro attack wasn't staged in order to create a pretense of right for the Russians to retaliate against whomever they finger?"

Carter loved it. A Tim Delancy[1] novel came to mind about how the KGB blew up the Russian parliament as a prelude to invading Europe.

"Sock-it-to-me, Ginger! Well, red-behind-the-ears Coverdale, stop fabricating excuses for Bushkuntosaurus Rex and rebut that one."

Becoming more habituated to her taunts, Lester calmly replied.

"Good call, Madam President. In our last meeting, we discussed self-sabotage as a possibility. But, we've firmed up the numbers and damage reports, it's very unlikely. This is a massive disaster to the people and the economy of Russia. They'd have never targeted their capital nor the Metro for such devastation. I mean, *Never*. They'd have faked a dioxin capture or orchestrated a minor but confinable incident in a small town that would be easier to decontaminate. The Moscow Metro system is the best place to kill its most educated citizens and the worst place to decontaminate. The absolute best and worst."

A contemplative lull took hold, and Chandler spoke into it.

"Madam President, sorry to report the connection's blacked out. Moscow's often had tech issues. But, no worries. I was on the horn with Ambassador Steele til I arrived here. I'm sure I can fill in the blanks if there are any."

Carter furrowed her brow — *Rooskie sabotage, no doubt!*

Relieved, Ginger sought to get the matter back on track.

"Madam President, I think Norman's plan to go eyeball to eyeball with Bushkin needs to be heard out. Mary-Ann?"

1 One of the owner-brothers of The Delancy Group, a multi-billion dollar US defense company. Tom's domain is the creation of literature validating the appropriateness of the vast sums America spends on 'securing the planet.'

Carter took in a prolonged yoga breath and relaxed — *Bushkunt, of course.* "Norman. Please, proceed."

"Thanks for your vote of confidence, Madam President. Bushkin is the key to resolving this impasse. As I was saying, the Russian people are furious that drugs are poisoning their society. When the reasons for the dioxin attack become public, their citizens will demand Bushkin step-up to the plate like the strong leaders Russians admire. Someone, like Potusson, our last president. Our satellite intel north of the Kazakhstan border confirms Bushkin is wedded to the agenda for action any red-blooded democracy demands."

Weissbrot cleared his throat and took a sip of A&W.[1] There remained a few loose ends that he wanted to cover before going out on a limb.

"Jeff, nothing controverts Mitchell's bone fides — correct?"

"Steele told me that all-in-all Mitchell's a straight shooter."

Weissbrot rested back in his chair so his hands were free to emote.

"Consider the reaction in Russia if the Mitchell DVD is made public at some future date. From their public's perspective, Mitchell, an American FBI agent, has testified ..." And Weissbrot meticulously laid out only those facts of Mitchell's testimony which the CIA was able to corroborate. He had almost finished when President Carter interjected.

"So, the upshot of all this is that the United States caused this disaster by facilitating the flooding of Russia with drugs and thereby turning Moscow into a trading post for both drugs and drug proceeds like diamonds and dioxin."

Weissbrot smiled — *At last, she's getting the picture* — and continued.

"Madam President, every Russian citizen knows America has a zero-tolerance drug policy. Hence, America and NATO have deliberately targeted Russia's youth with drugs. Operative phrase — *deliberately targeted.*"

The room was stunned.

All contemplated the obvious.

Lester stepped in to unload the next bomb.

"Furthermore, Madam President, we have no loop-hole. In the Russian public's warped mind, America is not a banana republic like Panama."

President Carter had been growing to detest the Director of National Intelligence. Day after day, Lester-the-Fester Coverdale habitually pestered her with his humorless outlook on world affairs. And, worse, he seemed to characterize Russia and China as countries the United States was impotent to bring to heel at Lady Liberty's democratic doggy-dish. Reeling from two perceived affronts, Carter again lost focus and became all snark-necked.

"Coverdale, you bet we aren't a banana republic! That cunt-fucking Cossack is juicing that treasonous pussy, Mitchell, for propaganda."

Chandler, no fan of Lester Coverdale, came to his defense.

"Madam President, be it roses, tulips or poppies, how do you hide half a million acres of open farmland producing flowers. The Russians have begged for peaceable access to Afghanistan to implement 'Operation Rambo'[2] and torch all poppy fields and end child slavery. We talk a good game about narco-terrorism

---

1 A famous American carbonated form of root beer. An American version of *kvas.*
2 Operation President Bushkin proposed in 2002 to eradicate Afghan opium plantations. US and NATO have repeatedly vetoed any such operation proceeding.

but in action we've done nothing. And, with Russia, we've stiffed them on Rambo, time after time. We have no excuse."

Worried how this scenario was only generating more paranoia in Carter's imagination, Ginger decided it best to get the worst case out on the table so it could be knocked down, and her friend might rest easy.

"So, the consensus is Russia plans to invade Afghanistan. And, if we don't accommodate their military like we accommodate drug lords, then it'll become a shooting war between us and Russia on the fields of Afghanistan."

Carter chopped in, more bellicose than Ginger had anticipated.

"*Screw that.* I'll eat the dried pickings out of my handkerchief first. We'll fight them on the beaches! We'll fight them on the poppy fields! I'm gonna shove *The Battle Hymn of the Republic* down Bushkunt's throat!"

Weissbrot and Lester stared at the NSC Director.

Suppressing her true feelings, Ginger soothed her friend.

"Mary-Ann, of course, we will. This isn't a press conference. You don't have to coddle neo-con rednecks. Let's hear what Norman suggests."

Once calm returned, Weissbrot walked the president through the larger issue step by step because the gravity of the situation demanded a clear-headed response. After giving the president a brief recap of the operative facts, he focused on public relations reality whenever a national security issue turns upon alien invaders who do as they damn well please.

"Madam President, here's our conundrum. Let's say the Russian military occupied Cuba, changed its government by force and green-lighted the production of cocaine on half a million acres. Next, the drug is smuggled into New York. There, oodles of profits are to be made. Then, some American or Canadian scientist wants his slice of the pie and sells the drug smugglers a weapon of mass destruction. But, for reasons unknown, it detonates in New York before the intended exchange takes place. What would our public's reaction be towards Cuba and Russia's complete military domination of Cuba?"

Carter remained mute.

Weissbrot took it as a sign of hope and followed through.

"Any Bolshevik bear-shit about 'Blame it on Fidel' would be an insult to our intelligence. JFK Sixpack, the average armchair patriot, would have no qualms about signing-up for war against Russian facilitated narco-terrorism."

Weissbrot watched Carter's face turn red as he kept plugging.

"Potusson's flower-power attitude to world peace and his refusal to spray poppy fields with herbicides is exploding back from Moscow. We're in a bind that's going to sink our administration. Democracy dictates we cannot permit Bushkin to invade. It also dictates that we cannot obstruct him from doing so."

Carter went from apoplectic to insane.

"Enough with the flatulence. Detail our strengths. Tell me how my troops are going to eat, piss and poop Bolsheviks — breakfast, lunch and dinner."

Ginger winced.

Lester flashed the faintest — *This president won't last* — smile.

Weissbrot remained unmoved.

"Madam President, this is the best we can expect to negotiate."

At that word — Negotiate —No one saw Carter's gut clench, but the fart was audible. Ginger stepped in to blunt any presidential interjection.

"Mary-Ann, please. Bushkin is the key. *Bushkin.*"

Carter saw nothing but spittle being served. She placed both her hands against the lip of the table and flung herself back into her chair.

Weissbrot followed up Ginger's baby-talk.

"Bushkin will release the 'Mitchell DVD.' Madam President? Ma'am?"

He remained quiet until she made grudging eye-contact.

"And, expect Bushkin to dish up other Mitchell testimony as well. All told, Bushkin's mission is to rally the Russian motherland to wage war on Afghanistan. America will divide between those who sympathize with the Russians and those who don't. Bushkin's forces will sweep across Kazakhstan, Uzbekistan, Tajikistan and Turkmenistan. They'll welcome resistance from those countries. As do we, I might add."

Weissbrot noticed how Carter was suddenly all ears.

"I'll cut to the chase, Mary-Ann. Our only option is to acquiesce to Russia's occupation of these onetime tsarist lands. However, even Bushkin knows a face-saving line must be drawn somewhere, somehow. Our administration cannot permit Russia to cross into Afghanistan. To save our bacon, we must start a major drug eradication program. This requires a surge of fresh troops."

Ginger's disgust kicked in.

"A surge! What of the forces already in place?"

Glancing over at the NSC Director, Weissbrot elaborated.

"Ginger, our veteran forces must blockade the Afghan border. No weak points, period. If we don't show man-for-man strength, the Russian people will demand to know why their troops sat on the border twiddling the hair on their testicles. Democracy compels Bushkin to prove he's no wimp. All sides must show massive strength. Operative word — *Massive.* Border duties might also fall on our surge troops, but otherwise, we need them to maintain local control, to prop up our man in Kabul and to eradicate all poppy plantations."

"So your plan is to buy-off Bushkin with oil territories so that he puts up a hard-nosed game face but no real invasion," Ginger chipped.

"But only if we're there in overwhelming force."

President Carter was rubbing her forehead furiously.

Weissbrot noted it, ignored it and pushed on.

"After US and NATO forces face down Russia's, Bushkin can play the role of 'Mr. Democracy' and take a prize he can really use — Kazakhstan, Uzbekistan, Tajikistan and Turkmenistan. Bushkin's pragmatic. Oil and gas logic says he'll confine his conquest to the Caspian Sea region. He might well decide to re-integrate all those republics back into Russia and liberate their citizens from the oppression of dynastic Islamic governance. Basically, bestow upon them the blessings of democracy, just as we're doing in Iraq and Afghanistan. Or, in the alternative, Bushkin might 'Do an Israel' and keep his conquered regions in legal limbo by playing 'Gotcha' games from one decade to the next."

Attorney General, David Hicks, saw the obvious hiccup.

"Norman, I can't see Russia embracing a huge influx of Muslims."

Secretary of State Chandler chimed in.

"David, right now, one in six Russians are Muslim. Only 35% of them favor democracy. 65% like 'Men-of-Iron' leaders, such as Bushkin. It's tenable. And, what Norman suggests has a sunny-side. It's called 'Soviet Satan.' Muslims go gonzo on Russia instead of us, for a change."

Weissbrot lent his affirmation and added.

"Cabinet, what I've outlined is classic superpower 'Fair-play Balanced with Hypocrisy.' No surprises, here. Also, under the US-Russia Anti-Terrorism Act,[1] Bushkin can indict these peewee Muslim countries as co-conspirators, facilitators and abettors of the Afghan drug trade. Thus, the Moscow dioxin attack falls on them fair and square. So, all in all, we're off the hook."

Hicks was stupefied. Rebuttal was essential.

"Norman, the region will become a Central-Asian Iron Curtain. Bushkin's Russia will be raking in revenues like an oil baron while Americans will be asking if we'll ever be removing our troops from Afghanistan. Furthermore, every Muslim on the planet will go berserk at the notion that we're going to be parked in Afghanistan for decades and did nothing to prevent Russia from over-running the Muslim states of the former USSR. In short, Muslims will scream bloody murder at the so-called Jewnited States across the globe."

Fuming, President Carter broke off her rubbing.

"So, Bushkunt plans to poop some 'Coalition of the Cossacks' electability crap down my pie-hole every which way from Shitday."

Chandler leaned over and addressed the president face to face.

"Mary-Ann, please look at the big picture. The Russians took a massive hit that was actually meant for America. *For America*, Mary-Ann."

Another long silence prevailed until Lester vented his exasperation at having to baby-talk a president over things that were entirely irrelevant.

"Whether Moscow was an accident or not makes no damn difference. Once the dioxin-for-diamond exchange took place, the Afghan drug lords intended to deploy this vile weapon of terror against the United States. That's how Bushkin can waterboard it, and the civilized world of zomboids will gulp down the slogan-spiked bear-jizz without a gasp of protest. Dioxin is cheap. Ragheads, stupid. America, the target. Done deal — Boom-Fucker-Boooom!"

And, Lester slammed his closed fist down on the table. Lester's outburst triggered a shift in the National Security Director's thoughts — *Dioxin is cheap.*

"Lester, just how cheap is cheap?" Ginger asked.

"A price of $200 per kilogram is entirely feasible for even kilo quantities. Remember, it's a pollutant, not a pharmaceutical. Purity is optional. One kilo of pharma or two kilos of amateur — same difference. Both insanely destructive."

1 After a terrorist nuclear attack on Denver, Colorado, as part of the 'Superpower Doctrine,' the United States and Russia recognized each nation had a unilateral sovereign right to hunt down and prosecute any person or entity engaging, planning, or aiding terrorism, codified into each nation's legal code as the US-Russia Anti-Terrorism Act.

You could smell the piss in the pants. Such was the silence.

Dismayed by this new distraction, Weissbrot spoke to endcap it.

"Let's not waste time on this. We're already seeing the collapse of financial speculation in Russia. No need for stress-tests to know how pollution is the cheap and easy way to eviscerate speculative pricing, starting with subways."

Treasury Secretary Earl Butz, a crusty, wire-rimmed bespectacled Vermonter with the bald pate of a Roman Emperor and best known by his nickname 'Groundhawg' for his uncanny sense about the future, was already disheartened by the monetary implications. And, much disquieted by that taunt — *Dioxinomics*[1] — on the flip side of Mitchell's note, which intimated the Russians had some sleazy game in play which he suspected sought to target the free market liberty of financially leveraged speculation, the treasurer chipped in.

"I'm meeting with Federal Reserve Chairman Arthur Frankenstein this afternoon. We're in the process of assessing the Moscow fallout to our economy. What we don't need is panic. We're hoping the public will remain ignorant until our major banks have offloaded most of their credit default swaps, options and mortgage exposure onto unsuspecting regional banks and mid-level investors, such as hedge and pension funds. Rest assured, the Big-10 banks have the power to do this because they can yank loans and put the screws to the small fish in our free market system. That's 'Fair-play Balanced with Hypocrisy' in economic action. We figure it's the only way to avoid a wholesale systemic collapse when people in major cities abandon their overpriced mortgages, once the reality of Moscow's toxic asset wipe-out is plain for all to see."

Realizing how the back and forth of this meeting could go on for a week, Weissbrot interjected to set the agenda for action — "Madam President, you now understand why I need to meet with President Bushkin post-haste. I've an excellent command of the situation. Defusing tensions is essential."

The president remained impassive.

To rouse her friend to action, Ginger endorsed the vice-president's plan.

"Madam President, can you see any reason for Norman not to fly to Moscow and begin working his magic on Bushkin? Mary-Ann?"

With everything out of her control, Carter murmured.

"Norman, do your best, sir."

Vice-President Weissbrot rose and said his good-byes. While shaking Lester's hand, he scratched the left side of his nose. The sign — 'Operation Mad Cow' would soon be wrapped up. Since the revelations of this meeting had caused more cabinet officers to become rattled, both men knew *Mad Cow* finality could not come soon enough. In turn, Lester promised him that Ginger and he would do everything to keep the president on a leash.

Before the next hour struck, Marine-One, a turbo-charged Sikorsky VH-3D Sea King, had ferried Weissbrot from the lawns of the White House to Andrews AFB, where he boarded a fueled-up Air Force One. By the time his plane touched down at Sheremetyevo the next morning, he anticipated Ambassador Steele would have lined up at least one meeting with President Fyedor Sergeivich Bushkin.

---

1 Portmanteau of Dioxin + (Eco)nomics. See also *Dioxinomics*® Series. www.dioxinomics.com.

Our Absolute Determination

Natalia's afternoon decontaminating at Moscow Central Hospital was cut short at 5:00 p.m. She returned to the Lubyanka complex to assist Olga and Dr. Soskrova in a fresh round of vampire intercessions on seven Afghan, Uzbek, Turkmen and Tajik terrorists, recently detained and rendered to Moscow. The doctor and her two vampires followed a script comparable to the Ursini intercession except they recited Qur'anic doctrines and invoked the wrath of Allah. Exiting the final session in a sour mood, Natalia was pleased to encounter Basil. He greeted them, palms wide open.

"Natalia and Olga, top job. In nine hours, our crew of imams will minister to our novitiates' need for contrition. May God help us harvest the peace-preserving intelligence these ragheads are withholding from the world. A second round of Al Guido scum are due in later. We hope—"

Racked with despair, Natalia mustered the nerve to cut in.

"You! You have more. When does this obscenity end?"

Sensing her call to mutiny, Basil chopped back.

"Agent Bogomolski, we must locate the second urn."

Natalia shrieked — "A second!"

"Which city? Wh … Where?" Olga blurted.

Basil let out a palatal snarl.

"Calm down, both of you. We're positive the target is a Doodle city. But, that's beside the point. Russia's a demokrazy. We must prove to the whole world our absolute determination to crush woppery. This second urn must be neutralized."

Basil sidled up to Natalia and held her close for comfort. Olga unfurled a discreet smile, turned about and became preoccupied with reviewing the video of her performance on the last Muslim detainee, Radzuleh Karzai.

With a modicum of privacy at his command, Basil softened — "Natalia, let me make small amends for another trying day. Would you be my guest for dinner?"

Natalia's consternation at the hard measures fate had dumped in her lap evaporated in a trice, and her mood brightened to embrace a beautiful hope. Tonight was the night. If they were destined for love, if their yearnings were genuine — time to act on it. Her reply tinkled as if from a crystal wind chime.

"I'd be delighted. I'll change and meet you there."

You Only Marry Once

An acre of land is worth no more than the cost to pollute it.
Dioxinomics: The Myth of Superpower by V. O. Litvinenko.

After a light-hearted, intimate meal together, Basil kept the second promise he made to Derek Mitchell. The American had known Natalia as a lover and convinced Basil it was vital for her to understand the full measure of the tragedy and the true black-heartedness of woppery before she could open her own heart to renewed love through more mature eyes.

Derek saw her confronting Ursini as a great gift.

Basil wasn't so sure. As an intelligence expert, he appreciated the many benefits, including putting an end to Natalia's protests about the cruelty of Russia's vampire intercessions. But, he also had misgivings that Ursini's naked disclosures might backfire in ways that could only be divined.

Basil led Natalia back down into the Lubyanka dungeons and opened the hatchway admitting them into the Honeymoon Suite. He stood in the room off-camera while Natalia walked over and dragged the interrogators stool closer to Alfredo Ursini's left. Exuding a menacing air of impatience, she waved the remote control which triggered the urushiol-laden 'Ivy' capsule stitched into his scrotum in front of Alfredo's eyes, then popped his gag.

"Hello, Alfredo. I'm back, no doctor and no Veronica. This chat is between you and me. Anything less than total candor and 'Ivy' joins the fun. Got it?"

Eyes on the remote, Alfredo stirred to life.

"I've … I've nothing to hide. Never had. But, if you insist upon candor, I doubt you'll like my side of this… uh, conversation."

She stared intently into his face — "Candor. I promise. Speak freely."

Alfredo looked ashamed, pitiable.

"I promise, too." Then he asked — "So? How can I help you?"

Natalia felt racked with affront by what she considered the world's most stupid question, but she held her tongue and laid it out calmly.

"Alfredo, why did you poison the Moscow Metro system?"

Exasperation, hot and raw, erupted from Alfredo's lips.

"Damn it! I gave you the video you demanded. Enough brainwashing."

"I haven't seen your stupid video, wop. I'm sure it's a spewl[1] of spasticism. This is me. Me. We made a promise, Alfredo — *yes* or *no*?"

"Candor? Yes."

"Good," and she waited for him to answer.

After a spell, and in a voice as implacable as Wolframite,[2] Alfredo replied — "Know this. I'm not interested in war of any form. Also, I had no intention of polluting anything or anyone. I merely brought a funeral urn to Moscow because buyers here were ready to exchange raw diamonds for it. That's all!"

Funeral urn! The detached insolence of the man rankled her beyond measure, and she let her tongue off the leash.

"This is about driving Ukraine into the arms of NATO — isn't it?"

"What! You have my video, you ball-sucking cunt."

She grabbed the plunger mechanism on his gag and shook it. Basil remained silent but waved his arms violently — *Nyet*. She recomposed herself and began with the only narrative she was certain about.

"This dioxin exchange is part of a tsarist coup — right?"

Alfredo calmed to his predicament. Becoming riled was pointless.

"Sorta like that. But, I … I personally accepted the task only to endow a fabulous betrothal gift upon my beloved fiancée, Julia. For a paltry $300 investment, how could any Prince pass up three kilos of diamonds?"

---

1 Portmanteau: Spew + Mewl. Means as it sounds.

2 Ore that yields Tungsten.

"What!" she almost choked — "What sort of Roman whore expects three kilos of diamonds?"

He became indignant — "Julia is a real Princess. The daughter of a Russian Grand Duke, who is a proper male descendant of the last Tsar of Russia."

Natalia glowered in silence at his response. Alfredo noted how chivalry appalled her. Jealousy, perhaps? So, he hit back with a reality she could verify for herself — "Natalia, go to the Kremlin palace and see all the jewels on display there. They did not come from the prop department of a Disney movie set. Those jewels were gifts of love between real people. The Romanov family, their lawful owners, were murdered in a rebellion cursed by the free world. Why does Russia parade the Romanov jewels before the proletariat? Please, tell me why?"

She remained stone-faced.

Alfredo's exasperation morphed to sarcasm.

"Is that museum there to poison peoples' minds with reality? Or with fantasy? So, why shouldn't I become the King of Bling to my dearest one, a woman with a real ancestry made even more spectacular and famous by Russia's own Romanov-jewelry propaganda department?"

Livid at what she smelt was red-herring intellectualism, she cut back.

"Why couldn't you just play the role of a romantic Prince?"

What's wrong with this vampire — he thought.

"You really want candor, Miss Vampira? I warn you. Be honest."

Natalia didn't hesitate — "Total candor. I promised."

"So your 'Miss Hottie looking for her Prince' rebuke to me is — Alfredo ignore the real-man crap. Be a player. Show your game. Not your blue-blood."

Natalia recoiled in shock. A micro-snarl flashed across her face.

Alfredo caught it. Such scorn coming as it did from the fembot world of undead air-heads riled him, and he vented without restraint.

"Play a role. *A role!* I don't hate myself. I'm *not* undead. I'm a real-life scientist with a real-life sense of moral order and self-respect. The sort of real-life champion who can only experience a feeling of living large if he wields the power to sculpt the real-life myth within himself."

Heavy with rheum, Natalia's eyes glinted under the bright lights.

Alfredo's undisguised contempt did not abate.

"Yet, I live in a world of fetid rubbish like that song *What a Girl Wants*. Or perhaps, *In the Midnight Hour* by Billy Idol is popular with you vampires. Or is *Maneater* by Nelly Furtado more your style of spastic. Veronica's anthem. Well?"

He stopped for effect.

In the silence that lingered, arcs of electricity sizzled and slashed the air. She glared at him, impassive and mute. He took it as a cue to resume his tirade.

"In the Jughead hour, she cried more, more, more. With a—"

Natalia whacked Alfredo across the forehead.

Alfredo smiled for the first time in days and stared down her vampiric beauty — "That'a nonsense merely glorifies materialistic crap, the siren song of the self-loathing crowd who suffer from 'Money Psychosis,' and think that moola is an opiate for health and happiness no different than blood is for vampires."

Natalia closed her eyes in self-reproach.

And, Alfredo kept barking like Hitler and Mussolini, rolled into one.

"Let me point out that if deprived of their money-fix, these self-loathers are a foot away from being fear and hate-mongers, ready to bankrupt whole societies with their psychotic inferiority and ego complexes. So, how do you like that for candor, Miss Rooskaya Vampira, Looking for her Armour in Shining Black. Or perhaps, splooging testosterone white is more your suck!"

Natalia felt heart-broken. Not only about herself, but about Olga. And, the crazy financial markets of Russia, with its golden-boy oligarchs, where the raw fear of ruination now reigned and validated everything this wop uttered. Breaking her long silence, she replied in a contrite voice.

"Alfredo, I do respect your honesty. Don't jump to conclusions. I'm not the same woman I was a week ago. Go on, please."

He, too, sought to connect rather than chide.

"Natalia, we've emailed. I'm sure you have a sense of my character. 'Player and Playette Fakery' is nothing more than a disgusting game by women to toy with men and men to toy with women. Psychologically disturbed crap."

He almost felt like crying. Every part of his body was strapped down. Then anger at both physical and social captivity boiled up and out of his mouth.

"*I never, never want to be polluted by such rubbish!*"

Natalia erupted as Alfredo's last remark exploded across her brain.

"*Polluted!* Polluted you say!"

He ignored her retort and stared at the ceiling, entirely sick of her thinly veiled derision masquerading as questions. As the moments ticked by, each of them started to realize they occupied a room becalmed into festering silence.

Derek was on her mind, and she truly wanted to reach out.

"Please, go on. Just understand, I'm hurting here," she whimpered.

Alfredo also wanted to find common ground. He took a slow, deep breath to mellow himself and then locked her eyes in a beckoning gaze.

"Natalia, look at all the fake people. Where's their sense of self-esteem? Their sense of heartfelt destiny? Women who think men exist to be part of their my-little-princess game are no different than those boys who play war with toy soldiers or sit on their bums and twiddle their thumbs with video games. Both of these groups of mental spastics need to grow up, yoke themselves to a heartfelt destiny and become part of the real world."

She closed her eyes momentarily.

"Spastics may be. But, heart-felt destiny? You destroyed Moscow. You're just an Oreo Prince chock full of sugary excuses," she cut back.

Unruffled, Alfredo replied — "You still want candor — right?"

She nodded — now aware how hot her cheeks were.

Alfredo knew her from emails. There was a deep sense of timeless honour in her blood. With this, he sought to connect.

"Natalia, I've never had any wish to hurt anyone, anywhere on this planet. I'm an idealist. I subscribe to absolutes. Either you're phony or you're real. Like any normal Grand Duke and Princess, the Romanovs of Italy were looking for a real prince. A reality no different than your government putting the Romanov jewels on display."

He stopped to let that bombshell sink in then resumed.

"Woman, don't be a hypocrite. There's nothing 'black' about that. Or wanting to reach one's true potential. In the modern era, the valiant Prince is one ready to heed the Reaganite call and slay the evil dragons bedeviling the lands of his father-in-law to be, the Grand Duke. I guess you Russians call the 'American Dream' of a peace dividend that can't be squandered soon enough — Fascism?"

She heard nothing but political smarm behind his words and hissed.

"Woppery. That's the new Russian word for your crap. W-o-p-p-e-r-y."

His eyes narrowed — "Racism in Russia. How fucking un-un-unexpected!"

"Aw — Witl-Witl-fredo kills Cossacks by the tens of thousands. He's a scion of Western civilization that spouts off about 'jihad,' 'jihadist,' 'jihadism' and all those cartoons mocking 'Islamofascism,' but," and Natalia dropped the baby-voice — "Wop — Oh My God! — Russians are racist dogs!"

She grabbed his face harness — "This ain't Iraq, Afghanistan or Niggertown, where you can waltz in with guns a'blazing. No, dumb fuck — This is Russia. Where's your passport *Signore*[1] Ursini? Or should I say *Signore* Borges. No wait — Ursini. In Amerika, WOP means 'With Out Papers.' The identity shell-game of woppery has nothing to do with racism. And, why should wop words permeate our language? *Fascism* is derived from Italian. *Woppery* is not."

He looked away, but she didn't care — "If you expect us Russians to use Zio-Nazi slurs like 'jihad,' you can get on your knees and pray to Allah because that ain't happening. Why?" She shook his face harness and screamed into his nostrils — "We're not self-loathing, Alfredo, if I may have Your Highness's leave to recycle your own queeving.[2] Words out of Roman mouths will never define us. 'Vopl' is pure Russian. 'Vopl' means 'Graveside Wailing.' Something Moscow enjoys in great abundance, thanks to wops like you. Now, get on with your ima-da-pwince mewling, Mr. Rich-boy Nerd of Romance."

And, Natalia sat back in her seat.

Alfredo was affronted beyond measure. He squirmed to no avail except to remind himself of the flanged tube mated hard into his anus, something that for hours now he had wished he could fart into the center of the Earth. His scrotum tensed, and into this Hell, he hurled back her nastiness.

"I'm rich but I intend to live on my damn talents. I ignore any bitch even remotely thinking of wealth. Those fuck-holes can get a job and drive some other self-loathing turd into an early grave. A peasant could be my soulmate if I could only know her true heart. And, don't bore me with some Woland videotape brainwashing that fascism set into motion the death of your Metro. Sexism killed your Metro. Men have equal rights. Equal rights for equal diamonds."

Natalia's eyes bulged like egg-yokes on a griddle.

Savouring her overt distress allowed him to tamp back his anger.

"Acknowledge the reality of being a true prince. If the Grand Duke could

1 Sir, gentleman, esquire (Ital).
2 Queef, hence Queeving — Vaginal farting (Eng).

find someone who would exchange three kilos of diamonds for an urn filled with three kilos of a simple carbon-based chemical worth 300 bucks, why not? It's commercial reality, not some Disney fantasy about magic beans and some pie-in-the-sky potential to find a goose that lays golden eggs."

Natalia whipped back.

"Is something about this amusing to you? Are you c-r-a-z-y?"

Her last word vacated her throat as if it might never issue.

Alfredo lashed back — "Crazy you say. You want reality — right?"

She nodded and steeled herself for god-knows-what.

He decided to become self-sardonic.

"In the modern world aren't all people entitled to be crazy in love? Or is that just more pollution 'Show Me da Baaling' Hollywood Jews transmit into my tender, idealistic and impressssssionable fassscist brain?"

And, the laugh that followed blossomed into sneer.

Natalia hit back — "Keep it about 'Prince,' Alfredo. Crazy, we'll cover later."

His eyes glinted with Italian pride.

"We have a famous author called Nicolo Machiavelli who wrote a classic called 'The Prince.' Every cultured president and CEO quotes Machiavelli like the Bible. It's considered very romantic to be the Prince." He paused to shift gears — "Now consider modern-era gender equality. Business or political, if men and women have equal rights, why should she *not* be a Machiavellian Princess?"

He focused hard into her flaring, red-rimmed nostrils.

"Equality, democracy and all that yummy gender-neutral lick-my-LGBT-ass stuff. And, it's not confined to Italy, you know. What about those romantic songs where a man professes he's a fool to love this woman or where she's his Princess? How many vain women do you know who describe themselves as Angels? Why be the stick-in-the-mud nerd who says 'bull crap?' Who has polluted me with such data transmissions — Who? The KGB?"

He stayed silent. She waited and waited.

Arcs slashed. The air tingled with ions.

"Self-loathing bitches! That's who," he roared. His anus felt like it was cramping — "If such 'Angelic Bitches' die by dioxin, I guess that makes it poetic justice for blaspheming the 'God' your cousin Veronica keeps cackling about. We have 'God' in Italy too, you know. But, we also have a proverb — 'All's fair in love and war.' I guess Italians are romantic jihadis like in that classic American anthem about 'Duke it out' dyke-fighting — *Love is a Battlefield*."

His snide jest triggered flashback. She clenched her fist and punch his harness. Her stool rocked back slightly, and the remembrance of how a valise shielded Ludmila from her assault swamped her sanity. Ludmila was doomed, but she, protected — *I'm betrayed! Self-betrayed*.

She shrieked in withering pain — "Fortune's fooool."

From his vantage point near the doorway, Basil started towards her. Natalia stretched out her arm, wiped her eyes and returned to Ursini, livid as ever.

"Keep dyke-fighting Amerika out of this. In that pathetic, paranoid, Doodle-Dandy crap-hole everything is a fuck, fuck, fuck, fucking battlefield."

Alfredo choked back a laugh. *Touché,*[1] he thought. Then he fired back.

"*Nye problema. Nye Amerika*[2] — it's nuke shit."

And, he cleared his throat to speak more piously.

"I adhere to religion too, MizBetty. In the Catholic faith, you only marry once. So, you must find your true, life-long love. I can be absolved for accidental killings and adultery but, without a papal annulment, it's excommunication for a second sinful marriage. I might be reviled in Russia, but I'll be immortalized in Italian ballads for centuries as the biggest fool whoever fell in love."

The naked purity of Alfredo's spew of invective clawed at her heart. But, unaware of any of this, Alfredo followed through — "Come on, MizBetty. Have you Russian vampires never fallen in love with the superb voices of our famous opera singers?"

Sensing he meant to taunt her, she tossed the remote control for the Ivy capsule on top of the counter. It landed button-side up. A let-God-decide moment. Alfredo shuddered. She remained aplomb and made brittle reply.

"Opera? Opera, you say. So, atheistic Moscow is but a Reaganite dragon slaying backdrop to a modern-era, wop opera about immortal love within the confines of the so-called True Church of Christ? That's your story — huh!"

While his tone sounded defensive, Alfredo flayed back.

"Christian love between the Prince and Princess is an ancient, universal, romantic ideal. It's not confined to Italy nor the modern era. 'Gen Y' defines a whole generation of citizens who have rights to feelings of entitlement. What Prince wants his Princess to not enjoy the finer things life has to offer?"

She remained mute.

Unexpectedly, an Albert Einstein saying floated across Alfredo's mind — *'The definition of insanity is doing the same thing over and over, and expecting a different result.'* He giggled at his oversight and retooled his delivery.

"Natalia, sweet lady, I'm a chemistry whiz doing a business major. I'm not a rock-star with a gyrating pack of G-string groupies. Dioxin and diamonds are just carbon molecules in slightly modified forms. One form is Noise, the other a Top-40 hit. Why should I refrain from using my abilities to turn $300 worth of Noise into a chemical that some cretin will buy for three kilos of Top-40?"

She still remained mute.

He ploughed on — "It's a crazy little thing called the reality of modern love. At least for talented, goal-oriented men and women in the West who feel entitled to pursue their ambitions and succeed in life. Such as myself. Why should anyone obstruct my path to finding my true beloved? Why? ... Why?"

He blinked his eyes and waited — *Silence* — *What a shocker from this ball-sucking cunt. Pure Envy!* he thought. And, he resumed ploughing.

"Be she a peasant or a diamond aficionado, I would love to transform my true, true beloved into the 'Kim Kardashian' envy of everyone. Don't you want to hear from the lips of your lunch buddies — 'Wow Natalia, look at the size of that stone, I envy you.' Or how about a more family oriented, 'Wow, Natalia, you have a great husband, I envy you.' Well, don't you Natalia? In the quest for

---

1 Sword fencing term - Your Point (French).
2 No problem. No America. (Rus).

wedded bliss, don't you want sincere," he paused, "unvarnished," he paused, "adulation like that from your gal pals?"

As Ursini spoke, her mind flashed back to the day she'd met Derek in his diamond store. The way he had disarmed her with his dazzling eyes. And, all the while, as Sergei was modeling each different ring on her finger for Tatiana, his fiancée-to-be, Derek had toyed impishly with the tender rump-muscle at the base of her thumb. So cherished was the memory, she expected tears. But, nothing came. In fact, as she dug deeper she realized how she was trembling from cold sweats. The spell was broken. Derek lay dying, and here — *Here* — Alfredo's mouth rattled on.

"Since I have these rock-star, scientific abilities, Natalia, why should Julia and I slum it in the phantasy that is the very quintessence of 'Barbie-World?' Be it Italy, Wall St. or the Joy-zee Shawzz — Why the Hell should we slum it?"

His unending jeers sickened her. She had only half a notion as to what Alfredo meant by this 'Barbie-World,' Joy-zee Shawzz gibberish. Her mind seethed with anger — *Pseudo-intellectualism! A pack of narcissistic wop-headed crap. 9,983 children — now dead. 30,465 adults — now dead. More cadavers to follow.* The televised evening account had come in during her dinner with Basil, a man she loved. And, now, the horror of 'Why' swirled like a maelstrom through her eyes, twisting her mind, sucking her sanity into the deep. And, her own hypocrisy also gored her. For, who was she to cast aspersions or assign blame? Adulation — that she understood. She had once subscribed to the so-called ideal, boast-worthy relationship. It was the Metro collision that had transformed her. She hadn't transformed herself. Her reply came out cold and aloof.

"Your concept of Prince and Princess is utterly pretentious. Utterly."

Alfredo blazed back and mocked her thoughtlessness.

"Oh really, Miz Suck-my-balls Vampira. Is that not fundamental to the humanity enshrined within the concept? In so-called 'role-playing the Prince,' is it not an honourable gentleman's responsibility to accept his gender-balanced duty of subscribing to a traditional romantic paradigm and adhere to it so that his Princess knows in her heart of hearts he is indeed her true Prince? There's a time for sackcloth, and a time to shed it and get real. Julia's father, Sergio, is a Grand Duke of Russia. When the *Lion King* finally reasserts his rights as Tsar, Julia will be a real hereditary Princess, not some *Little Mermaid*."

Alfredo felt a twang of Einstein again. But, after a momentary pause, he decided to persist because, surely, she had to get real sometime.

"Once Sergio is Tsar, he could, of course, rewrite the rules of the Prince and Princess paradigm. But, since the peacock-peahen syndrome in the human species embraces an element of lording it over lesser and more common sparrows, I doubt His Tsarness could make changes without incurring ridicule and derision. Mock the twats who love *Harlequin* romance novels? Hardly! Would you care to rebut that, Miz Four Hundred Years of Ball-Sucking Vampira?"

She stood paralyzed for a moment — *Why all this denaturedness?*

Her lips started moving.

"Did … Did Sergio Romanov give you this perverse outlook?"

Alfredo remained flagrantly unapologetic.

"Grand Duke Sergio helped me understand how easy it was to make his daughter into my perfect love, the woman of my dreams. He recognized how I possessed rare talents coupled with boundless ambition that were not being fully exploited within the confines of common-place plutocratic capitalism. I'm sure Marx and Lenin would concur, not to mention Friedman and Frankenstein."

Natalia's jaw dropped.

Alfredo rolled on obliviously — "Sergio castigated me for not living up to my full potential. In his opinion, I was coasting when I could be leveraging my talents into creating truly unique and magnificent things in life. He impressed upon me that Julia would love to become a true Russian Princess, not some fake Italian Princess. All I had to do was help him in his Reaganite ambitions to liberate Russia and re-institute a British form of government. He never required anything harmful from me. He merely wanted me to fulfill my potential. Disputed as Sergio's sovereign command might be, as Tsar by blood, I had every legal right to obey him and bring 2,3,7,8 tetrachloro-dibenzo-para-dioxin into Russ—"

Natalia broke her silence.

"Roman invaders have no rights. Say something sincere."

Alfredo shot back.

"Yes. Sorry. The sincere prince. When Julia realized my sincerity in wanting her father and our future family to be prosperous, she could not resist me." Then Alfredo slowed his delivery to engage her empathy — "Surely, men in Russia want to be with a woman who genuinely finds them irresistible. Don't you want a man who is irresistible to you, so you are madly in love? Don't you want your beloved to honour and respect your father and his family's heritage? Surely, your Count Dracul would understand that it wasn't outrageous for Sergio to have me transform 300 bucks worth of organic chemicals into something of stupendous value. Talent, such as mine, doesn't get anymore fantastically leveraged than that!"

Natalia intensified her glare.

He saw nothing but — *Russian xenophobe. No different than Raghead.* He fought back a smirk because reality intruded. Osama Bin Laden was a black prince. That Sheik of Islam had leveraged a one-shot $300,000 investment into a $300 billion dollar dividend, which hobbled his chest-thumping, superpower adversary year after year after year. In contrast, he was the white prince, who had leveraged a $300 investment to acquire three kilos of raw diamonds. Where was the harm in that? And the icing on his romantic cake included love, true, deep and abiding.

Natalia squinched her eyes — *What's he up to?*

When Alfredo noticed, he pounced upon the truth contained within his last utterance. His voice rang with glee before morphing into sarcasm.

"As those American bankers with their big fat 'Money Moustaches' say, 'If you've got leverage, flaunt it.' But I guess so-called humble Moscow doesn't air that American show hosted by Ronald Trumpet, the New York real estate tycoon. It tells you a lot about an American captain of industry's sense of esteem. They crave 'bling' and 'glamor,' otherwise you're a nobody. A big, fat zero. But, I … I wasn't born nigger in Kenya. I'm Italian. I have morals. I come from a wealthy family. I'm motivated by Cupid not cupidity. If I can leverage a meager $300 into a pot of diamonds, it's just business baby, so why the yippy-kai-yai hell not?"

Trying to restrain her rage, Natalia blurted.

"Just business! What Y-Doodle crap do you watch in Wopland? Why didn't you fly your urn to New York and parade your oh-so stupendous leverage there, you Roman prick?"

"A d-weam to die for. No sniffy-my-ass drug doggies in Manhattan. No potential for tragedy. But, reality is the buyer's diamonds were in Moscow. Your people told me they were Afghanis. Smells like the diamonds are profits derived from the US-NATO protected heroin trade. I'm right, aren't I?"

Natalia was flabbergasted — "You don't know who the buyers are?"

"Why should I?" he replied blandly — "But the second urn left me with suspicions. It's to be traded for 3,000 kilos of heroin. I guess that exchange will take place in New York. For some curious reason, the buyers want the urn delivered to America and Al Guido wants the 3,000 kilos of heroin delivered to America as well. So every camper will be happy, including 'Scully and Mulder' because they'll have the plum opportunity to interdict the heroin and the dioxin as it crosses over their 'Red, White and Bullshit' border. Collaring bad guys is something 'General Eisenhower' refuses to do in Afghanistan. Part of the Waffen-CIA's plan to poison Iranians, I'm sure."

Alfredo felt his anus relax. He farted heartily and laughed.

It was all hooks, barbs and rotten eggs.

And, oblivious to the colon squirting, he goose-stepped on.

"Regardless of 'Honest Injun GI-Joe' merit badges, I'm sure the 3,000 kilos of heroin will accumulate over time — interdiction or not. As for dioxin, any zombie running a methlab can cook up the goodies and swap it for hero—"

Natalia cut in.

"Once we alert the Doodles, what makes you think they can't stop this?"

Stupefied by her naiveté, Alfredo choked getting the words out.

"Boston arrogance. Marathon corruption. That's what'll destroy Captain A-Bomb. Perhaps, Al Guido will be charitable and permit the Lords of Krankhouse Money, the US Treasury, to tender a bid for the dioxin." He chuckled then became serious — "But, given their snooty 'We don't negotiate with terrorists' game face, I'd say they'll doodle around saying, 'kilo for kilo, dioxin and diamonds aren't the same.' And they'll probably lecture Al Guido about how the US Treasury can crank out vast quantities of dioxin at pennies on the kilo and don't need to buy the stuff at nuclear weapon prices."

And, noting how her cheeks had become white with shock, Alfredo let out.

"Candor. Americans love the liberty of candor. Yee-Haa!"

Her eyes narrowed in anger and tears flowed for the first time.

"Who? Who in Moscow wanted to purchase your urn of dioxin?"

Although exasperated inside, Alfredo noticed her pain and remained calm — "Sweet lady, I only have private suspicions based on second-hand appearances. Assuming that this diamond merchant I was supposed to see was really an intermediary then I guess I'm dealing with diamonds derived from heroin. As to 'Who?' Since its hard fact 95% of the world's heroin comes from US-NATO-occupied Afghanistan then 'Dr. Who' must be some US-NATO-protected Peace Corp program run by a drug lord from his Tardis."

And, for a change, Alfredo merely chuckled.

Natalia remained mute. A second set of tears rolled toward her chin. Arcs of electricity slashed away. In air, vibrant and fresh, Alfredo closed his eyes to sober himself before repeating the truth of the matter.

"Seriously, I never had the opportunity to meet the buyers or any buyer. I'm a scientist, not a sales rep. I only wanted to meet you for a romantic afternoon."

Natalia stared at him blankly.

Her silence was strategic.

A minute ticked by before a warm and comforting bladder release interceded during which Alfredo had a flash of recall — "Come to think of it, I remember Sergio making a joke. He assured me that the buyers met the definition of Section 3 of the February 7, 2002 directive of US President Potusson. Hence, as a matter of Amerikanski law, the buyers have the legal status of barnyard critters. Tada — no sale would legally occur. Why? Because a human cannot engage in commerce with a barnyard critter. That's America's psycho definition, not mine. Sergio is a lawyer and thought his joke hysterical. I laughed mainly out of politeness."

Natalia clenched her fist but held it by her side.

"Don't bore me with Doodle-shit. Why did your buyers want dioxin?"

"Why? You ask me — Why!"

He calmed because anger was just too damn tiresome.

"I can only speculate, Natalia. I assume ragheads want pollutants for a campaign of polluting the homelands and persons of all Satanists polluting Islam with crusader politics."

He suddenly laughed and sputtered.

"Gastrointerrogation.[1] The Steak of Satan — it's what's for dinner! It's not original because the Nazis used 'law' to classify certain 'critters' for experiments. Do you know it's top-secret in every court in America merely to inquire about how humane the US government's experiments on jihadi critters are?"

"Screw Amerika's woppery. You know dioxin's a toxic pollutant?"

Alfredo became as cool as a cucumber.

"I prefer to call it dibenzo-ortho-diether. That's its non-halogenated[2] structure. I say this as a chemist. I'm not trying to torture the language like most banks and governments do. But, after the Moscow mishap with Officer

1 Sanctioned in the Muslim scriptures - The Qur'an, The Spoils of War, Sura 8:69, Allah's 'Eat of your Enemy' edict. Gastrointerrogation is the process of acquiring battlefield intelligence by eating the cadavers of the enemy. See also: The Private Chambers, Sura 49:12, declares the appropriate penance for backbiting is eating the flesh of your dead brother. Like the defensive tactic of blowing oneself into atoms using bomb vests to prevent one's body coming under the control of satanic forces, gastrointerrogation is part of every rightly-guided Muslim's offensive kit to skunk out and get the drop on Satan. Gastrointerrogation should not be confused with 'enhanced interrogation' or 'torture.' Gastrointerrogation is more akin to CSI laboratory equipment consuming human flesh and thereupon making life or death evidentiary claims derived from such consumption.
2 Halogenation is an additive reaction involving fluorine, chlorine, bromine or iodine. It is what makes dioxin not merely poisonous but highly toxic and carcinogenic.

Fumblefingers in the Metro, I suspect governments will now want to play more word games and subject scientists to more public ridicule and—"

She cut in — "Yes, Roman prick, splooge on."

"Ha. See for yourself, MizBetty. Look up the website created by an American organization called the 'Coalition for Responsible Waste Incineration.' You'll see they and the US EPA[1] claim that the vast majority of dioxins are no more toxic than fresh air or water. Zero toxicity. *Zero, zero, zero.* So, you ask me what now? What? Just go to the website. Or, just whip out your phone and give them a jingle. Then discover what American maggots of truth look like!"

He took a breath and glared, daring her to take action — *Learn reality.*

Natalia remained furious but stayed on message.

"Damn your Y-Doodling maggotry. I'm told the substance in the urn is called 2,3,7,8 tetrachloro-dibenzo-para-dioxin. You knew it was toxic."

"Toxic is irrelevant because I made sure my EPA dioxin was properly entrained in a metal urn. Locked tight like Polonium-210.[2] I made it a funeral urn so that people would handle it with care and respect. Who? Yeah — Who, Natalia? Who tossed it onto railway tracks so that it could be smashed by a train and distributed over the Metro system? Me? Oh, no. Not me. No. It was Officer Fumblefingers. He's Russia's fuckhole."

Alfredo's anus tensed again, and he felt a glut of hurt well up inside. In a childlike voice, he chanted aloud in sing-song the angry thoughts that flooded his mind as he raced to catch the first train out of Metro Komsomolskaya.

"Fumblefingers, Fumblefingers, corrupt commie Fumblefingers."

Bewildered, Natalia slapped his forehead.

Alfredo stopped chanting and took a breath.

"Natalia, get real. I had three kilos of diamonds coming to me. Three damn kilos! Surely you don't believe I would suddenly change course and pollute the Metro system. And, even if I got stiffed on the exchange for diamonds, I still looked forward to the enchantment of meeting you. $300 is nothing. Three kilos of diamonds — yummy. But, enchantment is priceless, *mia ragazza dolce.*"[3]

Natalia pressed the flat of her palm against her nose. The tip of one finger massaged her brow as if warding off a migraine. She knew Alfredo was speaking the truth, whole, unvarnished — candid — as she had asked. And, into her silent distress, Alfredo spoke anew. His tone remained soft, but his words cut like carbide — "Confirm it with your government if you dare. But, I assure you it was a corrupt Russian police official who considered Mr. Viktor Fiksyonovich Magufinski's funeral urn no more precious than a plum opportunity to shake-down a wop for a pathetic fifty-euro bribe. He, Officer Fumblefingers, caused this whole disaster."

Natalia wasn't about to allow a corruption smear to blindside reality. Her lips moved under the base of her palm. Her airy voice brimmed with sarcasm.

"Did he ask for a bribe?"

1 US Environmental Protection Agency. Chemical industry friendly.
2 Radioactive high-energy alpha particle emitting metalloid. Ingesting 50 nanograms is fatal. In a perfect world, that's 20 million fatal doses in one gram.
3 My Sweet Girl (Ital).

And, as flinty as it felt, Alfredo's heart melted into surrender at the role cast upon him — *Being the patsy*. Locked in his mind was the face of true terror. An olive dress-hat adorned with a red star crowned that face. A scowling Rottweiler of a face without the slightest Aryan feature.

"Fumblefingers deprived himself of the bribe an airport official reaped. Two actually. Go ask Velcro and Pug-Eye for confirmation, *Miz Saputella*."[1]

She could do nothing but glare at him impassively.

He returned her gaze. "And pray tell, what is Officer Fumblefinger's real name?"

She ignored his question and fired off her own.

"Was it an accident or an attack?"

Her refusal to confront reality gnawed at him. *Why this ridiculous pretense of stupidity?* he thought, *Why conceal Fumblefinger's real name? Why?* But, despite his annoyance, he kept his reply even-handed — "An accident. No doubt. No one intended to pollute the Metro. Not I, not Fumblefingers, not Sergio Romanov, not Al Guido, nobody wanted that. Nothing to do with deploying chemical weapons or unleashing a terrorist attack. I swear before God, before the Pope and any priest who will absolve me — Any goof on my part was wholly unintended. This whole schamozzle is about accidental pollution, a fender-bender."

Natalia was aghast at his uncaring jabbering.

"A fender-bender. *A fender-bender!* So, Mr. Goof-off Roman Prince of the Church, you think you are a tragic, faultless victim of circumstance?"

Alfredo clenched his fists, before closing his eyes ready to weep.

"I swear. I swear. By the same standard that a politician or bureaucrat is faultless. I swear! Totally faultless, unless, of course, it's some undocumented Russian custom to distribute human ashes over the Metro. Then—"

She shook his head restraint.

"Arrogant politician — arrogant scientist, what's the damn difference?"

He opened his eyes. A sneer transected his lips.

"*Touché*. Pay-scale, I guess? Teenage prostitutes. Fat pensions, too."

Alfredo stopped and took a breath. Tired of coming across as cynical, he sought a return to a discussion about the controlling scientific and social facts.

"Natalia, wise up. Anyone can make dioxin. It's not expensive. It's not exotic. I'm no Martha Stewart homebody conversant with cookies and casseroles, so I used my talents to cook up other carbon molecules instead. Honorable toil to be traded for jewels which would express my deepest adoration for the woman I love, and all in a manner consistent with human morality. I'm not some nutcase looking for fame by polluting subway systems for sport. All credit belongs to Comrade Fumblefingers. Wha! — What's his name again?"

Natalia exploded, ready to rip his head off.

"Fumblefingers, my ass. You did this, wop."

Her outburst calmed his spirits, and he unleashed his lecture voice.

"As I said earlier, Natalia, I put the dioxin in a funeral urn so that it would be handled with care and respect. If living people cannot respect the bodies of the dead, why should the dead respect the bodies of the living? As a vampire, I'm guessing you are immune to dioxin. I'm sure you understand this sacrilege.

1 Ms. Know-It-All (Ital).

A moral lesson for the living and the undead, such as yourself. Miz I-Want-Candor, don't you see poetic justice in all of this?"

"*Poetic!* You've caused misery that knows no bounds. You—"

Straining violently against his restraints, Alfredo erupted.

"Typical Feminazi! You're *not* listening. Officer Fumblefingers, No-name Fumblefingers caused the Metro tragedy. The great love between Julia and I is shattered. Shattered — by a corrupt, cunt-fucking dildo. I'm just the one targeted for execution. The expendable alien ratbag — that's me. Torture, torture, torture — that's me. Trading carbon atoms for carbons atoms, I would do it again if some fool wanted to unload three kilos of diamonds or whatever. Carbon, it's everywhere. Carbon, it's forever. Ask De Beers. What was in that urn merely came out of an oil well. I just used my talents to enhance it with the chemical in table salt — chlorine. My diamonds had an honourable goal. Create a fabulous environment where my great love and I could nestle down to a life rich in peace and happiness. My motives, pure and family oriented. Now that is shattered. *Shattered by Fumblefingers!* I'll never know true love."

Alfredo's straining ceased, his energy all spent, now came weeping, hard and masculine. It was excruciating. It was horrendous. Hands at her throat with her own sense of guilt rising, Natalia's whole body trembled and she just stared, half in disbelief and half in anger.

Alfredo calmed, took note of her countenance and screamed.

"Bite off my balls, you stupid vamp. End this farce, before I go Islamic and become a suicidal nutcase. You're just a cow-wa-wa-ward! Go get Comrade Fumblefingers, give him a gun, give him a bribe, Romanov diamonds perhaps, and order him to take me to a secret well near Ekaterin—"

Natalia gagged him and paced the room — distraught.

The all-age death toll now stood at 40,448. All he knew about was Officer Fumblefingers, the convenient scapegoat for Mr. Ursini, a man in search of his one true love, a man with his ambitions circumcised to the fate of a common criminal awaiting a head-lopping guillotine, and thus, a prick who cares nothing for life anymore. Alfredo's bluntness worried her. The only reason tragedies like Moscow weren't happening around the world was that the great bulk of humanity were complete and absolute morons. Of course, what did any of this matter. She was immune to pollution, physical and spiritual.

She paced while her thoughts raced frantically. After having tamped down a storm of inner conflict, Natalia felt sufficiently composed to respond.

"Mr. Ursini, I cannot fault your world view. I've seen the George W. Beaver interviews about Amerikan fascists, the Al Jazeera 'Science of Gastrointerrogation'[1] report, and read the Islamic religious court decisions of hoity-toity Harvard educated Chief Justice Khalid Gharmin Al-Byabeeh about romancing seventy-two virgins in Paradise under the fundamental right enumerated in the Qur'an to blow oneself into atoms to prevent the forces of Satan from zombifying one's body."

1 Iraq, 2003, Al Jazeera broadcast the first experiments verifying the divine power of gastrointerrogation. Islamic science holds that gastrointerrogation affords warriors the means to learn about schemes Satan is hatching against the faithful. Like a battlefield version of CSI.

She bent lower, eyeball to eyeball.

Her nose grazed Alfredo's gag.

"I guess they're all your heroes. And, concerning your earthly theory of romance, I know vain Russian women who think that if their man is not living up to his bring-home-the-bacon potential then he's diddling her and his children. When I figure out who is the real vampire in all this, I'll let you know."

Eyes Rustling with Lust

Arm in arm, as if fleeing insanity, Basil and Natalia marched through the suffocating hell of the Lubyanka complex and out into the cold-sweat darkness of Moscow under martial law. Trudging along at a measured clip and steeling themselves against a biting autumn breeze buffeting in from the west, they headed north to Derek's apartment near the corner of Ulitsa Myasnitskaya and Ulinovskaya. After Alfredo's undisguised spewl, all conversation felt frivolous.

They walked for the longest time.

Natalia finally cracked.

"Basil, please hold me close. I'm … I'm so cold."

He draped his arm over her shoulders, and once settled he murmured what he knew to be her greatest hurt — "It's more than you wanted to know, isn't it?"

"Yes. And, surely all of Russia would like to know why this barbarism has descended upon us. I can't imagine their reaction to this Roman pig."

"I'm so sorry you had to confront this, Natash."

She kept venting — "And, such vile language too. He makes it sound like a noble soul was diligently painting in the romantic dots on a work of art aimed at creating a fairytale marriage between his fiancée and himself."

Another six paces later, she picked up again.

"Basil, did Olga and I cause this Roman dog to become deranged like this?"

Basil mused — *'Roman' it creeps in whenever she's angry.*

Two paces later, he replied — "No, sweet lady. Your vampire intercession merely drained all the pretentiousness out of what was once a moon-headed wop with stars in his eyes. Tonight, we heard a man in the land of the undead, scheduled for execution, stating the facts about a Western style of life centered around woppery." Basil took five more paces before he decided she needed to know — "Ursini genuinely considers himself a great romantic spirit."

Natalia bayed her bewilderment.

"He yaps about diamonds, Princes and Princesses as if reality is parody. Is this what so-called savvy women in the West refer to as 'a man with game'?"

Basil squelched an urge to laugh.

"Natash, consider this. Lacking artistic skills Alfredo sought the aid of a third party, Maestro Leonardo da Vinci, to woo his beloved Julia. Using his science skills to create a time machine fueled at the expense of one hundred thousand Russian corpses, Alfredo sends a note and a photo back in time to Da Vinci. He requests the Maestro to paint Alfredo and Julia as a married couple. Da Vinci is so astounded by the photo and notion of time-travel, he paints the famous '*Due Amanti*.'[1] And, it's passed down into modern times. There, hanging in the Uffizi[2] in the year 2004, the two lovers find each other miraculously betrothed on canvas by Leonardo himself. On his wedding night, Alfredo, the prince of romance, unveils to his beloved Julia the secret to winning the heart of a princess. End of Wop Fairytale! But, just like poppy-ninnies under woppery's Game of Hunger in Afghanistan, we live in reality. It's no fairytale. Ursini used his talent for romantic chemistry to swamp our city in death. The payoff — love and diamonds. So, yes. In the West the expression does apply — Dat wop got game."

She snarled against the heave of ice in her joints.

"We need to put an end to all this woppery."

Basil squeezed her hand and mirrored her outrage.

"We've already shut down Mattel, Disney and others. Woppery is not confined to Wopland. And, it's not just an Italian 'Prince and Princess' paradigm. Consider Derek's homeland. In Amerika, it's etiquette for an engagement ring to be worth two months of a man's income. Y-Ds consider it a dignified expectation."

"Why this obsession with the value of an object in the eyes of narcissists?" And, Natalia made a mental note to have Derek explain tomorrow.

Basil responded in an air of indignation.

"As opposed to the worth of a keepsake between two lovers?"

She squeezed his hand in solidarity.

"Exactly. In the eyes of others, such covetousness is about validation."

And, Natalia improvised a fairytale romance of her own.

"Basil, imagine this. A Muslim taxi driver in New York falls in love with a beautiful Arab Princess and offers her father an urn filled with a unique gift. He explains to the prospective father-in-law how the price of diamonds is controlled by an infidel diamond cartel. Their value is cooked-up. So he offers an urn that contains three kilograms of a carbon-based chemical worth $300."

Basil jumped in.

"Let me pretend to be the father-in-law. I'm a great Sheik and my daughter is a prize catch … Dear Sir! Princess Fatimah has many worthy suitors. I have a reputation and you offer me an urn worth only $300 — *By the beard of Allah!*"

Natalia giggled at Basil's over-the-top delivery and responded in kind.

"Good Sir, I'm a hard-scrabble taxi driver. In terms of money, $300 is a great gift. Two months of hard work and savings. My feelings and intentions toward your daughter are very true. My love for her deep, strong, and noble. Although I appear to you as poor, I aspire to become an Amerikan 'Genghis Khan' of military science, leech off the paranoid Y-D taxpayer and be a husband, worthy of the fountains of Doodle-boodle that will flow my way in future."

Basil laughed without restraint before making crackling reply.

"The father — He softens to the taxi driver's sincerity. Honourable lad, I'm well pleased that your character is so fine. It's truly more important than your gift. However, I'm afraid that your offer in marriage cannot be accepted because

1 The Two Lovers (Ital).
2 World renowned art museum in Florence, Tuscany, Italy.

in the eyes of conventional society, my wife, daughter and I would be considered fools to allow this union on the basis of so paltry a token of engagement."

Natalia felt the warm glow of love-affirmed swaddle her body.

"Sir, I have told you the contents of this urn are worth only three Benjoes,[1] but let me also reveal to you that it contains in weight and chemistry the exact same substance that polluted the Moscow Metro system three days ago. Surely, my wise Sheik, any heroic-hearted Arab prince might consider the worth of this gift from a lowly Muslim the equivalent of an urn full of diamonds freshly scooped by infidel labour from the vault of the DeBeers diamond cartel?"

Basil tamped back laughter and countered.

"My future son-in-law, you may be a humble taxi driver but you're living up to your potential as a Prince walking amongst MICE — the Military Industrial Computerized Empire. Welcome to our noble family!"

Natalia loosed all the day's hardships and joined his laughter. Mirth soon trailed to silence. And, for the longest stretch, shoes clapped on pavement before Natalia reset the mood — "Basil, it's beyond sick. Do you think Disney would make a romantic rags-to-riches movie like that? They could call it *Mujahideen in Manhattan* or maybe a musical *Jihad on the Jersey Subway*."

Basil restrained an urge to snicker.

"I doubt it, sweet lady. DeBeers would do a Stalin and find a way to gulag that movie. It ridicules their 'Diamonds are Forever' propaganda. For Hollywood and the Bling-bling wanna-be aristocracy, the mystique of the Prince and Princess romance requires third persons to pay court and to put a value on the objects of veneration that are exchanged because, like death, diamonds and love are forever."

From deep within, Natalia's body shivered.

"You know Basil, if some beast-like Minotaur was to ask my hand in marriage and in consideration gave me an urn of anti-dioxin that could reverse all the carnage, I would accept in a minute." Recalling her assault on Ludmila, she sighed — "I would do it with all my heart."

Basil's voice thrummed with warmth.

"You like the Beauty and the Beast fairytale, don't you?"

"Yes, but our modern day Arab Prince story is better. I like its egalitarianism because the gift created from two months of the income of a lowly Muslim cab driver is equivalent to that created from two months of the income of the greatest Muslim oil Sheik. Both are different, yet both are two months of savings and so, according to the Doodles' validation theory of wedded bliss, both are esteemed in the eyes of third persons as equally precious. Our Arab story is about true classless, social equality, not bling-bling depravity."

Who started laughing first — neither knew. But, they laughed because the irony of the whole matter, both social and political, was so utterly hideous.

Basil was the first to calm.

"I also prefer our Arab Prince story because it's about the real world of human vanity. Never overlook the fact that oil, dioxin and diamonds all consist of carbon. The only difference is their inter-atomic bonding. Like the bonding

---

1 A US$100 bill (American).

between a man and a woman and parents and children differ from family to family. Some are like oil. Some are diamond. And, others, toxic like dioxin."

Three paces later, Natalia's voice sprang to life.

"If the bond is nurturing, even if the family poor, the relationship is precious. If toxic yet the family rich, the relationship is worthless."

Basil added — "Also, diamonds have rigid bonds that can chew up steel. Yet, diamonds burn as readily as charcoal. Dioxin has weaker bonds, but it survives high temperatures. Like sand, diamonds cannot integrate into the human body but dioxin is organic and invades human cells like DDT."[1]

Natalia tugged Basil's arm before responding — "Another observation. In the desert, say the Sahara, an urn of water is worth more than an urn of dioxin. But, in New York City, an urn of dioxin is worth more than an urn of water."

The *First Law of Dioxinomics* came to mind, and Basil elaborated.

"Natash, that's what makes this attack on our Metro a global calamity. Dioxinomics holds that cheap carbon chemicals exist that make two pieces of real estate equal in value in the eyes of covetous humans."

Natalia halted — "Diomics? What's that?"

Basil nudged her to keep moving.

"That's Dioxinomics,[2] Natash. We can discuss it later. Reality is about to intrude into the capitalist fairytale called Economics. Dioxinomics is a fact of science. It isn't Marxist-Leninism. Nor is Dioxinomics unique to Moscow. Or to Washington. Or Paris or London or Beijing or New York." He stopped speaking to fill his lungs with cold air — "Nor is Dioxinomics confined to Metro systems. The critical thing is that over the coming days, the world faces permanent real estate price collapse. It's ultimate cause — woppery and a Prince-Princess system of romance focused on what Ursini calls 'Barbie-World' and its 'Money Psychosis.' Global calamity at the expense of cheap-to-come-by shared happiness is the true face of the capitalist me-me-me economics of woppery. Wall St. — its prime exemplar."

Natalia flashed him a look of disbelief

Basil raised her hand to his lips and kissed it.

"Panic not. Sit back. Watch. And, keep it all in perspective, my fine lady. Dioxinomics only shatters the 'Barbie-World' crowd. Soon the myth of superpower will be what it always was — Myth — so much asymmetric, wind-bagging from a warmongering media elite. Captain A-Bomb and GI-Joe Doodle is in for a less than humble slice of dioxin pie."

To purge all the horror behind their banter, Natalia cut loose.

"Basil, I'd like to think I had a unique gene called 'Miroxin' inside me. And, better. Like Eve leaving the Garden of Eden, if I polluted the world with 'Miroxin' then it would cure all maladies and infect people until they brimmed with love for each other. Within a few generations, Miroxinomics would dissolve all international borders and end the rule of greed, graft and government."

"Miroxin and Miroxinomics — Hmm." And, Basil warmed to her phantastical vision and replied in jest — "Blessed with 'Miroxin,' you say? To

---

1 DDT - Dichlorodiphenyltrichloroethane. (IUPAC 1,1,1-Trichloro-2,2-bis(4-chlorophenyl)ethane.
2 Portmanteau of Dioxin + (Eco)nomics. See also *Dioxinomics*® Series. www.dioxinomics.com.

me, it seems to confirm how CIA has poisoned you with Mad Cow disease."

Alarmed, Natalia stopped and grabbed a nearby lamppost.

"Do you know something you're not telling me?"

Basil tweezed his chin, milking her anxiety for all it was worth.

"My sweet, sweet Natash. Of course, I'm talking about the Committee of Inspired Angels. Maybe they infected you with a mad cow prion because you are a cow who is crazy in love."

Natalia swung her hand free of the lamppost.

She slapped his chest — "You scamp! I love it."

They clip-clopped along. Not a word was spoken. With so much trifling burnt away, both now felt the deep premonition in the air between them. It was a stillness, glowing with caprice, glowing with the expectation of sexual bliss yet to come. Having crossed the intersection south of Derek's apartment, they stepped onto the next sidewalk and Basil broke his quiet deliberations.

"Seriously Natalia, you might be onto something. There's no question an unexplained miracle is at work inside your body. Any scientist might well speculate you do have a 'Miroxin' gene." He looked at her askance — "If this disaster were to befall any city on the planet, you and presumably your children would consider such wastelands your private playgrounds. To you, they have value, to all others woppery makes them worthless."

Basil took several paces before fine-tuning his point.

"A puff of dioxin, real or imagined, and 'Barbie-World' is all gone — zippa-roo — nada. That's the invincibility of Dioxinomics in a nutshell."

She replied mischievously — "Barbie-World or not, I don't need any more phantastical miracles. But, I would love a true miracle at work inside my body and I'd like to think that you were attached to the other end of my treasured wish."

She came to a halt and tugged at his coat.

"We're here. The front door," and she gestured.

Basil looked up at the eight-story edifice and then down onto a beautiful, satin-skinned face bejeweled with eyes that sparkled like blazing saphhires. The moment of truth. His heart shuddered then thumped back to life. At the edge of the abyss, he basked in the exquisite power radiating throughout his body. And, smiling from deep within, he was amazed at how the piling-up of years had no power to dull the poignancy he felt. Their sense of oneness already transcended the physical. He could not deny it.

Almost in whisper, he replied — "I'm ready. But, I must confess I don't want to rush anything. I savour our connection. It's so ... extraordinary."

She blushed at the caring delicacy behind his words.

"I'm in no rush myself, sweet man."

She tapped the security code into the door-lock keypad.

"But truly Basil, I want you so close it hurts."

The lock's solenoid hasp buzzed like an ovarian alarm clock, yielded and a less than chaste steel-plate door cracked open, which threw a tracing of light across Basil's left shoe.

"Let's go in and become who we're meant to become," she said.

During the ride up the elevator, Basil made small talk about the art-nouveau decor. When the elevator lurched to a stop on the sixth floor, Basil tucked his overcoat to one side and pulled keys from his dress jacket. After swaggering down the corridor, he arrived at a typical 'Plate and Rivet' door. Opening it afforded him, an opportunity for silence. Even for a seasoned FSB General, it was always a coin toss if the knobby brass key for the outer door had to be turned left three times or right three times. Since Elena had given him the keys, the fumble-time of the correct guess was his, including a quiet respite to be preoccupied.

Once the cumbersome security door was relocked and the inner door closed with a snap, it was all action. Basil pulled Natalia close and drew a kiss across the threshold of her lips that turned her blood into corked-pop champagne. After several minutes, a woman whose eyes were rustling with lust broke the press of a man whose breathing had been reduced to abdominal pants.

She excused herself to the bathroom.

Basil prepared their *boudoire*.[1] He stripped, removed the blanket and fluffed up three pillows before sliding under a tented sheet. The shower's sudden silence alerted him to a nagging concern about not wanting to come across as overly intense for her. So he relaxed into that fuzzy feeling of destined yet detached anticipation, where one senses oneself as a fuse of carnal cordite sizzling shorter and shorter.

Natalia emerged from the bathroom with her fulsome locks trussed up. While her hair was dry, she had not dried her body at all. And, sashed around the trunk of her sinuous waist like a set of wetted fairy wings, a knee-length chiffon robe clung exactingly to her every curve. In the marginal light emanating from the bathroom, the diaphanous fabric amplified the sexual shock-waves thrumming hard from her breasts, waist and hips.

Like a tax-collector, Basil lay in quiet ambush.

A reckoning was long overdue.

"I see you like to purloin government property, Miss Bogomolski."

Her eyes lit up like moonstones and she smirked at his bold jest. And, as if a butterfly emerging from its chrysalis, she peeled the government's property off her shoulders until her bosoms bobbed into view. She loosed the sash so it hung free, and she pranced tenaciously over to him, all the while teasing the robe to slough to the floor under the influence of her bouncing gait and the clawing drag of the carpet.

She came to a stop adjacent to him, entirely naked. Her midriff loomed close and like summer radiance off an adobe brick wall facing a setting sun, Basil's whole face tasted the blast of hot sex coming his way. When she had discerned that the heat in her mons had melt the resoluteness in his eyes, she made full confession of her scandalous act and her desire for him to confer absolution.

"My dear General, you have caught me completely naked in my crime. Probity demands I offer you the best bribe that you've ever had."

Basil flicked off the sheet — "Then straddle me."

1 Connubial Chamber (French).

She complied by mounting his trim abdomen then wiggled her way down toward his groin, bringing her moist lips closer to his.

But, Basil intercepted her impulse — "Not so fast, my sweet rogue."

And, he placed his right hand then his left hand over her back.

"Now do the same with me," he murmured.

She beamed with unbridled anticipation and placed first her left hand and next her right hand on his back and over his heart in the opposite location. They pressed themselves close — until nipple kissed nipple, and navel kissed navel. And, they closed their eyes in repose, and putting all utterances and declarations of love to shame, they projected their feeling thoughts, one to the other. Thus did they consummate their true-hearted desire to know each other fully, before moving on to the incidental intimacies of their first night together.

My Wife Died in Labour

The first to wake, Basil rotated his head left and watched her eyeballs flicker wildly inside the gorgeous pink-white pupa of her eyelids. Her hand lay over his chest, and as if the paw of a cat locked in the dream world of a mouse safari, her fingers quivered and flinched, tickling him every so often. But, more astonishingly, he sensed her unconscious moods. He put his hand atop hers and closed his eyes in an attempt to elicit a deeper sense of the drama unfolding in her dream. But, what he felt remained vague. To enhance the effect, he placed his hand over her left breast. Any improvement was imperceptible. Her dream seemed neither happy nor sad. It seemed pregnant with hope but also resigned to fate, and left him wondering whether two great wills were in conflict or just conflicted? It was hard for him to know what to think. Getting nowhere, he broke off.

The day had dawned.

Basil was brewing a pot of tea when his mobile rang. Without warning, President Bushkin had scheduled a meeting. He quickly dressed. And, not wishing to disturb Natalia, scribbled a note, and plastered it to the fridge door before flying out the door to meet the car dispatched to collect him.

In anticipation of a trying day of presidential business, Basil's mind was everywhere making ready to dissect the weeniest of details. As he strode into his office, Elena informed him that both Derek and Teodor, the Patriarch's son, had passed away. The Patriarch was in the Infirmary. With five minutes to spare, he grabbed his files and dashed off to offer his condolences. During the brisk march to the Infirmary, he grew more and more overwrought with how Mitchell had died — halfway into watching the video of the chew-the-fat confrontation between Natalia and Ursini. Derek had assured him that he could help more if he knew more. It was a mistake. The unintended consequence he dreaded the night before had come to pass. The heartbreak of discovering Ursini's fixation with diamonds sent the gemologist into a coughing fit from which he never recovered. Basil felt as if he had strangled the man to death with his bare hands.

And, Natalia's reaction? — *This, she could never know.*

Her mission was world peace — *Keep her focus on woppery.*

Heavy in heart, Basil held his head low, and mindlessly watched the toes of his two black shoes clip-clopping in and out of his eyesight. On reaching Teodor's room, he stopped inside the doorway and lifted his head. The Patriarch stood huddled in a corner. His shoulders trembled with grief. Basil felt more disarmed than ever — *What comfort could he offer a man such as this?* He readied himself by projecting empathy throughout his body, hoping that whatever words came out, they would come out right. And, from the safe harbour of the doorway, he spoke into the anguish before him.

"Kolya, my only wish is that Teodor went to God peacefully."

The Patriarch turned about.

For Basil, the sight was wrenching.

"Thank you, Basil," he blubbered. "My wife died in labour. Teo was my last attachment to her and to this world. The hurt is beyond comprehension."

The sting of divorce, his own children hundreds of miles away rolled over Basil before he mustered himself — *Take the matter elsewhere.*

"Kolya, did you know Derek also passed?"

"Yes." And, the Patriarch wiped his face — "I've so much work today."

Basil's eyes started to feel heavy — *at last* — but he beat it back.

"Patriarch, yours makes mine look routine." He felt horrible about the abruptness, but time was running low — "Kolya, I'm going to be with the president most of the day. May I ask of you the great favour of consoling Miss Bogomolski. If you'd both like to meet our President for lunch, I can probably finagle that. Please, let Elena know if you're in better spirits by midday."

"Thank you. Let me decide later."

"Of course." Basil paused — "Look, the president is expecting me. I have to run. I'll have my driver take you to Miss Bogomolski. She's at Derek's apartment and doesn't know about him yet."

"What! She doesn't know. So, you want—"

Basil nodded blankly, bared his watch and tapped.

"Kolya, I'd do it but I have no choice. I must go. Now."

Basil wheeled about to end all equivocation — *Take the day elsewhere.*

While sprinting to Director-General Besstrashnikov's office, Basil phoned Ivan, his driver, to inform him about the day's schedule, the Patriarch meeting Natalia, and the possibility of a lunch-time trip to the Kremlin. Being the last to arrive at Besstrashnikov's office, Basil tendered a snap apology, and the contingent of FSB Generals made the subterranean trip to Bushkin's Bunker.

Green on the Outside Yet Red All Over

Cutting Western flesh with the keen edge of a shepherd's marking knife, that same cold and cloudless morning Ambassador Steele greeted Vice-President Weissbrot at Sheremetyevo Airport. The engines of jet aircraft pealed hard all around them, but neither man believed in the delusion that such noise afforded them any privacy. On the tarmac, they exchanged handshakes and small talk because both well knew that until they sat within the acoustic security of the embassy limousine and got underway, infrared cameras and infrared lasers would pick up everything they did and everything they said. Once the car was in motion, Weissbrot launched into the thick of it.

"First off, I'd like to see Mitchell. He's at the Lubyanka, right?"

Ambassador Steele's reply concealed his exasperation.

"On the way to the airport, I was informed that he passed away last night. At least, that's the story the Russian's are putting out."

"Damn." Weissbrot paused. "Have an attaché confirm that in person."

"Already in process, Mr. Vice-President."

"Please Mr. Ambassador, it's Norman. Norman is fine, Rodney."

He waited for Steele to acknowledge him before continuing.

"Next item. Any breaks establishing an insider within Russian intelligence?"

"No. And, to be frank, given the current environment that's a fool's errand. Also, Lester asked me about an informant code-named 'Squirrel,' and whether he might've made contact. I'm clueless. Do you know what that's about?"

"During my stint in Moscow. He's a longtimer with very deep cover. No one knows his true identity, but he's been 100% in the past. He hasn't resurfaced with Langley. Perhaps, at your end?"

Steele shook his head. Weissbrot did not want to linger on the mystery of Squirrel because there was too much at stake to leave to happenstance.

"So what's my schedule with Bushkin?"

"He's on a very tight budget. His timetable dictates yours, sir. Expect a call at any hour." Steele shifted in his seat to face Weissbrot eye to eye — "Norman, things are extremely tense. The death toll announced at midnight stood at 42,637, and Lester's boys have projected deaths at 7,500 today. With a head of steam this huge building up whenever the Kremlin releases their spin to the Russian people about the Whos, Hows and Whys, it's gonna be a pogrom response."

The ex-Moscow Ambassador in Weissbrot reflected momentarily.

"Thanks for your read, Rodney. My job is to vent as much of the blood'n guts as possible. But, first, we need to improve our relations with the Russians. Something more substantial than the Boy Scouts and Girl Guides National Parks Clean-up Program Comrade Bushkin is currently sponsoring."

Feeling unexpected relief, Weissbrot chuckled.

Steele relaxed and snickered in unison.

"Funny that one. A classic 'Rooskie riddle' wrapped inside an 'Ivan enigma.' Green on the outside yet Red all over. I'd put money on any bet that says 'Fearless Leader' Bushkin is hinting we should do the same in Afghanistan."

In response, Weissbrot simply smirked.

Steele read Weissbrot as very approachable, and because relations with Russia had soured into what he considered an 'All the Days of Our Presidency' soap opera, he decided to ask an outwardly impertinent question.

"Norman, on the up and up, for no objective reason, President Carter has taken a disliking and, dare say it, an openly hostile attitude toward Bushkin and his governance. What the Hell is going on?"

Weissbrot grimaced and blushed slightly.

"Rodney, I can't discuss that. Consider it a good-cop bad-cop strategy in play. And, whatever you thought I just said, I didn't. And, it's all 'Top Secret.'"

Steele winked in acknowledgement — *Better to exchange staged melodrama rather than nuke-tipped ballistic missiles*, he thought.

"Of course-ski, *tavareesh*. [1] Never heard a thing! It's a play to get you here with access to Bushkin." And, he reclined back into the folds of his seat — "By the way, I offered to host a function at the embassy, but Bushkin has no time. I do know he's delighted to meet you. But, for now it has to be on short notice. Impromptu lunch or dinner at the Kremlin, I'm guessing."

"It's good to hear he's open to cordial relations. As am I." Weissbrot's voice grew wistful — "So, how's Moscow handling the medical issues?"

"Bushkin has pulled out all the stops. The Army mans clinics all over the city. They're chasing down all the injured to prevent them from declining further into ill-health. Norman, there's going to be an avalanche of collateral death from immune deficiencies and opportunistic diseases. To compound the disaster, in eight weeks, we'll be in the grip of a Russian winter. Like a Rocky Mountain forest incinerated by fire and which dies back further from blizzards, such will be the ongoing misery racking Moscow."

On that note, their conversation lapsed into morbid silence.

As President Potusson's political appointee, Weissbrot had been the US Ambassador to Russia for three glorious years. The thought of Moscow and it's now crippled populace enduring a harsh winter numbed him. He had always taken time to speak with the simple folk, people thrilled at listening to his mangled attempt at speaking their language. And, while he prided himself a well-seasoned military man, the experience of living in Moscow had quite unexpectedly transported him back into the realm of wondering youth — One open to fresh discovery. A time of great happiness and dear friends.

How was Yulia Fyedorovna faring? he thought.

And, what irony it was that Afghanistan had brought him back to Moscow. Yula's husband, Yuri, had died in Afghanistan during a decade of Soviet occupation when Russian President Brezhnev had sought to create a beacon of godless communism within a Muslim nation. His jowls filled with warmth as he recalled how he first met the widowed grand-dame. Plying a survival trade under the ever-bustling Ulitsa Konyushkovskaya, she sold flowers to passersby in the *perikhod*[2] that furnished pedestrian access to Metro Krasnopresnenskaya.

Yula was not the most robust of women. But, what she lacked in physical stature, she made up for in earthy warmth. She had pegged him as a man of distinction. Rising from her seat with the elderly charm of a fifty-year old going on eighty, she intercepted him and placed a carnation into the button hole of his left lapel. He protested, but she asserted her courtesies ever so graciously. To decline was impossible within the confines of the diplomatic foreigner. And,

1 Comrade (Rus).
2 Subterranean crossing (Rus).

it was Yula who had offered him his first insight into dealing with Russians, something that over the months served him well as his nation's ambassador.

Nor could he forget how the soldier in him warmed to the curious liberation of being commanded by a Russian babushka, one who had no idea of his true station in life. All she knew was that he would become bound to her as a customer during his three-year stint. She'd seen all she needed. His eyes had given him away. Each day, he went out of his way to take the long route and practice his skills at haggling in Anglo-Russian. He knew that to glut Moscow with foreign money would soil people's perspective. But, while he insisted on paying the local price, he never celebrated victory. Rather like a son worried about an elderly mother, with a stern yet tender insist, his last words — *Sokhranitye dla novuyu platu* — Save for new dress. And, he always left extra change once the real transaction was complete. Of course, there never was a new dress. He knew she probably spent the extra money on Oleg, her grandson. Tennis lessons for sure. Her 'Olegin' was going to be the next Sampras.

As Weissbrot turned to look out the limousine window, he caught his reflection smiling back at him. And, it deepened as the beauty of a treasured remembrance washed through him. With a stark winter looming, every act of grace became all the more poignant. For in Russia, survival was a matter of provisions or wealth. Ukrainian President Eunatovski had survived dioxin assassination. Obviously, the dose wasn't fatal. But, still, Ukraine spent a fortune on the treatment of a solitary man at a clinic in Austria. He knew many of Moscow's injured could not even obtain an Austrian visa, let alone Austrian medicines.

Now, here he was, back in the 'Motherland,' among a community of survivalists, where joy had become as frigid as Stone-age ice and anger as pyroclastic as Jurassic magma. Dioxin's invisible fangs gnawed at the flesh and health of the everyday people he respected the most. His heart was ill at ease. This poison had come not from Soviet-occupied Afghanistan but American-occupied Afghanistan, a so-called beacon of Western democracy in the Muslim world.

There were no excuses.

The red storm brewing promised God-knows what.

He knew only this — It would shred Martensitic stainless steel.

A Soviet Santa with Bushy Eyebrows

With the morning's 'Bushkin Bunker' meetings concluded, Director-General Besstrashnikov and General Novimirov, marched grimly along with their president to the larger salons of the Kremlin Palace for the next set of meetings. All of them, hot-blooded 'World Peace in Camoflage' affairs.

Hour by hour, over the last three days, panic had crept into the Russian people and the once vibrant Russian economy. A brisk walk to the stores to get essentials became a stampede to convert whatever value was left in paper money into some tangible product that within days might not exist on shelves anywhere. Dioxinomic chaos had thrown the country back into the darkest days of the Soviet-era — both psychologically and economically — a time when throughout whole apartment complexes hoarding and barter was common place. Softcover books of toilet paper could be traded for spongy fresh soap. Souring milk for rancid sausage. And, hardcore bread for wilting vegetables.

Bushkin had kept his top generals heads down formulating their nation's military response shielded from Dioxinomic reality. He needed their hardscrabble focus, untarnished by anger. But, today, the curtain of civility was being lifted because the nation's elite had a duty to commiserate with the nation's rank and file.

When Bushkin, Besstrashnikov and Novimirov arrived at the Ivan-the-Conqueror Ballroom, everyone was already seated and chatting among themselves. While the room's magnificent marble and gilt paneled walls were crowned by a ceiling that appears to the eye the continuation of those very walls so as to form the impression of a massive spire to heaven, all earthbound eyes were impatiently locked onto the man at the podium. Echoes were on the dwindle by the time Bushkin raised his hands — The Summons to Order.

Bushkin called upon General Litvinenko to make the opening presentation. As he anticipated, Litvinenko's report refused to be anything except grotesque. The general's projections were becoming more inescapable as more data was amassed, more human behavioral systems observed and more computerized models of Dioxinomics verified. He was like a meteorological nerd-bot in the sky piercing the dust-cloud of woppery, and detailing the hurricane force agonies of a poisoned formicary that his fellow ants once called 'Moscow.' Bushkin welcomed Litvinenko's candor because the motherland needed her generals indoctrinated with the caliber of bloody-mindedness essential to crushing all her enemies. And, with the mood set through Litvinenko, Bushkin returned to the lectern and launched into the true purpose of the meeting with agenda item: Number One.

"General Tendinov, how are the Army's clinics doing at recruiting the walking dead for our Bzombie brigades?"

"The response has been excellent, Mr. President. Now called the Feralia Brigades, we currently have 8,348 in training, with the ranks swelling by some 3,000 new recruits a day. We anticipate 20% will die within three weeks. The rest will linger on between the sweet spot of four to ten weeks."

Bushkin attacked a niggling concern.

"Suicide looks dandy on paper. What of hesitation when the time comes?"

"First off, we refrain from any mention of the word 'terror' because we don't want our boys getting the notion that this is bluster fit for Hollywood and Western news-papsters. All recruits are schooled how Russia is at war with woppery. And, how *woppery* is derived from *Vopl. Nash Materni Yasyk.*"[1]

Bushkin interposed — "General, I'm concerned about *hesitation*."

"Sir, because the 'Wops from Wopland' story remains a state secret, it's all about *Vopl*. Right now, we can't point to a map and say — 'Go fuck'em.' The—"

Bushkin chopped in.

1 Literally, Our Mother Tongue. Idiom for 'Vulgar Language' (Rus).

"You've already got a taste of Litvinenko's idea of 'stark.' Trust me, when the time comes, I'll do 'stark' plus 'drama' to ensure every peacenik on this planet goes berserk. Bzombies are essential to minimizing bloodshed in the opening hours of our mission to preserve world peace. General, fill us in, please."

Tendinov dipped his head out of respect.

"Sir. For the first twenty-four hours, recruits are indoctrinated with feelings of broken-heartedness to fully engage their reptilian sense of the Almighty's Holy vengeance. Next, they nurse victims for another twenty-four hours while those victims ceaselessly beg for a quick end. Only when the nursing period concludes, are they allowed to vest up the victim, who then euthanizes without qualm. In addition, audio-video about what woppery looks like, steels them with the fortitude necessary to punch the button. We tap into rational 'vopl-pollutes-you' emotions so they feel undead like real zombies. When presented with a juicy target, these heroes of world peace will tap into the slow-death anguish they witnessed, scream *'Death to Woppery'* and euthanize without a second thought. At the 'Peace-Out' hour when all our Feralia forces come out of hiding, the enemies of the motherland won't know what atomized them."

Bushkin rose onto his tingling toes and nodded approval.

"Excellent. I also hear we have re-designed bomb vests — yes?"

"Mr. President, we call them HSCs — Human Shaped Charges. Recruits are trained in various abdominal postures to optimize destruction to tanks, armoured personnel carriers, pipelines, fuel depots, and steel or concrete structures. We're using aluminium infused silicon carbide disks mounted within Kevlar swaddling. By creating a flexible 'Dragon Skin' blast plate, their bodies don't simply shatter but rather focus a directional blast to maximize the shockwave and eject a supersonic armour piercing beam of molecular copper. We also have retirees in the process of adapting automobile airbags to further asymmetrize the blast effects. When it comes to ending their dioxin-riddled lives, our Feralia forces will make all those Islamic martyrs you hear about on the news look like boy scouts brandishing firecrackers. For woppery, there's no such thing as safe distance from the heroic forces of world peace."

Rising even higher, Bushkin draped his chest over the lectern.

"Brilliant. We need to restore a nationwide sense of esprit-de-corps. When the order to preserve world peace is given, woppery must know that the blow-out of the motherland's intestinal fortitude is unstoppable."

And, Tendinov felt a need to elaborate.

"Sir, from a military standpoint, it will be interesting to see how this plays out. I suspect once the enemies of world peace realize that any civilian could be a Bzombie, they'll have all civilians go naked anywhere their troops tread. Sort of like the ancient of days of clothing optional warfare in Greece."

Bushkin gloated quietly at the prospect — *Naked wops*.

"Which reminds me." Bushkin looked to his left — "General Novimirov, what's the status of 'Operation Chili Balls'?"

"We have thirteen seasoned Veronikas[1] deployed, currently refining our field methods. The rest are working on Siren recruits, many of whom suffered

1 Russia's Amateur Spy Corps. In honor of Veronika Lewintsova, captured by 'Capitalist Pigs' in 1998.

spontaneous miscarriages after the Metro attack. They could not be more psychologically ready to give birth to peace upon our planet."

Bushkin nodded his approval to Basil — "And, what of logistics?"

"Each Veronika leads a platoon of twenty-five Sirens. All are selected for their ten-week life spans. The Sirens cannot wait to screw the enemy in ways undreamt of before. Hot sex for hot vengeance. They're currently mastering the art of how to inject the rear of the scrotum to best avoid detection and minimize nerve damage. By the time the 'Peace-Out' hour arrives, the army can expect 85% of our time release urushiol capsules to have opened and the other 15% within hours thereafter. Expect US-NATO infirmaries to be crammed with as many sad-nad excuses for soldiers that our Siren units can seduce before then."

Bushkin laughed hard with relish.

"That'll show those US-NATO pricks what chemical warfare feels like! I wonder if they'll ever discover that half of our urushiol supply is being harvested by Amerikan Boy Scouts and Girl Guides doing voluntary cleanup of poison ivy and poison oak over the many parklands in the United States and Canada."

A white-haired Soviet Santa with bushy eyebrows bustled himself onto his feet to amplify his presence. Regaled in full-dress olive uniform, Marshal Ogrom Mikhailovich Palachnin, the Supreme Kommander of the Armed Forces was the 'Klassic Komrade' — green on the outside yet red all over. He expressed misgivings — "General Novimirov, how can you guarantee every single injection procedure won't be detected? The element of surprise is vital."

Basil turned and faced his komrade-in-arms — "Marshal, at the point of orgasm the soldier is electrically stunned into temporary unconsciousness. The Siren has ten seconds to inject the capsule. The tear in the skin is miniscule and she has superglue to seal any lesion. When the soldier regains consciousness, she raves about how she never had a client who had such a monstrous orgasmic blackout before. The soldier takes it as the perfect compliment and spreads the word to his buddies that there are some super fuck-you-dead whores in town."

Basil directed his gaze into the assembly.

"Any doubters are welcome to verify the process for themselves. No charge."

The room exploded with laughter.

The first to sober, Palachnin voiced continued skepticism.

"General, sounds great in theory. But, given the ever shortening periods of time between injection and the 'Peace-Out' hour, what makes you so confident the capsules will release almost simultaneously rather than haphazardly?"

Basil faced Palachnin again.

"Marshal, the capsules are micro-ampoules sealed with a biodegradable plug of various lengths. The capsules are preset for each day and during the day can be filed down to obtain synchronized release within fractions of a day. The release will occur over a matter of several hours before and after the designated 'Peace-Out' hour. Some 5% of scroti will experience premature release six hours beforehand. But, we expect 85% of all injected scroti will need emergency medical care by the time the clock ticks 'Peace-Out.' The debilitation factor for those in the field will be enormous. Incapacitation will last from four up to fourteen days."

Bushkin raised his arm — "General, what's our expected Siren strength?"

"I'm looking to field twenty-six platoons by week's end and over forty platoons in all. The sooner they canvass towns near military bases, the better. As an added bonus, this will be an enemy funded operation. For a military op, *Chilli Balls* might even turn a small profit."

The generals laughed for a solid half-minute before Bushkin cocked his arm, brought his hand to his forehead and extended Basil the ultimate accolade.

"General Basil Andreivich Novimirov," Bushkin snapped.

Surprised, Basil faced his president and stood at attention.

"On behalf of the Russian taxpayer, I salute you!" Bushkin finished.

Applause resounded across the room.

Once the raucous died down, Basil added.

"One other suggestion Mr. President. If a certain nosey Y-D Vice-President wants to know when Russia will be making a military strike, evade the question by telling him this — 'That's a secret but I assure you before it goes down, the enemy will feel us coming in his balls.' That should get him thinking."

Everyone roared with laughter again. Bushkin raised his hands. The room calmed. And, the meeting proceeded into dissecting and coordinating the many resources being mobilized for the ambitious mission to preserve world peace the Russian military was planning. Twenty minutes before the scheduled luncheon appointment with US Vice-President Weissbrot, Bushkin excused himself and turned the chairmanship back to his able Minister for Defense, Buran Boyanovich Smertvopski.

For the Sake of World Peace

Bushkin made for his office, with Director-General Karl Besstrashnikov and General Basil Novimirov in tow, for a pre-lunch rendezvous with Russian Foreign Minister, Radinka Ivanovna Klintova. Once seated, Bushkin initiated deliberations.

"Komrades, it's obvious Weissbrot is here to mend fences and snoop. Field your opinions about what I should and shouldn't discuss with him?"

The lack of prepared talking points bothered Klintova.

"Mr. President, if he gets too nosey, let me deflect the issue. 'The Heroin Holocaust' out of Amerikan-occupied Drughistan being the most obvious. The civilized world's moral compass should dominate discussion."

"Good Rada. When I tap your stiletto that means do exactly that and when you do, focus on finding common ground, such as Chechen terrorism. Don't confuse Weissbrot with that dinkle-berry strutting around the White House. I know Weissbrot personally. He's pragmatic and would make a fine president."

Perceiving 'mans-squawlking' at work, Klintova went for the high ground.

"Sir, with woppery on the march, we can't entrust world peace to monsters. Amerikan democracy is just a ruse for the abdication of moral order. Even if a darkie-Doodle like Oprah Spinfrey were president, I doubt we'd get any

'Truth' or 'Justice' or the 'Amerikan Way' in the Eisenhower sense, as the rule of civilization in Drughistan."

"Rada, save this for lunch, please."

"And can you imagine Y-D children doing school history reports comparing Abraham Lincoln and his generals, like Grant and Sherman, to sick Y-Doodle psychos like Potusson, Carter or Noriega and their inauguration of starvation enforced poppy-ninny slavery in the twenty-first cent—"

"Cut the 'conspicuous compassion,' Rada. Focus on Weissbrot."

"Mr. President, my point is alien decadence and immorality continues shredding every citizen's konstitutional right to national security under Article 61(2). Internecine gender-tantrums in Western rabble-ocracies must never trample on our people's konstitutional rights, freedoms and liberties. Just as Potusson once publicly berated us as barbarians for defending our sovereignty against Chechen terrorism before Amerika's '9/11' incident, that slag in the Oval Office felates her 'anti-Rooskie redneck' constituency and upbraids us for our so-called anti-narco-terrorism jingoism. And, doing so at the expense of the cordial relations Weissbrot once established between our nations. For the sake of world peace, Mr. President, prudence militates regime change."

Bushkin sighed — *Chainikov's assassination agenda.*

"Calm down. I'm reviewing things. It's a simple fact that presidents come and go. But, nations endure and their relations need to be the same — Enduring."

"Gods may do what cattle may not," Klintova quipped.

"And the bear never asks permission," Bushkin parried back.

Klintova sat erect and stone-faced. The message, clear.

Bushkin tilted back in his chair, heavy in thought.

"Rada, would you leave us and greet Weissbrot. Use your feminine charms to get a better read of the issues he'd be inclined to discuss at lunch. Above all, we must move forward. Also, show more leg. Intel has it Weissbrot is stoofing their Director of National Security and has a thing for legs."

Klintova left, certain her boss was now primed for action.

After the door eased shut, Bushkin turned to Besstrashnikov and Basil.

"Komrades, no more coddling starvation enforced poppy-ninny slavery. If children all over this world knew better, they and I would scream as one — *'Carter must be assassinated.'* World peace demands regime change. Is there anything I can do to have Weissbrot help us help him become president?"

Karl Besstrashnikov knew this outwardly open question was really one directed at him. For months now, in several private meetings with Bushkin, scenarios for Carter's assassination had been thrashed out at length. The prime mover was Russian Vice-President Chainikov, who had championed the cause the moment Carter won the election. Only after Carter had rebuffed every overture to implement 'Operation Rambo' and derided the Romanov-Al Guido Pre-Emptive Action Notice[1](PAN) as nothing more than a gambit squarely designed to subvert democracy in Russia, did Bushkin begin warming to the idea. Because Russia was on the path to demokrazy, Besstrashnikov restated

---

1 The name for the Notice Russia gave the UN Security Council on March 15, 2005 concerning the 'Romanov Conspiracy.'

what he considered common cause — putting rights and obligations inherent to all demokrazies into their proper global context.

"Sir, our intelligence profile on Weissbrot confirms he's as like-minded as you about Carter being another in the long line of morons the Wank-me-Doodle two-party system puts into office. The Y-Ds had the first cut of their two-party deck. As a demokrazy ourselves, it's about time the people of Russia exercised their elektoral franchise to cut that deck again. This time in Weissbrot's favour."

"Karl, I'm sold. Time now for action. So?"

Besstrashnikov lurched forward — "Sir, I have the plan as well as the man."

Bushkin's eyes brightened — "Out with it, Karl."

"Ivan Polakulakov resurfaced after hearing about Moscow. Avenging his daughter's death from a heroin overdose remains his priority. But, once I explained the involvement of Al Guido and gave him the gist of our plans for Afghanistan, he's back in the fold. In fact, he was instrumental in the capture of that narco-wog Radzulah Karzai."

Bushkin's face shone with approval.

Besstrashnikov continued — "As luck would have it, his mission of vengeance to penetrate Amerikan defenses and take out Supreme Kommander, US General Fidel Noriega has provided us a wealth of intel. Nor has his suicidal mindedness wavered. Carter is simply a more juicy target for his revenge."

Unrepentant glee gushed from Bushkin's lips.

"Suicidal. We're talking about as polished as the MI6-Al Yamamah financed operation on September 11, 2001 — right?"

"Definitely, sir."

"There can't be a whiff of evidence connecting Polakulakov to us. Our two nations are approaching the brink, so it must be much cleaner than the Oswald fiasco. Karl, can this truly be done? Truly?"

"Bzombie style, yes. I'll draft the details as soon as I return to my office."

Bushkin leant forward and extended his arms across his desk.

"Get Polakulakov airborne. I want him in Washington, prepped for action. Tell him, if we don't proceed on Carter, he has presidential authority to take out Noriega. I'll be demanding that four-star drug-wop to be pulled out of Drughistan as an act of contrition. Ivan can leave his signature half-empty box of bullets and return home with all accounts squared, all grievances settled and pardoned. Karl, he's in a position to travel — right?"

"Yes, clean identity — Matt Bauer. Ready to go on command."

Coming as a bolt out of the blue, Basil felt uneasy about the subject. While he considered the assassination of the Commander-in-Chief responsible for 'The Heroin Holocaust' that kills off 30,000 Russians each year a moral imperative indispensable to world peace, he also knew assassination was fraught with peril.

"Mr. President, if I may."

"Yes, Basil?"

"Don't neglect to implement the 'Oswald Ploy' as backup. Our best play is to salt in evidence, which suggests Weissbrot was in on the plan to snuff Carter.

That way when he's president, he'll have every incentive to do the smart thing and shut down all the hoopla, except the usual entertaining conspiracy theories."

Bushkin laughed derisively.

"Yes. Presidents come and go, but nations, cockroaches and crazy conspiracy theories are enduring," And he looked to his right — "Something else, Karl?"

"Mr. President, if Polakulakov does the Carter job, combined with our evidence tying him to the hit on that New York Times reporter and other evidence we generate as well as the fact he mysteriously came from Afghanistan, we'll have every Dood screaming — '*Al Qaeda sleeper cell*.'"

Almost as soon as he had finished, Besstrashnikov sensed he'd over-reached. Both he and Vice-President Chainikov had promoted the assassination of Times reporter, George W. Beaver. Initially, Bushkin had been reluctant, but decided to proceed and had organized the affair himself. But, in death, the curse remained. Beaver's posthumous exposés about J. W. Potusson, the corrupt incumbent president, had propelled Carter into the White House. Whacking Beaver remained a sore point, a perfect case study in assassination backfiring.

And, Besstrashnikov was not alone. Basil also noticed the sudden, cautionary mood descending over the president, making it clear to him that these men had discussed this whole subject at great length well beforehand.

Bushkin tweezed the underside of his chin.

"Perhaps Karl, but let's keep handy-dandy Chainikov thinking out of the loop. I'm not going to jump the gun with dire *what-if-we-don'ts*. Got it?"

Besstrashnikov nodded obsequiously.

Bushkin brightened and rose from his seat.

"Time to knosh with Weissbrot. Once I get a read of what intelligence fish Mr. Veep is angling for, we can decide what eel head to toss him. I'm looking for anything to boost Weissbrot's prestige, expose Carter as a slathering warmonger and rebuild strong US-Russia relations. Be ready for a post-luncheon meeting."

"Sir," Basil said, "Let's aim to toss a crab claw in Yogi's picnic basket."

Bushkin doubled over in hysterics and put up his hand.

"Let me. Claws — because the CIA assigns greater credibility to tidbits that are hard to crack. The harder, the more succulent the meat. Then CIA butters up this dish and serves it to their president as 'Hard Won Truth.'"

Basil twisted his palm and finger in a corkscrew gesture — *Touché*.[1]

Bushkin wheeled about and made for the door — *Friends are priceless*.

Basileus, Basileus, Basileus

Returned to the Lubyanka, Basil and Director-General Besstrashnikov conferred about the proposed assassination of Carter for half an hour. An incoming call from Basil's driver, Ivan, confirmed that the Patriarch and Miss Bogomolski had arrived back. Basil excused himself to attend to the mystery surrounding Natalia Bogomolski. He caught up with her at the cafeteria entrance.

1 You got it! (French)

"Natash, I'm very sorry I could not be with you this morning. Derek's passing must have come as an awful shock. It was for me, sweetheart."

Natalia remained stone silent, as if she had not heard one word.

Basil shifted to the positive.

"The most recent crop of 'Jugheads' have been confessing everything since five this morning. President Bushkin conveys his deep appreciation for your mission of peace and righteousness and the many lives that will be saved because of your perseverance. Today, the Amerikan vice-president showed up, so lunch was not possible. I'm sorry I had to rush off, and—"

Natalia wanted to remain in the simple present, so she interjected.

"I'm sure President Bushkin is horribly overloaded. Derek's passing reminded me of the urgency." Speaking his name hurt. Her larynx felt petrified. But, just as quickly a spirit within annealed her — "Basil, please let's not discuss it. Lunch together is the best medicine. Here comes the Patriarch."

Patriarch Mudretski held out his hand.

"Basil, I hope you've had a good morning. I have. The Lord's work cures all."

Basil replied with equal heart.

"Your work has such purpose, Kolya. And, thank you for being there for me this morning. Please, Your Eminence, join us for lunch?"

"Your hospitality is kindly noted," the Patriarch replied, "but I'm sure you two would prefer to eat alone." And, the Patriarch glanced down at Natalia — "Talk to Basil about what we discussed."

She felt somewhat ambushed.

"Certainly. But, in that case, you must join us. Basil might wish to ask religious questions. Patriarch, please. Don't leave me defenseless."

Basil winked, and his left cheek plumped in half-smile.

"Well Kolya, it seems Special Agent Bogomolski has issued your 'Marching Orders.' Come, I also insist. I owe you lunch and much more."

Seated in seclusion in the officer's dining hall, Basil told Natalia he had watched her eyes moving in REM sleep that morning. Wondering about whether he would be able to sense her inner thoughts, he confessed how he had put his hand atop her left breast close to her heart. She giggled and made teasing reply.

"I suspected as much, General Basil Andreivich Novimirov. 'The Grope of Hope,' no doubt. Did you enjoy the feel of my D'D'Dreams?" she stuttered.

Basil tweezed his lips at this C-cup scamp's sultry boast. But, with the Patriarch present, he confined himself to under-the-wire riposte.

"Special Agent Natalia Vladimirovna Bogo-milk-ski, I sensed generalities pregnant with concepts, but nothing I could put language[1] to."

The Patriarch rubbed his hands — "That's interesting news."

Pulling his eyes from Natalia, Basil flashed the Patriarch a quizzed look.

"Basil, you may have influenced her dream. Why don't you explain, Natalia."

She leant forward across the table.

"Basil, the difference between this morning's dream, and the previous night when I slept alone, was that today the Roman soldiers did not prevent me from

---

1 A ribald play on the Russian word Yasik - meaning both Language and Tongue.

touching the lower legs and feet of Jesus. He was already dead, so a centurion ordered them to let me pass. Still nailed in place, I stroked every wound as far as I could reach." She clutched Basil's hand and beamed — "Basil, they all healed."

The Patriarch nodded in shared jubilation.

"Now Basil, from what you've just divulged, and what makes this interesting, is that Natalia's dreams may not be memories of the past but allegorical dreams that her mind is fabricating to acclimate her to her powers of healing. And, all in terms of the tragedy of Golgotha. To put it another way, God is sending his Special Agent emissary a mission statement."

Natalia sat upright. While it warmed her to know how the Patriarch looked upon her as God's Special Agent, this constant back and forth about what to her were very private matters from the distant past was exasperating.

"I accept the plausibility of cathartic dreaming. But, I honestly think my dreams are direct recollections."

Feeling remiss for not consoling her about Derek's passing, Basil squirmed in his seat at the prospect of coming across as Mr. Cynic. He wanted her to find peace and reconciliation because it was clear to him she was suffering from a vast overload of personal guilt, only made worse by the vampire horror show thrust upon them. To stymie argument, he crooned as fondly as possible.

"Sweet lady, keep in mind, the purpose of sleep is to embed memories into the brain's glial-neuronal structures. You're trying to recall these dreams. It's true you sense them when you're awake as memories. But, memories of a dream."

"Oh! And, just how do I understand several languages in my so-called cathartic dreams?"

Basil smiled — *This argument was becoming very, very stale.*

"Really! *Basileus, basileus, basileus.* Would you care to explain?"

"Yes. Jesus spoke to me in common Hebrew. He said—"

Basil chipped in — "*Basileus, basileus, basileus.*"

"No. No, he did not say that," she lashed back — "What's wrong with you! I want to talk about—" Then the thought struck her — *Perhaps, he did hear something.* "So … so, you heard Jesus address you by name?"

On its upbeat, Basil's heart felt bathed in a hot spring of hope. Her delirious optimism kindled his deep admiration for her. But, on its downbeat, his heart crumpled to hard disconsolation, for this hope was naught but delusion. He felt hurt. He felt ambushed. While his mind insisted she ought know one truth, his love for her insisted upon another.

"Slow down, Natash." And, Basil's voice became as satin — "Ancient Greek was one of the languages used on the placard attached to Jesus' cross. From biblical accounts of witnesses, it read 'Jesus of Nazareth King of the Jews.' So from your specific dream about Jesus, if you knew only four words in ancient Greek then '*basileus*,' which means 'king,' would be one of them."

He extended his hand to her.

"I'm trying to make you realize that you're having dreams. You're not having 2,000 year old recollections that include linguistic abilities."

Sporting a face baffled by it all, she replied.

"I thought you were speaking a name. *Basileus*, your own ancient name."

Basil continued to twinkle charm.

"Natash, you're right. Basil is derived from the Greek for 'king.' However, as you know, in Russian it means 'courageous' or 'brave.' In fact look at my complete name. Basil Novi-mir-ov means 'pertaining to brave new worlds.'"

She seized the opening to match wits with her lover.

"In a Shakespeare play about love and power called *The Tempest*, there's a line by Miranda, a woman overwhelmed by the new wonder of visitors, especially men: 'Oh brave new world that has such people in it.'"

Basil was relieved she'd not taken his response as a put-down.

"Natash, we must read it together. Have you read the Aldous Huxley novel *Brave New World*? It was written before nuclear weapons were invented. Based on his experience with the cheap annihilative power of chemical weapons in World War I, Huxley speculated that to survive, mankind would need to erect a worldwide utopian order."

Her mood remained a yarn ball of playful.

"My dear Basileus, I haven't. So let's read that as well."

Sensing that he had just been pet-named, he quipped back.

"But only if you promise not to dream about it!"

"Now, I'm smelling Basil-leos, the cowardly Lion of Teasers."

Basil immediately parried back in jest.

"And, I think it's now obvious, you're no Greek geek."

Natalia abruptly became serious.

"So you agree with the Patriarch — My dreams are cathartic?"

The Patriarch spoke into the looming spat — "Natalia, Don't brood. It's the General's job to be open-minded, to ask searching questions and not jump at the first convenient explanation. Tell Basil about what Jesus said to you. I'm sure he'd love to know."

Basil smiled encouragement into her eyes — *Please do.*

Natalia's mood brightened eleven degrees — "It's beyond extraordinary. Near the beginning of my dream. This I remember without fail. Jesus said not to be afraid or sad. Then his words — I would have a son. He was very specific — '*Mother behold your Son. Son behold your Mother.*' But the Patriarch told me the Apostle John recorded this statement in the Bible and it's related to Mary and John becoming mother and son at Jesus' command."

Basil oozed solidarity with her but stayed on message — "My sweet Natash, if it's Biblical record, you obviously had a dream about something you read. I truly believe Jesus spoke to you. But, through a wondrous dream meant to help you cope with this tragedy. Trust me, the great spirit of love within you knows your mission in life and is helping you get over your feelings of guilt."

No sooner had he finished speaking than Basil became pensive. Ultimately this whole subject reverted back to Derek Mitchell. And, with his demise, what dreams would come tonight.

Natalia noted the fret on Basil's face. She winced because defending herself against skepticism was becoming tiresome, especially when she had gone to great lengths to differentiate what she considered premonition and what she considered memory. She felt like unloading.

"Basil, I'm asking you to trust me. I don't expect you to believe me but please don't ridicule me or think I'm crazy."

Basil put his hand over hers. But, she kept unloading — "Who has done what I've done over the last 48 hours? Who? In the Metro, while I was half unconscious, it seemed only momentary but I definitely heard a voice tell me that within three days I would find my greatest love and would be with child."

Basil's ears twitched — *Three days.* This was specifically what Derek had told him during the debriefing in his office. He now comprehended the distress Mitchell had spoken about — *rabid female territorialism — three days — a great love —* and now — *with child! These sperm-sucking vampire intercessions are getting out of hand*, he thought.

"And Patriarch, where's your faith?" Natalia snapped.

The Patriarch addressed the winnowing glare Natalia threw his way.

"Please don't question my beliefs. You're very correct. Every day is a day of continuous proof that you are a miracle walking amongst mankind. But, I would like to keep the grace of God rooted in the present day. We don't need to twist accounts from the life of Jesus or conjure up prophecies cut from biblical sources when we have eyes to see and ears to hear."

Natalia's voice was deadpan — "So, you do heed the words of the Lord!"

The Patriarch was taken aback. He hadn't realized what he'd said. She was very correct in her upbraid. Indeed, he was heeding the teachings of Jesus, but it was a novel experience for him to have a lay person chide him with a scriptural censure. The Patriarch decided upon a diversion — "Miss Bogomolski, calm, please. Time to leave Jesus out of this and tell Basil the real news about the present day," and he flared his eyebrows in encouragement.

While Basil's face went on alert, Natalia's glowed with prospect, for it was news she was busting to get off her chest — "Basil, please don't be alarmed but I think … I'm very certain that I'm pregnant. The signs are there, vague but," and upon noting Basil's sudden stupefaction, she switched gears to make the matter more jocular — "and yesterday like the rumble of a train coming down the Metro, I could feel my eggs bouncing along ready to form a baby."

Basil remained mute — *Riposte was one thing — but not this.*

Sensing that with a pregnancy in the offing, three was way more than a crowd, the Patriarch made graceful exit. Basil bided his time and watched the Patriarch shamble off. Then he turned to Natalia and broke his silence by joking that while her eggs might be rumbling along like duckies at a carnival concession stand, he might be shooting blanks. She laughed. She knew otherwise. But, his jest about dodgy carni-ammo presented a perfect opportunity for her to insist that he continue shooting, and right now in his office would be an excellent time to practice FSB marksmanship — on-the-house.

And, in the process of standing, she had a flash of recall.

"Basil, I almost forgot. I touched his body. I have that vague sense that I somehow revived him back to life. Can you believe it!"

Basil was caught unawares — "What! Derek is still with us."

Splendor unfurled across her ruby lips.

"No. No, I mean Jesus. My child. Perhaps I'll recall it better in another dream. But, near the end of my last dream, when I stroked his feet on the cross, I had this premonition … There's more to it. A life force stirred and then I felt rejoicing." She sighed as she noticed Basil's gaze — "It's so hard to explain."

Basil's temples tingled with delight at the boundless absurdity of miracles streaming pall-mall from the mouth of this sweet lady. She was raw exaltation, so he spoke not a solitary thought. What did it matter that if in her delusions and rationalizations, Natalia thought she was the mother of Jesus come back to life here in Russia. Compared to the vile Tsar, Tsarina, Prince and Princess pretensions of the wops imprisoned in this very building, this meek woman had something exquisitely serene about her. Like Derek Mitchell's marveling thoughts after one long telephone call, one long summer ago, Basil's thoughts waxed the same — *Here is a woman I could grow to adore.*

Damn Rooskies Y-Doodling Your Chain

From the comfort of his office, President Bushkin provided Director-General Karl Besstrashnikov and Basil a summary of his lunch meeting with Weissbrot before eliciting their suggestions for a follow-up dinner with the vice-president that evening. Basil was simply itching to know.

"Sir, what was Weissbrot's take on Mitchell's GPS note?"

Bushkin eased out a half-smile in Basil's direction.

"I sensed Weissbrot was dubious about that lucky break and smells the possibility we orchestrated it. Given the 'Mallory Wilson Affair' slamming the door on Amerikan intel and their suspicion over every morsel of snot we choose to blow their way, any intelligence officer worth a glass eyeball might have formed the same conclusion. How Weissbrot handled it makes him smart."

"So, you're thinking he'll put other DVDs we offer up into play during the next White House meeting hashing out the 'Crisis in Russia.'"

"Bear in mind, no one will be fooled that we gave him an intelligence coup." Bushkin lurched forward — "The critical news is we agree on Afghanistan. What's going to happen is going to happen. He knows our elektorate must blow-off steam. And, he prefers bellicosity from a disciplined leader rather than some whack-a-doodle demagogue screaming bullet Bushkuntosaurus through the eyeball, as if our fledging demokrazy protecting the world from godless nuclear annihilation means nothing to those Jewnited States pagans. It's something horrifying he saw in Potusson. Now, to his dismay, he sees it again in Carter."

"I assume we're keeping Romanov and Al Guido's involvement secret?"

"Not a damn peep. Carter still cracks jokes about our Pre-emptive Action Notice. Focus on Al Qaeda. It's no stretch for Weissbrot to peddle that crap."

"Fine. We'll go from 'Afghan drug lords' to Mitchell specifically identifying the Afghan, Uzbek, Turkmen and Tajik terrorists we have in detention as the scumbags he was holding the diamonds for. Since Romanov remains off-the-radar, I guess you've also decided against informing Weissbrot about the dioxin urn destined for the United States."

"Agreed on everything. But, I'm thinking of letting the Doods know about the second urn. That disaster will rear its head at some point. Once we go public with Romanov, the Amerikans will put two-and-two together. Then they'll know we held back, and once again our improving relations will sour."

Basil responded pensively — "I understand, sir. Might I point out that if we load up Weissbrot with too much information, it comes across as glaringly unsubtle. Cynics in the White House could conclude the whole thing was staged."

Bushkin and Besstrashnikov burst out laughing.

Basil shifted moods and followed suit.

Bushkin dusted off his 'White House Elmer' falsetto.

"Oh, those wenegade Wooskie Wascals!" He mellowed — "If only those Voshington cheeseburgers knew that our Afghan, Uzbek, Turkmen and Tajik confessions are confected out of pure koko-loko. Zero correlation to reality. Bravo for your vampires, Basil. Someday when you retire you can make real money producing a television show. Give it a sexy name like *'Basil's Vamps'* where you play some faceless old fart on a speaker-phone pulling all the strings."

An unexploited idea flashed across Basil's mind — "Sir, since the dinner tonight is more social, why not invite the Patriarch and Miss Bogomolski? Based on his profile, it would be good for Weissbrot to see the so-called godless Pastafarian[1] President of Cossack-land embrace Christian values."

Bushkin leant forward in his chair.

"*Bolsheviks*! Excellent idea. Also, the Patriarch would see the inestimable stake both he and his Christian fraternity have in promoting world peace."

"Mr. President," Besstrashnikov interposed.

"Yes, Karl?"

"Why don't I take Weissbrot to one side and show him the Mitchell testimony about the urn destined for the US. I can act as a behind the scenes agent, like you did with President Zeltsin during the Denver nuclear disaster.[2] It relieves you of the dilemma of handing over too much information in one sitting."

"Perfect. If Weissbrot mentions it, I'll elaborate. It also serves to remind him about how the Denver crisis was defused via back-channels. The man needs a reliable forecast about our sincerity and how cynics inside the White House compel us to remain cagey about our sources of intelligence, including the dioxin disaster headed for Amerika. He can see. He'll understand. He doesn't need White House poodles snarking — 'It's the damn Rooskies Y-Doodling your chain.'"

---

1 Religious sect. Deacons adorn their heads with colanders.
2 After a terrorist nuclear attack on Denver, Colorado, as part of the 'Superpower Doctrine', the United States and Russia recognized each nation had a unilateral sovereign right to hunt down and prosecute any person or entity engaging, planning, or aiding terrorism, codified into each nation's legal code as the US-Russia Anti-Terrorism Act.

A knock. The door cracked open. The odor flooded into Bushkin's office. Evgenia entered with tea service for three and a platter of shortbread, fresh-baked from Nigras Patisserie on the grounds of the Kremlin.

Bushkin's glee was almost instantaneous.

"Nigras! *Devushka, tebya loobloo.*"[1]

And, who didn't love eating Nigras. Discovered and encouraged by Tsar Alexander II, the bakery's founder, Constantin Nigras and his family, had emigrated from Thessalonika to Moscow in 1863. With an imperial patent to set up shop in the Kremlin palace, the talent behind their motto 'Nigras make the best pies' carried the family through seven decades of Stalinist purges. As they say in Russia — '*The way to Koba's*[2] *heart is through the codger's stomach.*'

Bushkin took the tray from Evgenia's grasp and issued instructions.

"Evgenia. Rustle up a gift tin of Nigras finest for Weissbrot, please."

"Certainly, sir." And, she left the men alone once again.

After a cheery round of tea and Greek shortbreads, the meeting turned to the here and now; the means of Carter's assassination. High on a sugar buzz, Bushkin endorsed the plan Besstrashnikov laid out. But, success was essential and that made solid intel essential, so Bushkin assigned himself the dinner-time task of probing Weissbrot for possible vulnerabilities.

After the logistical details of her assassination had been thrashed out, deliberations focused on the political. And, the more they discussed how America's two-party, two-timing version of democracy elevated slag into high office, the more these men appreciated how the apple of America's eye, it's children, deserved far better — such as the benefits of a new world order inaugurated through Weissbrot. And, after another round of tea and Nigras, they convinced themselves that, as repugnant as it was, the assassination of Carter was an indispensable element to the advancement of world peace. Something even Oprah Spinfrey would applaud.

A Mystery Wrapped Inside a Jeroboam of Enigma

Upon her return to the Lubyanka complex, and in a spare twenty minutes, Natalia dressed into a black satin evening gown hastily requisitioned from the Veronika division. Elena escorted her to the northern garage where she joined Basil and the Patriarch for the journey to the Kremlin. With the aid of a special escort, they arrived some thirty minutes ahead of schedule, which provided them ample time to set up and demonstrate the dioxin decontamination equipment.

For two days, Bushkin had been itching to know more about Miss Bogomolski and the decontamination process, so he dunned her for a preview before their guest of honour arrived. Natalia had just finished showing the president how her skin could decontaminate dioxin when the stately twelve-foot high doors to the grand parlor room swung wide and regally open. In walked a small processional that included Director-General Karl Gregorivich Besstreshnikov,

---

1 Young woman, I love you. (Rus).
2 Nickname for Joseph Stalin, Head of the Soviet Union (1922-1953).

US Vice-President Norman Ousley Weissbrot and US Ambassador Rodney Francis Steele. And, bringing up the rear, marched a stiff-kneed Kremlin porter bear-hugging a wooden crate the size of an airline carry-on bag.

Bushkin extended his hand — "Norman, welcome back."

"Fyedor, thank you for your continued hospitality in these trying times." Weissbrot motioned toward the porter — "*Moi tavareesh,*[1] a gift of champagne. The least I could do given my unceremonious arrival in your lands." The Vice-President formally presented the crate to Bushkin and continued his tone of bonhomie — "The White House inventory indicates a *jeroboam*[2] of France's finest with two Lalique stemware inside, waiting to be ravished by you, me and Uncle Joe's ghost."

Heeding the call to camaraderie, Bushkin dipped his head in Weissbrot direction. Weissbrot returned the sentiment and cemented the mood — "With your approval Fyedor, I'd like to crack it open and make a pre-dinner toast."

"*Harosho*! An excellent idea, my friend." And, Bushkin addressed the porter — "Put it on this table, Oleg, and pry it open."

While the porter and the wine steward wrestled with opening the crate, President Bushkin formally introduced his guest of honour to the other attendees, starting with Basil. Next was Natalia. But, before he could get to the crown-jewel in his Christian Fabergé, the Patriarch of Moscow and All Rus, the last wooden slat lifted free and the focus of attention returned to Weissbrot's gift. Bushkin held off because the Patriarch was a crucial introduction deserving of no distraction.

Inside, nestled between pine-scented wood shavings lay a massive three liter sea-green bottle. It bore no label. The pedigree of its contents had been acid-etch and gilded into the frosted glass in a flamboyant Louis XVI, Roi d'Or,[3] typeface. Bushkin picked up the hefty bottle and passed it to the wine steward, who then disappeared into a Kremlin anteroom, long converted into a modern-era bar.

Bushkin placed his right hand on Weissbrot's shoulder — "Norman, I'd like you to watch a demonstration. You need night-vision goggles. Basil, if you would, please."

Basil set a pair of goggles over Weissbrot's head while Natalia donned her own pair as well as one latex glove to mask her secret power.

Bushkin grabbed his own pair and ordered.

"Everyone stand still. Dim the lights, please."

An infrared scanner became the only source of illumination.

"Miss Bogomolski, proceed, please," Bushkin directed.

Natalia was about to pick up a pre-contaminated demonstration sample when she noticed faint flecks of light emanating from the crate.

"Look! One of the glasses is fluorescing."

Bushkin peered into the box — "Yes. On the right. In the bowl."

Natalia picked up the glass by the stem and held it closer to the infrared light source so they could all study this curiosity.

Bushkin pointed it out to his guest.

1 My Brother (Rus).
2 A 3.0 liter bottle (French).
3 King of Gold (French)

"See the fluorescence. It's very distinct now Norman?"

"Ah — why — Yes."

Then Weissbrot's tone hardened in mock indignation — "So, that's dioxin?"

"Definitely," Natalia replied.

"Norman, where did you get this gift?"

Discerning an accusatory snip in Bushkin's voice, Weissbrot hesitated.

"It … It comes directly from the White House cellar. A Christmas gift from the French Ambassador, so I'm told. It should've been protected under diplomatic seal at the airport. All I can say is that some bloody busy-body has been snooping to see what the box contained. This is extremely embarrassing."

Fortunately for Weissbrot, the room was so dark and the goggles so large, no one noticed the raw agitation on his face. He remained on edge but considered that he had provided a plausible explanation. Bushkin poked around the wood shavings inside the box like a pheasant scratching for grubs.

"I see no other contamination. Miss Bogomolski, please double check."

Bushkin felt ambushed. He had secretly rescinded diplomatic protocols. It was very possible yet another inept official at Sheremetyevo airport had caused this. And, far worse, the bungling appeared like an assassination attempt.

"Norman, I apologize if some fool at Sheremetyevo has done this. It's beyond stupid. You have to understand we're under extra security since the urn containing dioxin was released in Moscow. In theory, that three liter jeroboam could conceal a lot of dioxin. I'm sure you can appreciate our nation's anxiety."

And, while Bushkin was talking, a cork popped in the darkness.

Already unhinged, his mission a total failure, Weissbrot jolted at the unexpected sound. And, a new worry had his heart racing. Soon the room's lights would be on and his guilt-ridden demeanor would be plain for all to see. His only remedy was to become hyper-agitated while darkness prevailed. Contriving to redden his cheeks as well as delay any return to proper illumination, he clamped his eyes closed, clenched the muscles in his neck and spoke gruffly.

"Fyedor. It's terrible. For all I know, the snoop could have been an Embassy employee. I do apologize. Apologize! This pollution is insidious." He raised his voice and stiffened his shoulders — "Insidious! Russia has my heartfelt sympathies. This dioxin contamination is spread by sticky-beak bumpkins. This curse must be snuffed out. Snuffed out!"

He stopped. Surely this was ample to pass as indignation.

Weissbrot did not know it, but Bushkin had his own issues and felt relieved by his guest's outburst. Indeed, Weissbrot's voice expressed a heartfelt anger towards a common enemy. Bushkin replied to allay further anxiety and put baseless and scurrilous suspicions to rest.

"Norman, now you understand up-close and personal. That's what counts, my friend. Let's not trouble ourselves with speculation. Miss Bogomolski, decontaminate the glass, please."

Natalia confirmed the mood of reconciliation.

"Already done, Mr. President. See?"

Bushkin crooned with satisfaction — "Excellent. Lights, please."

Bushkin and Weissbrot removed their goggles and exchanged words in follow-up while Natalia sought out the wine steward. With the two glasses filled, she returned and addressed the president about protocol.

"Sir, etiquette requires we serve our guest first — correct?"

"Yes, of course." And Bushkin gestured for her to present the glass in her right hand to the Amerikan vice-president.

Weissbrot stared coldly at a glass bubbling with sweet champagne as if it were an Erlenmeyer flask containing triacetone-triperoxide[1] solution boiling its way down to detonation. Assuming the glass still remained contaminated, the matter was fifty-fifty. If he died, Carter would go ballistic and doom the whole planet. He looked Bushkin in the eyes.

"Fyedor, I don't wish … I trust that you've decontaminated the glass, but I can't permit this. Both these glasses must be discarded. I represent the President of the United States and we find a toxin on the glass of a gift that was supposed to be under diplomatic seal. It looks very bad. Could you ask your steward if the champagne was completely sealed, we heard the cork pop, but—"

Bushkin cut in cordially — "Of course, Norman. Right you are."

Bushkin swiveled to his left.

"Oleg, was the champagne properly wrapped and sealed?"

"Yes, Mr. President. No indication of tampering. Wired in place, the cork required a substantial amount of twist to release. All very normal, sir."

Bushkin faced his guest — "Well Norman, it's your call. What do you think?"

Weissbrot took his time.

"Fyedor, I'm probably overly anxious. Let's toss the glasses and go with Kremlin stemware. If you think the champagne is compromised, let's toss it too."

Bushkin laughed and winked — "As long as it's handsomely compromised with alcohol, I'm happy to drink the stuff. Of course, I still expect you to take the first sip as my poison-tester tonight. After all, it is *your* plonk."

Weissbrot relaxed and quipped back in half-chuckle.

"I'll consider that a promotion until I become president of some banana republic. Then you'll have to dig up a replacement."

With a sense of camaraderie firmly re-established, a jovial spirit pervaded the room once more. The wine steward returned with an ornate silver tray jostling with the Kremlin's finest gilt-rimmed crystal ware and while the champagne flowed freely, Weissbrot was once again introduced to the small circle of attendees, but most especially the Patriarch this time around.

During the next twenty minutes, both the Patriarch and Natalia provided the Vice-President of the United States a deeper appreciation of the tragedy. For his part, Weissbrot was elated to see the dawn of a new attitude — Bushkin paying homage to the blessings of Christian religious intervention. Everyone was well past introductions when the Master-of-the-Table heralded them into the Azurite Banqueting Hall. Amidst the crackle of wetted oak burning warm and festive in the belly of an enormous hearth of Carrara marble inlaid with

---

1 Highly sensitive, twitchy explosive.

black jade and polished azurite, the conversation between all diners continued brisk and hearty, considerate and sincere.

Weissbrot tactfully divulged to his host that Director-General Besstrashnikov had let him view the Mitchell testimony concerning a second urn of dioxin headed to the United States. Bushkin pretended to be a little troubled by this presumptuousness on the Director-General's part, but quickly moved on by explaining the dilemma of releasing too much intelligence. He re-emphasized the point that Weissbrot needed to be very discreet because in his estimation too much data too soon would make it appear things had been orchestrated.

Weissbrot let Bushkin know how much he understood the predicament and thanked him for the mature way he was handling the shortcomings of the current White House. For — How could Bushkin invite impartial American spies back into Russia's security apparatus — Impossible. In the post-'Mallory Wilson' world, the two men concurred that trust was at a premium and distrust was only aiding the cause of their nations' common enemies. As a matter of joint national security, in openly recognized baby-steps, Bushkin and Weissbrot strove to forge a deeper personal relationship. Both men harbored the expectation that if the information came from the top, was trustworthy, was verifiable to a reasonable degree, and was confided one to the other solely to assure peace and stability then what need was there for espionage.

Ready to test the boundaries of a *Blizki-Drugi*[1] relationship, Bushkin acquired a modicum of information about President Carter's schedule, but nothing sufficiently concrete that assailed his nagging sense of caution. Assassination was always a tricky business. This, the onetime Intelligence Tsar of Russia knew well.

For his part and with like confidence in the budding camaraderie between the two men, Weissbrot ventured to put out feelers for more specifics about the impending Russian assault against her enemies. Bushkin's cheeks turned ruddy in smile, his eyes betrayed sheer pleasure at his new friend's presumptuousness and he responded without hesitation.

"Norman, I assure you of this. Before a single bullet is fired, the enemy will feel us coming in his balls." And, he roared with laughter.

Weissbrot gradually broke into polite chuckle, all the while reflecting on the Winston Churchill adage — '*Russians are a mystery wrapped inside an enigma.*'

By the end of the state dinner, one thing was clear to Weissbrot — Bushkin understood the situation in Washington. And, plain as day, Bushkin was rallying to heed a Christian God, rallying to reduce his people's suffering, and rallying to inaugurate a new world order, in which superpower governments would unilaterally dictate what lesser countries may and may not do. Feeling refreshingly liberated from all the politically-correct hokum of the onetime 'Fair-play Balanced with Hypocrisy' doctrine, Weissbrot's final thought for the night was reduced to the only specter which promised to frustrate the life, liberty and happiness of both nations — *Democratic chaos must never stand in the way. Far better if Carter is out of the picture and Bushkin is in the picture.*

1 Close and trusted friends (Rus).

Stupid Doesn't Last Forever

The afternoon of the sixteenth of September, 2005 was miserably wet. At CIA headquarters, a meeting involving the senior intelligence staff from every branch of the Office of National Intelligence was thrashing through the additional information the Russians had provided their so-called new Amerikan friend. Decisions needed to be made as to whether Bushkin's disclosures were sufficiently credible, and thereupon actionable so that their nation's responses and policies could be designed and implemented.

Director of National Intelligence Lester Coverdale wasn't in attendance.

He was at Andrews Air Force Base. No sooner had Air Force One come to rest within its hanger then the boarding stairs were butted firmly against the fuselage and the aircraft door swung open. Lester stepped out of his limousine and extended his hand in greeting the moment Vice-President Weissbrot's right shoe hit the hanger slab. Because events were moving even faster in the political imbroglio Lester and Weissbrot were targeting personally, a private meeting was essential. As the car lurched into motion, Lester ribbed Weissbrot.

"*Gaspardim Veepski*, ready for five hours of meetings in *Angliski*?"[1]

"*Absolutna tavareesh!* Good for six but then a solid night's sleep."

"And your read of Bushkin?" Lester asked.

"To call Bushkin readable is to call the tax code *Green Eggs and Ham.*"

Weissbrot put his attaché case on his lap, and his mood shifted to serious.

"Lester, we need to make some irrevocable decisions. There are huge strategic issues over the long-term that might be better accomplished by making trivial concessions in the short-term."

"I sensed you had a change of heart during our last call. Fire away."

"Bushkin is the President and acts like a President. Of course, he remains a slippery piece of sturgeon but he's pragmatic. In fact, his current Director-General acts like the slithering eel I expected Bushkin to be."

"So you aborted the operation?"

"Son of a Cooter! I was good to go. Especially after a lunch, which was nothing but a tirade against Carter. Although now I reflect on it, that giraffe on stilettos, Klintova, did most of the carping." And he explained in detail the demonstration at the Kremlin and how the Russians were using tunable infrared scanners to detect dioxin contamination. He turned in his seat to address Lester, eyeball to eyeball — "That was how the Mad Cow derivative lit up like a lighthouse."

Knowing the score, Lester was polite but aloof.

"A close call, Mr. Vice-President. And, I take it, you now appreciate the foibles inherent in any so-called surgical assassination."

Recalling his past abrasive criticisms, Weissbrot's heart mellowed.

"Easy on paper. I apologize if I came across too harshly about the operation against Bin Laden, and the 9/11 blow-back from that."

Lester's eyes winced out a smile in acknowledgment.

Weissbrot resumed his train of thought.

---

1 *Gaspardim Veepski* - Mr. VP. *Angliski* - English. *Absolutna tavareesh* - Absolutely comrade (Rus).

"Also, that word, *Dioxinomics*, seems just as we assumed."

With a look that would make Darth Vader piss a hole through his acid-proof armor, Lester closed his eyes and muttered — "I know."

Weissbrot waited until his friend opened his eyes again.

"Lester, I lived in Moscow for three years. Inflated by the bloat from oil revenues coupled with an inefficient building sector, five days ago, that city's real estate was the most overpriced on the planet. Days later, banks are in the process of being scuppered. What moron is going to pay off a mortgage for five million roubles when the property in question is not worth a tenth that?"

"Norman, I don't know if you've had a chance to read Groundhawg's report or the 'Eyes-Only' paper authored by US Fed. Chairman Arthur Frankenstein, but the Moscow junk-mortgage effect is fanning out into the major cities of many other countries, especially our own."

"I'll read their reports, later. On the flight back, the petro-dollar issue disturbed me most. Without a Metro system, if the Russians depend on gasoline powered transportation alone then before the year is out, Russia will stop exporting oil and gas, and hoard it for their own domestic needs."

"Speaking of fuel, the price is back at $3.80 again. Take a look outside when we pass the next gas station."

Weissbrot grimaced — *If ever I become president, what a frack!* But, right now, there was a crazy lady in the White House. Resolving that impasse to global peace and prosperity remained job number one.

Lester pulled out a small notepad loaded with talking points.

"Norman, time to squeeze brass from the balls. What's your best guess about when the Russians will launch their military strike?"

A wave of levity rolled over Weissbrot, and he let out a laugh.

"Bushkin made this strange crack. 'The enemy would feel it in the nuts long before Ivan fired a solitary bullet.' While we aren't the enemy, I assure you from the man's tone, I'm certainly feeling it in the Cossacks."

Weissbrot switched seats so he could face Lester.

"Seriously, I got no hints on that front. Assuming the Cinderella scenario, we have Bushkin's pledge that he'll give us and NATO a week or more to get our forces prepped to defend the Afghan border."

"Do you trust him to hold to the deal?"

"Given the choices both our nations face — Yes. What worries me is that we may not be able to keep our end of the bargain. Bushkin's aware of our problem."

"Carter?" Lester sputtered.

"Yep." And Weissbrot let out an extended, audible breath.

Lester nodded resignedly.

No words were spoken.

None were needed on that score.

"Next item. What about Mitchell's testimony?"

Weissbrot countered — "Our chargé d'affaires in Moscow inspected his corpse and took a DNA sample? Death is fully confirmed — right?"

"Yes — and the FBI labs have re-confirmed as well."

Weissbrot flexed his spine to relax.

"We're out on a yardarm here. Besstrashnikov with Bushkin's tacit approval showed me testimony about a second urn of dioxin headed for us. Bushkin explained why he was compelled to do the hokey-pokey. More 'Mallory Wilson' fallout. If he loaded me up with all the facts, every anti-Russian cynic in the White House would scream I was being played like a monkey and the whole thing was staged for whatever new game of organ grinding Bushkin was concocting."

Lester vented — "It's nuts. Real informants don't exist and losing Mitchell adds to that curse. What we have now are informants of convenience. People, any intelligence director worth a dildo would call double ass-fucking agents."

"Precisely. Squeeze the source, we're slurp'n on splooge. Hit up our so-called informants we're being pegged. Basically, unless we fuck the facts out ourselves, believe nothing. Remind me when I'm president to have Grover Karlson[1] discreetly drop-kicked into a nice, toasty volcano."

Lester broke into laugh. Plans already drawn up, he had no scarcity of CIA patriots ready to escort a list of White House cronies down the aisle to be mated with Pele, the goddess who lived in the lava dome of Mt Kilauea on the big island of Hawaii. Weissbrot smirked on noticing how Lester's eyes said it all.

No words were spoken.

None were needed on that score.

Once an easy moment of silence had passed, Lester went to the heart of what troubled him most — "Norman, Mitchell's testimony isn't really critical because we have two problems. First, Mitchell was a diamond fence. How can he genuinely know about a second urn destined for the United States?"

"Mitchell swore he listened in on the confessions of his Afghan drug lords. But, that means nothing because anyone could contrive a confession. Mitchell may be completely honest, but such honesty means nothing. And, the second?"

"Let's take the cynic's view, Bushkin's trying to buddy up to you by telling you Russia's trying to hunt down a second urn. So what! There's always a so-called second urn. It's classic television drama."

"Lester, this is no joke."

"Bear with me. Transporting one or one hundred urns into the US is similarly irrelevant because Tim McVeigh could cook up any number of urns."

"Huh — McVeigh?"

"Home-grown *Dioxinomics*[2] is the real problem. It's where science in the hands of Tim McVeigh crushes economic fantasy in the hands of Wall St. wankers."

"Doesn't Groundhawg have that covered?"

"There is no cover. Take that literally, Norman."

Weissbrot flashed Lester a bemused look.

"Ok. What don't I get?"

---

1 Deputy Chief of Staff to US President Potusson, responsible for CIA-WMD Malory Wilson outting.
2 Domestic Disaffection, as per *Domestic Disaffection* chapter in the *Dioxinomics®* Series.

"Dioxin is like gold. But, to Economics, it's negative gold. Gold plus dioxin equals a big fat zero. But, no biggy. Gold can be scrubbed clean on the cheap. Real estate plus dioxin equals a big fat zero. Real estate can also be decontaminated, but only by spending millions or billions of dollars."

"Holy Shit," Weissbrot sputtered.

Lester saw his friend was picking up the matter fast and rolled on.

"Asymmetry is what makes pollution potent. It's cheapy-cheap. Doesn't require pharmaceutical quality. Is hard to detect and easy to deploy."

Weissbrot cinched the bridge of his nose between thumb and index finger. Lester plowed on.

"On the other hand, bombs are expensive, require pharmaceutical quality, thus, hard to manufacture and also hard to deploy. Easy, easy, easy versus hard, hard, hard. That's *Dioxinomics* in a nutshell."

"Fuck." Weissbrot muttered — *Game changer to History.*

And, Lester kept at it — "Bombs fizzle. But, pollution! Pollution never fizzles. *Never*! Even if it's amateur Tim McVeigh crap spilling out the back of a motorcycle going through Lincoln Tunnel or any other tunnel or building. That's also *Dioxinomics* in the nutsacks."

"Double fuck."

"And, Norman, *Dioxinomics* isn't a creature of human fantasy like Economics. As science, *Dioxinomics* lives forever in the human imagination. Not as a fantasy like the S&P Stock Index, but as science, immune to graft and manipulation."

Having no comeback and numb with denial, Weissbrot tweaked the subject.

"How's Groundhawg doing stabilizing our financial markets?"

"He and Fed. Chairman Frankenstein are hard at the razzle-dazzle routine. Fortunately, our markets remain staffed by business school wankers behind computer screens. They're too dim to catch on to the scientific ramifications of the Moscow disaster and the hard-science Dioxinomic reality headed our way."

Weissbrot laughed to relieve tension.

"Some predictable news from 'Barbie-World.'"

"I give Babs-for-brains less than a week, Norman."

"Yeah," Weissbrot replied glumly — "Stupid doesn't last forever."

Weissbrot's grim feelings on the plane journey from Moscow flooded back. Soon, every US citizen would wake up to the reality of Potusson's fifty-year crusade against terrorism. If a pollution weapon fizzles, who was off the hook? Nobody. A whopping few Franklins[1] wasted, but the panic would never end. New York, London, Paris, Beijing, and all major cities with their quaint mortgage issues were just getting a whiff of *Dioxinomics*. The key to surviving America's crusade against terror was not to be living in plum targets like major cities. Simple is simple, and stupid is stupid. The science behind *Dioxinomics* was simple. The reality of financial collapse — brain-dead simple. Bankers and wankers — stupid.

And, unlike science — *stupid doesn't last forever.*

1 The US $100 federal reserve note features Benjamin Franklin — a Franklin — a Benjoe. Franklin is famous for the saying — "You have a republic if you can keep it." Dioxinomics is crunch time.

223

Blow by Blow

On arrival at CIA headquarters in Langley, the two men joined the meeting in progress. Blow by blow, they rehashed the meltdown in Russia and what the expected reactions might be, once the Russian public was informed. Weissbrot detailed what Bushkin had told him in general terms and how Russia needed America to keep a level-head and act to support Bushkin's mission to diffuse Russian anger and tamp down calls for escalation. Weissbrot presented the free world's conundrum in such a way as to deliberately elicit the maximum alarm around the conference table because he wanted all assembled to fully envision how President Carter, now thick in the flow of menses, was going to explode.

After the formal meeting ended, Weissbrot and Lester pulled aside Dr. Glorioso, the Secretary of Defense, for an informal pow-wow in the Director's Office. Weissbrot made it clear his primary duty was to ensure the United States picked its enemies wisely. Glorioso couldn't agree more.

To the Best of My Ability

The gloom of the previous day blossomed into a sunny but unseasonably frigid Washington morning. Every cabinet officer, without exception, had risen early. For those souls without earmuffs or head cover, the sky buzzed a vibrant azure blue. The air was crisp on the inhale, and creamy on the exhale. And, while an alpine zest invigorated attendees as they strode across frost-covered White House lawns that crunched cleanly underfoot, upon entering the Cabinet Room, all felt entombed by the suffocation of the place. Even the toasty allure of Colombian roast, Carter's favorite blend, smelt bitter.

Norman Weissbrot and Lester Coverdale were the exceptions. Deference and caution would no longer be pandered too. The Dioxinomic peril unfolding upon the world demanded bold and valiant action.

After President Carter read from minutes prepared by her secretary, Norman certified that he had taken the roll-call and confirmed that every principal officer of the executive branch was present. After thanking him for his diligence, the president read the final sentence.

"Norman, would you please present the findings of your meeting with Russian President, Fyedor Sergeivich Bushkin."

"Madam President, contrary to our last meeting, I'm compelled to report that Bushkin does not respect you. In Russia, you're known as Krankhouse Karter, a warmongering loon who panders to America's anti-Russian rednecks."

Carter's day-old tampon launched into orbit — "What! That drunk Brewskie son of a bitch, how dare he. As leader of a two-century democratic superpower, it's my duty to score points with my electorate as I see fit. No wonder Russia's democracy is slowly descending into the grave under Bushkunt."

Carter's outburst gave heart to Weissbrot. But, Lester remained cautious. She had ingeniously wrapped her insanity in the flag and professed a right to exercise democratic dementia. Both men knew they would have to persist in order to outfox her knee-jerk cunning.

"Then on that note Madam President, as I faithfully serve my country as Vice-President, let me also inform you that Bushkin said you'd make a fine President of Russia in this it's time of troubles."

Weissbrot waited for her to react.

Carter's nose crinkled, her eyes narrowed in squint, her fingers stretched their full length and her long, manicured nails unfurled — Cantaloupe Green.

"I assure you, if I was Madam President of Russia, I would not be sitting on my ass name-calling, sending action notices to superpowers about some Italian who wants to be the damn Tsar and jibbering rubbish. I'd be out whomping into the ground those Raghead fucks and every cunt of a country that gave them aid, harbor or financial sup—"

Carter's spine locked up.

She clutched her throat — *Is Allah calling on me?*

The room went silent.

Like a stunned calf hanging inverted on meat hooks in an abattoir, minutes away from the cold steel pincers that would clamp shut and crush its neck with guillotine ferocity, President Carter's eyeballs stood apart from her sockets. The beryl irises of her eyes seemed lacerated by a deep, nameless woe — As if they were looking backward and in upon their master-tormentor, bewildered and straining to know where all this jungle anger came from. Striving to stay clearheaded, she choked back every thought about Ebola; about her migraines.

"Norman, please. … Please, root me in reality. Can you at least report that Bushkin is going to do the right thing by his people the way I would?"

Weissbrot remained implacable — "No Madam President, I can not. I can report that he considers your bellicose anti-Russia tone reminiscent of President Reagan. He claims that your vindictive temperament and hostile rhetoric towards Russia is the very thing that has given terrorists a license to attack his so-called Evil Empire. He assumes you funded the so-called forces of democracy like President Reagan did in Nicaragua and Afghanistan.[1] Remember, we're dealing with the Russian government, not Joe Americano. While our administration continues the censorship of the full 9/11 Commission Report, Al-Yamamah speaks volumes, so Bushkin says. And, in that light, he reckons that pro-Carter and pro-NATO terrorists have heeded the Reaganite call to put down the godless atheists in the Russian government, subvert it, and bring Russia into the parliamentary mold common to Europe. Yes — it may sound tutti-frutti, but all of Russia." And, Weissbrot stopped to make extra emphasis — "Every Russian considers you a Russia-hating buffoon. That, Madam President, is reality."

Ginger was beside herself. Norman and Lester had promised they would do their utmost to mute the President's worsening condition. She glared at Lester who remained impassive. It was that time of the month, as a fellow woman Ginger knew her president was taking it badly.

Carter's stupefaction lasted less than a pin drop — "No Bushkunt will mock me like this in front of my electorate. Why the hell am I having a Cabinet

---

1 In the 'Annals of US History,' these freedom fighters are denoted Contradora and Muhajideen.

meeting! I need to assume the Commander-in-Chief role. Miles, get my Generals assembled in the Oval Office. I need to address the Russian menace that seeks to invade my Constitutional right to talk at any electorate in any way I deem appropriate. Including the right to warmonger against any empire I designate as 'Evil.' And, Mr. Red, White and Blue Vice-President of these United States, if the Cuntsack[1] electorate doesn't like it then Cuntsack don't gotta vote for me."

Ginger chopped in frantically.

"Mary-Ann, you have these rights but Bushkin certainly isn't attacking the United States in any military way. He doesn't even warmonger against the US, except to demand that we stop facilitating heroin and opium production."

But, Ginger's attempt at calming her friend only infuriated Carter more. The President was in her own realm of invasion and justification — "Pure poppy-snot. As President of the United States, I declare that my right to speak and hold any opinion I wish is a right of the executive branch protected by the Constitution. I also declare that no nation, including Russia, or any ginned-up, alien electorate for that matter, shall encroach on the Constitution while I'm president. I also declare that alien encroachment on the electoral sovereignty of the United States has occurred and that Russia has made such encroachment."

Lester eagerly chimed in.

"And is it not the President's oath of office and constitutional duty to defend and protect against alien encroachments on our Constitution, Madam President?"

The nudge was trite, the abyss vast.

Carter became apoplectic — "Because encroachment is tantamount to invasion, the US Constitution demands from its sitting president faithful execution and war. The Constitution, which I pledged my honor to defend and protect, and Russia's encroachment upon the rights enshrined therein have collided. I've no discretion when war is our constitution's express salvation. My oath ties my hands."

Vice-President Weissbrot's ears twitched with disgust.

"Salvation? What about our nation and its life, liberty and the pursuit—"

Carter cut him off.

"If you ever take the oath Norman I hope you remember the words and apply them as religiously as a tea-jerk Republican. 'I do solemnly swear that I will faithfully execute the office of President of the United States, and will to the best of my ability, preserve, protect and defend the Constitution of the United States.' In case you haven't noticed, the constitution is a document, like the Bible, like the Qur'an, like the Torah. I'm duty bound to preserve, protect and defend the Constitution to the best of my ability."

Weissbrot cut back — "Surely our nation is one of humanity. One of people. Their lives, homes and liberties are what's paramount."

He waited for Carter to spew more unreality. Oblivious to the concept that Wall Street and Main Street had joint interests, Carter turned on her lecture voice — "While good politics protects life, liberty and real estate, I'm under no legal mandate to do so. That's discretionary. As the Republicans say — That

1 Derogatory term derived from Cossack, the Russian ethnic group, most credited as the manpower behind the tsarist pogroms against Russian Jews. Alludes to President Carter's problem appeasing the Jewish voters and Israel's yearly demands for the pardon and release for Israeli spy Jonathan Pollard.

would be pandering to what the cut-and-run sector of the US electorate might want protected."

Sensing this vein of argument was a dead end, Weissbrot refocused on 'Bushkin,' a word that always sent Carter haywire.

"Madam President, Ginger spoke justly. Bushkin poses no threat. You're fabricating an alien invasion — slash — encroachment because you hate Bushkin."

Realizing her words were being twisted against her, Ginger blushed crimson and was about to weigh in when Carter raised her voice — "From your own mouth, Norman. Your *own* mouth! According to Bushkunt, my constitutional right to pander to the US electorate gives him the right to invade the document that I'm sworn to protect against all enemies, foreign and domestic. If the constitution falls, these United States become a juicy piece of real estate sandwiched between Canada and Mexico. To protect real estate, our constitution must never fall. Don't confuse me with Potusson, I won't flip off our supreme law or spurn my oath of office because it suits 'my gainsaying legacy.' For every true-hearted president, the law and the oath always come first. Absolutes are absolutes, Norman. No Brewskie shall induce me to shirk my oath or my duty."

Weissbrot looked at Lester. Clearly, the president was laboring under an acute case of 'Presidential Megalomania Syndrome.' Weissbrot squared his jawline, time to apply the classic test — crazy or just moody.

"Madam President, with respect, you're just suffering from PMS. Only our greatest leaders have proven immune to it. If you must hunker down with your generals, surely the Surgeon-General is the one best suited to remedy the bloody situation which threatens to afflict your country?"

Carter's taut lips turned a bright scarlet. She rose to her feet, hands clamping the edge of the table as if she were a two-a.m. barfly trying to right herself. She started mouthing words, but nobody recalled hearing anything coherent. Ginger sat shocked at Weissbrot's chauvinistic slur about 'Presidential Megalomania Syndrome.' Any decent woman instinctively knew the nation's cherished leader was suffering from another condition.

Defense Secretary Miles Glorioso closed his phone.

"Ginger, please escort the President to the Oval Office. The Joint Chiefs will be here in twenty. It's best she recompose herself first."

Ginger snapped — "*What!* What have you done? You idiot!"

Glorioso looked puzzled.

"Ms. Arnold, the President called for a meeting with the Joint Chiefs. I merely put her directive into action. Everyone here can attest to that."

"But — But, she wasn't herself. You had no right to make that call."

Glorioso extended his arm — "Here's my phone, Ms. Arnold. If you honestly think President Carter wanted the Surgeon-General, please, make the call."

The room remained frozen. Like figurines locked within a rotating, musical snow-globe, Carter was blubbering, Glorioso, arm out stretched, was offering his phone and Ginger, now standing, was rocking to and fro with indecision.

To clear the air, Weissbrot addressed Ginger.

"Take Mary-Ann to the Oval Office. Calm her down. If she decides to cancel the meeting, that's her prerogative. Miles has faithfully executed the president's lawful command. It's not the end of the world. *Just yet.*"

Still Ginger hesitated. Lester rose from his seat.

Weissbrot growled — "Lester. Ginger. Escort Carter out. Now."

Trail of Evidence — Linkage to Al Qaeda

While Washington slowly warmed from the frigid start to its day, Moscow was yielding to the prickly cool of approaching evening. Gibraltar[1] had finally returned Basil's phone call. During the thirteenth minute, the caller concluded his dissection of their options. Basil interposed some additional questions and was jotting down his third page of scratch notes when the caller's report came to a close and Basil made reply.

"Excellent. This means the operation is feasible. It's essential that we establish a trail of evidence back to ETA, the Basque Separatist movement. And, better still, linkage to Al Qaeda."

Basil fingered his lower lip, as the caller elaborated on his suggestions.

"Leave Al Guido out of the equation. But, be prepared to salt that in if Moscow decides otherwise. Also, don't overlook any opportunity to exploit Western paranoia."

As the caller spoke next, Basil flicked back to page one of his notes.

"Brilliant! The Doodles will go for that hook, line and sinker. I'll start coordinating with our men in New York to prime the target."

Basil made some notes in the margin as the caller proffered enhancements, after which Basil responded with caution.

"No promises. But, I would say if Italy doesn't pan out in the next day or so, it's 80% likely that it's a go. I still need to run the whole thing by the Director-General, then the President."

The caller did a verbal double-take, and Basil replied.

"Yes Captain Vitrenko, you heard correctly. President Bushkin. *Poka.*"

No Better Than Torturers

The last to leave, Lester Coverdale locked the door interconnecting the Cabinet Room with the President's Secretary's Office behind him. Weissbrot opened the corridor door and summoned Greg Lambert, the chief of his Secret Service detail, into the cabinet room. Lambert handed Weissbrot the black gift-box, bound by a white cotton cord, he had been entrusted earlier. As he did, Weissbrot quietly informed him that he was convening a cabinet-officers-only meeting. Weissbrot walked to the head of the conference table and made the

---

1 British territory and naval base on the southern tip of Spain.

announcement. Everyone except cabinet officers started shuffling out. As they did so, Weissbrot retrieved a military command-issue manila envelope from a side table. Returning and leaning over the back of the president's executive chair, he placed it and the mysterious box on the conference table. When the room was almost clear, Weissbrot pulled upwards on the box's cord and moved his hand to his right. Its top and four side panels plopped onto the table, revealing a five-inch, navy-issue brass bell. When the door latched closed behind Lambert, Weissbrot wasted no time exploiting the unease in the room.

"We no longer live in an age where royal houses can settle scores between each other using bombs, bullets and poison gas, as in two World Wars. We live in an age of nuclear annihilation. Because national security and world peace are one and the same, egocentric games of brinkmanship ensuring re-electability are vanities democracies can no longer afford."[1]

Coming from behind the president's chair, Weissbrot made a formal show of sitting, and as he did so, he pulled a black walnut bell-striker from his suit. Once his body came to rest, he gave the brass Admiral's bell three distinct raps.

"I hereby call to order an Amendment Twenty-Five tribunal."

He made another blow before depositing the striker on the table.

"The Constitution imposes upon every Vice-President a duty to decide whether or not to convene a tribunal to discuss and then call upon the cabinet to vote on whether a sitting president is able to discharge the powers and duties of the Office of President."

Hicks and Chandler, Carter's staunchest allies, looked at each other in dismay. They had heard and dismissed office rumors about a Weissbrot clique becoming more emboldened as Carter became more embrittled within a deepening, anti-Russian malaise — one that had now hardened to the point of insanity. Weissbrot disregarded their whispering and flipped the manila envelope over. Moving his hand back and forth in a figure-eight motion, he unwound the red cotton twine.

"The first check on any president is our constitution. She must be a native born citizen over the age of thirty-six. The second check is the electorate."

He opened the flap and removed two sheets of card stock.

"The third check is Amendment Twenty-Five."

And, he handed the first sheet to Attorney General Hicks on his left.

"David, please, verify the text is correct, then pass it on."

As Hicks did so, Weissbrot steam-rolled along.

"When each of you read it, take note that Section Four merely requires a simple majority of the cabinet declare a president unable to serve. Nor do we have to provide any reason. To be specific, we need only state that President Carter lacks the ability that any prudent citizen would expect of their president in this day and this age. Carter herself cited the Oath of Office just minutes ago. 'To the best of my ability' she said. As if we all needed reminding about what 'Best Ability' in the thermonuclear age means. So, keep Carter's scolding rebuke about 'Best' in your hearts because this cabinet's duty is to ensure our nation has a capable leader, especially when two superpowers are on the verge

1 Uppermost in Weissbrot's mind are the non-voters — Children destroyed by adult vanity.

of facing each other down militarily. At least that is what Carter, now awaiting the arrival of the Joint Chiefs, seeks to do."

Lester re-entered the Cabinet Room directly through the President's Secretary's Office and bolted the interconnecting door behind him. Weissbrot slapped the second sheet of card stock on the polished oak table.

"This short declaration will memorialize our vote about whether President Carter is incapable of discharging the powers and duties of the Office of President. Please note, it does not say she's mentally handicapped or anything derogatory." Weissbrot handed the sheet to Hicks and finished — "Please, take note where you record your vote on the matter, be it yes or no."

The succinct declaration made the rounds. No different than the first sheet, some officers did not bother to look down before passing it on.

"Because some of you might be feeling squeamish about the obvious, I'll ask Dr. Glorioso to say a few words. If you would, please, Miles."

While various officers perused the declaration, Glorioso presented his medical assessment. Mary-Ann was suffering from a neurological breakdown. Decency demanded she get prompt and formal diagnosis at Walter Reed Hospital. He cited the movie, *A Beautiful Mind*, to let everyone know the gravity of the matter, and the sooner the treatment, the better the outcome for both her and her return to duty. While the doctor spoke, Lester extracted a black cloth bag from his briefcase and stood by Weissbrot. When Glorioso finished and the declaration once more lay in front of Weissbrot, Lester upended the black bag on the table, and a jumble of coins fell out. Lester made a great show of turning the bag inside-out, shaking it and holding it open-mouthed while Weissbrot continued explaining the process.

"I respect every person's right to have an opinion. I propose we vote anonymously at first. Each cabinet member is to place either a dime for a vote of 'Able,' or a quarter for a vote of 'Unable,' into this bag. I've put spare change on the table in case someone doesn't have both coins. Let me demonstrate."

Lester held the bag, mouth open to Weissbrot's right.

"With both coins in my hand, I dunk it in the bag and release one coin. I'd like to get an immediate poll. I've voted. Lester's turn."

And, Weissbrot held the bag for Lester and then he walked the bag around the table, anti-clockwise. Hicks was the last to drop a coin. Weissbrot tendered the bag to the nation's numismat-in-chief — "Groundhawg, please, do the honors."

Treasury Secretary Earl Butz inverted the bag. By the time he had finished folding it inside and out to prove to all present that it was empty, the last coin had ceased its chattering. All eyes looked down.

Weissbrot rapped the bell once and maintained a sober tone.

"A lawful majority votes 'Unable.'" He ceremoniously placed the striker down on the table — "Since this is the first time in our nation's history an Amendment Twenty-Five tribunal has convened, I'd like to reduce the number of dissenters from four to no more than two. First, as a layman, I fully endorse Dr. Glorioso's opinion. Human decency compels all of us to get Mary-Ann the treatment she deserves as soon as possible. To do otherwise, makes us no better than hypoxia-inducing torturers. Now … turning to duty."

He took a deep breath to ensure everyone knew how painful this was.

"Just as President Carter has asserted a duty to defend and protect the Constitution, I'm under the same elected obligation including the duty to protect what our constitution expects of 'Best Ability.' This is not a matter of discretion or pandering to the electorate. In front of our constitution is the human face."

He jostled his chin between thumb and fingers for emphasis.

"This face. For thousands of years, the nobility inherent to human life has always been the paramount law of civilization. In the nuclear age, this truth applies most especially rather than some two-century parchment from an era when travel from Washington to Moscow took months and months."

Weissbrot leaned forward and held his hands open like a bread-basket.

"The president serves the people and the people don't expect to be thrown into nuclear war on Carter's whim about how some alien demagogue has encroached upon our nation's constitution. But, let me cut to the chase. I think it's clear that President Carter has lost her grip on reality. She hates Russia for no other reason than vanity. I served as a US Ambassador there for three years. I don't like everything the Russians do, but they're not virulently anti-American. We all know this."

He took a sip of A&W to allow his warm-up to soak in.

"Look at the comments that Carter has made to us in private — 'We will fight them on the beaches and on the poppy fields.' Do you know how offensive that is to Russia or any normal Western nation plagued by heroin? Not to mention 2,3,7,8 tetrachloro-dibenzo-para-dioxin."

That word — *Dioxin* — Everyone squirmed in their seats.

"Elected leaders are bound by responsibilities. Fantasy or not, Bushkin is elected. And, when he finally goes public with the whole chest-thumping story, here's what he might reveal to make his electorate berserk for war."

Weissbrot rested back in the chair before resuming.

"History first. The US and NATO invaded Afghanistan under the pretext of catching an alleged criminal mastermind so he could be brought to New York and face trial for the crimes he was indicted of by a federal grand jury. Thereafter, supposedly looking for more criminals, the US and NATO occupy Afghanistan. Whereupon, opium plantations pop up left, right and center. Thereafter, we install our own *Puyi*[1] and pretend everything is situation normal."

For emphasis, he lurched over the table.

"*Our* president trumpeted to *our* electorate that *our* troops would ensure that death would never again be exported out of Afghanistan back into *our* homeland. For Russia, Afghanistan, going from 1% to 95% of the world's supply of heroin, is a submarine launching intercontinental ballistic missiles tipped with weapons of mass destruction. Each year, the nihilism of narco-terrorism puts 30,000 Russian citizens into an early grave. The very existence of Mitchell — The fact our own FBI sent Mitchell to Moscow to combat drug smuggling

---

1 Datong Puyi, the 'Last Emperor of China' (1934-1945) was a puppet installed by Japanese Emperor Hirohito and the Imperial High Command, over seven years before the bombing of Pearl Harbor.

is proof positive. Ask any Russian — Who is to blame? Castro? Noriega? The Medellin Cartel? Oh — wait — let's blame Al Qaeda!"

Weissbrot thumped the table and held his fist down as if restraining inner anger and calmly scanned the room to re-establish eye contact as well as personal rapport with his peers. His voice boomed with emotional vigor.

"*Yamashita*[1] says otherwise."

He fixed his gaze on Attorney General Hicks, Carter's biggest ally — "Violating the US Supreme Court holding in *Yamashita*, as commander-in-chief for nine months, Carter continued President Potusson's policy of turning down 'Operation Rambo' to crush this Made-by-Crusaders obscenity in Afghanistan. Now, a killer toxin has polluted the Moscow Metro system and its roots hail from US-NATO war criminality locked and loaded on the backs of starvation enforced poppy-ninny slavery."

He took a sip of A&W to wet his lips.

"An FBI official has testified that the proceeds of Afghan drug sales accumulated in Moscow in the form of diamonds in his safe keeping. He has testified that some mysterious cargo destined for Afghanistan was being exchanged for the diamonds. It's obvious to me that American and NATO servicemen in Afghanistan, Iraq and America were the real targets. The DVD confessions of Afghan, Uzbek, Turkmen and Tajik terrorists furnished by the Russians corroborate the obvious. America was the target."

Weissbrot pounded the table to let that bombshell sink in.

"It would have been better for our country to have occupied a nation of Muslim pig farmers. Starving Muslims are permitted to eat pig. But, that's just food-on-the-table fiction. Reality is much worse. Opium isn't food. Furthermore, Muslims are under a holy duty to abstain from all addictions that make them unmindful of Allah and his prophet, Mohammed."

He stopped and breathed rapidly to hold in check the temptation of saying the words — *We are so, so, so fucked!* He steeled himself and resumed.

"So, what would you call an alien Muslim invader of our country that inaugurates starvation agriculture, and through heroin dependence, makes Americans unmindful of Jesus and the Christian covenant? … Invaders bent on Satanism that's what. Under Potusson and Carter and for the rest of recorded history, every Russian and every Muslim on this side of fucking Paradise knows American Crusaders inaugurated the 'Heroin Holocaust' in Muslim lands."

Weissbrot brought his hands into spread-finger prayer opposite his nose.

"If America has a hankering for heroin, we have ample agricultural capacity. We don't need to palm that off on third-world countries or use starvation enforced poppy-ninny slavery or smuggle surplus Pentagon-protected heroin into foreign nations. And, talk about fucked-up smuggling. We benefited from the heaven-sent circumstance that this urn of dioxin never made it out of Moscow. An utter fluke! So, what honorable cause have we to hate the Russians?"

1 US Supreme Court holding a Commander-in-Chief has an affirmative duty to supervise, and if he neglects to supervise his forces, he becomes criminally responsible for the consequences of such neglect. See In Re Yamashita, 327 US 1 (1946). Yamashita is pronounced Yah-mushsh-ta.

Weissbrot slapped both his hands flat on the table, swiveled to his left and faced Secretary of State Chandler, another Carter loyalist.

"The Russian government has been very subdued in their criticism of us. But, I tell you that is only because Bushkin understands the nature of the menace of telling his countrymen the unvarnished facts in their entirety."

Weissbrot balled his right hand into a fist.

"This isn't Homeland Security blather."

He slammed the conference table. The Admiral's bell ting'd.

"This isn't Rooskie sloganeering."

He slammed again and kept it there two seconds, sliding it to and fro.

"This isn't a theory. It's a reality that debases and kills thousands of Americans as well, and not just the reported 12,000 youths who croak from Domestic Minor Sex Trafficking[1] each year. Bushkin is about to expose the US news media for the useless, child-hating, slathering warmongering organ that it is. I made a pledge to Bushkin to start burning every damn poppy field without delay. He's given our nation one-week — one fucking week! And, hear this — Poppy-ninny slavery stops with me!"

He pressed his knuckles hard into the table, and his cheeks flushed pink.

"And, the export of death … That stops with me!"

Sensing too many precious seconds had flitted by while he'd reined in his anger, Weissbrot spread his fingers, knuckle side up and spoke hurriedly.

"The Russian people don't want to hear one excuse from our president and nothing about eating dried-pickin's from handkerchiefs and how our decent, hardworking citizens will fight Russians on the beaches and on the poppy fields. Don't pull Ginger's excuse and remind me how Carter is not right-minded. The issue of 'right-minded' is bloody well why the US Constitution *compels me* as Vice-President to convene this tribunal and demand a vote."

He calmed and nestled his clenched right fist against his chest.

"Today it's essential that our country does not permit Bushkin to go hog wild with retaliation. I promise as president I can do that. Carter cannot and won't."

Weissbrot blanketed his left palm over his right fist and watched as the seated Cabinet mentally replayed the scope of the stakes. A shuffling stillness gave way to the eeriness of pulse-behind-the-ears silence. And, into this bystander-to-history mood, Lester Coverdale made his statement.

"I have little to add to Norman's hard-nosed assessment. Our personal knowledge about Mary-Ann Carter is unassailable. If she was the President of Russia, mouthing off like a Cossack demagogue and using the Russian military to defend the right to institute narco-colonialism over Ukraine that exports death into our homeland, we, Americans, would go ballistic. Even a feminazi whore juiced to the nines with slave-made, happy-hour heroin from third-world countries financed by her 'spread the legs, it's my cunt-fucking body' lifestyle sees the three-ton Dioxinomic elephant in Barbie's Dollhouse. We should thank providence that a disciplined leader like Bushkin is in control of Russia."

1 Domestic Minor Sex Trafficking (DMST) is US domestic law enforcement term for US citizen child slavery rings. Age range 8 to 18 years of age. 12,000 is a lower bound estimate of the annual death rate.

In an appeal to hearts, Lester softened his tone — "We elected a bright and capable president. Every American had that expectation. But, now the leader we elected is no longer the expectation we elected, but some other," he paused for strategic effect — "Let me be blunt. From out of nowhere, our president has become some crazy lady who deserves prompt and effective medical care. She has already told you what she would do if she were President of Russia. I quote — 'whomp those Raghead fucks and every cunt of a country that aided, harbored or financed them.' Well folks, that would be us Americunts, especially the uniformed ones in Afghanistan. We cannot delay. With the Pentagon on the way to the Oval Office, Carter stands ready to antagonize and ridicule Bushkin in front of the people of the world and goad every so-called Rooskie redneck to go psycho, march into Afghanistan and smash us as best they can using every conventional weapon in the Russian arsenal and then some."

Lester paused then repeated in a snarling tone — "*And then some!*"

He glared at David Hicks before resuming.

"What's more pathetic than a strung-out heroin whore?"

He drew a ballpoint from his suit and jiggered the air with it.

"Us, right here — the US Cabinet — sitting on our democratically elected bums doodling about. That's going to change. See this pen?"

He grabbed the declaration and signed it — "I'm the first. Who else is ready?"

Secretary of Defense Miles Glorioso raised his right hand — "Here."

Handing him both pen and paper with a big show of arm movement, Lester broadcast a wave of emotion and urgency that was not to be stopped.

"Signed!" Miles declared and he looked up, saw Lester pointing to Groundhawg, and pen atop paper, Miles slid the unity across the table.

And, back and forth the declaration shuttled with no additional comment.

The four original holdouts remained unknown. Seeing how the whole matter was a *fait accompli*,[1] they decided that withholding concurrence only made them look foolish. The anonymous coin vote proving that a majority would pass the declaration combined with Weissbrot's arguments had worked their charm. With his Marching Orders in hand, the Acting-President thanked them all for coming to their country's defense, dissolved the tribunal and instructed them all to carry on their day as usual. Lester Coverdale, Chandler, Hicks and Glorioso remained behind chatting in the Cabinet Room.

Weissbrot unbolted the door to the Oval Office and entered. He was soon back in the Cabinet Room with Joint Chiefs Chairman Army-General Harvey L. Kilburn. After perusing the declaration, Kilburn issued a deep sigh of relief. Next, he scanned the faces of Coverdale and the others. They all nodded affirmatively. Weissbrot directed Kilburn to return to the meeting with Carter and do nothing to antagonize the situation, but rather to keep taking notes about her errant behavior.

All five officers, Weissbrot, Coverdale, Chandler, Hicks and Glorioso took the acting-presidential limousine to the Capitol Building, where they were immediately met by the Speaker of the House and President Pro Tempore of

---

1 Done Deal. (French)

the Senate. Secretary of State Chandler, thereupon, certified the propriety of the Amendment Twenty-Five tribunal and confirmed the unanimous vote given in the declaration.

America's true constitution was preserved.

"You have a republic, as long as you can keep it," once said Franklin.

A Sick Media Gag

President Carter was delivering a scathing lecture on the hidebound nature of the US military when her secretary, Naomi, burst into the Oval Office and turned on the television. Over the course of a long, silent minute, it dawned on Carter that she had been removed from office and Weissbrot was now the Acting-President. When she made some flip remark that it was a sick media gag without any force of law, General Kilburn spoke up.

"Remember when Acting-President Weissbrot interrupted the meeting, Ms. Carter? He showed me the declaration in the presence of the Attorney General, the Secretary of Defense, the Secretary of State and the Director of National Intelligence. From this moment, it is you, Ms. Carter, who is a guest in the White House. The Acting-President should be back shortly with an official acknowledgment from Congress. Ma'am, please remain—"

Before Kilburn finished his sentence, Carter slumped into the arms of Secret Service Agent Elaine Genrette. Without further fuss, this allowed her Secret Service detail to discreetly confine her to the White House infirmary until further arrangements were made.

A Pitbull with Lipstick

Weissbrot's day vanished in a long sequence of urgent meetings. Only well into the black of night did he and Lester get to relax in private. Shoes off and lying back on two Oval Office sofas, they sipped on twenty-year oak-cured bourbon liberated from the White House cellars. Savoring their first glass, they chatted with great relief about the upward surge in the financial markets.

Enjoying the repose that comes with a second glass, and with the vice-presidential fig-leaf now history, they eased into reviewing the darker events of the day. Lester stirred first — "Norman, the CIA lab report concerning the fingerprints pulled from the coins has come in. It's as expected."

Weissbrot remained silent. Concerned about 'Operation Glass Ceiling,' his eyes scanned the plaster moldings of the Oval Office, as if searching out the buzz of an errant mosquito — "Lester, you sure the room isn't still wired?"

"Everything's spotless, including the hormone sniffers."

Weissbrot belly-laughed. The ice jiggled in his Old-Fashioned tumbler — "Chemical weapon detectors — yeah. I watched them going in." He calmed and vented his real concern — "How long do you say Mary-Ann has?"

"Two weeks, at most. The new agent is fast compared to the stuff you administered her back in November. With her going bonkers in fits and starts, this fluke crisis in Russia gave us no choice."

Weissbrot picked up on Lester's larger meaning.

"It's great to know we can now 'Veep' the scarecrows any nation throws up as their so-called leader. It's one thing for a party's candidate to occupy the chair, but another entirely for a leader to fulfill the duties of the Office."

Weissbrot suddenly jammed his glass to the floor as if about to gag and roared with laughter. Lester shot him a worried look, and before he could sit up, Weissbrot's voice mocked a women crying as if in the throws of orgasm.

"Oh, Thomas, T-h-o-m-a-s." He looked at Lester — "Remember those tapes? How Jefferson was her rippling, red-haired Viking prince?"

Lester almost choked on his bourbon — "Talk about wet dreams gone Nordic. A more pleasant side effect of Mad Cow disease. I guess we can assume where all those screwy 'seventy-two virgins in Paradise' fantasies come from."

Both men laughed so hard each almost rolled off his sofa. Righting himself, Weissbrot turned his head again to address Lester.

"Mister Director. Should I circumvent an autopsy?"

"Don't worry, Mister Acting-President. The original agent appears in the brain like Alzheimers. Given the many months of cerebral degeneration, the knock-out blow you administered after our last Arlington meeting will leave few damning signs. When the old bat finally clocks-out, we'll harvest her brain to get a better read on how to optimize the process to minimize detection and accelerate death for future peacekeeping missions."

Weissbrot remarked almost nonchalantly.

"Don't forget there's the Ginger Option, if things go south."

Lester turned his head to Weissbrot.

"Any idea what you might do with Ginger?"

"Not really. She has a superb figure. And, I like how she has such wonderful long hair but keeps it trussed up so elegantly. She'll be politically lost once Carter kicks it. Her psych profile and ploys peg her as a raging power junkie, so I might keep her on as my cabin boy."

Lester chuckled at the turnabout in fortunes — "Norman, you're remarkable. Ready to take out Bushkin. And, taken out our own whack-job." Lester changed his accent to mock Russian — "On her hands and knees, comrades, Carter's little better than a pitbull with lipstick."

Both men roared hysterically, recalling that night when a comedian from Alaska speaking in a thick Eastern European accent had appeared on *Late Night with Conan O'Brian* with a pitbull puppet that sported an oversized 'Allen Burns' cigar. Derived from the antics of a prior president, the comedic sketch left its audience with the impression that Carter's agitation was a direct result of the bitch not receiving the sort of presidential-sized medication she really needed.

Weissbrot settled down, looked over at Lester and extended his drinking arm. His elbow locked as he proffered his glass for a refill.

"Tavareesh, whiski, pajalsta."[1]

Lester did the honors. After, he proposed a toast.

"To Carter I say — Thanks for helping us get the operation against North Korea resolved. To Norman Ousley Weissbrot, President of the United States, I say — Congratulations America, you've finally got a decent and capable president at the helm. Hoorah and about damn time."

There was a clink of tumblers and the two men lapsed back into sedate conversation about the day's problems and tasks yet to come. In the weeks ahead, both men needed to groom a very loyal, very imaginative and very capable new Director of National Intelligence since it was understood who had the support of the acting-president to become the next vice-president.

More Precious Than Children

Opwop for short, the telephone conference orchestrating a joint US-Russian mission called 'Operation Wipe Out Pollution,' now ticked into its second hour. President Bushkin had already given Acting-President Weissbrot many verifiable guarantees. The most critical concession was all Russian warships located in the Indian Ocean would set sail for the Mediterranean. And, to further assure Weissbrot that he meant what he said, Bushkin confided that this naval flotilla would become part of a convoy escorting a two billion Euro gold bullion shipment steaming from the Russian port city of Sochi to an unnamed port in Italy. This gold was set aside to guarantee payment on several massive contracts Russia had recently signed in Italy. He also intimated that several vessels would be made available to the Italians to assist them in their quest to recover Silvio Calamari, the kidnaped son of the Italian Prime Minister. And, Bushkin let slip how he had a Russian filmmaker in Italy pestering him about using surplus navy vessels in an upcoming project. All in all, both presidents knew Russia had solid reasons for moving its navy back into the Mediterranean. The many ties between Russia and Italy made it clear to Weissbrot that neither nation harbored ill-will towards the other. And, US satellites could openly verify every win-win promise Bushkin made.

With the major issues behind them, the two men returned to the thorny politics of crowd control. The conversation became laboured briefly, and when all seemed resolved, Bushkin strove to wind up the proceedings. But, at his end, Weissbrot aired several nagging misgivings. Bushkin hammered back.

"Keep in mind the dynamics of demokratik victimhood. Katharsis[2] is essential. Please, Norman, run that by Oprah Spinfrey. I can hold back a public announcement for a few days and a few days after that I can pretend to still be planning our military response. But, the peril remains. The longer I suppress the facts about Drughistan, the larger the buildup waiting to explode. Don't pretend Russian anger won't be directed at drug facilitators such as the US military and its so-called elected civilian oversight. Timing is everything."

1 Comrade, Whisky, Please. (Rus).
2 For effect, heavy use is made of 'K' russification in this chapter.

Weissbrot voiced his concerns while Bushkin thumbed back five pages in his notepad before he dove for the jugular.

"Our boys are fielding over 100,000 veterans. Remember — many have afflicted loved ones. They'll be backed up with heavy-armour. You've surely had a good glimpse," and Bushkin chuckled to allay tension — "I'm offering you ample time to put similar forces in place. As we've agreed, the Indian Ocean is all yours. But, my order to stop at the Afghan border will be demokratik suicide unless you install a force of comparable strength to hold it. That border, you must keep with the tenacity of a Muslim martyr. And, I'm sure your MIC armament oligarchs will love the ka-ching of clashing shields. Bonus pig-fest!"

Weissbrot, a man mired in misgivings about the danger of blowback, kept venting. Bushkin empathized with his American friend's frustration, but reality was paramount — "Norman, think. My nation is faced with an onslaught of Russians enlisting in the army. I, too, must heed the kick-ass ferocity of patriotism. It's only proper in placating nuclear-powered demokrazies that the brunt of demokratik katharsis and the preservation of world peace fall on the runt nations of our times."

As Weissbrot spoke, Bushkin sensed he was in denial, so he fired back.

"It's about Kossacks, Norman. Kossacks on the verge of riot. And, don't forget, by the time my army reaches the Afghan border, we both need to produce satellite photos publicly verifying that at least 20% of Drughistan's poppy fields are torched or burning. Think of Eisenhower's movies about Hitler's concentration camps. Visible truth is essential. And, the timetable is limited. Your Pentagon needs to get cracking. Only like military force and demonstrable kontrition can hold in check the savagery of Rooskie demokratik resolve. Talk up a storm about Russia's Dioxinomic Zombies if that makes it easier for your elektorate to phantasize about the heavy-lifting that awaits them."

Bushkin flexed his jaw to relax. Weissbrot was succumbing to the message. And, when it came his turn to speak, Bushkin broadcast his approval.

"Agreed. Only a few Ironman vs. Ivanman skirmishes, here and there. My friend, it's good to live in times when superpowers can accomplish great things with only marginal casualties while still giving the world audience a good gorilla-thumping spectacle. Also, a handy reminder about how superpowers have the wherewithal to squish any zit they please. Such as Al Qaeda."

Weissbrot said his piece about Al Qaeda.

Bushkin, who loved Al Qaeda for its calming influence on Amerika's militaristic psyche, chuckled at his friend's predicable glee about stomping on 'Camel Plop' like bubble-wrap rain-puddles.

"Too, too funny, Norman. Now, get your troop schedule faxed to me as priority so I can organize escorts for NATO transports across our airspace. After that, all airspace must be closed to commercial planes. We need to minimize regrettable kollateral damage and all the media monkey-skunkey."

Bushkin made notes while Weissbrot broached another concern.

"*Da*, Norman. Secrecy at my end is beyond reproach. So, when Kongress finds out, it will make it impossible for them to reinstate Carter."

Another uneasy pause ensued.

"All my best, Mizda[1] President. Bye now."

Bushkin floated the Soviet-black Bakelite handset back into its cradle and scrawled his final recollections on a pad before relaxing into the folds of his chair to catch breath and give matters further thought. Certain there were no loose ends, he pressed the [ACCESS GRANTED] button. The elevator doors opened, and Director-General Karl Besstrashnikov and Supreme Kommander Marshal Ogrom Palachnin stepped into the president's office.

"Gentlemen, sorry to keep you waiting. I just wound up a lengthy phone call with Norman Weissbrot, the new Doodle President. He was filling me in about the details. Carter's whole Cabinet declared her unfit to be president and ousted her. It's simply the best news possible."

Besstrashnikov expressed caution.

"Sir, be aware it's provisional. Only a two-thirds vote in Kongress can make Weissbrot the permanent president. But, I think it'll stick because Amerika's financial markets have rebounded, their lobbyists have noticed, and so must their poodles."

"Norman explained the doggy-dish intricacies. Strange how Doods make a whopping production of a small adjustment. He's the better man for the job by far. I assured him, we'll do anything prudent to help him secure what world peace expects of two nuclear-powered demokrazies. Only something out of the ordinary can derail his ascendance. And, I won't let that happen."

And, Bushkin winked at Director-General Besstrashnikov.

Supreme Kommander Palachnin spoke into the mysterious interlude.

"Mr. President, if we may. I need to get the updates worked in."

"Right you are, Ogrom." Bushkin scooped up his pad and launched into the meeting — "Gentlemen, it's agreed. The small fish in the system will pay the price."

Palachnin interjected — "Sir, the Doodles have a track record—"

Besstrashnikov cut Palachnin off — "Ogrom, superpower conflict would be the death of civilization. Scapegoating is now rule of international law. Look at the financing of 9/11. Did Amerika march on Britain or Saudi Arabia? No. Did they sue the Al Yamamah slush-fund for billions in compensation? No. Thor's hammer fell on candidates for Western psychiatric intervention — 'suicidal Muslims.' As well as that undertapped runt, oil-rich Iraq. In Yahweh's Almighty 'Jewess of A,' elektoral outrage was scripted to suit a Zio-Nazi feeding frenzy."

Bushkin motioned for Besstrashnikov to be silent.

"In short, Ogrom, when Romanov or Osama plays, the wops and wogs must pay. That's Captain America and Kaptain Kossack operating hand-in-fist. A Superpower Justice League, any Joe Doodle and Ruslan Rooskie can be brainwashed to admire. All thanks to Jewish media experiments on the Western elektorate. As a world leader, accountable for elektoral dividends in Russia, there is no way I'll frustrate our citizens' expectations regarding the maintenance of world peace with anything less than a world-class superpower show of strength with all the trim'ns, fix'ns, back-stabbing and payback."

---

1 Russian portmaneau Miz + Pizda means Ms + Cunt. In English, the Russian accent Mizda sounds innocuous - Mister. But who can say?

"So, what's the military play now, Mr. President?" Palachnin asked.

"Just tweaks. Pursuant to Russia's membership in NATO's 'Partnership for Peace' program, I gave NATO a right of over-flight across Russia for one week. Here's the gist. Weissbrot will be dunning France, Spain, Greece and Wopland for veteran troops. They'll be assigned to eradicate the poppy fields. NATO's heavy-arms veteran forces, mainly German, Austrian, British and Amerikan, will arrive by sea and they'll take up border duties. Weissbrot knows we'll be fielding a 100,000 man heavy-armour force against Drughistan."

Bushkin flopped back in his chair — *Time to relax.*

"I dangled the ultimate carrot, so the wabbit had no choice."

And, Bushkin cocked his eyebrows and cracked one of his wicked *What's-Up-Doc* smiles. Palachnin was puzzled, but Besstrashnikov laughed hysterically and lifted the veil of cypher-spiel.

"Demokrazy! The preservation of the art of running the circus from the monkey cage. Unlike their blue-bloods with direct access to power, from birth to death, the Y-D proletariat are hostage to demokratik sloganeering. Their 'Dee-fen-sof-Lee-burr-tea' is more precious than their children or social security."

Bushkin nodded to Palachnin in affirmation and sat bolt upright.

"Now gentlemen, to prevent Russia's fragile demokrazy from backsliding." And Bushkin chuckled before resuming — "I made it klear to Weissbrot that Amerika and NATO need to come up with a comparable force. Because without it, any order I issue for Russia's forces to stand down at the Afghan border would be the suicide of Russia's demokrazy. I'm no dictator and I'm certainly no idiot!" And, Bushkin thumped his desk.

Palachnin's eyes squeezed tight in glee as Bushkin continued explaining.

"Weissbrot and I, both agree a titanic show of strength will be necessary in order for me to pander to our ultra-nationalist element, the so-called red-behind-the-ears Kossack. Unlike that dingbat Carter, the man in Weissbrot understands we need to soften our elektorate's demand to mete out hard justice while preserving demokrazy. And, world peace, too. Of course."

Palachnin's tittered his unvarnished admiration.

"So, NATO will have hoards of heavy-armour barreling through Pakistan and Drughistan to get to its northern border on time and a large number of wop and other NATO southern command troops from Greece, Turkey and Wopland swatting away at poppy fields by the time we pounce on Wopland?"

Coming in a voice of utter bewilderment from an old Soviet war-horse like Marshal Palachnin, Bushkin could not restrain himself.

"You'd think that by now I could stop laughing at that thought, but that's correct Ogrom. It's all coming together and much faster with Weissbrot calling the shots. I see only marginal bloodshed thanks to klear-headed leadership."

And, Bushkin finished with a jovial burst.

"In a world of runts, it's classic superpower win-win."

Palachnin focused on the real deal.

"And the fate of Kazakhstan, Uzbekistan, Turkmenistan, and Tajikistan?"

240

Bushkin leant triumphantly across his desk.

"Weissbrot and I have finalized our secret pact. Amerika keeps Drughistan as its client state. We're free to take back Kazakhstan, Uzbekistan, Turkmenistan and Tajikistan and, by way of kompensation for their involvement with 'terrorism', strip off the oil and gas fields in the western half along the Caspian Sea. In due course and concomitant on Amerika exiting Drughistan, under the 'song and dance' of bowing to international pressure, Russia will gradually reinitiate sovereignty in these republics on a redrawn map. Turkmenistan will become extinct, so we'll always have a border with Drughistan. I also assured Weissbrot that Russia wouldn't menace the border any longer than one year. Our only demand is all poppy fields be flattened."

"Do any Konventions of War apply?" Palachnin asked.

Bushkin flared his eyebrows.

"Legal is still gold-mining that. Needless to say, Russia will be following the example of our Y-Doodle komrades, as ratified by the Y-D electorate. So first off, no konvention of war applies to any Doodle. Treat them as kritters. Or do what the spit-treaty-in-your-eye Australians do. Embed 'non-signatory kontractors' like the Waffen-CIA to make 'enemy kaptures', then we're off-the-hook — Aussie-style. A true-blue, dinky-di dodge — huh, mate?"

Besstrashnikov laughed. But, Palachnin's gut stiffened with contempt. He'd been under the spank-me-doodle microscope for his command of the suppression of jihadism in the Russian Republic of Chechnya, and he let rip.

"So! So, Russia aspires to exalt Western hypocrisy, Mr. President?"

"Exactly, Ogrom. That's the heart of the superpower 'Fair-play Balanced with Hypokrizy' doctrine at work. Always remember, Italy is part of NATO and adheres to the Geneva Conventions. But, like Al Qaeda, Al Guido and the Taliban, Wopland is signatory to nothing. And, even though Afghanistan signed onto the Geneva Conventions in 1956, and did so every year thereafter, US President Potusson decreed on February 7, 2002 that no such conventions applied to Talibanistan. In short, the soil a nation's patriots defend is protected by nothing more than the demagoguery of the alien invader. Palestine and the Raghead Semites of Palestine invaded by Nordic Semites from Europe is another classic example of long-running fascist hypocrisy in act—"

Alarmed, Palachnin chopped in.

"What? A third front, sir?"

"No, Ogrom. It's about Russia's legal framework. As German is to Austrian,[1] the Semites called Palestinians are genetically indistinguishable from the alien invaders who refer to themselves as 'Semites', or more precisely 'Semites from the North' — Nordic Semites or Ashke-nazi, if you prefer. Let Israel drag Y-D into the grave as they both fall on their own warmongering swords. That fight against fascist runt-on-runt hypocrisy and anti-Semitic extirpation isn't our affair."

1 *Jewish and Middle Eastern non-Jewish Populations Share a Common Pool of Y-Chromosome Biallelic Haplotypes*, M. F. Hammer et al., US National Academy of Sciences Vol 97:12 (2000). In short, the genetic difference that distinguishes a German from an Austrian is the same genetic difference that distinguishes a Palestinian from a European Jew. This is no joke. Ref: www.pnas. org/content/97/12/6769.full So, if ever you hear an adherent to Zio-Nazism claim that something called 'Palestinian race' or 'nationality' is a fraud, have a good laugh. To paraphrase Abraham Lincoln, "Those that deny Semitism to others, deserve it not for themselves."

"I see. So, what's our final lawfare status?"

"As President of Russia, I've decided that Drughistan will be the official name for the region formerly known as Afghanistan until such time as all poppies have been eradicated. Hence, no Konventions apply to Drughistan, even if Westerners refer to the place where the Geneva Conventions of War were doodled into non-existence as Afghanistan. At least, those Westerners whose sons and daughters haven't snuffed it from drugs or drug induced HIV/AIDS — 'The Heroin Holocaust,' as we Russians know it. Now, the patch of dirt between Russia and Drughistan, that's our turf, Ogrom."

"So, we finally have proof that the Kazakh, Uzbek, Turkmen and Tajik people aided 'The Heroin Holocaust' as fascist proxies for US-NATO and are implicated in the attack on Moscow?"

Bushkin smirked.

"Ogrom, since when is that relevant. In any case, we have shown the US government the general DVD conversations given by their favourite nemesis — gastrointerrogating Muslims. Once we invade Kazakhstan and the rest of the Oilngas-o-stans, we can always 'Gitmo' konfessions by the truckload."

And, all three men roared with laughter.

Because the choirboy in Palachnin seemed removed from the stage of global politiks, Besstrashnikov decided his komrade needed the klarity of altruism.

"Ogrom, ignoring the Jewnited States's public display of bigotry against mother Russia, Amerika and Europe will quietly embrace us as heroes for pacifying the Muslim strongholds north of Drughistan. Our invasion of Central Asia is good for everyone. Honourable and unmuddled superpower 'Fair-play Balanced with Hypokrizy' politiks at work."

Bushkin nodded his concurrence and emphasized the salient truth behind any kompromise that preserves world peace.

"Ogrom, every superpower face-off must be designed to be win-win. After a tidy round of chest-thumping with the agreed upon skirmishes that we all know are indispensable to maintaining taxpayer approval ratings for outlandish military budgets in any well-balanced demokrazy, US and NATO will have victoriously defended Drughistan. As for Russia, we will have the blessings of the world because we forced all opium production to cease, thus saving the lives of hundreds of thousands of heroin addicts worldwide who die year-in year-out. For ourselves, we get back the old tsarist regions with all that delicious oil and gas."

Palachnin mused aloud.

"History and heroics marches hand in hand then?"

"That's the classic legacy of win-win," Bushkin replied.

And, the rest of the meeting focused on getting forces mobilized in the west and along the Black Sea for the armada that was being assembled to sail against Italy. When the Supreme Kommander was confident Bushkin understood and approved of the essentials, he excused himself to rejoin a meeting of the nation's generals and interweave the benefits of the Bushkin-Weissbrot Pact into his nation's larger mission for world peace.

Something Honourable

As soon as the elevator doors cinched shut behind Marshal Palachnin, Bushkin dunned Director-General Besstrashnikov for his take.

"Ogrom seems to have things under control."

"But, he remains concerned about the risk 'Operation Chili Balls' poses to ruining the element of surprise. Have you set a time and date for zero-hour?"

"I'm still awaiting Ogrom's invasion schedule for the seaports of Bari, Genoa, Livorno, Salerno and Ancona. The date is also a function of what Weissbrot can accomplish in terms of moving his forces into Drughistan. I also ordered up more exercises for our SM-21 and SM-23 brigades, so the Doods can verify they've undercounted our full armoured capability."

Besstrashnikov relayed his concern — "Sir, we need to start setting aside SM-21 and SM-23 decoy kits for the Wopland front. Can I assume the buildup of decoys in the east is now over?"

Bushkin twinkled with delight — "Yes, we don't want to crack satellite lenses with too many heat signatures. Weissbrot now thinks we have 80% of our Smertimolat units in the Caspian region. The 20% we actually have there and the 20% along the Baltic Republics should keep what's left of NATO's military on their side of the EU divide. That will leave us a full 60% to hammer Wopland with. So, Karl, how are we going with finances and covert operations?"

"The Ursini Group payment of 500 million Euros for their purchase of a three percent stake in Gazprom has been received. With Ursini Group Trucking Services sold off to us, our men will soon know the highways and byways of Wopland as intimately as the veins on their girlfriends' buttocks."

"Splendid. Any upcoming wop-ops?"

"Using explosives liberated from Ursini's 'Project Gladio' bunker, we're giving the wops a daily Al Guido-Al Qaeda suicidal incident here and there. And, tonight, two Bzombies will sabotage Ursini's Milan and Foggia breweries. This will cause Ursini's keg inventories to be deployed. Keg beer that we've contaminated with dysentery. All in all, Wopland will remain focused on internal matters so our covert forces can penetrate the country with less likelihood of detection."

Bushkin beamed his approval — "CIA munitions being Al-Yamamah'd against woppery. Poetic justice! So, what's our force count now, Karl?"

"We've smuggled some 7,800 into Solini Farms south of Bari, and some 4,500 irregulars are mixing into the country, 1,600 or so are Bzombies. Then there's the 3,780 personnel working for various enterprises we own or have purchased interests in over the last few days. That includes Rustalia SpA, our trojan-horse phone company."

"And, the status of 'Operation Chili Balls?'"

"Basil has the prime locations in operation. They've not deployed any urushiol ampoules. Sir, again — we need to establish a date and a zero-hour."

"By days end. Any updates about the second dioxin urn?"

"Sir, bear in mind, we have to balance hunting down Al Guido with the need to remain invisible until our regular forces hoist the Russian flag. The sooner we start the overt invasion of Wopland, the sooner we help our Doodle komrades by finding the urn headed their way."

Bushkin cast the Director-General a look of frustration.

"Karl, while we aren't responsible for their political crap, we still need to put on the right song-n-dance to shore up Krankie-Doodle's superpower status. Wopland is a runt and therefore subject to the doctrine of 'Fair-play Balanced with Hypokrisy'. But, it's still going to be messy. A second urn floating about makes things even more messy. I'm also worried because there's no guarantee it's actually headed towards the United States. It could be anywhere, damn it!"

As preliminary as Basil's plan was, Besstrashnikov decided to voice it.

"Sir, Basil and I have been talking about using some of the remaining 1,2,4,5 tetrachlorobenzene seized from Ursini's lab to cook up another urn. Put Ursini's fingerprints on it and ship it to New York. There, we'd interdict it and give the Doods a hearty dose of woppery in action."

Bushkin jolted like he'd swallowed Moses' staff.

"*Bolsheviks*, of course! Karl, give Basil another twenty-four hours to process the most recent crop of Al Guido detainees. If there remains no break, start planning a script for thwarting woppery in the act of sabotaging the New York Subway. Design the operation to maximize press exposure. If it's not a public spectacle like a Tim Delancy movie, you know the Y-D White-House will Watergate it to avert panic. We need thumbs-up from regular Doods for our heroic mission of world peace. You must stage a real public horror show. Which reminds me, what's Agent Polakulakov's status?"

"In Washington. The Amerikan identity Matt Bauer is serving him well. Milking the GI buddy system and putting into play a means to take out Carter in an orgy of explosions that guarantees to erase any trace of his existence in the process."

"Good, an absolutely clean hit."

And, Bushkin hunched over his desk for emphasis.

"Karl, remember, that operation is not yet green-lighted. I'm worried it might backfire like 'Operation Beaver Whack.' I'm also thinking Bauer might be a useful operative to put into play in this dioxin urn interdiction. After it goes down, we need to put a face on CNN and the other television networks, one sympathetic to Russia. Bauer was undercover in Afghanistan, has Y-D buddies there and has that rugged TV-crime-fighter reporter look to him."

"Bauer?" Besstrashnikov grinned — "You mean Polakulakov, sir."

Bushkin chuckled — "Now my head's off in TV land!"

And, Bushkin clapped his hands on his desk.

"So, what do you think, Komrade Director?"

"Polakulakov's an excellent choice. We can always use Bzombies to take out Carter. Our problem is that the Wopland front goes hot ten or so days from now when Kongress might be deciding between Carter and Weissbrot. She'll strut her madcap Bushkuntosaurus outlook and accuse Weissbrot of being in bed with the enemy. Remember sir, he needs two-thirds to become—"

Bushkin cut in.

"Got it. A stacked vote. … Too close for comfort," and Bushkin reclined into the folds of his chair and rocked — "Karl, the only way to prevent a miscarriage to world peace is to eliminate MizzFrumpty-Doodle."

"Agreed, sir. The Twenty-Fifth Amendment and Frumpty mustn't interfere with the checks and balances Y-D's founding fathers contemplated in 1787. You really shouldn't call it assassination, sir. As a rabid Jeffersonian idealist, even Carter would appreciate the glorious irony behind her own demise."

Bushkin roared with laughter.

"Karl, you make it sound like I'd be an anti-demokratik tyrant if I diddled a great Y-D statesman, their first kunt for a president no less, out of her crowning moment in the history of world peace by refraining from pulling the trigger."

Besstrashnikov joined in the president's mirth.

"Good one, sir."

Bushkin settled into the demeanor of a man reconciled to the fallacies of international statesmanship — "Karl, a year from now, I'll do something honourable to kommemorate Carter. But, for now, just as Oswald crowned his president, it falls on my watch to krown Carter."

"Can I get a final decision, sir?"

"Get a script in play for the dioxin attack in New York. It's code name — 'Operation Rescue Democracy.' We'll pick operatives later. For the moment, Polakulakov stays in Washington to perfect 'Operation Presidential Veto.' If it even smells like some Krock-a-Doodle Kongress will override my presidential veto then that operation must proceed without delay."

And, the rest of the meeting focused on the many covert operations to seize control of the Italian mobile phone system, the railway system ….

An Able Commander

Phone handset at his right ear, Basil was ecstatic.

"Bravo, Colonel. As soon as they've cleared Italian airspace, administer a healthy dose of urushiol. By the time they get here, I want them begging to have their scroti hacked open and their agony relieved. Is that clear?"

A short pause — "Excellent. *Poka.*"

Re-cradling the handset, Basil could hardly suppress his glee. Rome had reported that the 'Rolfino Effect' had narrowed the search for the second urn to four Al Guido suspects. Each still pointed the finger at the other. Within the hour, they would be airborne and on their way to Moscow, where, balls-in-hand, they would experience the persuasive power of a vampire intercession. Basil asked Elena to schedule Olga, Natalia and Dr. Soskrova for evening work.

Reclining into his horse-hide chair, Basil set aside a moment to relax. Natalia and he had enjoyed another romantic evening last night. But, this morning, when she mentioned new details about her recurring dream, he had come off abrupt. This he regretted. Life was already far too harsh. With her, he sought only purity and tenderness. And, he knew she sought the same with him.

In her new recollection, Natalia described in detail the riotous conditions the College of Jewish High Priests fomented and how a crowd-savvy Roman centurion on duty decided to nail Jesus to his cross. If the worst came to the worst and the soldiers were forced to retreat then the mob would have to rip this pretender to the sovereignty the Jews now owed to their sworn King — Tiberius Caesar — off his crucifix. And, in so doing, cause him to bleed to death. It was a smart call by an able commander at Golgotha because the Jewish high priests took pains to accompany the throng. And, there, they goaded the crowd to hysteria by claiming that any Jewish Messiah sent by a Jew-loving Yahweh had the power to come down from pagan Caesar's instrument of execution, nails or no nails.

Torn between wonder and concern, Basil always listened intently as Natalia delivered her recollections. There was no denying it. They were in love. And, that's what hurt. Whenever she spoke about her recollection-dreams, her sweet voice bristled with emotional force. Her descriptions had a disturbing authenticity to them. But, as always, he ultimately ended up pointing out everything she detailed was logical or described in scripture.

Annoyed at him, she had gone on the offensive about his 'Basileus' theory. She reasoned that once upon a time she might have been Chinese and could read a Chinese menu but only as a matter of recalling past experience and not as one who could compose her waking thoughts in Chinese. How could her dreams be an active imagination at work? An active imagination required linguistic fluency not recall.

Against her sharp new insight, he had no sound rebuttal. And, without doubt, she truly possessed a miraculous power, something she had been plying tirelessly all day now. He reached for the intercom.

"Elena, is Miss Bogomolski on the line yet?"

"Her mobile phone is ringing now, sir."

And, Elena connected the call to Basil's desk-phone.

The chirp-chirping stopped — "*Privyet*, Natash."

Basil smiled at hearing her speak his name.

"I also missed being with you for lunch today, sweetheart."

A lengthy pause ensued before Basil replied ever so warmly.

"That's good, *Daragaya*." She had mentioned eating-for-two, her so-called pregnancy, a matter still days from being verifiable. "At least, you have a wholesome appetite. I only called to say that I may have come across too harsh this morning. Please excuse me if I was. You made a good point about the language issue. Please pass that on to the Patriarch."

Basil laughed as she spoke her piece.

"So he agrees. *Touché*. About tonight, we need you here at 8:00 p.m."

Natalia quizzed Basil, and he fired back.

"It's four Al Guido terrorists. You'll finish around ten, darling."

Basil's mood hardened as she sounded off.

"Yes, it's critical. They know about the second urn."

Basil winced as he heard his beloved's voice crack with conflict.

The light to Line-2 started blinking — *Reprieve!*

"Natash, must go. The director's line's flashing. Above all, never forget, it's about world peace. I love you, my princess. *Poka.*"

He pounced on the button to connect to Besstrashnikov.

"*Privyet*, Karl. Just off the phone with Rome. The four are airborne. Hopefully, by tomorrow, we'll have the second urn. Has the president vetted my proposal about cooking up our own?"

The Director-General first stressed that the second Ursini urn was still out there, and so its capture remained paramount. But, he quickly relayed the good news. Bushkin had authorized 'Operation Rescue Democracy.' A bloody death for Carter always had the prospects for casting aspersions on Weissbrot, in light of the 'duel of presidents' before Congress. After further reviewing the plans, the president realized how a staged dioxin interdiction might take her out in the best way possible — no bloodshed — because in any demokrazy, assassination in primetime was more surgical than blood and guts reality. And, Besstrashnikov laid out the additional public-trust building goals that 'Operation Rescue Democracy' needed to achieve.

As soon as the call ended, Basil organized a chemical engineer with General Litvinenko's group to generate another urn of dioxin from three of the remaining fourteen kilos in the twenty-kilo drum of pelletized 1,2,4,5 tetrachlorobenzene taken from Alfredo's subterranean laboratory at the Ursini Vineyard in Tuscany.

Sometime in the coming week, Carter's petition would establish the exact day on which Congress would debate and vote her fit or unfit for office. Hence, Basil would know well in advance the prime time to stage 'Operation Rescue Democracy.' The goal — inoculate the American people with an act of woppery, and steel them for war against their true enemy. But, the real beauty of Basil's operation was that it would also tip all Amendment Twenty-Five debate in Weissbrot's favour. With the loss of so much independent intelligence caused by the 'Mallory Wilson Affair,' Weissbrot could conclusively prove to Congress that hospitable and open channels with Russia had enormous national security benefits.

Matrushkas in Waiting

September drew to a close on good news. US President Carter had lodged her Amendment Twenty-Five Re-instatement petition with Congress, and a hearing was scheduled for Monday. Despite Natalia's anxiety about Basil being absent on some secret mission, the spirit of Derek Mitchell continued to work its charm. In the process of healing others, she found catharsis and started embracing the Heaven-sent beauty within her power.

"Perhaps, this is what my gift is for," she said.

Swallowing the last piece of crust of what had once been a slice of stale Freedom-with-Pepperoni Pizza, Tatiana sat high and replied.

"A thousand heroin addicts in one day!"

"Phenomenal, isn't it?"

Tatiana was about to respond when Olga sashayed over to them, trilling. "Ladies. It's official." She dragged up a seat — "Call me Miss Matrushka!"

Natalia hugged Olga around the neck while Tatiana, whose pregnancy had been confirmed the week before, picked up Olga's left hand and sandwiched it between her own in solidarity. Olga was raring to ask.

"Natash, any updates on your situation?"

"My period is due, more or less. But, nothing so far. It's claimed the urine test strip is reliable six days prior to menses and it confirms what I sense myself. But, I'll have to wait until next week to be absolutely positive."

Tatiana interposed.

"Give it forty-eight hours and do a second test. A 99% clincher."

Natalia replied nonchalantly — "Next week, just to be dead certain."

Natalia felt taxed because, unlike sloppy sex, when it came to pregnancy, Basil was the type of man who expected persnickety exactitude. But, the Major in Tatiana knew Basil would not be around next week. With pregnancy on the line, action was essential. Tatiana leant over.

"Natash, do it Sunday. Right now, the General thinks this pregnancy idea is a wonderful possibility. But, the best thing for him is to embrace reality."

"Tats, if it were so simple. I love him, typical man and all. But, I don't need any special power to distinguish male enthusiasm from polite offhandedness. Next week won't hurt. Then Daddy Baz can confront science instead of me."

Tatiana smiled in empathy.

"Yes — typical man. But, I tell you this. While woppery is weighing down everyone, being a father-to-be has given my Sergei a new lease on life. Natash, there's a Kremlin ball Sunday. Pretend I never told you because I'm sure the General will break the news to you when he returns. So, why not give him a Sunday surprise of your own? Do the second test and tell him on the way home. Expect a huge night of romance starting at the ball. But, most important, give Basil a gift that will lift his spirits in the days ahead."

Natalia flashed Tatiana a fretful look.

"I'd love to Tats. Love to. But, he's very stubborn."

Tatiana winked.

"Let me taser the old mule. This Major will set one Kossack straight about the accuracy of a second test. 99% — assuming your second confirms the first."

Natalia clasped Tatiana's hand — "How perfect. Just perfect."

"My pleasure. And, make a special night of it."

And, in an air of mock formality, Tatiana turned to Olga.

"Ahem! Lieutenant Olga Nikolaevna Krovsoska, I believe tradition dictates that you treat your esteemed komrades to a celebratory toast. Let's go, and I'll order your extravagant selection from the senior officer's wine cellar."

The Laws of Counter-Defense

On the morning of Saturday, the first of October, for the forty-eight generals, admirals and air marshals in attendance, the last echoes rippling across the magnificent Ivan-the-Conqueror Ballroom in the Kremlin Palace petered to silence. Bushkin opened the meeting with several routine preliminaries but soon turned his focus onto the dark heart of their nation's great quest.

"Komrades, henceforth, our combined military missions are to be publicly called 'Operation WOPPERY,' meaning *Wipe Out Pollution*, its *Perpetrators, Enablers, Radicals and Yahoos*. Our military forces are to proceed into the lands of our nation's enemies on a mission to secure world peace in our time, as well as protect the assets of the motherland, especially our sizeable gold bullion reserves soon to make dock at Bari."

Bushkin stopped to re-establish eye contact with his audience.

"As you know, Italy is a member of NATO. And, under NATO Treaty Article Five, an attack on Italy is considered an attack on the United States. NATO is in Drughistan under the Potusson laws of war because on September 11, 2001, and financed by moneys from the Al Yamamah slush-fund, nineteen nutcases committed suicide in a manner that caused 'collateral damage.' Did Doodle-land celebrate how fifteen Saudi terrorists, as well as two from Yemen, one from Lebanon and another from Egypt were whacked out of existence in a single morning without the use of Predator drones and Hellfire missiles?"

He stood tall and slapped the lectern.

"Hell — no!"

Bushkin waited until the reverberation of *no-no-no-no* died.

"In its propaganda designed to mobilize the forces of good collateral damage against the forces of evil collateral damage, Y-D declared 'collateral damage' resulting in the death of a terrorist was a violation of the laws of war. These hypocrites claimed an Article Five attack under the NATO Treaty occurred, and hence all of NATO suffered theoretical 'terrorist-snuffing collateral damage' too. Pursuant to Amerikan legal doctrines, I have come to some critical decisions about what Russia's legal framework will be."

He slowed his delivery and fingered the front of the lectern, making sure his hands, curled shy of a fist, were noticeable to everybody.

"I've decided to adopt the mindset of President Potusson of the United States. We are not at war. We are at counter-defense. Our adversaries are not Muslims nor Italians. They are wogs and wops. And, the fundamental rule of law in our counter-defense against woppery is — When in Rome, do as Nero would."

He clasped the edge of the lectern and boomed.

"Once upon a time, there was a locality called 'Italy' but by the authority granted in the Russian Konstitution to me as the nation's president, I declare 'Italy' a failed-state, an illusion, a multiplayer videogame. As such, the land on any map denoted as 'Italy' is in law to be treated as 'terra nullius.' For Russia and all civilized nations, there exists only Wopland, a patch of dirt, inhabited by Wops. Wopland and Drughistan are equal and the same. As per Kranky-Doodle on his shit-in-your-face pony, there is no law in Drughistan. No Geneva Konventions. No Torture Konventions. No Slavery Konventions."

He waited for renewed silence and thumped the lectern.

"So be it for Wopland!"

Moving his body arms-length from the lectern, he resumed.

"Komrades, never forget, our business is securing world peace."

He perused the room from left to right, biding his time.

"Anyone who opposes our state of counter-defense against the global forces of woppery is not a lawful combatant but rather a wop and subject to Russian tribunals of martial law. And, under the Doodle's theory of aiding and abetting, it goes without saying that if you are not with us in our global counter-defense then you are against us. Soon we'll know which nations coddle woppery."

He elevated his voice to make his declaration raw.

"As terrorism is to the Amerikans, woppery is to us. As the Taliban is to the Amerikans, the Wops are to us. As Al Qaeda is to the Amerikans, Al Guido is to us. I repeat — War konventions are not applicable. Legislation to authorize war is not applicable. The UN Charter concerning war is not applicable. Russia is in a state of counter-defense aimed at preserving a world already at peace. *Not war!*"

To permit the boom of his last blast to wither into silence, Bushkin took a swig of *kvas.*[1] Then, he softened his tone. "On the issue of espionage, komrades. Again, Doodle President Potusson is our legal eagle. Mobile phones constitute two-way radio transmission equipment. A lawful spy is one on the payroll of a legitimate government but an ad-hoc spy is a civilian, who by possession of radio equipment has the opportunity to report our counter-defense actions. Ad-hoc spies are to be treated like persons who think they have a right to carry machine guns, be they loaded with ammo or not. Any person caught with radio transmission equipment is to be arrested, summarily tried and sentenced to be shot. No exceptions. That means all wops and any foreigners lock-and-loaded with mobile phones have automatically violated the unwritten but obvious laws of counter-defense, whether or not transmission occurs or batteries are drained. Is that clear?"

A chorus of aye-ayes echoed across the room. Everyone understood 'Unlawful Espionage' was nothing more than an extension of the pre-existing US-NATO 'Unlawful Combatant' doctrine. Bushkin took another swig of *kvas,* turned to his right and clutched the base of the microphone in his left hand.

"On our eastern front in Central Asia, I've decided as a matter of grace that we will adhere to the Geneva Konventions of War until we reach the Drughistan border. Across that border, where US-NATO declared on February 7, 2002 that the Geneva Conventions of War don't apply, or in any US or NATO engagements on our side of that border, you are to adhere to the laws of counter-defense."

Bushkin turned to his left — "General Litvinenko, it's time for you to make your presentation quantifying the reparations due the motherland."

While Litvinenko stood and repositioned the lectern microphone, President Bushkin made his way to his seat on the right. Towering over the lectern, General Vadim Olegovich Litvinenko waited for quiet to return.

---

1 Made from stale Russian black-rye bread scraps, a drink comparable to Root Beer.

"Komrades, since Russia is adopting an eye-for-an-eye policy, let me start with human lives destroyed or upended."

Litvinenko's first slide appeared on the projection screen. And, he launched straight into the state of carnage for the twentieth day after the Metro attack — 66,921 dead; 15,853 cadavers were once children. He provided a wealth of detail before boiling the loss of their productive labour into man-months.

"Komrades, it comes to 24,444,447. This is equivalent to owning the productive labour of 100,000 wops for 20.4 years or owning the productive labour of 203,703 wops for ten years. Sir, have you made some decisions?"

And, he pivoted his shoulders to face President Bushkin.

Remaining seated, Bushkin raised a hand mic level with his chin.

"Yes, General. I've decided Russia prefers not to keep convicts for more than ten years. Our captures should focus on the eighteen to twenty-five age group so we can release them before age thirty-five. Once returned to Wopland, they can knuckle down to breeding. In the West, it's common for women to have children at such an advanced age. This gives us the longest duration of use under our ten-year reparations policy and affronts no Western reproductive sensibilities. A classic case of win-win."

"Sir, I'm now about to report reparation figures that will require you to dial back your program to execute all spies, ad-hoc or legitimate. It's a matter of numbers, sir. We need spies alive as additional manpower."

Bushkin nodded.

"Quite correct, General. Reparation comes before blood lust."

Bushkin stood up to ensure his word was treated as edict.

"Komrades, I'm commuting death sentences on any ad-hoc spy age thirty-two and under who confesses their 'unlawful espionage.' Without a signed confession, all those convicted are 'spies by profession' and are to be executed by firing squad. All commuted sentences will be served in Russia. Fifteen years of labour. However, as a carrot to encourage good behavior, I'll even reduce that accommodating term to ten years if the convict proves himself. The FSB informs me that when we invade Wopland, we can expect a flood of ad-hoc spies dressed up as civilians who claim a right to possess two-way radio equipment. We'll deal with this scum under the laws inspired by US-NATO."

Bushkin raised his open left palm to indicate he wasn't finished.

"Now, for wop spies over thirty-two and all foreign spies regardless of age, all commanders can still polish up the firing squad and execute them as the laws of counter-defense provide. Or, they can seek my one-on-one clemency. All in all, we need to bring in the reparation harvest as priority. Any questions?"

General Tendinov, head of the Feralia Forces spoke up.

"Sir, I'm left with the impression that we're being overly indulgent towards spies. I don't question your generosity and largesse. What concerns me is that our definition of a spy is needlessly confined. In Drughistan and elsewhere, Yankee-Doodle considers daggers, knives, swords, flintlock rifles and gardening tools the paraphernalia of an unlawful combatant. In fact, even if a child defends himself from certain death, Y-D considers that an act of 'unlawful combat.' Recall that Canadian civilian child? That darkie was convicted of 'unlawful self-preservation' for throwing back a live Amerikan hand grenade."

Bushkin gestured for Tendinov to make his point.

"Sir, just as a rifle transmits potential combat injury, we should define data transmission along the same lines, as a potential espionage injury. We should include landline telephones, flashlights, and for that matter keychain lasers. Can't we have the Russian Ministry of Justice cook up a more extensive definition of 'unlawful espionage' armament?"

"General, nose hairs are grinding stones as we speak. I just presented the most egregious situation as example. Treat all persons as spies until they can prove they're lawful civilians. Let Russia's military tribunals decide who is firing squad material and who is not. Sifting out spies is not a soldier's job. So, Litvinenko, what's the total number of wops we need to harvest?"

Litvinenko cleared his throat — *Crunch time*.

"Sir, I need to emphasize that my estimate is a lower bound. I suggest taking an additional 10% in live captures. Now the big numbers. We have citizens dying in the coming months as well as hundreds of thousands of citizens slowly degrading. Their lives are shortened, their industry is lost, I estim—"

Bushkin chopped in — "Litvinenko, cut to the chase."

"Mr. President, we'll need 2.5 million wops aged eighteen to twenty-five under your ten-year policy, sir."

Bushkin stopped reaching for his *kvas*.

"So, we need a fifteen-year convict policy?"

"Mr. President, ten years is feasible. It amounts to approximately one-third of all wops on the Italian peninsula aged from eighteen to twenty-five. We may need to do hit and run raids on Sicily. Worse comes to worst, you can always stretch out the ten into additional years. Your ten-year gift was predicated on good behavior, sir."

Mic in hand, Bushkin rose to his feet.

"I hereby declare and order that our forces need to capture 2.5 million wops, preferably aged eighteen to twenty-five. In addition, I'm told some 800,000 Moscow women can no longer carry a fetus as a result of dioxin poisoning. So be on the lookout for prime young wops. Breeders with healthy uteri. Is that clear?"

The room nodded. The order was straightforward — oodles of wops, one-third to be breeders, preferably young, field-tested and healthy. It was pretty obvious to the most retarded grunt what their nation expected in terms of quality control. Supreme Kommander Palachnin stood.

"Sir, in Wopland, as far as breeding goes, the age of consent is fourteen. No one could take offense if our captures are fourteen and upwards."

"*Konechna*."[1]

Air Vice-Marshal, Valeria Rodchenko stood.

"Sir, we'll be ostracized in the West as sexist. Boys in that age group should also be harvested. It expands the motherland's range of convicts."

1 Of Course (Rus).

"Vice Marshal, I'd never choose to be politically incorrect. My order is modified. Our target range is now fourteen to twenty-five years of age. This should now make it easier to fill the quota of 2.5 million. And, all spies must be able-bodied. If not, they're fodder for the firing squad."

Bushkin re-sat and posed the next issue.

"General Litvinenko, we need to address resurrecting Moscow's transportation infrastructure. What are your recommendations?"

Litvinenko dreaded this question. Life-for-life reparation was easy to quantify, now came the sort of intractable choices that involved a complete re-organization of society itself. He spoke into the mic but fixed his gaze on the president.

"Sir, the problem has two components — population density and the capacity to expand above ground transportation. Moscow has an unofficial population of twenty million. Once, our Metro was a fast and cheap—"

Bushkin hammered his glass of *kvas* on the table.

"Make your point, General!" He calmed. "Please."

Litvinenko hesitated. Now came the riotous moment of truth, the fight to remain civilized while maintaining a just face on the nation's righteous counter-defense to salvage world peace out of the ravages of woppery.

"Mr. President, it's a fact of Dioxinomics that all Metro systems are gas chambers in waiting. With millions vulnerable in a Metro system, that can be readily polluted—" Litvinenko noticed Bushkin drumming his fingers. "Moscow is far too tempting a target for a fascist holocaust should we get a third dose of it in the future. Given that in this age of woppery, megacities are Dioxinomic dinosaurs, our only option is to radically downsize all our major cities."

Bushkin rose to his feet, his tone was black, almost a snarl.

"Komrades, this gets back to the larger issue of social upheaval. Russians have no business living like Gypsies. We need to decentralize and build at least twelve one-million-man cities. Litvinenko, any rough numbers to do this?"

"Sir, there's much civil engineering work involved—"

Exasperated with arse-hair counting, Bushkin cut in.

"So, let's simplify this. We need another one million wops, preferably with building skills. We'll need to erect roads, water and sewer systems, and housing and industrial infrastructure. In short, building at the snap of the fingers a series of one-million-man cities, scattered about so that they are not tempting targets for future acts of woppery."

Bushkin then turned to his Supreme Kommander.

"Marshal Palachnin, can you bring home the bacon — the transportation of 3.5 million wops to mother Russia?"

Palachnin waited for the last echo to subside and replied with gusto.

"Yes, sir. But, it requires that we commandeer every plane and piece of wop shipping we can lay our hands on. At best, it'll take us ninety days of non-stop shipping back and forth. Also Mr. President, keep NATO in mind. This scenario means we can't provide naval escorts to all the anticipated convict convoys."

Bushkin gave a left-handed thumbs-up.

"No problem. Each ship will be a floating legation, bearing diplomatic insignia and carrying one diplomat as well as diplomatic papers. If NATO attempts to molest these vessels, they'll be demolished so violently that they'll sink like a rock. I want every ship packed solid. Our counter-defense against woppery doesn't end until 3.5 million or more convicts set foot on Russian soil and clean up their wop-owned mess. Our motherland needs a morale boost. We need to start rebuilding our infrastructure. No excuses. No doodling."

Bushkin swiveled to his right.

"Director-General Besstrashnikov, are we prepared to tag 3.5 million wops with radio ID?"

"Definitely. It's the system used to tag pets. Besides our production, we have a wop semiconductor foundry tooled up to pour out a million chips starting Monday. By the time our forces unfurl the flag, chips should be streaming off their production lines waiting to be requisitioned by our military."

Bushkin followed through — "And what of our other contracts?"

"All going to plan. With Gazprom and the gold bullion about to land at Bari as collateral, we have plenty of Euro loans from wop banks financing these contracts. Production that we've outsourced to various wop industries continues streaming off assembly lines. They'll be ready for military confiscation the moment our forces kick-down the doors."

"How are we for cash when we get there?"

"Again, no problem. We've done another surreptitious round of charging some ten million wop bank issued credit cards with draws ranging from 40 to 200 Euros. We'll be swarming over Wopland long before any billing dispute arises. We're flush with Euros to purchase any black market products we can't confiscate first."

Bushkin's tone turned even more gruff.

"Good, we're already dioxinomically screwed. Let's share the wealth. Which reminds me, is General Novimirov's brothel network turning a profit?"

In Basil's absence, Besstrashnikov stood and made reply.

"The so-called cultured nation of Italy nicknames itself 'The Beautiful Brothel,' *Bel Casino*. So, by wop standards, I am most pleased to report, sir, it's earning a respectable profit."

The room exploded into thunderous laughter.

President Bushkin returned to the lectern with a black shoe in his right hand, and as if he were wielding a gavel, brought the heel down hard on the lectern. By the fifth blow, he had calmed the room to residual echoes. When silence returned, he reminded them why this had to be.

"And let this appear in the historical record. I could submit Russia's written demands to Wopland for 3.5 million wops for ten years of hard labour to wipe clean the pollution they unleashed on the motherland along with a bill for damages of 1,500 billion Euro. This would save everybody the need for military conflict. But, like the pre-emptive action notice concerning the plot being formulated by Romanov and Al Guido, which we honourably submitted to

Italy, France, Britain, China and the United States six months ago, I know that we'd be laughed off the planet."[1]

The rest of the meeting focused on the army's task to confiscate or fabricate the hospital, medical, construction, agricultural equipment and other supplies that would need to be transported along with 3.5 million convicts.

Specto Patrem

On Sunday, in the wall-to-wall mirrored vastness of the Paul-the-Peacemaker Ballroom, a grandiose evening function at the Kremlin waltzed along magnificently. Because many among the attendees knew of her special powers, almost every general came up to Special Agent Natalia V. Bogomolski to make introduction and pay her their highest regards. As the evening progressed, Basil, who had returned that afternoon from his quest to save Amerika, felt more like Natalia's escort, because she was dunned for dance after dance. And, what shameless pleasure these generals came away with, after each waltz drew to a close. Her immense delight at their rapt attention simply radiated out of her body and into theirs.

Uncharacteristic for a Russian ball, this regal affair ended promptly at 10:30 p.m. because Monday would be a flurry of unfolding operations. On the chauffeured drive back to Derek's former apartment, Basil and Natalia had their first opportunity to converse in private.

"Well sweetheart, you were quite the belle of the ball. Did you meet any eligible bachelors? Any reason for me to be jealous?"

She kindled bright with mystery.

"Well, I must confess I was completely smitten with a certain bodyguard tonight. The president has good taste in choosing his men."

Basil laughed uneasily and fired back.

"Remind me to convey your assessment to our president. So, sweet lady, what of this handsome fellow?"

She held his arm and whispered.

"Words would do no justice describing this paragon. All I can say is that if I were the President of Russia and this guard had to safeguard my privacy in the Kremlin ladies-room, no power could prevent me from jettisoning my reserve and know him completely."

"So — which of his guards do you yearn to seduce?"

Hand on his inner thigh, she arched high and close to his ear.

"I already am, my darling."

"Why you minx! I should take you here and now. Remind me to make you the head of the Veronikas when I get back."

She was giving him a little show pulling up her dress when it registered.

1 Akin to America's Iraq/WMD report of February 5, 2003, on March 15, 2005, Russia's UN Envoy Tamberlin Tsarnaev presented his nation's 'Pre-Emptive Action Notice' (PAN) before a closed-door session of the UN Security Council. Russia claimed Sergio Romanov and other fascists, Italy was providing safe-harbor, were hatching a plot to overthrow the government of Russia by force or similar unlawful means.

"'Back!' Where are you going, now?"

"*Bolsheviks*! In the morning—"

Basil paused to rein in his sentiments then spoke soberly.

"Natash, in twenty-four hours, Russian military forces will be fanning out across both Wopland and Central Asia."

She clenched his hand. Feeling her trying to restrain her shivering made his heart sink. Then came a wrenching tick, and Basil spoke into her bereftness.

"My dear Natash, the day has come to put many plans into action. This time tomorrow, I'll be in a secret location in Wopland. I'll be safe. Much safer than many others." He attempted a joke, unleashing a tone patina'd with reassurance — "Natash, you know Bushkin can't afford to lose his best bodyguard, can he?"

He ventured a look. Her eyes shimmered with fearful solidarity yet blooming across her face dawned the faintest of smiles. She stared hard into his stolid gaze. Reconciling herself to what must be, her cheeks plumped under the strain in her jaw and they squeezed free two half-tears that drizzled lazily sideways before wicking into her hair. Distraught within but stoic without, Basil's tone remained soothing.

"I'll probably be gone for one or two months, perhaps even three. I cannot begin to describe how hard it will be for me to be away from you. I, I—"

He stopped trying to explain. What had to be, had to be. She remained silent. Overwhelmed, he blanketed his left hand tenderly over hers.

"My dearest Natash, I love you more than words can say. I will be safe. Safe, do you hear. Danger is nothing to me." And with a bitter-sweet smile, eyes heavy and on the verge of betraying sentiments best unseen, he finished — "Surely, you see how painful it is for me to even think of being apart from you."

His last words vanished swiftly into silence and filled the air like stardust.

Natalia felt his inner need for fortitude and stuttered.

"Oh, sweet man, I know. … Basil, my darling Basileus, I love you. My life is nothing without you. I've seen so much misery and death. It hurts. Hurts."

She raised his hand to her lips and kissed it. Her lips remained quivering against his knuckles. It was pure agony. Basil went to stoop lower to re-establish eye contact when she abruptly sat up and looked him breathlessly in the face.

"Basil, if you ask for my services I can go. Surely, I would be indispensable to the wounded. How obvious. Yes, it's so simple!"

He swallowed the sudden lump in his throat and shook his head.

"No, Natash. It's not safe. The president wouldn't permit you to leave. And, there's far too much important intelligence work still to be done. We'll be sending prominent terrorists to Moscow. You and Olga are going to be very busy."

Her eyes implored for more. He clasped her hand firmly in his.

"Natash, your work in Moscow will save many lives."

"Then all the more reason for Olga and I to be by your side," she protested, "field interrogations are faster, more efficient."

He smiled and kissed her salty eyes.

"Sweetheart, what a shameless *boudoire* I would make of my command bunker if I could have you by my side. But, it cannot be. We have two fronts, Wopland and Central Asia. It's all been prudently considered."

Sensing that it was pointless arguing, she remembered something that would cheer them both. She wiped her face and fumbled through her purse. Basil watched in amusement, enjoying the quiet respite.

Extending a quaking hand, she said.

"Here, darling. It's for you."

In her palm lay a stately white box secured by a thread-worn red ribbon.

He gushed.

"Natash, you got me a pen and pencil set. Where did you find it?"

"No, Basil. It's not that. But, if you'd like to guess, I'll drop a hint — It's something you should be expecting."

He had a flash of recognition and chuckled.

"A medal of honour. That fox Bushkin gave it to you to present to me in private, right?"

"Just one medal! You deserve ten my hero. No, not that. Another hint — I now know it's not premature. It's kind of a birthday gift from me."

The box seemed too narrow for a man's watch. Perhaps, it was some modern era love bracelet for men. Something given by one's girlfriend. Then his left eyelid flared as if saluting a silent thought, and he seized the opportunity to lift both their moods.

"My last guess. I'll make three. It's a watch. It's a love band. It's Harry Potter's magic wand, so I can protect us and defeat all our enemies. *Res Ipsa Loquitor!*"[1]

Her face brightened at his crazy humour.

"I love what you're thinking, darling. The wand idea's a good approximation. Hold it and I'll untie the ribbon."

He looked on in silence, savouring the dexterous way her delicate fingers tugged and collapsed the once pretty bow. From a floppy petal bloom into a knurled corn kernel — *Pop* — the knot vanished and the ribbon fell free. He held onto the base while she gently lifted the lid free.

There the mystery gift lay in the dim light.

A laugh took hold of Basil.

"Another riddle. I love it. It's curious you chose a digital thermometer. Oh, I get it. 'Doktor.'" And, Basil playfully jostled himself against her side, and kneading her thigh above the knee-cap between finger and thumb, he asked — "Are you going to be the 'Nurse' or the 'Patient?'"

Caught off guard, she peered over his hand and giggled.

"Basileus, it … it's flipped over. There. That's better. Last hint darling — *Specto Patrem!*"[2] she said in a voice dripping with glee.

He squinted and looked closer.

The light in the backseat was far too dim.

He remained mute.

She roused to explain.

"See that blue cross? There."

1 The matter speaks for itself (Latin).
2 I see a father(Latin).

With her fingernail, she rapped the now crucified 'Circle of Hope,' something Basil perceived as cross-hairs on a snipers scope.

"My second shot, Basil. It's 99% certain, I'm pregnant."

He remained mute. Gratski's words echoed in his mind.

She looked up into his heavy eyes.

"I'm bearing your child, *Daragoi*."

Basil felt suspended in time and space. Such was the seesaw of his sentiments, burnished by a heart that wasn't beating, but spinning over and over in somersault. Until now, it had all been crazy talk — charming crazy talk — but science had intruded — the second test — 99%. *Bull's Eye*. Elephant down.

"My sweet Natash. I—"

Thwarted for words, Basil dropped the box in his lap and placed her hand over his heart and his left hand over her belly.

"Compared to this connection, words are monkey squawk. I'm so sorry I doubted you. My leaving's beyond cruel. Can you feel my ... my love, *Daragaya*?"

And, the love that Basil's touch expressed was one of those ineffable admixtures of both pain and happiness which the most rarified language framed as the most elegant poetry could only approximate in its intensity. She could feel the tremors in his heart as it oscillated from the groaning despair of impending separation to the deep rapture of his new life with her. Her being radiated into his, and slowly calming, he smiled. And, then, it happened. An unseen hand seemed to float out of her belly and grip his wrist-joint as if the hilt of a sword. Basil recoiled in shock.

"Natash, do you feel it. I'm sure it spoke to me."

"Oh Basil, there's an angel inside me. I feel it. I know it. I just know it, my love."

And, as one who has finally discovered their true destiny, tears of pure delight streamed from her eyes. And, Basil, once a doubter, almost to the point of taunt, was seized in a fit of panic.

"Natash, we've so little time. While I'm away, talk to the little one for me. Russia will be victorious. Tell the little one. I'll be safe. Safe, you hear."

She beamed and stroked his cheek.

"I promise, *Daragoi*. Now, be still. And, be at one."

She placed her hand over his and firmed it against her belly to soothe his subconscious anxieties. She knew that Basil knew something. He'd been given a message. Even Basil sensed he'd been given a message — a warning rank with peril. But, what?

Basil relaxed and melted into the welcome of oneness. It wasn't until the car had remained parked awhile that Ivan, his driver, had mustered the pluck to shake his superior's shoulder. Basil and Natalia came to their senses, and he noticed Ivan's discomfort.

"Thanks. Busy day catching up. Natash, time to go sweetheart."

Dazzled So Black

That night Basil made love most tenderly.

Natalia reminded him that she would not break and that he could do as he pleased. In fact, it pleased her for him not to hold back, to bring it on. Their little remaining time together was so spare — so precious.

Basil placed his thumb in her mouth, canted her head right and lowed in her ear — "Sweet lady, I had intended to tear up this bed tonight. But, I want this. The long pleasure of being inside every part of your beautiful warm body. The only thing I want to hold in my heart while I am away is a memory of you that can only be experienced in a lingering intimacy. To me, this is everything now."

He retracted his thumb, straightened his arms and ground himself as close to her as possible. She met his gaze and spoke into his yearning for tenderness.

"Basileus, How perfect. Let me relax into the magic of it."

Basil leant in, nuzzled against her neck and whispered in her left ear.

"There, you see. We're moving beyond the mood for lust. We're simply two children at play. Throw away preoccupations. Let it be what it will."

Basil put his arms under her shoulders and took hold of both her hands drawing them close to the side of her neck so that her arms flexed back and splayed open their fragrant silkiness like the tracings of a butterfly's wings. And, pouncing upon the milkiness of her right inner arm, hovering across the crescent of her upper armpit, to her neck and to her face and across to the other arm, as if in search of truffles, he laved her flesh with tender puckering kisses, stopping occasionally to babble about the delight of it all.

For in the weeks of separation that lay ahead, where ecstasy might be found in echoes, and where letters would be their only intimate contact, both wanted to be sure that they could draw fortitude and fidelity from a cavernous cistern of shared recollection about what this brief night of deep and abiding love meant for the other.

And, as wave after wave of Basil's searing tenderness licked over the flesh of a woman glued to his every touch, it became inevitable that she came to that state of states where the most subtle change of his tempo sent her into rapture and where it was everything he could do to capture the moment for himself without succumbing to the urge to explode inside her.

And, thus, hemmed tight in kiss, pelvis to pelvis in motion and dancing with ecstasy, the sparkle of molten starlight traipsed across the back of their eyes. And, around the circumference of their inner skulls, an aurora borealis shimmered bright against a backdrop of liquid obsidian that dazzled so black it appeared to cannibalize light. And, in that vision of a shared firmament, both felt the insistent beauty of the spirit that sought to unite them and sought to re-emerge into this world through them.

A spirit that would not be denied.

The Octopus of Evil

On Monday, at 8:00 a.m. Washington time, Acting-President Weissbrot called a snap cabinet meeting to discuss the sudden crisis in New York. The financial futures markets were freaked, and he needed to get a multitude of facts squared away before addressing the nation at a hastily convened press conference, sixty minutes away.

The first issue on the agenda — How did this happen?

Revered throughout Dixie as Bulldawg, the room's focus fell squarely on Holroyd Ashfelt, the Secretary of Homeland Security.

"Missa President, we now know the urn came over in a shipping container. Furnishings from a Spanish estate sent to a brother in Brooklyn. The container cleared customs and was put in storage for pick up. The perpetrator used a false power of attorney to enter the area and only removed the urn."

Weissbrot sat glumly listening to what he already knew one way or another. Mitchell's DVD testimony had come to pass — the second urn — the shores of America — *Dioxinomics* in action. Sooner than he'd hoped, he would have to shut down every subway in America. Not just New York and Washington, but Atlanta, Boston, San Francisco, … the list of closures was long and grim.

President Bushkin of Russia had provided the United States with solid intelligence, against which, he'd had to endure a prattling pack of Carter's naysayers — people more attuned to blathering on about Russia and Bushkin's schemes to upend its nascent democracy than come to terms with Dioxinomic reality. Now, he felt fully vindicated, but vindicated at an awful price. On the one hand, there was the expected, but on the other the unexpected. Every detail Bulldawg confirmed made his blood boil in fury, but worse, his gut curdled with dread.

"Sounds like Al Qaeda," Weissbrot snapped — "Are the family legit?"

"When you can see kernels of truth in it, cornshit passes the smell test, Missa President. At present, it seems only the terrorists were expecting the shipment. But, we never accept any cornshit at face value and have discovered that the family are not simply of Spanish ancestry but actually Basque—"

Weissbrot cut in.

"I assume you're investigating whether they've any affiliation with ETA,[1] the Basque separatist movement. Bulldawg, surely there's a strong link to Al Qaeda?"

Bulldawg focused on the clear-headed pursuit of unmasking the facts.

"Missa President, I assure you as spitchcock is to eel, such connection is plausible. We are pursuing. Even collecting information about Al Guido. Y'awl know over a week ago, the Itai[2] government publicly stated Al Qaeda and Al Guido are tight. The 'Octopus of Evil' could be larger than we reckon."

Both Lester Coverdale and Hicks shot Bulldawg stares of disbelief.

Weissbrot countered.

"That's debatable, Bulldawg. And, 'Octopus of Evil?' Let's stay clear of the Wodka spiked 'Cool Aid' Bushkin has concocted for Bolshevik bozos. Follow the leads, but I doubt much of that Al Guido hoopla will pan out."

---

1 Basque separatist movement — Euskadi Ta Askatasuna.

2 Pejorative: Italian.

Hicks stifled a snicker and Weissbrot shot him a dirty look.

"Excuse, sir. P-A-N,[1] Pre-emptive *Action Notice* and Tsar Romanov."

Weissbrot chuckled to unwind and nodded.

"Right you are, David. Anyway, let's not re-visit Romanov land looking for fruit-loops. We'll leave that for Carter when she comes out of her stupor."

Hicks smarted in quiet. Carter was an old friend.

Bulldawg remained sober in his assessment.

"Missa President, call me a coonskin coyote, but Romanov conveniently became 'disappeared' the same time Italian Prime Minister Calamari's son was abducted. And, people supposedly associated with Romanov and this Al Guido have also vanished or I could say 'gone into hiding.' The dawg in me's a'smellin there's a connection. Why would Itai piss away good pork on such a huge manhunt? Plus all the suicide bombings, here and there. Sir, as piglet is to porkette, these are Al Qaeda tactics."

"See what you mean. OK. Keep investigating this Al Guido. We must put aside the 'Made-for-Carter' pre-emptive action notice the Russians threw at us."

"Trust the process, sir. We're hump-tee-doodle on every peck of cornpone."

"Back to New York. How'd the Russians buy into this?"

The acting-president already had his own theories, but time now to verify. Given the damage, no stone was going to be left unturned.

"Ivan's poop passes the whiff test, sir. Imprisoned in Moscow, the terrorist's partner made a call to our terrorist's mobile phone in New York. I'm smell'n the man broke after days of torture. Anyway, the Rooskees told us they traced the call and pegged his location this morning. They began tailing him for a squeeze play. The two Rooskee teams converged when he got to Rockefeller Plaza. About this same time, the gomers at New York Homeland Security finally picked up on the fax sent by the counter-terrorism coordinator at Russia's New York mission an hour before. Now hear it straight, Rooskee promptly faxed us a summary dossier and artist's sketch. But, we were slow to go."

Weissbrot wiped his hand over his lips in annoyance. The problem was that very few people knew about a second urn, and many of those who did, took it as hypothetical rather than actionable intel.

"Anyway, the scallywag saw a squeeze coming, and hightailed-it into the Rockefeller Center Plaza and mingled with the 'NBC *Today Show*' audience. The Rooskees were on the verge of nabbing him when he decided to break into the set to make a do-or-die escape. As a diversion, he slammed the urn onto the concrete. An Ivan, named Fizbitszdvenchnikov, got off one shot. A flesh wound."

"Bulldawg, tell me we got a blood sample."

"Yes sir. A good'un. But, y'awl know the cooter got away. Fortunately, Rooskee covered the urn immediately. The release of dioxin in a big crowd all on national television—"

1 Akin to America's Iraq/WMD report of February 5, 2003, on March 15, 2005, Russia's UN Envoy Tamberlin Tsarnaev presented his nation's 'Pre-Emptive Action Notice' (PAN) before a closed-door session of the UN Security Council. Russia claimed Sergio Romanov and other fascists, Italy was providing safe-harbor, were hatching a plot to overthrow the democratically elected government of Russia by force or similar unlawful means.

Weissbrot interjected — "Yes, luck — raw fuck-a-duck luck."

A pause ensued, allowing Weissbrot to hate that word — *Luck* — even more.

"So, no one intercepted this fucker?"

Bulldawg felt like a sher'ff with a spiked-collar donut kicked up his ass.

"Missa President, Ivan shooting into a crowd of Yankees is politically sensitive. Especially with Carter and y'awl dookin it out. Rooskee was under strict orders to fire only if it was cleaner than a tampon in June. In front of TV cameras, the varmint pulled out a dead-man switch and showed he was bomb vest to blow. Both police, NBC security and Rooskee had no choice but to back away. A whole mess'a folks were in peril."

Weissbrot rubbed his thumb over his forehead.

Bulldawg plowed on.

"After the varmint disappeared from camera range, NBC focused on that weird mess'a coats stacked on that urn. Y'awl need to know, Rooskee and all other security staff covered the spot so that not the slightest trace of dioxin could blow away. It's 'Fly'n Cow Alley' in downtown New York, sir. Winds are fierce. Ivan saved the day. And, once NBC understood the enormity of the story, they interviewed all the Rooskees and broadcast the artist rendering of the terrorist. When Homeland arrived on scene, we shut down the squawk. Missa President, it rates up there with 9/11 in its public visibility."

Weissbrot remained incensed because, other than a blood sample, all that was harvested so far was a story — *Just a damn story.*

"Bulldawg, how did this bastard vanish?"

"Gotta smell the piss in the pantaloons on this one, sir. One blast from a bomb vest and that mess'a coats would've blown to noth'n. We're dippity-dawg lucky he wasn't a suicidal nutcase. Anyway, the coon made the typical gitta-way. Run, duck, cover and vamoosed his keister into the subway."

"Christ! So that's it?"

Weissbrot exhaled in exasperation. Of course, he was relieved overall. That dioxin could have been a hop, skip and jump away from being slammed into an oncoming train. At least, only some psycho in a bomb vest had made it into the subway. Even if he had detonated, all up, the damage would be a few dead bodies, mangled carriages. A simple repair job — no doubt about it.

Secretary of State Chandler felt a need to clear the air.

"Mr. President, Russia's counter-terrorism coordinator from their New York mission called State to apologize for their men's on-camera foolishness. He sent them packing to Moscow with a stern reprimand. They were already airborne before I had a chance to request waivers of their diplomatic immunities so that we could interrogate them."

"I know. I spoke to Bushkin. He also apologized." Weissbrot calmed and drew more reflective — "Gentlemen, this is no surprise. All in all, it's an excellent day when you consider what might have been. So, Bulldawg, what's the chance of catching this prick given the details the Russians gave us and the blood sample?"

Bulldawg replied without hesitation.

"The Department of Defense Chemical Warfare Division is decontaminating the urn, so we can pull prints. Regardless, using both the FSB sample, which Ivan supplied the day after y'awl became acting-president and the samples we secretly harvested from contaminated clothes in Moscow, we've concluded within a scientific degree of certainty that the New York dioxin came from the exact same chloro-benzene source as the Moscow dioxin. This means the second urn has surfaced and is defused. Thank Gawd."

Weissbrot flexed his neck to relax, nodded his solidarity with Bulldawg and quietly reflected. Sure enough, the two countries had a common enemy. The same chemical fingerprints, no right-minded skeptic could cry 'Rooskies yanking your chain' any longer. Moscow had been walloped good and hard, New York a near miss. But, the renewed tremblings of financial crumbling — That was no near miss. That was dead on target.

Gut still in knots, Weissbrot reached out for discussion about what worried him most. This morning's press conference had not been scheduled for the purposes of doing a round up the posse song-n-dance, but to address the real freaky stuff. For days, Wall Street had been speculating — If Moscow, why not us? Nor was it a matter of 'If' any longer. Quick as a slam on the ground, two Dioxinomic facts were proved.

It was a matter of 'When.' And, 'When' means Today.

Before primetime *NBC Today Show* television cameras, located a Dioxinomic puff north of Wall Street, the turds on the stock exchange living out their glamor dreams inside their 'Barbie-World' of wall-to-wall stock-index-derivative monitors and golden parachutes had their answer. Party's over. Time to hand your clients' cash back to your clients because New York is an urns-throw from Moscow.

Weissbrot's voice became deadpan. He knew that he would need to speak like that to the press for the rest of the day. His choice of words circumscribed if not downright bland. He addressed Treasury Secretary Earl 'Groundhawg' Butz.

"Groundhawg, is there anything I should say in particular to alleviate the panic that's creeping back into the financial and real estate markets?"

"Mr. President, I would say nothing. Better not to highlight anything. But, by all means field questions without appearing too evasive."

Weissbrot rolled his eyes — *Field questions? Silence? As-if!*

Groundhawg stayed on message.

"If you're asked about China, say you can't speak for China. I'm doing my best to convince the Chinese not to dump $935 billion dollars worth of US Treasury bonds onto the market. They're after liquid funds to feed like vultures on the Russian carcass. Months of record oil prices and Russia's Gazprom collateralized Euro borrowings in Italy are fueling their lust to buy into oil with similar on-the-cheap terms Russia offered the Italians."

Weissbrot nodded his concurrence.

"Yes, we don't need oil getting in the way of our dollar. I asked Bushkin about that. He's completely rebuffed China. Russia wants its oil, 100% Russian. So, gentlemen, any other suggestions before I confront the press?"

Lester Coverdale felt the call to duty.

"Mr. President, I know that you were planning to make a formal response to Carter's demand for re-instatement two days from now, but this disaster in New York gives you no latitude for chivalry. Today would be an excellent time to lean on Congress to vote up or down on Carter's Twenty-Fifth Amendment protest. Tell the press that Congress' schedule is already shot to hell, so on behalf of the country you should insist that they debate and finalize the matter this afternoon. The principle point you need to stress is our constitution expects a definitive leader, not some acting-president. Our physical security demands it, our economic security demands it and our political security demands it."

Weissbrot pretended to remain unmoved — *Above-the-fray.*

Lester played the mood and softened his tone.

"Sir, bless her heart before the press. Yes, bless her heart. But, be frank about the facts. Carter's getting worse. We cannot afford to hold national interests hostage over one person when our constitution protects us all with a backup."

Moved by Lester's compassion, Groundhawg spoke in support.

"Sir, Lester's on the money. Carter has the right to be revered, but no right to be our president. We need your leadership to pull our financial markets out of this on-the-brink trillion dollar Dioxinomic funk. Carter must become history. I mean *must*. Sir, insist that today *is* decision day."

The room was roused to aye-ayes and all cabinet officers looked over at the great statesman in Weissbrot. The Acting-President twiddled his lips with his fingers as if vacillating and with an air of deliberative resignation, he finally nodded his concurrence and acquiesced to what must be. Today was perfect. Carter once had firm supporters, but not now, not even sympathetic friends.

Aware of Weissbrot's inquiring gaze, Ginger made her break public.

"Mr. President, Groundhawg's right. You've been more than deferential to Mary-Ann. I'm going to put together my own statement for members of Congress. Whatever hold-outs for Carter still exist, I'll do whatever it takes to see they fold. I also suggest a larger tactic. In your press conference, inform the American people that, tonight, you intend to speak to them in a national address, but only as a full-term president revealing his plans for the remainder of his term. If people tune in and find only the nightly news, they'll know Congress is dickering. Between our lobbying and voter expectations, Congress has no choice but vote today."

Weissbrot's eyes twinkled with delight. Here was Ginger at her political finest.

"Excellent, Ginger. If Mary-Ann was more lucid I know she'd salute your wisdom." And, Weissbrot rose from his seat — "Everyone, follow Ms. Arnold's lead. Start lobbying Congress on my behalf. For me, the vultures await."

With that, Weissbrot exited and spoke to the American people. During the press conference, he promised if Congress willed it, he'd make a follow-up address that evening, during which he would outline a long-term plan for the crisis of confidence now polluting America and making most of her assets, Toxic.

Conspiracy Theories

Off Du Pont Circle in Washington, DC, two news reporters, sitting in a dingy 'Smoker's Corner' of Ali-Bar-Bars and halfway through their third Anchor Steam, were engrossed in a televised broadcast.

Appalled beyond malice, Ernie was first to rouse.

"Gummit! That whelp got the news conference of the year and the only question he asks is how some Russian nerd saved the acting-president's life at a dinner function."

Bert felt the same sting — "Yeah, un-bloody-believable. Weissbrot did a half-decent deflect not to give Big-Red all the credit."

"I wouldn't call that a deflect. Our government furnished the gift in its entirety. Any blood spilled would be on our hands."

"Every journalistic bone in my body tells me Rookie sabotaged the gift then staged a show to unmask the poison. I'm a Carter fan. Just because she's in la-la land, doesn't mean she isn't right. Those Bullshitviks are sly mothers. Both the poison and the poison detector. Ha! All so conveniently placed at the last minute."

"Speaking of staged, how'd you reckon Bauer got wind of that incident?"

"Dunno. Ask that Nu-Nork prick Friesen, who overrode our seniority at the Washington bureau for that puppy reporter whoring his Afghanistan scoop. The sooner Mort is out of the hospital and back at the helm, the better."

"Here, here!"

Two beer mugs clattered. Froth slathered down the sides.

While Bert and Ernie continued with their conspiracy theories, CNN switched over to the financial desk to report how the markets were staging a mild recovery. By the time the pair left Ali-Bar-Bars, all channels were reporting Congress would be taking a vote on reinstating Carter.

Within the same hour, sensing the tide flowing against her, Carter moved to withdraw her protest until a more opportune moment came to bare her claws. Upon the media's report of her maneuver, the markets reacted and so did the Senate and the House of Representatives. After a thirty-minute debate to resolve procedure, both Houses voted and unanimously found Carter unfit for office.

That same night at 6:30 p.m. EST, the first president ever inaugurated under the Twenty-Fifth Amendment, took the oath of office before a wheel-chair bound Chief Justice of the US Supreme Court.

The moment was unique in so many ways. Viewers the world over watched in silence and in great relief. But, some viewers were less silent and less relieved than others because in fits and starts, reporting to infirmaries all over Italy, US and NATO servicemen were contending with their own unique moment in history. Like Tater Tots[1] sizzling on a griddle, a crippling torment raging inside their scrotums seemed intent on frying their testicles. Only through a spinal nerve block did they find a modicum of relief with the rest of humanity.

---

1 Deep fried, nugget-sized, grated potatoes.

Having been sworn into office and subsequently delivering his first presidential address to the nation, Weissbrot took special pains to get an early night. Despite his ascent earlier that afternoon after Carter was voted down and his continued best efforts to project calm into his people, all capital markets had closed the day down 13%. And, there remained the smell of panic tomorrow.

However, amidst the horrendous news, there was a spot of good news, and best of all, a spot of fabulous news.

The horrendous news was that terrorism was on the boil in Italy. But, that could wait until 3:00 a.m. when his generals came back with something more definitive. A counter-reaction most likely, something that he and his generals might have foreseen if only their intelligence were better. *If only* — he hated that nagging antecedent almost as much as its dooming predicate — *the 'Mallory Wilson Affair.'*

The good news was that the Russian invasion of Kazakhstan had begun in earnest. All Russia's troop strengths were within specifications and all their movements were proceeding to the agreed-upon schedule. The Afghan border was not in peril. This was a great relief. Trust was paramount and trust had been earned. If Al Guido did have ties to Al Qaeda, the attacks in Italy now made sense.

The fabulous news was that Moscow had a hit on the fingerprints lifted from the New York urn. State secrecy was involved, but Bushkin's email had assured him a big picture was emerging and a full report would be on his desk by morning. The email ended with a common and mutual plea — coordinated action to snuff out mutual enemies was essential.

With Bushkin, Weissbrot could not agree more.

So at last, with upbeat news from a trusted friend as sedative, Weissbrot fell hard and fast into a slumber that sheared him away from the most wearisome day he had ever known.

The Olive Wags the Branch

On that same Monday, an hour after Weissbrot concluded his morning address, the sun melted into the horizon over the Caspian Sea. From naval ports on its west shoreline, an amphibious armada sailing east inserted Russian SM-23 tank and SM-21 armored personnel carriers into western Turkmenistan. Paying no heed to the precaution of securing a land corridor through Kazakhstan, these shock forces fanned out and overran that half of Turkmenistan laden heavy with oil and gas. Russian air superiority across the narrow Caspian and the open scrub-land wilderness of western Turkmenistan ensured that any approaching Turkmeni forces were raked to shredded metal before they had an opportunity to position themselves close enough to fire upon Russia's trans-Caspian ground forces.

Leaving Astrakhan, the main body of Russia's heavy armor crossed the Volga River and fanned out across the Caspian Depression. With so many mobile regiments now plainly in sight, what little element of surprise once existed came to an end. The invasion was on in earnest.

Entering Kazakhstan from its north-western flank, the Russians headed east to the Ural and Embe Rivers. From there, they swept south onto the Tupqaraghan Plateau and through the west of Kazakhstan and occupied the thinly populated Ustyurt Plateau which skirted the border with Uzbekistan. In this way, the combined land and amphibious Smertimolat regiments secured the whole Caspian Depression, a vast tract of oil-rich territory extending from Russia to the northern border of Iran. Across this arid land, the Russian forces drove eastward at breakneck speed to take possession of every Turkmeni district deemed strategic.

After three days of sporadic resistance in the Karakum Desert, the main body of Russia's eastern forces arrived at the north banks of the Amu Darya River, the Garabil Plateau, and the Badkhyz Steppe. There, on the eve of the third day, they stopped and faced off against US and NATO forces, which had recently arrived in large numbers, ready to secure the integrity of the border separating Turkmenistan from Afghanistan.

Nothing Seemed Amiss

In the course of counter-defense, no expected outcome is ever certain. However, when the defender doesn't know who or what is coming, for he who is the counter-defender most things will usually go as planned.
Treatise on the Laws of Counter-Defense (1'st Ed.):
Introduction, p11 — Buran B. Smertvopski (Editor).

On that same Monday, hours before Weissbrot closed his eyes in slumber, Italy came into play. On a spit of land, four hundred miles in length, eighty miles in width, with mountainous terrain for a spine and surrounded on both sides by sea, the invasion of Italy was far more problematic. And, worse, teeming with westerners, Italy was defended by a modern NATO trained military with access to first-class weaponry, transportation and communications infrastructure.

Italy required special handling — Novimirov's touch.

The ill-will and alienation between the two nations caused by Russia's accusations leveled against Romanov and Al Guido had been adroitly reconciled over two weeks before. Bushkin confided to Italian Prime Minister Aurelio Calamari that his pre-emptive action notice of March was conceived less to scare Al Guido into realizing that all heroin trafficking was being watched and more to rattle the cage of the 'Dotty Bitch in the White House.' Since the Italian Prime Minister subscribed to fascism with a compassionate face, the two nations soon found common cause against a whack-a-doodle liberal.

But, this was merely the ice-breaker.

The next day, Russia turned over Guillermo Forchesi, a reputedly high-ranking Al Guido lieutenant in all his uncircumcised glory. But, the videotaped clincher was 'Forchesi's Conversation,' where he boasted how Al Guido had an alliance with Al Qaeda and how he had helped orchestrate the abduction of Silvio Calamari, the Prime Minister's son to Sicily. Over the days that followed, this terrorist was adamant about his innocence before the Courts of Italy and claimed to know nothing about some nonsensical phantasm called 'Al Guido.' Rather, he asserted that he was the real victim — abducted then tortured by vampires. In court, Forchesi jumped onto the advocate's bench and pulled down his pants as proof. Proof of his lunacy, most snickered. There wasn't a stitch or mark on the man. To all, it was clearly a transparent ploy to plead insanity and thwart Italian justice.

So it was that the relations between the two nations were as if France and Belgium. And, Russia's Indian Ocean fleet was welcomed in every port. But, even better, to Sicily, the Russian navy ferried vast numbers of Italy's police and military as well as healthy numbers of civilians, who all denied they were Mafia, and yet, curiously sought to curry favor with Prime Minister Calamari by putting as much distance between themselves and this 'Al Guido' outrage as was demonstrably possible.

In Sicily, the search for young Silvio heated up, because here and there, cornered Al Guido hoodlums detonated themselves. Fortunately, clues about other potential Al Guido-Al Qaeda locations survived their suicide, so the Italians were able to continue hunting without relent. With Al Guido-Al Qaeda strong-holds confirmed through martyrdom, Italy poured more and more men into restoring order on that island. And, the Russians were only too happy to aid their new Komrade. Thus, on Monday evening when Russia unleashed 'Operation WoppaDaWop,' the Italian front in 'Operation Woppery,' with Italy's forces stretched between NATO poppy eradication duties in Afghanistan and the search for Silvio in Sicily, Russian forces encountered few disciplined adults on the Italian peninsula able to wield firearms, public or private.

Bushkin ruthlessly adhered to the doctrine that military commodities in the hands of an enemy were subject to immediate confiscation. By contracting out much of their military needs to Italian industry, the Russians designed their invasion to reap a boon of military hardware, lawfully confiscated upon arrival. As a spoil of counter-defense, international law recognized no obligation for Russia to pay for any of these goods. And, given the level of Italian corruption over the preceding week, Bushkin viewed the right of confiscation as reciprocal justice. Because, like schools of piranha, those in the Italian police who had evaded the call to duty in Sicily had been nipping away at the lucre being generated by Russian industry — 'Operation Chili Balls.' Freebies and bribes were corruption. Confiscation was lawful and patriotic. But, on invasion night, Bushkin considered all accounts squared when the investment made in *Chili Ball* freebies to Italian officials started reaping handsome dividends.

It came as wretched surprise to the Italians that the city of Bari, with its large port, massive petroleum refinery and an international airport at nearby

Palese, had been covertly honed into the tip of the spear for Russia's invasion of Italy. Over the prior ten days, Bari's many industries had been pumping out equipment indispensable to the Russian counter-defense machine.

Night and day, the city's aluminium[1] plant had been churning out the powdered metal. Ostensibly, this civilian ordinance was the flash powder used in mock explosives in a large war-movie project. But, when the Russians took delivery by confiscation, these stockpiles were impressed into use in a variety of very huge and very real thermobaric incendiary munitions.

Under a similar contract, the Bari steel plant had stamped out hundreds of vehicle panels for additional SM-21 and SM-23 decoy kits. These panels were designed to be fitted onto several common varieties of Fiat and would replicate the appearance of fully armored SM-21 and SM-23 vehicles.

Nothing seemed amiss about any of this because across the docks of Bari behind secure chain-link fencing already lay much accumulating military equipment of Russian origin. This imported Soviet-era hardware was ultimately destined for employment in a movie project that Kino-Rus was gearing up to shoot in the Puglia region. Furthermore, in Bari and Foggia, the sight of many people regaled in Russian military wardrobe had become commonplace, as movie scouts sought out Italians in the thousands as movie extras. Thus, no local knew exactly what extra was wearing what uniform.

AT 6:00P.M. EU time, while America's east coast was digesting lunch and deciding who might be their full-time president, at Spinletti Farms, a casting call of over three thousand was finally winding down. Given the unglamourous nature of their routine work, Kino-Rus had no difficulty enticing the majority of their movie extras away from the ranks of the police and fire-fighting departments of the Puglia region. Pretending that a shoot the weekend following would involve hundreds of handcuffed and hooded Islamic detainees, and providing a one-hundred Euro bonus to any qualified policeman for merely showing up, this manly cross-section of Italian society had arrived in droves all afternoon for audition.

BY 8:20 P.M., when Congress voted in Weissbrot's favor (2:20p.m. EST), the casting process had bound and gagged the last batch of one hundred Italian extras seeking their fifteen seconds of cinematic fame. By 8:25 p.m. these tail-enders were securely anesthetized, tagged with subcutaneous pet identification chips and ready for transport to Russia along with their unlawful espionage equipment. Thus, it was that 2,371 uniforms were conscientiously recycled for an unfolding campaign of stealth in the process of unwinding over the length of Italy.

Most critical in Russia's campaign were the contracts let to Telefono-Vesti SpA and Electro-Telefono SpA, a third of which had been paid up front with money secured from fraudulent credit card transactions. These Italian companies had been enlisted to manufacture circuit boards to control transmission towers for a planned expansion of Telefon-Siber's system in eastern Siberia. With the exception of a few custom security features designed in, the circuit boards and the whole system itself appeared to be an exportable carbon-copy of the Italian mobile phone system. Unlike the confiscation contracts, these components

---

1 Aluminum.

were delivered early to many Russian technicians already in Italy doing final quality control. This stockpile, supplemented with Russian-made units as well as re-worked Chinese knock-offs, allowed the Russians to put the first phase of their telecom stealth operation into play long before the shooting started.

At 8:30 p.m., Bzombies, the Russians had planted throughout Italy over the prior ten days, simultaneously went to their assigned mobile-phone towers, broke into the controls and replaced all circuit boards with new Telefon-Siber ones. The en-masse black-out of Italy's phone system came as complete surprise.

Region by region, while standard Italian mobile phones were going off-air, encrypted SMS messages on Russian military phones started crisscrossing the country. Other Bzombie interventions knocked out the broadcast of radio and television whenever the programs departed from their regular schedule. Internet sites were hacked while land-line telephone nodes where surreptitiously seized, disconnected and blockaded by Bzombies. The many synchronized assaults across the length and breadth of what the Russians had designated the 'Wopland Occupation Zone' (WopOZ) tornadoed the bulk of this Italy's communication systems within thirty minutes.

The black-out even included a Russian upstart telephone service called Rustalia SpA, which had handed out some 800,000 mobile phones with free 90-day trials. Rustalia had entered Italy on the heels of the goodwill generated by the surrender of Forchesi. And, a hefty bribe, parceled off from the proceeds of false credit card charges, expedited telephone license approval from months to hours. The unique feature of the Rustalia phone was how each had a thumbprint-recognition security feature. This ensured that only the legitimate owner could operate the phone. Only on the morning before Russia's invasion did a Rome newspaper cry foul and accuse Rustalia of age discrimination when it uncovered that the vast majority of its thumbprint-secure 'free' phones were targeted for Italians in the 14 to 25 age range.

With the regular Italian phone system knocked out, many discovered that Rustalia phones were a life-line. The company's private channel remained open for several hours to help the youth of Italy find places of refuge, but refuge with their nemesis. Upon the capture of these agents of 'Unlawful Espionage,' the confiscated Rustalia phones were SIMcard-reset for Russian military use.

No resource went to waste.

And, whenever technicians were dispatched to repair faulty phone towers or disabled electrical supply nodes, Bzombies in police wardrobe made quick capture. One by one, Spetsnats brigades, Russia's Special Operations forces, entered into the mix, donning the uniforms of captured technicians, which kept the invasion rolling. And, each captured phone-repair vehicle was outfitted with a custom radio identification transponder, which enabled each to identify itself as friend. All others were foe. This subterfuge allowed more Bzombie and Spetnats brigades to drive deeper and deeper into Italy and interdict more and more telephone and electrical specialists. Thus, the night was one rolling juggernaut of ambush and capture against an enemy deprived of essential communication and the capacity to coordinate against hard to detect invaders, who always self-detonated whenever cornered in a fire fight.

Against Bzombies, resistance was suicide.

BY 9:07 P.M., the port of Bari had been secured and Kino-Rus Studio vessels steamed en-masse to join the Russian bullion convey already at dock in the harbour. While military equipment transports occupied several docks, the personnel carriers occupied a single one. Roped side by side, the forces of the motherland crossed from one vessel to the next and disembarked. Units not unloading equipment were assigned to harvest detainees. This process was repeated at the smaller port cities of Ancona, Ravenna, Salerno, Piombino and Livorno.

BY 9:20 P.M., Russian forces, augmented by those surreptitiously in place on counterfeit Latvian, Estonian, Lithuanian, Romanian and Polish passports, had overrun Bari, Livorno and Foggia. False reports of sabotage to rail bridges were sent up-line from Foggia. And, city by city, all civilian railway traffic at terminals across the south came to a standstill. Only now, did Italy proper become increasingly aware of a massive wave of homegrown terrorism. During the course of the next three hours, those residual military forces not sent to Sicily, Afghanistan or hospital were mobilized to guard railway facilities. Doing so, made their capture by Russian forces simple.

The only trains rolling out of Foggia were numerous freight trains carrying Russian military personnel and equipment. Bzombies in Italian uniforms stood ready to render assistance to their fellow Italian brothers in guarding the railway infrastructure from suicidal crazies dressed like civilians — the foot soldiers of Al Guido and Al Qaeda. The tactic was simple. A Bzombie would blow out the guts, and regulars would finish off the dazed remnants. In this way, Russia was able to preserve all of Italy's vital railway facilities for their exclusive use while mowing down the bulk of Italy's remaining military reserves.

At **9:30 p.m.**, winding up a four-day official visit, in the VIP lounge at Leonardo Da Vinci Airport, Italian Prime Minister Aurelio Calamari bid a most heartfelt farewell any father could offer an esteemed guest, Russian Vice-President Andrei B. Chainikov. Apart from the gifts furnished by the good people of Italy, the vice-president's plane was loaded with many extra-large crates, containing more drugged and hooded Italian parliamentarians, including four ministers. Upon rendition to Moscow, they would bring the count up to 212. No different than members of the Taliban, all Italy's members of parliament were accused of aiding, abetting and providing safe harbour to woppery, as well as possessing unlawful two-way radio transmission equipment used in espionage.[1]

AT 9:36 P.M., as soon as he reached his limousine, Prime Minister Calamari was handed a file about how terrorism had gone on the boil. A minute's drive out of the airport, Russian Spetsnats units masquerading as Italian special forces flagged down the Prime Minister's motorcade. Aurelio Calamari was whisked back to the airport and secreted aboard the vice-president's plane. Thus, it was, in a final gesture of good will and friendship, Chainikov's return

---

1 Government officials possessing espionage paraphernalia are automatically professional spies. Hence, like terror suspects, the presumption of guilt makes them fodder for firing squad/beheading justice.

flight to Moscow would bring to fruition a touching father-son reunion for the Calamari family. And, for Bushkin, an extra bonus. Both Calamari and he shared the same shoe size.

BY 9:45 P.M., the petroleum refineries in Bari, Livorno and Ancona started serving new masters. Offloaded at all three ports, shipping containers placed onto railway flats made their way to the refinery terminus where each was filled with gasoline in one bladder and diesel in the other. To prevent chaffing, the bladders were protected by powdered aluminium, which served in place of sawdust. While retaining the function of an improvised fuel tank, these shipping containers provided a more sinister purpose: enormous tamper-proof fuel-air bombs designed to explode at ground level. And, unlike air-dropped fuel-air bombs, these 8x8x20 ft 'Fuel Depots' possessed a solid steel stanchion welded at the explosive epicenter that clamped the roof panel, which created a topside blast deflector. By shaping the explosive fuel stream horizontally, each depot could generate horrific side-ejecting doughnut-shaped thermobaric blasts capable of obliterating ground-level masonry. Placed in town squares all over Italy, if the fuel depots were ever tampered with, the Italians could kiss their ancient brick-and-mortar heritage — *Arrivederci.*[1]

BY 10:00 P.M., fuel-depot freight trains supplemented with armored vehicles, tanks and men, started rolling out of all captured refineries on a regular schedule. They fanned out across the Italian rail network and were unloaded at various destinations.

BY 10:45 P.M., Russian planes were landing en-masse at the international airport in Palese. They carried officers and the remainder of Russia's senior commanders, including Marshal Ogrom Palachnin and General Basil Novimirov. Thus began an eight-hour period of the continuous disgorging of airborne troops. Once emptied of men and materials, these planes were rapidly packed solid with drugged, hooded and handcuffed detainees, the vast majority of whom were accused of unlawful espionage.

AT 11:00 P.M., while Weissbrot shared a late-afternoon whiskey with his Director of National Intelligence mulling over the satellite intel coming in from Central Asia (5:00 p.m. EST), full-scale control of Italian civilian areas began. Enhancing the benefit of night cover, the electric grid in each city was blacked-out, block by block. Bari was first, with Foggia soon to follow. Bzombie brigades swept through both cities, building by building, arresting spies in every nest. Sporadic gunfights sundered the darkness, now and again. Because they were charged with making forced entrances and demands for spies to surrender, Bzombies took the brunt of the resistance.

While the pre-invasion intelligence had mapped out Mafia hotspots for brute force handling, civilian resistance was still expected, and from time to time, encountered. However, once muzzle flashes betrayed the position of shooters, regular army support snipers quickly eliminated the menace. By dawn's early light, the Bari harvest had yielded 62,384 spies from age 14 to 25, with total losses amounting to 246 Bzombies in the 72,371 locations raided. Civilian and

1 Good-Bye (Ital).

espionage casualties were guesstimated at 3,000. Detainees under age 33 were systematically handcuffed, dispatched to the airport at Palese or the seaport of Bari and there, teams of Army Judge-Advocates charged them with crimes against the laws of counter-defense. In Russia, these agents of woppery would be afforded the opportunity of a proper and speedy court-martial as a prelude to sentencing and, if eligible, the mercy of President Bushkin's commutation of death, and in return, gift the motherland with a term of convict labour.

Joining the 25,677 Russians already smuggled into the country over the proceeding ten days, the nine-hour period from 9:07pm to 6:00 a.m. saw an inflow of 129,739 additional troops. All aircraft and ships that carried in troops or supplies were taking convicts out. Packed into every available space in outgoing aircraft and ships, the first 24-hour convict rendition exodus amounted to 266,827.

By flying over the airspace of Serbia-Montenegro and Bulgaria, the thousand-mile, two-hour hop between Palese and Rostov-na-Donu in Russia allowed most jets to make three trips on invasion night. Bushkin had anticipated that Bulgaria would make the customary international protest the next day as a matter of proper form. Relying on the element of surprise, the first night would be Russia's sole opportunity to fly transports in comparative safety. It wasn't until 1:00 a.m. that the unusually heavy air traffic in the skies over the Adriatic Sea registered with Italian air control. But, by then, there was little they could do.

AT MIDNIGHT, the general operations to overrun all of Italy's airports employing stealth or false flag attacks got underway. Malpensa Airport serving Milan, as well as the civilian airports at Turin, Genoa, Verona, Bologna, Venice, Rimini, Pisa, Naples, Brindisi, Palermo, Catania, and Cagliari were given special attention. Lecce and Cosimo were disabled as well, in case they might be re-opened. But, the biggest and most worrisome prize on the list was Aviano.

Al Qaeda, Al Qaeda

Within the dimly illuminated cockpit of one of five cream-white turbo-prop UN air cargo planes that had been droning their way back to Europe from relief work in northern Africa, a UN squadron commander radioed the US airforce base at Aviano. He reported engine dwells typical of fuel blockage and urgently sought permission to land. In command within the control tower, a defensive Major Leitner, demanded an explanation. Amidst the crackle of static, an East European voice radioed back, speculating how their problems had been caused by tainted fuel or sedimentation when they had refueled in Algeria.

Leitner diligently reconfirmed the planes' transponder signals. They were authentic G222 UN cargo planes.[1] But, he hesitated, paced to the control tower windows and mulled over the situation — *Five planes all at once.* The emergency had to be fuel-based. The peril, genuine. Given the public relations nightmare of refusing to assist a fleet of UN planes, Leitner picked up the mic.

1 Made by Aeritalia, and used by the UN, the G222 is also known as the C-27A Spartan.

"Permission to land — Granted."

While banking hard to make approach for an emergency landing, the planes' signatures suddenly disappeared from the tower's radar screen. No transponder signals, either. Leitner froze in bewilderment. Seconds earlier, he had dithered away precious time. The tower crew strained through binoculars, scanning the darkness for flames where the planes may have gone down. Leitner reached for the phone and as he started dialing, a low rumble, like exploding thunder, reverberated against the tower's enormous panel windows. He swiveled about to face the northern quadrant of the airbase. A sequence of bright lights erupted over hanger row. Vaulting over and pressed hard up against the glass to get a proper view of the spectacle, he and the tower crew watched as a chain of roof blasts were accompanied by hanger doors buckling or blowing outwards.

Two UN planes were flying in low. Spooling out of their rear-door ramp-ways were charges tethered together by a steel cable. Once the anchor charge was ejected, the tethered munitions packages exited the rear of the plane over the hanger roofs, all perfectly spaced and coordinated. Each one, a three-stage bomb. The first blast mined a hole through the reinforced roof. The second fusillade dispersed dozens of cluster bombs into each hanger. After one bounce, they exploded at head and chest height mashing whatever the hanger contained. The demolition fly-over relied on solid munitions design and a brainless ribbon of greasy Soviet steel. No intelligent electronics. No laser targeting.

After the fourth roof-door blast combination had brought reality home, Major Leitner dashed back to his station and hit the scramble button. The base was roused to immediate and full military alert.

Completing their bombing runs in less than fifteen seconds, the two planes banked and homed in on their final objectives. The control tower crew failed to notice that one plane was heading for the base's command center because with its light fixtures rattling and blinking and its huge plate-glass windows pulsing from the roar of oncoming propellers, there in front of them was a plane on collision course.

Hijacked planes from Algeria! — Of course.

"Al Qaeda, Al Qaeda." Barked one brave US major into the air-log microphone. And, thus, were Major Leitner's last words memorialized on the air traffic control tower's equivalent of an aircraft's 'Black Box' recorder.

In the pandemonium the hanger-run bombardment afforded, the third and fourth UN planes landed unnoticed at the far end of the main and auxiliary runways. Slowing to jogging speed, each plane deposited a cruciform trailer onto the tarmac from off its rear ramp-way. Each plane taxied on and deposited another trailer and then another as it proceeded down the runway and closed in on the bombed and burning hanger area.

Only two feet in height, each trailer was equipped with six squat cannons aimed downwards. They were not motorized, but rather pushed along by six Bzombies dressed in US Air Force uniforms. Every two-hundred feet, a muffled explosion drove a cobalt steel shell loaded with HMX deep into the tarmac slab.

A Bzombie bringing up the rear installed a signal amplifier to ensure perfectly synchronized detonation. Within six minutes, from six trailers, six shells were blasted into the high strength, steel-reinforced concrete runway slabs. On the seventh minute, all Bzombies vanished into the darkness. When the minute struck eight, the tarmacs of Aviano erupted into a criss-cross terrain of yawning craters rimmed by shark-tooth concrete fragments. The ninth and tenth minutes heralded in sporadic attacks on radar and other infrastructure. To the trained ear — backpack explosives.

Salted with plans and dispatches between Al Qaeda and Al Guido alliance members, the fifth UN cargo plane carried two platoons of Bzombies as well as the final Aviano sabotage units — motorized trailers containing six ultra-high-powered down-blast cannons housing six PTFE jacketed shells tipped with depleted uranium. Once on the runway, their electric engines powered them over the smooth pavement from one jet-fuel bowser access-point to the next. One by one, each blasted its cargo into the concrete above the underground fuel tanks. Once the last shell was driven, a ground-penetrating detonation signal was transmitted. No special synchronization was required. The area shattered and Aviano's vast fuel reserves erupted in red and orange flame and billowed acrid soot-laden smoke into the black of night.

On their suicide runs, the remaining three UN cargo planes targeted emergency generators, munitions, above ground fuel depots, barracks and most importantly, Aviano's advanced radar systems. And, thus, the base was expeditiously reduced to flame-lit, darkened chaos.

Unidentified snipers felled servicemen reporting for duty. And, in the ultimate indignity, wherever platoons formed up into full strength units, they perished when some fellow serviceman inexplicably committed suicide.

The Aviano attack was a full-on 'No Bzombie Left Alive' mission.

The Russians sought use of only a handful of airfields and repeated the Aviano attack pattern using regular civilian planes and smaller Bzombie forces to sabotage all other airfields. Russia's generals had no illusions about being embedded in the belly of Europe and trying to control the skies over Italy, except through the extensive use of S-300 spoof-proof[1] anti-aircraft missiles.

Done Their Damnedest

Situated 90 kilometers north of Venice, the Aviano attack took place at 12:30 a.m. EU time — the same instant Weissbrot's face appeared before television cameras at 6:30 p.m. Washington time. After his swearing into office and his first address to the nation ended at 7:00 p.m., President Weissbrot was appraised about the catastrophe. Recovering the air control tower's digital recorder and having had less than half an hour to make sense of the carnage and audacity of the attack, military investigators had made excellent headway. From one of the wrecked G222 UN cargo planes, a laptop computer and four surviving documents confirmed the control tower's assertions — Al Qaeda.

1 Immune to jamming and signals masquerading as missile control commands.

Combining this damning evidence with Mitchell's DVD revelations and the Al Guido-Al Qaeda alliance Italy was combating as well as Bushkin's email about a fingerprint match on the New York urn, President Weissbrot needed no other information. As clear as day, he was dealing with North African jihadists, ones who used unsophisticated stealth, steel and explosives, not trained armies.

Al Qaeda's ragheads had done their damnedest.

Spent their energy. Died as martyrs.

Were porking in Paradise. One down, seventy-one to go.

Already dog-tired, this disaster only exacerbated his need for sleep. So, Weissbrot decided that his generals would have the next eight hours to provide a damage assessment and formulate their nation's response, before he weighed in on the matter himself when he woke shy of 3:00 a.m.

WMD — Western Made Demo^{n}cracy

Seven and a half hours passed in undisturbed and refreshing slumber before Weissbrot rose to prepare for his 3:00 a.m. 'Terror at Aviano' meeting. He arrived outside the White House Situation Room at 2:45a.m, to confer with his secretary, Naomi. Had she received a report from Bushkin? No — but she did alert him that Bushkin was on the verge of giving a Russian press conference. Weissbrot took the obvious in stride and ordered her to break-in on the meeting the moment Bushkin's report came in.

Naomi next pressed the [CALL HOLD] button and handed the president his office mobile. With European markets about to open, US Treasury Secretary Earl Butz appraised his president about the world's economies withering under free-market Dioxinomic forces.

The hallway clock struck three. Weissbrot donned his Admiral's chapeau to refocus his mind on matters purely military. Upon entering the Situation Room, he found the Joint Chiefs and their adjutants huddled around the room's direct-feed television monitor. They were watching breaking news live from Russia via Canadian Broadcasting Service satellites. No sooner had he asked all attendees to take their seats than Naomi stuck her head through the door and hailed him.

"Sir, Bushkin's report. Just one line — 'Watch the news when you get up.'"

A grim-faced president scratched his crotch and faced down the television monitor more than a little miffed. *Just one line — that's no full report. Watch the news — that's no state secret.* He scratched his crotch again.

Within moments, the screen flashed to live coverage. The setting — the Cathedral of Christ the Savior — *Interesting choice*, Weissbrot thought.

Bushkin and Patriarch Mudretski emerged from the sanctuary through the Templon[1] gates. The Patriarch sat off to one-side while Bushkin came to rest at an ornate lectern. President Weissbrot relaxed to the pageantry and almost chuckled on realizing the irony that all over the world he was now just like any other man in any other 3:00 a.m. democracy, glued to the television awaiting

---

1 Iconostasis, the ornate wall separating Nave and Sanctuary.

the political crumbs as they dropped. Fortunately, he was the president of the world's only meaningful superpower. He knew better — for inside the bad news was the good news.

When the flash photography died down, President Bushkin cleared his throat and stated that his paramount duty as president was to protect Russia from the ravages of terrorism, government sanctioned or otherwise.

"Today, we face a world of unconventional challenges from the spread of stateless terrorist networks and weapons of mass destruction to the grave dangers posed by failed states and rogue regimes. Furthermore, in the absence of action, terrorism has unleashed a devastating Dioxinomic crisis that will become more difficult to contain with time. Our world also labours under a multitude of nations, many weak and overextended, and as such, breeding grounds for devastation to larger humanity. In all of recorded history, what remains beyond doubt is that certain national superstates are too-fat-to-fail, and as such, they must take decisive action on behalf of the future of all the peoples of the world."

Weissbrot snickered under his breath. Bushkin's opening reminded him of a speech he had heard Arthur Frankenstein, the Chairman of the Federal Reserve, make before a closed session of Congress where he doggedly rebutted the puissance of hula-hoop 'Dioxinomics' over good-as-gold 'Economics.'

Without a hint of trepidation, Bushkin announced that 'Operation WOPPERY' [1] was in full swing. And, without pause, he launched into a detailed explanation of how and why Russia had dispatched its peace-loving military into lands rife with woppery.

Woppery? — Weissbrot's brows set deep and hard.

Whatever happened to good ol' phrases like 'crusade against jihadism,' he thought. Again, he scratched his crotch and shifted in his chair. He sat amongst men whom he had tasked to respond to the raghead outrage on Aviano Airforce Base. A flurry of military adjutants left the room and started making frantic calls to their superiors' fully staffed mission control centers at the Pentagon to get a handle on this new threat to world peace called 'Woppery.'

To Bushkin's left, a Liberty-Bell-sized globe of the Earth, two bear-hugs big and round, was wheeled up close to the lectern. Various countries were electrically illuminated in green. After another flurry of flash photography subsided, Bushkin explained green meant 'Green-Light' and he plunged into the rationale behind Russia's unilateral 'Go it Alone for World Peace' policy.

For the first time, the public was told about Russia's Pre-emptive Action Notice served on Italy and the major powers, Britain, France, China and the United States on March 15, 2005 as well as the resulting closed session deliberations before the UN Security Council. With a remote in his hand, as he spoke, locations and arrows on the globe pulsed with multi-colored laser-light graphics to emphasize Russia's attitude on positive, neutral or negative geopolitical issues. Bushkin asserted that while the other major powers had heaped scorn on his government, only Russia had acted responsibly to try and peaceably defuse 'The Heroin Holocaust' and the Romanov-Al Guido and Al

1 Acronym — 'Wipe Out Pollution, its Perpetrators, Enablers, Radicals and Yahoos.'

Qaeda alliance. The globe flashed red with hot spots. The world audience had their first glimpse of where Wopland and Drughistan were located on Russia's map of the New World Order.

Weissbrot stood bolt upright, out of his chair. He placed his hands down flat, lurched over the conference table, and glowered at the screen as if seeking to merge himself into a pressroom adorned with frescos located half a world away.

Bushkin next fired up an overlay video. From the mouth of FBI Special Agent Derek Anthony Mitchell, the world learnt about Romanov, about Ursini, about Al Guido, about an Al Qaeda–Al Guido alliance, about the involvement of Italy, about his pure-hearted mission as a widower and a diamond fence attempting to interdict heroin flooding into Russia from Afghanistan, about 'Operation Rambo' and about the US and NATO sponsorship of the cultivation of vast quantities of opium in Afghanistan on some 500,000 acres of farmland produced on the backs of starvation enforced poppy-ninny slavery. 'The Heroin Holocaust,' a moral obscenity and overt crime against humanity, was open to the naked eye, open to Google Earth and open to Russian and US satellites.

Rebuttal was impossible.

Weissbrot hawed from one foot to the other. On screen, a series of slides and videos broadcast the facts. They culminated in photos of the children of Drughistan living on the brink of starvation and all around their emaciated bodies were panoramic views of agricultural land where not a skerrick of food was growing. To make the case about eating poppies and eating barbed wire clearer, Bushkin's video presentation flashed between the black and white photos from Soviet and Eisenhower archives during the Nazi-era and the modern color photos of the US-NATO occupation of Drughistan. Bushkin did not conceal his disgust when he addressed what US-NATO and the fascist press in the West called 'Western Made Democracy,' better known in Russia as WMD and how WMD targeted non-voters, such as children, for starvation enforced slavery.

Next, while the estimated number of each month's fatalities caused by the Heroin Holocaust rolled up the screen like film credits, video footage of the crop-duster fly-bys of wheat fields flashed on screen. Then, corn fields. Back to wheat fields. Then, poppy fields. Then, corn fields. And, then, poppy fields interspersed with wheat and corn fields. Against a symphonic track of 'America the Beautiful' ripped-off from the end-of-day audio broadcast by KMTV in Omaha, Nebraska, Bushkin's accompanying narration disclosed how time and again Russia had presented 'Operation Rambo' to the US-NATO alliance. The joint mission *Rambo* contemplated — to snuff out the Heroin Holocaust. But every time and no different than its pre-emptive action notice of March, the Carter adminstration had laughed off *Rambo* as a not-so-veiled Russian hose-down of American values.

Bushkin emphasized that any unbiased observer of history knew who had orchestrated the growth and export of heroin onto Russian soil and who had created the Dioxinomic opportunity for Al Guido and Al Qaeda to accumulate the funds needed to purchase deadly dioxin pollutants. Bushkin omitted all mention that cheaper than cooking a bag of meth, only $300 in finances was all it took to stew up a few kilos of dioxin. Better the common ignoramus living in 'Barbie-World' think of dioxin as a rocket-science substance, diamond like in cost.

While the first phase of Bushkin's evidence targeted the global audience with facts sworn to by FBI Special Agent Mitchell, CNN amongst other US media leviathans censored the broadcast under the excuse that 'America bashing' would incite the nation's redneck radicals into fits of patriotic apoplexy. However, the people of Russia, as well as people watching in many other countries, were all ears. For them, the whole world was witnessing exactly what they assumed the media-savvy American people were witnessing. Except for Canadians, few in the world knew that press self-censorship south of the Canadian border, was providing most US citizens only a media-orchestrated 'news report' conforming to the agenda of those in control in New York and Washington.

Weissbrot stopped his jostling. Joint Chiefs Chairman Harvey Kilburn stirred but the Commander-in-Chief motioned for him to stay still.

Bushkin's attack on Western fraudulence shifted focus. He invited the global audience to access the www.crwi.org website [1], a so-called science-oriented public health site based in the United States. Since it was 3:00 a.m. in the homeland of that website, much like the White House censorship of the American Industrial Hygiene Association website which for a handful of hours published the H. P. Environmental Services Report about asbestos contamination from office samples taken at 150 Franklin St and 200 Rector Place in the wake of 9/11, one or two hours remained before www.crwi.org became similarly 'China'd.'[2] To prevent censorship at the global level, the salient webpages Bushkin referred to were flashed on screen — US EPA reports concluded most dioxin isomers had the toxicity of distilled water — *zero*. Bushkin asserted that fascist-loving special interests sought to use the Internet to pillory science, engage in fraud and gin up public confusion. He suggested all this so-called zero-toxic dioxin dust, as www.crwi.org claimed, be dumped into the Metro systems of Washington, New York, Atlanta, Chicago, San Francisco and Los Angeles.

Let Dioxinomic truth speak for itself — uncensored.

Attacking America's corporate establishment, Bushkin felt on a roll. He accused fasco-capitalist forces of targeting Moscow to eviscerate Russia's currency, its banking system, and the value of its fixed assets. War on a nation's currency and its underlying assets was the new battlefield of woppery. Conservative government in the US meant it was liberal toward drug running, liberal in under-taxing an elite and liberal in looting the US treasury reserves to preferentially fatten America's 'Royal Monetarchy.'[3] So-called Federal Reserve

---

1 Coalition for Responsible Waste Incineration.
2 To Censor or Black-hole (Slang)
3 The Royal Monetarchy is a nobility of large consortium Western banks. The Monetarchy consider the stage play called 'Economics,' something they own and can write or rewrite as they please. The 'Monetarchs' define the degree and timing of joy, fear, survival and sorrow in any given 'Economic performance.' Furthermore, the presumably non-economic game humans have erected called 'Democracy' is likewise a stage play subject to the Monetarchy's pleasure. *As You Like It*, Act II, Scene VII: "All economics is a stage. And, all the men and women are merely players." Benjamin Shalom Bernanke. *MacBank*, Act V, Scene V: "Economics is but a walking shadow, a poor player, that struts and frets his hour upon the stage, and then is heard no more. It is a tale told by an idiot full of sound and fury signifying nothing." Fyedor Sergeivich Bushkin.

Monetarism was designed to enthrone an American aristocracy, corrode other nations' currencies and make the US dollar an overvalued currency of last refuge so that a money-fatted nobility could go on a Third World buying binge when the value of assets were chopped to Dioxinomic pieces. He refrained from calling such capitalist sabotage part of a larger Zionist banking conspiracy because Tsar Nicholas II had tried and failed on that front a century earlier. And, while Bushkin observed how the West's pro-fascist media and banking empires foisted their agenda on the western proletariat, Russia's vampire intercessions had not ginned up the quality of evidence needed to justify a claim of a 'Jews of Amerika Konspirazy' — as yet. So, while he was itching to use his presidential authority to order the extraordinary rendition of US Federal Reserve Chairman Arthur Frankenstein to amass more evidence of state-sponsored woppery, Bushkin confined himself to presenting only the indisputable proof currently available.

Dioxinomics was the Monetarchy's guillotine, said Bushkin.

US President Weissbrot's face turned ashen. His body, as if paralyzed by a bolt of lightning, plunged back into his chair. Over the last seven days, Groundhawg and Frankenstein had promised economic revival, expostulating before the public about how the worst of the nation's financial crisis was behind it. But, despite the fact that few Americans have access to uncensored media news feed, Weissbrot knew for certain that in six hours the overpriced markets in most advanced nations would be *permanently* hammered to dust.

Denial was over.

Dioxinomics supplanted Economics.

The wanton production of opium had made it so.

To corroborate his Dioxinomic contentions, Bushkin narrowed his assertions down to observable reality, starting with what preceded Drughistan and the currency wars. Bushkin reminded the world that for lesser countries with hard to destroy currencies, such as Panama, when Manuel Noriega was its president, superpower hypocrites issued drug facilitation and money laundering indictments as the pretext for a surprise midnight military invasion. An assault that, besides generating countless and uncounted Panamanian dead, gratuitously blew or burnt the guts out of hundreds of homes and buildings all over Panama City. All done for the inestimable purpose of nabbing a one-man outlaw amongst a sea of drug lords. All the facts about Panama were documented in US Congress' post-invasion reports. Citations appeared on screen.

Hot off his scalding Drughistan and Panama power trips, Bushkin next disclosed the airport photos of Alfredo Constanzo Leonardo Ursini entering Russia. An Italian passport under the name 'Umberto Julio Borges' flashed on screen. He accused the Italian government of favouring an Italian aristocracy, all of them rich and adhering to fascist philosophies. He stated that Wopland, under the guise of 'Italy', coddled billion dollar extremists and provided them with fabricated 'Italian' identities and passports, no differently than if some Arab regime might hand out bogus passports to Muslim elites. As President of Russia, Bushkin unilaterally called out Wopland's actions as harbouring, aiding and abetting woppery. Public opinion was irrelevant. International opinion, self-serving.

A series of document images flashed on screen demonstrating Bushkin's claims of the Wopland regime's complicity in smuggling the Octopus of Evil's urn of dioxin into Russia. First, a photo of Alfredo and the letter from the 'Italian government' stating the urn contained ashes of a deceased Russian, one Viktor Fiksyonovich Magufinski. Second, Alfredo holding the Magufinski urn next to his face. Third, footage of the 'Italian Embassy' car that had been dispatched to pick up Wopland's human-ashes trafficker 'Umberto Borges,' a man in a green sequin dress, identical in appearance to Alfredo Ursini. Fourth, a video statement by Carlo Rolfino about the Italian government rescuing Alfredo Ursini as well as a photo of the *dva pediki*[1] together.

For those viewers permitted to watch this portion of Bushkin's address, he stopped the presentation. Relying on the same legal reasoning advanced by the United States as well as Ayatollah Khomeini of Iran, Bushkin reminded viewers that just like America's Talibanistan legal fiction, 'Wopland' was not a signatory to any treaty such as the Vienna Conventions on Diplomatic Rights and Privileges or the North Atlantic Treaty Organization.

Bushkin's Show-and-Tell resumed.

Alfredo Ursini's videotaped conversation detailed his role in the Octopus of Evil and how he was expecting payment of three kilos of uncut diamonds which Derek Mitchell's Diamond Emporium held on behalf of Afghan drug lords. Then Bushkin played the secretly recorded conversation between Natalia Bogomolski and Alfredo Ursini disclosing the particulars of the sale of two dioxin urns. Alfredo made clear how his pious Italian belief in 'Only-Marry-Once' romance sanctified the intended urn-for-diamonds exchange. He also admitted to synthesizing the second urn destined to be exchanged for three thousand kilos of Afghan heroin in New York City. Natalia's conversation with Alfredo omitted how dioxin could be cooked up for several hundred dollars. Like gold bullion in Fort Knox, dioxin had to remain in the fictional realm of heroin-like in cost, even if the true, open-for-sabotage market value of real estate was as clear as the *Second Law of Dioxinomics*.[2]

Bushkin's voice dripped with menace and resolve.

For the sake of engaging the gullible American viewer Madison Avenue style, Bushkin fell back on the dogma that the United States was the intended target of both dioxin urns. He released the fingerprint images secured from the New York City urn by the US Department of Defense WMD taskforce. Using 'CSI-Cam' overlay imaging, Bushkin showed the prints were an exact match to Ursini's prints. There was no doubt — the Octopus of Evil was gunning for America.

But, why?

Bushkin next elaborated how the Romanov plot to incite nation-busting anarchy required the haughty United States to get hammered mercilessly. With the so-called flower of democracy prostrate to a handful of Who-dunnit whackjobs, its citizens and its courts of rubber-stamp law would accommodate, if not pine for, the replacement of blowhard liberties with the institution of a more autocratic regime. Sergio Romanov, Aurelio Calamari and the rest

---

1 Two faggots (Rus)
2 An acre of land is worth no more than the cost to pollute it.

of Al Guido could then more adroitly supplant the current form of Russian demokrazy with a tsarist monarchy based on the British model. Because, with the US in collapse, their plans for Russia could be accomplished with less violence, destruction and turmoil.

At this time, over Perth, Australia, a high-altitude stealth MQ-1 Predator drone, the CIA Media Circus Division had dispatched, was spraying the exterior of the US Consulate with .50 caliber sniper rounds. Because it had reporters on scene, CNN cut in with **Breaking News**. Bushkin's address went 'dark' on CNN.

Bushkin then introduced the unimpeachable testimony of other 'high-value' Al Guido and Al Qaeda detainees, including the drug and would-be dioxin smugglers from Kazakhstan, Uzbekistan, Turkmenistan, and Tajikistan. All the testimony corroborated Bushkin's claims about how and why America was the primary target of the Octopus of Evil and Russia the secondary objective.

For its part, Wopland was to receive many benefits, including access to vast amounts of Russian oil and gas at below-market prices. Silvio Calamari, the son of the Prime Minister, Constanzo Ursini, Sergio Romanov and Ernesto Colonna all confirmed Wopland's involvement with the Octopus of Evil. Finally, the roll-call of evidence ended with a comprehensive statement from Al Guido's main patron, Wopland's, El Duce, Aurelio Calamari. His disclosures affirmed the specific testimony of the others, and most especially his nation's deliberate silence before the United Nations about Russia's Preemptive Action Notice as well as the falsity of the Niger uranium documents, which ex-US President Potusson used to justify America's unilateral invasion of Iraq. Calamari then proceeded to explain the link between Al Guido and Al Qaeda and how he had thought he had been back-stabbed by his son's abductors, who he surmised were in search of greater benefits than those already promised.

Bushkin concluded by explaining the purpose of the judeo-subversive Islamofascist crusade of the Octopus of Evil.

The dioxin dust in the Metro spoke for itself.

But, the Russians were not done.

Threat of World War III loomed.

Breaking News: CBS, ABC, Fox and NBC cut to Perth. Bushkin's address went 'dark.' While CNN focused on witness interviews, every other US channel broadcast aerial footage from various Australian affiliate news-copters.

Bushkin tore into NATO and asserted the acronym really stood for 'North Atlantic Terrorist Organization.' Every one of NATO's members would be held to account like the Taliban and Al Qaeda, like Wopland and Al Guido, and would be treated no differently than Drughistan and Wopland. Given the territorial extent of the North Atlantic Terrorist Organization, Bushkin swore on every nuke in Russia's arsenal that he could see no other recourse but to deploy the obvious 'maximum' weapon.

As the president of Russia, Bushkin declared he was exercising the right to follow in the footsteps of US President Potusson as of February 7, 2002. The executive power to decree any region on Earth a 'failed state' was a right vested in the president under the Konstitution of Russia, a right he, as commander-in-chief, was prepared to defend by force, nuclear if necessary.

President Bushkin, thereupon, declared Wopland a 'failed state' and as such considered 'terra nullius.' Just as no treaty concerning 'Afghanistan' applied to Talibanistan, no treaty concerning 'Italy' applied to Wopland. As a consequence, Wopland had no legal capacity to adhere to any treaty, be it: diplomatic, a war convention or a military alliance like NATO.

Breaking News: CNN's crew under fire. Shards of glass rained down on — OMG! — Tom Snowclaw, CNN's first Apache-Korean-American reporter. CNN overlay Muslim 'jihadist' monkey-bar footage for its bigotry effect.

Bushkin's version of peace-loving Russia wished to extend an olive branch to NATO as well as absolving NATO from any legal obligation to aid Wopland as opposed to a former NATO member once called Italy. Bushkin stated that if NATO represented free nations rather than hypocrites, NATO would not merely applaud Russia's peace preserving mission in Wopland and Central Asia but would rally to aid Russia in its heroic counter-defense against the global forces of woppery. Thus, did international law and common cause afford the means to avert a nuclear confrontation between Russia and the North Atlantic Terrorist Organization.

Breaking News: CBS, ABC, Fox and NBC ran the Tom Snowclaw drama.

Then, like a Coca-Cola Santa come home out of a Christmas blizzard, Bushkin's cheeks flushed Soviet-red with the spirit of giving and the man softened his tone. In consideration for what he expected would be their good behavior, Bushkin gave NATO permission to occupy Sardinia and Sicily and garrison northern Italy as a check on any further expansion of Russian occupation beyond the Wopland-Italy demarcation line that he proposed at the forty-fourth parallel. Russia and NATO had done this years before in Bosnia. They could be allies once more.

Their joint mission — obliterate woppery.

Woppery — Weisbrot's brows set deep and hard at the idea. This Rooskie 'olive wagging the branch' sleight-of-hand would confuse no American patriot. A flurry of military adjutants re-entered the Situation Room eager to brief their superiors about Italy. While the room buzzed with murmurings, Weissbrot's complete attention remained on the Canadian broadcast.

Breaking News: ABC — two victims now confirmed. Details to follow.

So that the people of the world could better understand the pestilence of anarchy the Octopus of Evil represented and how the term 'woppery' applied to this species of terrorism, Bushkin next played videotape of the Moscow Metro system being contaminated by a white cloud of dioxin. Next came footage of face after face blistered beyond recognition, followed by row upon row of corpses. Black and white Soviet footage of liberated fascist camps from World War II was interspersed with crisp, color footage of the ravages woppery had visited upon Moscow. In voice-over, Bushkin likened the scenes to gas chambers fascists had built and put to use decades before. He announced the cadaver count of

'Concentration Camp Moscow' now stood at 68,897. A prominent counter appeared on screen, and the count ticked upward, second after second.

Breaking News: **America was glued to the television. On screen, aerial footage of Perth SWAT and AFP[1] commandoes showed them fanning out, canvassing larger and larger zones endeavoring to skunk out the sniper(s).**

Once the Metro Gas Chamber footage concluded, Bushkin, standing behind his lectern, reappeared on screen. He pledged to the people of Russia that if their nation encountered any NATO interference then in subways, shopping malls, sports stadiums and TV studios all over Europe and Amerika, 'Snow Bzombies' would do made-for-primetime, tear-gas-like re-enactments using innocuous aerial compounds such as flour, baby powder, dry ice or white phosphorous.

Breaking News: **A third injury confirmed — a Jewish Holocaust survivor. Perfidy knew no bounds!! Fox immediately juiced the anti-Semite angle.**

Bushkin promised that aside from white-powder psychosis, there would be no physical harm. None. Just keeping it real, just keeping it wop — With Out Pollution — he said. Against a backdrop of irrational exuberance, the sole intent of 'Snow Bzombies' would be to remind all dissenting nations each and every day what Dioxinomic chaos looks like, in case Westerners clung to some strange notion that Russia was being less than even-handed with Wopland. He also reminded the world audience that while 'Snow Bzombies' would do no physical harm, he could not speak for the 'Tim McVeigh' nihilists out there.

Who knows what those nutcases would do?

Breaking News: **The American viewing public learned how a SWAT team found a discarded .50 caliber Barrett M99A1 sniper rifle. All American TV commentators reported the perpetrator was assumed to be on foot.**

Bushkin closed his presentation with a prospective accounting of death. While well shy of the eight million murdered by fascists decades ago, the death toll displayed on screen now stood at 68,908, making the Metro attack currently twenty-three times worse than what America called the '9/11 Attack.' He presented a synopsis of the demise of some 800,000 Russians over the next six years and the debilitation that an estimated 1.5 million Russians would experience over a truncated lifetime. Referencing his electronic globe, he next walked through General Litvinenko's simulation of the ruination facing the economy of Russia and by implication the potential ruination to the smug city-centric economies of Europe, America and Asia that woppery had yet to directly target for extinction.

Breaking News: **A Ten/Fox[2] news-copter spotted a suspicious figure duck into a car park. On NBC, retired General Jamison detailed sniper strategies.**

Bushkin announced a new science of human reality. He christened it — *Dioxinomics*. Woppery had ushered in the 'Age of Dioxinomics.' Long gone was the 'Gilded Age' of billion dollar militarism with death wrapped up in fancy metal casings and priced as if plated with gold. Might had nothing to do with tanks, planes, smart bombs and robot weaponry. Nukes — a billion dollar joke.

Pollution trumped every such weapon.

And, Dioxinomics was its fallout.

1   AFP - Australian Federal Police
2 Australia's main TV networks are denoted by numbers, Channels: Seven, Nine and Ten.

Breaking News: **Nine/NBC and Ten/Fox news-copters were following a speeding black Yamaha Star Roadliner. Lights blazing, AFP red and silver Holdern Chargers were in hot pursuit.**

With the 'Captain A-Bomb' fallacy about national security inculcated into America's brainwashed masses now exposed, Bushkin next detailed the demise of a system of economics which enriched a 'Royal Monetarchy.' Western capitalism was a scam orchestrated by Zio-Nazi aristocrats who owned the exclusive right to shackle serfs to the playbook of 'Central Bank Monetarism.'

In his next breath, Bushkin revealed one of the eighteen laws of Dioxinomics — *An acre of land is worth no more than the cost to pollute it.* Be it a solitary acre or a Manhattan Island-sized clutch of acres, no amount of playbook monetarism could detox the 'real value' of Dioxinomic reality.

Again, Bushkin underscored the point.

Pollution nuked every asset.

And, Dioxinomics was its fallout.

Bushkin reminded the world.

"Economics is all in your head. A stageplay to amuse the Royal Monetarchy."

Breaking News: **American viewers watched riveting helicopter footage of AFP officers wailing on a biker. Once his helmet was removed, Ten/Fox got the scoop. An Aborigine. Batons were holstered. Cuffs came out. Sheila Kurupuru, head of the Australian League of Indigency picked up the phone.**

Bushkin's message was simple — Just as cheap pollution kills military fat, as well documented in Iraq and Drughistan, cheap pollution kills economic fat. Dioxinomic tycoons don't require oodles of paper splooged with green ink.

Any blue-blood nutcase can be J. P. Morgan.

Any blue-blood nutcase can be Genghis Khan.

Breaking News: **NBC stuck with Jamison, a credible pundit. Fox went with Miguel Bachmann's take on national security. ABC scored big — Senator McCain of Arizona — Torture is in the eye of the beholder — he now claimed.**

Bushkin's sense of demokrazy was simple and homegrown, and Russia was its flower. Galvanizing his elektorate in the way of righteousness was everything. Alien nations were nothing. Because it was his duty to defend the Russian Konstitution from all encroachment, alien encroachment most especially. To this end, Bushkin concluded his televised address with words made famous by ex-US President Potusson four years before. Bushkin, however, expanded the quote to embrace the complete menace the Octopus of Evil posed to the peoples of the freedom-loving, democratic world.

"Know this core principle of my presidency. If you threaten Russia, you'll find no safe haven. In our global counter-defense against terrorism, fascism and woppery, either you are with us or you are against us."

Breaking News: **Wrap up. America's media made simple P and J choices. Both crustless, white bread. The crunchy Peanut in the pin-strip suit on CBS bemoaned how Australia's restrictive gun laws had failed their nation then expostulated about the anti-American white-fella-complex behind the trigger. The bespectacled Jelly in an XXL Argyle cardigan on Fox accused the Australian Labour government of coddling terrorism because they were too damn liberal.**

285

Loose-Canon Democracies

Airforce General Eugene Aldrich turned off the monitor. Seated in silence, the Joint Chiefs looked askance at their president. When Weissbrot finally stirred, he checked his watch and hailed his secretary on the intercom.

"Naomi, rustle up a full cabinet meeting for 5:00 a.m."

"Yes, sir. A full cabinet meeting in one hour."

Weissbrot punched the disconnect button, gestured for everyone to remain silent, reclined deep into the folds of his chair and perused his fingernails. He sat motionless, stewing in cold and calculating thought. All in all, the Bushkin presentation had been professional, and as a result, highly persuasive. It was loaded with unassailable evidence when compared to the 'read my lips' drivel ex-US President Potusson had whipped up to deceive the UN Security Council and Congress. Weissbrot's heart thumped as he realized how most viewers around the world would have come away with the knowledge that when demagogues running loose-canon democracies go after terrorists, they don't play games, don't tolerate hypocrisy, don't lie about reality, don't deceive the electorate or hide the truth. Head bent, elbows on table, thumbs on his cheeks, he massaged his temples with his fingertips. Candor replacing the high art of propaganda was too frightful to contemplate.

Half-Caste Glory

Returning to his office, Bushkin took time to relax and catch up with social news. His secretary laid a silver tea service on the president's desk.

"Thank you, Evgenia. Some alone time."

For the next ten minutes, Bushkin reviewed a document he intended sending to the US president. It's title: International and Constitutional Law Must Capitulate to the Greater Imperative of World Peace. He put down his cup and pressed the intercom button.

"Evgenia. No amendments. Get it off now."

Bushkin next accessed the *Dallas Times* website and the October 2, 2005 Sunday edition news story about the opening of the Russo-American Friendship wing at Potusson's presidential library. There were the three dignitaries of the day: ex-US President Potusson, Russian Ambassador Igor B. Meshok and 'Homo Potus'[1] standing tall in all his naked Pro-Magnon — Neanderthal half-caste glory. Even after this unique gesture of friendship as well as providing US and NATO over-flight rights to Afghanistan, any great outpouring of American sympathy for the calamity Moscow was suffering had remained begrudging and piecemeal — *How predictable*, he thought.

---

1 Unearthed in a Siberian peat pit in 2003 by coal miners, after reconstruction and much argument, the Russian Academy of Sciences assigned this ancient hominid a distinct biological classification - *Homo Potus*. Bushkin has Madame Tussauds make a wax replica, which he presents as a gift to the United States.

After a second belt of caffeine, Bushkin's mood lightened and he reflected on why he admired Potusson. This founding father of the new millennium had created the moral and legal high ground so essential for the demokratically inclined demagogue to rally the patriots of the free world to embrace the heroic fifty-year mission that was 'Operation WOPPERY.'

His direct line rang. He snapped it up.

In less than a minute, all was made clear.

"Doktor, see you in sixty. *Poka.*"

Money Shot to the Eyeballs

After Bushkin's address drew to a close in his mind, a more steely Weissbrot felt ready to digest the options the United States had at its immediate disposal. Central Asia was one thing, but this invasion of Italy presented a completely different impasse, something that Bushkin publicly threatened would take out Metro systems all over the West and possibly go nuclear if the anger of the Russian people was not assuaged. Twenty-five frustration filled minutes later, Weissbrot decided the Joint Chiefs and their staffs needed to thrash the matter out as a coordinated group before seeking his involvement. Moreover, the president needed to focus on the full cabinet meeting, he had scheduled for 5:00 a.m. because the most pressing issue was domestic. Relative to the spirit of uptick in Moscow, the US financial mastodons were on the verge of sinking into a tar pit of lawfully over-leveraged pessimism.

On his way to the White House Cabinet Room, Naomi handed him a freshly printed email from Bushkin. After absorbing the gist of the document, he instructed her to delay the cabinet meeting while he gave the matters Bushkin raised thorough review and quiet thought of his own.

Convened ten minutes behind schedule, the cabinet debate grew most heated around 5:25 a.m. as Carter's old guard of Jeffersonian idealists tried to come to terms with the Dioxinomic predicament the people of America and Europe faced. Attorney General Hicks hammered back.

"But Mr. President, our directive of February 7, 2002 is coming home—"

Flaring hot with exasperation, Weissbrot's graveled temper sought to terminate Hick's pointless argument.

"Spare me, David, this isn't about international law."

"But Mister—"

"Hicks, only one fact is relevant. Because the blow-back from the 'Mallory Wilson Affair'[1] decimated the CIA's capacity to get independent and credible intelligence, we've taken a money shot to the eyeballs. And, this is the result — A handful of Islamic psychos tweaked the nose of our fucking vain 'gotta-have-legacy' presidents who exposed the United States to the potential for exploitation in Iraq and Afghanistan."

---

1 Occurring on July 14, 2003, the 'Mallory Wilson Affair,' put every CIA informant around the globe on notice that the US White House would stab anyone in the back, including their own government personnel. The upshot - the CIA lost informants (human intelligence HUMINT) left, right and center.

"But in Afghan—"

"Zip it! Not one peep," Weissbrot barked.

There was an excruciating pause before the president, deeply ensconced within his executive chair, adopted a clear-headed tone — "In Afghanistan, we have 245,000 veteran US and NATO forces fighting the so-called War on Terror, hunting down Osama bin Laden and Al Qaeda, smashing the Taliban regime, and now eradicating poppies and securing the Afghan border against invasion. Bushkin's case speaks for itself. Yet there we sat, green-lighting Afghanistan's rise as the world's biggest drug-flower producer, all inaugurated on the backs of poppy-ninny slavery. Abe Lincoln must be rolling over in his grave."

Still needing to spout, Weissbrot pointed his finger at Hicks.

"And look at Iran. They're still getting opium from Afghanistan. They convert profits into munitions, which then get exported to Iraq to kill our forces there. So it's not just damn opium addicts dying. It's our citizens — my bloody troops."

Hicks could not possibly know how harrowing the prior 3:00 a.m. meeting with the Joint Chiefs had been for Commander-in-Chief Weissbrot, let alone the contents of the email that President Bushkin had sent, and Hicks tried to chop back in. But, Weissbrot motioned for him to shut up — "In Iraq, David, I have another 145,000 men. 'Coalition of the Willing' forces invaded Iraq because the UN's *Inspector Clouseau* inspectors couldn't find a chemical weapon if it teabagged their pie-hole. Until our puppet regime in Iraq finishes their mission of training Iraqi troops to defend their fledgling democracy, our forces remain bogged down."

Weissbrot rocked to and fro — "Remember the newly invented grand theory of Potusson and his cronies in Congress was and remains — Iraq will become a beacon of change in the Middle East. Even though I'm skeptical, I'm not going to undermine a trillion-dollar mission so close to completion."

"But sir, unlike Iraq, we have a treaty commitment to NATO."

Weissbrot lurched forward and fired back — "We are honoring our treaties, consistent with new realities and new threats, as per Section 1 of Potusson's February 7, 2002 directive. Also, the US-Russia Anti-Terrorism Act obviously modifies our onetime treaty obligations. David, you're the Attorney-General. For Christ's sake, you know a recent statute always trumps an older treaty."

"Yes, but—"

Weissbrot pounded the table — "*Fuck Buts.* NATO understands that Iraq and Afghanistan cannot relapse into terror-friendly states. Europe has forces on the doorstep of Italy." Weissbrot tapped down hard on the table with his index finger — "Americans are nobody's GI-Joe-poodles. It's do or die time for Signore Dippity-Do-Euro. And, let's not forget, wops have that quaint joke about how every Italian is prepared to defend Italy to the very last American. Well, ha-dee-ha-ha, but we Americans won't defend tsarism being exported from the homeland of fascism into Russia through the use of terrorist toxins that were actually aimed at us — these damned United States."

Weissbrot jerked back into his chair. His chest hollowed as he exhaled.

Secretary of State Chandler spoke into the imbroglio.

"Mr. President, why play Russia's game? If we really need to free up troops, why not withdraw from Afghanistan? Bluster aside, I can't see Russia repeating its invasion of 1979. Too much emotional baggage."

Weissbrot stifled a look of incredulity.

"Jeff, we're stuck in our own superpower fantasy there. With the exception of Spain, France Ireland, Holland and Denmark, most of NATO's tank and heavy armor was offloaded in Karachi, Pakistan, two days ago and is now barreling along at break-neck speed to the Afghan-Turkmenistan border. Lester, would you remind us all why we cannot turn tail and leave the Afghan border thinly defended as a matter of peace-preserving diplomacy."

Still smarting from the triggering of 'Operation Rin Tin Tin'[1] in Perth without running it by him for confirmation, Lester Coverdale pulled his nose out of the 'Eyes-Only' file containing Bushkin's email that the president had handed him in the hallway. He slapped it closed. The file only added to his fury because a secret CIA black-site at San Severo, Italy holding the notorious 'Ground Zero' had gone dark. All the signs were not good. And, he had yet to pass on this potential calamity to the president. That could wait until solid confirmation came. Lester growled.

"Nobody wants to start World War III over two intersecting streams of piss like Italy and Afghanistan. Bushkin is adhering to his commitments to decompress the riotous anger in his nation and preserve some semblance of democracy. Excluding this underhanded invasion of Italy, he's doing everything to plan. The Kazakhstan, Uzbekistan, Turkmenistan, and Tajikistan invasions are proceeding in accordance with the agreed upon timetable. By tomorrow, the bulk of our troops and incoming armor will be in place to hold the border, regiment for regiment, division for division. America stands resolute so Boris Bolshevik can blow off steam. Democracy must be preserved — Period."

Lester shifted gears and shifted mood.

"On the Italian front, we're in the process of orchestrating a song-n-dance that the freedom-loving peoples of the world will accept. And, as Director of National Intelligence, I remind and re-emphasize to all of you that our complete surprise by this invasion of Italy is the direct result of the loss of reliable intelligence caused by the 'Mallory Wilson Affair.' One that started when the Italians faked up documents that Potusson insisted proved how Niger was shipping uranium to Iraq. So I agree with our president, Wopland's deceptive bowel movements means they get to eat the shit they aimed at others."

Treasury Secretary Earl 'Groundhawg' Butz, spoke up in support.

"Here-here. And, don't neglect the money shot aspect. We're facing systemic failure. Not just financial, but political. No different than small debt-leveraged banks, it's just as Bushkin said — Lesser countries such as Afghanistan, Iraq and Italy need to be declared as 'failed states' and overrun to ensure that the solid democratic systems in those countries that hold the promise of a better future for all mankind remain solvent. I'm talking about simple market forces,

---

1 American TV show about how a German Shepherd is the military-industrial-complex's best friend.

'Fair-play Balanced with Hypocrisy' at its finest. As a democratic, nuclear-powered institution, Russia is too-freaky-to-fail."

The president sat cleanly upright — "Thanks, for the analogy, Earl. And, let me add that I'm of the opinion that the halcyon days when vain, back-stabbing mankind reveled in the psychosis of money are drawing to a close."

A cold earnestness pervaded the room. Weissbrot cleared his throat and addressed an issue Bushkin raised in his 'Eyes-Only' email.

"Now, gentlemen, speaking as an admiral let me lay out the bloody facts of World War III. With the Russian fleet dominating the Mediterranean, if we fantasize about turning tail in Afghanistan and ship our forces back to Europe, we can expect a Russian blockade of the Suez Canal and probably the Straits of Gibraltar. Furthermore, removing our troops from those theaters signals capitulation and invites greater jihadi insurgency. And, even without retreating, I expect resistance in Iraq and Afghanistan to escalate because even to the most moronic Muslim, it's plain as day we're stretched too thin."

He paused for persuasive effect.

"Hence gentlemen, as I said before — we're being exploited."

He drummed the table four times while that truth sunk in.

"As for the Italian peninsula, moving forces into Russian-occupied Wopland is a quaint exercise on paper. Aviano is ripped to pieces by what I'm sure were Russian suicide forces. Not to mention that all of Italy's airstrips south of Bologna are captured. In fact, we've got an on-going mystery, NATO aircraft being shot down over northern Italy. Miles, any explanation?"

Secretary of Defense Miles Glorioso moved his mobile phone away from his mouth — "Sir, No, not yet. Missiles come out of nowhere. We're using AWACs out of Ramstein and sending in decoys with large radar signatures to see if we can trigger launches and trace the missiles to their point of origin."

Weissbrot nodded resignedly and motioned Glorioso to silence.

"Gentlemen, here's my decision. Fascist-coddling nations can fend for themselves. Given over two hours to respond, the Italians have not come up with anything but blather to rebut the extensive and hard evidence the Russians have provided. America is always happy to destroy CIA videotape before the eyes of US Federal judges and substitute song-n-dance claims about how we act on the 'Top Secret' confessions of Muslim terrorists we've black-holed. In comparison, Russia's video confessions of the Italian terrorists, who created the dioxin with the intent of selling it to Muslims who confirmed the United States was their real target, is vastly more persuasive."

National Security Director Ginger Arnold rapped the table with a pen.

"Mr. President, sir, we shouldn't put any credibility on those confessions Bushkin calls 'conversations.' Barbara Walters material? Hardly. We must assume what every patriotic American will assume — The Russians imitated our policy under Potusson and tortured the hell out of all their detainees. And, the so-called Viktor Magufinski 'Urn Letter' and that 'Umberto Borges' passport should be considered forgeries like the Niger-Iraq uranium letters the government of Italy conjured-up for our amusement."

Lester rounded on Ginger — "Norman and I have conferred about 'credibility' for days now. We agree. Perhaps, it's true. Perhaps, it's false. But, look at reality. We invaded Iraq based on a whispering campaign maligning Saddam Hussein, including 'Top Secret' confessions about him and Al Qaeda forming a terror alliance. The US hasn't produced one shred of solid evidence regarding Al Qaeda or Iraq, nor one videotape or anything remotely close to the quality of public disclosure the Russians have procured from their detainees. And, now, Rooskie rednecks are as mad as cunt-fucking Cossacks. That's reality, and that's the *only* reality that matters."

Ginger, whose protest wasn't about the political drive for 'Good TV ratings,' felt her point was lost. She anchored her elbow on the table and hunched to her left as if a break in cleavage to orthodoxy was called for.

"So, the upshot is that democracies are best served by dialing up the torture to get a good Bubba-Wubba 'conversation' out of whomever for rebroadcast to the viewing public in order to get their patriotism juices flowing hot and plenty?"

Lester was not amused. But, the pragmatist in Weissbrot, seeking a modicum of relief, let out a good belly-laugh and made crackling reply.

"Welcome to *realpolitik* in the new millennium, my dear Ginger. We're dealing with Russians facing their own 9/11. That reality is *not* fake. And, when it comes to the US of A, never forget, we destroy our own videotape confessions so we can deceive the public and lie to juries. That's judicial record."

"But—"

Weissbrot waved her off — "And, forged letters you say. Urn versus Uranium? If I were a red-behind-the-ears Rooskie, I'd call that poetic justice. Italy had ample warning six months ago. That Russian Pre-emptive Action Notice named bloody names concerning the Romanov-Al Guido plot. We laughed it off as the rants of a megalomaniac bent on subverting democracy in his country."

Hick's cheeks blushed. Weissbrot did not relent.

"This absurd three-penny wop-opera exchanging an urn of dioxin for an urn of diamonds has ruined our economy not to mention the economies of most of Italy's NATO allies. City real estate will soon take on Dioxinomic prices. To quote Bushkin — '*One acre of land is worth no more than the cost to pollute it.*' That, Ginger, is reality, too. Fuck, it's hard science — *Dioxinomics.*"

Weissbrot squared his jaw — "Lady Liberty's job is to dance with a flea-sack of a bear and avert World War III. My address this morning will explain the salient facts to our fellow citizens, so they can decide if we should diddle away resources to liberate Wopland and piss off every Russian in the process."

Weissbrot reclined back into this chair.

The silence was only momentary. In case certain cabinet members still lived in the 'Barbie-World' days of military adventurism, Director of Homeland Security Holroyd 'Bulldawg' Ashfelt added his opinion to the mix.

"Missa President, we're exposed to millions of home-grown hoons who hate New York and Washington's Zionist imperialism and arrogance. Look at the attack on our consulate this morning."

Weissbrot stared at Bulldawg — *Huh?*

Lester cut in — "Mr. President, I'll brief you later. Small potatoes."

And, Bulldawg resumed — "Many nutsos gunning for America are ethnic Rooskees. Chechens, the worst. Right now, homeland security reality is about how some Brooklyn babushka carrying groceries, such as a one dollar bag of flour into the subway, which — 'oh what a silly old dingbat' — accidentally drops onto the railway tracks and the subway gets shut down." Unnerved by the simplicity of *Dioxinomics*, Bulldawg paused. "With us being only in year four of our fifty-year crusade against terrorism, beatniks dusting down subway systems with flour power or any amateur pollutant annihilates everything. Poof — worthless."

Ginger felt compelled to weigh-in.

"Actually the American news media blanked out dioxin-death chamber footage amongst other parts of Bushkin's presentation. Bulldawg, you have to keep in mind that we, in the White House, watched Canadian satellite coverage."

Weissbrot lurched in Ginger's direction — *What?*

Ginger pre-empted the president — "A sniper shooting outside a US Consulate in Australia. That story sidelined much of Bushkin's address."

Weissbrot squinched his eyes. His cheeks reddened.

"*Screw that.* Ginger, get on the horn. The rest of the world thinks regular Americans see the real news. I'm not Potusson. We ain't the Soviet Union. I'm sick of the excuses behind censored, skewed and bias coverage and the hooligan media's agenda of manipulation designed to divide the US electorate. No more US press making our country look as brainless as beheaded journalists."

"Sir, that's American norm—"

Weissbrot slammed his fist on the table.

"No more Matzo-balls[1] out of New York and Washington goy-boying[2] the news. We aren't a nation of 300 million puppets. World War III is screaming into my fucking face. I want the whole, unvarnished Bushkin report aired. Tell them, I'll publicly endorse *RT.com*, the *Russia Today* website if I hear one fang-fucking hiss of protest. Now, hop to it."

"Yes, sir," and Ginger rose from her chair.

As she made for the door, Weissbrot finished his point.

"Before I deliver my 9:00 a.m. address, the public needs to understand why the Russians are pissed as hell with us. Got it?"

David Hicks considered clarity a danger — "Sir, sometimes less is more and sometimes more is more. Often the public needs to be deceived more so that they feel more secure, regardless of reality. Our banking system is a paragon of stability because it's secured by deception. More truth only amounts to more panic."

Ginger stopped at the door, hand perched on the knob.

Weissbrot looked from Hicks to Ginger and back again.

"Bulldawg's got the catfish by the whiskers, David. Homeland security is paramount. I'm going to ask our citizens to think about what matters most before they exercise the one-time option I'm giving them to vote by phone, fax, text message and email. I'm not shying away from telling them that if they

1 Pejorative: Jew.
2 Goy is Hebrew for Subhuman/Untermench/Gentile.

want to fight Russia 'on the poppy fields,' I'll activate conscription. If I don't get two-thirds support from the people and a two-thirds resolution from Congress to invade Italy proper then we're going to confine ourselves to securing the unoccupied north of Italy as well as Sardinia and Sicily."

Ginger closed the door behind her.

Secretary of State Chandler was alarmed that this could be misinterpreted. After explaining his concerns, Weissbrot gave him the nod, and he beat a hasty exit too.

The rest of the meeting focused on economic and legal issues, such as reformulating the legal memoranda of the Potusson era to address the Russian invasion. The meeting adjourned at 6:30 a.m. so that Weissbrot, Coverdale, Glorioso and Ashfelt could confer with the Joint Chiefs.

On the way to the Situation Room, confirmation came in — 'Ground Zero' was in Russian hands. Lester Coverdale passed this on to the president. The feast of made-for-primetime Octopus of Evil conversations about the fourway linkages between Al Guido, Al Qaeda, Drughistan and Wopland was now completely served, not to mention how this additional capture had the potential to expose 'Operation Mad Cow.'

The Bogomolski File

Within the confines of his office, President Bushkin hit the [ACCESS GRANTED] button, and Dr. Chernikrov stepped from the elevator. Bushkin directed the doctor to hand him the Eyes-Only report about the pregnancy of 'The Princess of Peace,' Special Agent Natalia Vladimirovna Bogomolski.

The third paragraph floored Bushkin. He looked up and dissected every option at great length with the doctor. After Chernikrov confirmed that except for fabricated records, there were no copies of his report in the Infirmary, Bushkin informed him that until countermanded, the provisional protocols they had discussed at their first meeting were now permanent.

Bushkin strolled over to his walk-in office vault and added the report to the *Bogomolski* file. Hailing the doctor to join him, he made a beeline for the elevator. Bushkin was eager to see his nation's new jihadi guest face-to-face, including the two CIA handlers who had survived the firefight outside San Severo.

Bushkin smelt 'major coup' was close at hand.

Collateral Damage

Over the course of the first hour, the Joint Chiefs presented President Weissbrot a plan of attack and detailed the estimated manpower and munitions required to oust the Russians from the Italian peninsula. Their plan assumed Bushkin was bluffing about nuclear weapons.

During the second hour, updated information from Aviano confirmed suspicions raised by the CIA's Counter-Terrorism Unit. Trace amounts of dioxin had been found in the remains of the pilots of the cargo planes and Y-chromosome genotyping confirmed Slavic ancestry. Covert Russian suicide units had attacked Aviano. A follow-up CIA report concluded that NATO could expect some 30,000 to 50,000 dioxin-dead Russians to be embedded in any number of countries.

The news left the generals speechless.

The Pentagon's experience with suicide bombers in Iraq and Al Qaeda's 'Devour Satan' terrorist offensives made it plain that there would be enormous losses from suicidal Bombie brigades. The mauling at Aviano was a prime example of what a handful of determined counter-defense bombies with proper military discipline, training, tactics and basic weaponry could do. Only time could defuse this Dioxinomic Bombie apocalypse. The sane tactic was to sit pat for three months and let the bulk of Russia's suicidal capacity wither away naturally, before cranking up a war machine based on the tried and true doctrines of American offensive warfare.

The good news was that the Air Force had located over fifty stratospheric hydrogen-filled balloons that served as launch platforms for missiles that continued to rain havoc on NATO air patrols. The bad news was there was currently no easy way to shoot down these balloons using conventional aircraft. The good news was that they would travel out of range within a day, assuming more weren't secretly launched and could reach the safe, high altitude of thirty-two miles. The bad news was that once they had left their range of air attack, the balloon-based missiles launched on missions of last resort. Like bats, the released missiles glided westward until they reached a designated area. After a specific target had been acquired, they went into rocket-powered dives that were destroying railway and highway bridges all over northern Italy. Be it against air or ground targets, no Russian ordinance was going to waste.

Other bad news confirmed the second item in Bushkin's email. The Russian fuel depot system, located in almost every historic site in the Russian zone of occupation, was tied to the US military's GPS system, specifically to the civilian C/A code channel. If any GPS-secured fuel depot detected that it was being disturbed, the antenna disabled or the signal scrambled, then the 8x8x20 foot container would self-destruct. To permit the United States to verify this fact, the Russians programmed a one-time fifteen-minute blank-out option into all detonation computer controls except for a solitary demonstration unit.

The US military called Bushkin's bluff and turned off the C/A code channel the US NAVSTAR satellite system transmitted. A proof-of-concept fuel depot at coordinates 43° 04' 26.3" North, 12° 36' 27.7" East instantly went hot and smashed every building within a two hundred meter radius.

A crime under the laws of counter-defense?

The long-settled laws of war said — *No*.

First, the United States had pushed the 'collateral damage' button — 'World Heritage' sites be damned. But, regardless, the law was the converse. Theft of fuel was an offense. This method, as strident as it was, lawfully deterred theft. The message: Tamper with GPS — Watch fuel depots all over the Russian zone of occupation explode, including the one jammed into the Carlo Maderno designed entryway of Saint Peter's Basilica in Vatican City.

Of course, the Russians had their own GPS system called GLONASS. However, the Italian company that had made the GPS receivers for delivery confiscation by Russia only made cheaper mass-produced NAVSTAR units. Bushkin, ever a red-tag blue-light politician full of frugal irony, had given the US and NATO complete freedom to decide the extent of so-called collateral damage. Bushkin's reasoning went, surely the US president was a man more experienced with collateral damage, and so ought to have his finger on a WMD button such as this. In any case, if push ever came to shove, Bushkin certainly had his own button — a more surgical one.

Operation Bushkin

At 8:40 a.m., President Weissbrot left the meeting to rehearse what he was going to disclose during his emergency morning address to the nation. Earlier, around 6:50 a.m., pursuant to a Presidential Order, Ginger had finally set the US news media straight. From 7:00 a.m. onwards, the nation had been receiving the complete and uncensored report about Bushkin's unilateral decision to use military force in what Russia called 'Operation WOPPERY.'

By 9:00 a.m., most Americans were insanely eager to hear their new president's response, and how he intended to deal with this assault on America's exceptionalism. On his way to the podium, Weissbrot got his only laugh for the day. Medical tests had determined why over 35,000 US and NATO personnel were hospitalized hours before the Russian invasion of Italy. Doctors north of the zone of occupation were removing capsules containing trace amounts of urushiol from their patients' scroti. Reasons still under investigation.

The President gave a measured and exacting address. In light of the urn attack on the NBC *Today Show* set, he could not fault or controvert Bushkin's evidence as to who created the dioxin and how the United States was the intended target. He could not fault or controvert the now public Russian Pre-emptive Action Notice of March 15, 2005, nor the regime of starvation enforced poppy-ninny slavery that 'Operation Rambo' could have snuffed out under Potusson or Carter.

Rather than carp on Russia's unilateral excessiveness, Weissbrot laid out the Dioxinomic harvest World War III would bring. His first counter-measure for self-preservation was simple. By Presidential Order, all foreign creditors with more than one million dollars in US assets would only be permitted to witdraw their import-earned dollars from the United States by buying American-sourced exportable products or assets. Non-exportable products included real estate, American corporations and raw resources like gold, oil, unprocessed materials and commodities subject to speculation. All these were off the table. The president explained that his intent was to circumvent destructive speculation by credit-glutted foreign nations. For example, the vast horde of $935 billion in Treasury bonds held by China and the huge billion dollar treasury holdings of other countries was not going to flood into the lives of the American people and create inflation in the price of essential goods. Alien assets had only one purpose, to balance US trade ledgers after decades of trade imbalance.

To the horror of the public, Weissbrot bluntly informed his countrymen how the Octopus of Evil had ushered in a new age of warfare. Evil sought to exploit the 'Obese in America' paradigm. Dioxin accretes in the human body in fat cells and lipid complexes. The brain is 95% fat. And, it wasn't about dioxin, rather more about dust, any dust. Airborne pollutants in 'Battlefield Subways' were as brain-dead simple as silica dusts infused with ammonium dichromate. No amount of wishful totalitarian thinking could assuage the brain-dead simple science of terrorism's optimal tactic — Cause death by toxicity in the short-term or by cancer in the long-term. Evil's dividend was autistically simple. Since every American knew how 5% of the population was already wolfing down 50% of health-care dollars, Weissbrot asserted the US would soon descend into a permanent state of health-zombie feudalism, an elitism, terrorists could exploit on the cheap.

By Presidential Order, all subterranean traffic corridors were shut down.

Weissbrot continued his socio-political slant and assaulted viewers with more candor. He voiced his nation's frustration at how many slacker countries couldn't cobble together the sort of advanced standing armies Western powers fielded, so out of frustration, the runts of the world would freely resort to covert, cheap and miserable methods of warfare as their means of keeping superpowers on a tight leash. He reckoned Americans would soon pine for the good old days when Iran and North Korea squandered vast resources on exotic, budget-busting weapons like nukes. Weissbrot went on to state that, by every measure, the democracies of the world were in the process of sinking into an era of voter endorsed totalitarianism. He warned that if such pollution kept spreading, the need for voter endorsement would end at some point, just as it had ended in the fascist countries of Europe once they had gone onto a 'Blood, Honor and Fatherland'[1] war footing.

Turning to the issue of military ruination, Weissbrot reminded his nation that their military were already fighting the Taliban in Afghanistan, chasing down the notorious Osama bin Laden and his Al Qaeda cohorts, including the Al Qaeda forces that President Potusson claimed were training in Iraq. Weissbrot explained that these regions might see redoubled terrorist activity in the wake of the Moscow attack and the thwarted attack in New York by their Octopus of Evil ally — Al Guido. He laid bare how the nation's forces were already efficiently locked into protecting some semblance of the American way of life from a handful of Islamic jihadists.

The fiscal conservative in Weissbrot switched gears.

1 Hitler Youth Oath. Nazi sloganeering.

In case it had not dawned on anyone how the Social Security Trust Fund was invested in military despoliation on foreign shores, he spelled out the facts. Not content with over one trillion dollars each year from regular taxes, Potusson had mined the Social Security system for all it was worth. But, now, with a national debt exceeding $6 trillion, Dioxinomics brought America into an era of fiscal cash on the barrel-head reality. The Dioxinomic foundation under cash capitalism was set anew. Barbie bought it, Barbie owns it. Good luck. No derivative, option, put or swap could be interposed to fob reality off onto others.

By Presidential Order, all derivative contracts were void.

Winding up his address, Weissbrot invited the people to ignore Afghanistan and Iraq, and vote-from-home on the issue of a third front in Italy. If they wanted to expand the military manpower and resources of their country, they would have to disregard the currently depressed and collapsing state of their economy. They would need to buckle down, pay additional taxes, as well as support military conscription. By the will of the people, these patriots would be conscripted within one month and after a minimum of two months of training, would be available for combat. What was left of Europe after three months of gearing up to face down Russia, who could say. And, the conscripts would also be deployed to other countries where the president saw fit to take the fight against the Octopus of Evil.

If the people of America wanted full scale war, so be it, said Weissbrot.

In essence and fact — World War III.

Softening his blood and guts conscription scenario, Weissbrot dangled a carrot. The US and NATO would not enter Turkmenistan or the other former USSR republics in Central Asia and would allow the Russians unfettered use of Italy for three months. But, after that, if the Russians did not exit Italy then the US and NATO alliance would unify and go on the offensive wherever it pleased.

Weissbrot's candor and call to 'Vote from Home' jolted many viewers. It smelt like a 'referendum' at the point of a Russian gun. A president had never spoken publicly in such straight-up terms. By midday, as citizens conferred with other citizens, many Americans started pining for the good old days when, without any qualms, guileful politicians told them only the good news even if it was crap. To them, Weissbrot seemed like one of those neo-con-libertarian spoilsports who took WMD — 'Western Made Democracy' — far too seriously.

Fortunately, President Bushkin, ever astute about the real Amerika, had foreseen this. And, in the second section of his email that morning, he outlined for Weissbrot's consideration a course of action within the confines of the US Constitution that would save and solidify both their political careers. Weissbrot concurred with Bushkin's objectives. And, because Bushkin's proposal had many of the idealistic aspects that, in her onetime lucid days, Carter held so dear, Weissbrot toyed with the thought of naming it 'Operation Carter.' However, given the threat woppery posed to world peace, Bushkin's plan would establish a more sane and pragmatic sense of government in the United States.

So, in honor of its architect, he titled it 'Operation Bushkin.'

Home for Christmas

Four days after both presidential addresses, the United States, NATO, Italy and Russia formalized arrangements to avert pointless carnage. As in all things requiring massive compromise between different cultures, the devil always remained in the details. From his command center in Bari, Basil was winding up a lengthy phone call.

"Excellent, Mr. President. 'Camp Carter,' it is." Basil stopped scribbling notes. "Now, the personal stuff sir — How can I help?"

While Basil remained silent for the longest time. His face revealed the whole father-to-be story. Scratching down words he might put to use, he smirked from time to time as Bushkin recounted Special Agent Bogomolski's intransigence. After a moment to compose, Basil launched into the voice-mail the president sought.

"Natalia. I miss you dearheart." And, Basil exhaled audibly. "Right now, we're fully embedded within the maws of woppery so communication is only possible through the highest channels. Fyedor has brought me up to speed with the wonderful news. Follow Doctor Chernikrov's schedule, darling. Also, there are some high-value detainees rendered to Moscow — CIA goons who wounded one of my men and almost hit me too. Natash, expect lots of CIA to come your way. Your vampire intercessions are truly vital sweetheart. No father, myself included, need to take a wop bullet to prove anything. Always, think of Derek and the drug scum at the CIA. And, think of the thousands of addicts awaiting your healing touch. And, ask the president to brief you about CIA money funneled to Karzai and 'Project Gladio.' Also, if Fyedor, our president — and Natash, know this — Fyedor is a dear personal friend and the most honourable man I know. So, if our president asks you anything, please do it without qualm or hesitation. But, dearest, most of all — I can't wait until woppery is crushed so I can hold you in my arms and give you all my love. *Tebya Loobloo, Daragaya.*"[1]

Basil glanced at the rattling door while Bushkin finished off the call.

"Thank you, sir. *Poka*," Basil returned. And, he hung up, scooted to the doorway and beckoned Marshal Ogrom Palachnin inside. While positioning a chair for the Marshal, Basil passed on the good news.

"Ogrom, our counter-defending posture is to become an occupying force. Stewardship, civility, and convict-harvesting are now our focus."

Returning to his own chair, Basil kept the briefing in motion.

"Amongst the terms of the negotiated plan for the Wopland front of 'Operation WOPPERY,' we have unfettered action until the sixth of January."

Palachnin cried gleefully. "Home for Christmas!"

"Yes, Ogrom. The best Christmas ever."

And, Basil momentarily lapsed into a daydream about reuniting with his Natash, a woman that the president had confirmed was pregnant. Ultrasound printouts would follow in due course — *News could not be more perfect.*

Palachnin leant over the desk.

---

1 I love you, dearest (Rus).

"Rounding up 3.5 million convicts in ninety days will be a push."

"*Da*," replied Basil, still locked in daydream.

"What about Pantelleria?"

Basil remained mute.

"General?" Palachnin prodded — "General?'

Basil snapped back to the here and now.

"Yes, Ogrom. Pantelleria. NATO has confirmed that Russia has lawfully entered into a perpetual lease with the 'Restoration Government of Italy' for the island of Pantelleria. I'll be dispatching convicts from the Military Counter-Defense Tribunal here in Bari to start construction on 'Camp Carter,' a proper naval base, similar to Y-Doodle's in Cuba and the Pommie's[1] at Gibraltar."

"And is it now agreed that the northern occupation limit is latitude forty-four degrees with a ten kilometer demilitarized zone?"

"Yes. Skirmishing should end. I'll be heading to Florence to consolid—"

Basil stopped speaking. The apparition, which had overwhelmed him in the car on the last night he and Natalia shared together, wafted over him. In dreams, he had sensed flashes. Now, the implacable haunt returned. There was more — *Something about northern Italy. Something yet to happen. The second urn? No, not that.* He strained to summon the premonition into being, but Palachnin's voice intruded — "Basil? General Novimirov?" Palachnin rapped the desk.

Basil blushed momentarily and resumed.

"Ogrom, yes. My job is to consolidate our gains. Your priority is convicts. Remember to keep an eye out for breeders. Also, your forces need to wrap up operations in the south, especially at Reggio di Calabria. We don't need wops fleeing to Sicily and out of reach. And, as a show of good faith, we're ordered to remove all fuel depots around St Peter's Basilica. Your turf again."

"Good. I'll get a decommissioning squad on it today. And, ..."

While Marshal Palachnin spoke his piece, Basil opened a bottle of Stolichnaya, righted two inverted shot glasses used as paperweights, filled them with vodka and handed the Supreme Kommander his libation.

"Ogrom, to the motherland's triumph over woppery."

Two glasses clinked, were upended over unshaven faces and their contents emptied. Next, Palachnin refilled them and did the honours.

"Basil. A toast to the eight in ten Doods who acknowledged Russia's right to counter-defend against woppery."

"And, the wisdom of not going nuclear," added Basil.

"And, convicting 3.5 million wops for espionage," Palachnin pressed.

"And, world peace." Basil rejoined.

"And, our world's beautiful 'Princess of Peace.'" Palachnin finished.

Basil's eyes twinkled noticeably in the moment that followed before two glasses clinked, were upended, and their contents drained to empty. Aware Basil was coming into side-bet money, Palachnin was itching to know.

"What made you so sure the Amerikans and NATO would acquiesce so soon and in the enlightened way they did?"

1 British citizen (Slang).

"During President Zeltsin's administration, I used to represent the 'Highway' faction in our modeling of Amerika's two-party shit fight. Like President Bushkin, who once represented the 'My Way' faction, I have a deep dispassionate insight about the real Yankee-Doodle, not the crap Washington and the Jewnited States media dish out to the Y-D proletariat for their happy-meal consumption. A centerist, subscribing to the superpower doctrine of 'Fair-play Balanced with Hypokrizy,' Weissbrot is All-American beef balanced between buns of bullshit."

Palachnin laughed. Basil snickered and resumed.

"President Bushkin and I wrote many of the talking points in Weissbrot's address to his proles. The pragmatist in him doesn't want his nation prostrated by politics which hands out favours to an elite at the expense of the majority."

"It's fabulous," Palachnin remarked, "how President Bushkin maintains strong international relations with talented world leaders. But, elitism? It seems to run counter to what the Doodles proclaim in public as their ideal."

Basil chuckled at how the Walt-Disney-effect of Amerika's propaganda mill had left its mark on a gullible old Soviet like Palachnin. Basil put down his shot glass — "Ogrom, you must stop thinking like a *Mishka-Mish*.[1] In Amerika, Yankee-Doodle doesn't ride his cronies, rather cronies ride Y-D. In this age of woppery, the city-slicker mortgaged lifestyle amounts to sabotage no different than tobacco smoking. Are those smokers and city-slickers paying extra taxes or set-asides to support their self-destructive lifestyle? No. Have Y-D's 'Royal Monetarchy'[2] paid FDIC insurance or engaged in real commerce as opposed to leveraged price speculation with commodities essential to humans like oil and real estate? No. As any informed Dood would say, they suck trillions from the Y-D proletariat through the taxation mechanism of the Amerikan government to feather-bed their amp-up-prices speculation."

Palachnin gushed — "Perfect! Less boodle for the Doods to throw into their stinking military machine. Gotta love those Royal Monetarchists."

Basil restrained a laugh and shook his head.

"Not really. Royal Monetarism gives woppery annihilative leverage. Y-Doodle's Pentagon calls it 'Asymmetric Warfare.' Woppery need only target the 'Royal Monetarchy,' and in turn they will suck dry Amerika's serfs. Consider the health-care subject Weissbrot raised. Ideally, Amerika should have a system affordable to all citizens with health loving lifestyles. The reality is vampirism. An elite 5% of Doodles suck dry half of all medical infrastructure. Not to mention that 3% of beers, the malt variety, account for 50% of that country's emergency room interventions. And the same goes for their banks. 3% scoff down 50% of the paper money printed."

Basil beamed like a father on realizing how this old Soviet-era war-horse was getting hands-on experience about how the 'Barbie-World' model of credit capitalism compared to the Raggedy-Ann model of cash capitalism. For an elitist in 'Barbie-World,' power could be inflated and then concentrated into the hands of an aristocracy while in the other, power was dispersed amongst those

1 Mickey Mouse (Rus).
2 The Royal Monetarchy is a nobility of large consortium Western banks. The Monetarchy consider the stage play called 'Economics,' something they own and can write or rewrite as they please.

who actually produced real hands-on wealth. The psychosis of money was the classic divide between the elite and the egalitarian.

"I think that eight in ten Y-Ds are slowly seeing the long-term prognosis. If 5% of Amerikans destabilized and consumed 50% of the resources, what would any rational citizen call these elitist zombies?"

Palachnin answered — "Zio-Nazi saboteurs."

Basil nodded — "Nazis aren't shown the firing squad as in Stalin's day. In the Jewnited States, they are pandered to with trillions looted from Y-D proles under the ruse of averting so-called Katastrophic Krisis. But, just like asbestos fucks the Deutscher Bank in Manhattan, Dioxinomics fucks their whole playbook."

"Asbestos. Dioxinomics ... What?"

Basil realized how it had come out confused. "Ogrom, dioxin, asbestos, heroin — it's one and the same — *Pollution fucks all assets*. Consider 'The Heroin Holocaust.' It's not confined to Russia, nor merely the financing of the dioxin pollution of our Metro. It's been polluting the whole world with death for years. The CIA use heroin to poison Iran, much like they did with cocaine in Amerika using Manuel Noriega of Panama, before they stabbed him in the back. Superpower 'Fair-play Balanced with Hypokrizy' is how the Doodles control their puppets. Fourteen years later, Noriega still rots in an Amerikan prison. And, Potusson? He's hammering golf balls around the links of Dallas."

Palachnin vented his own opinion of Potusson.

"As part of 'Operation WOPPERY,' we need to render that *svinya-pizda*[1] Potusson and stuff his balls down his pie-hole until he chokes."

Basil smirked. Certain scuttlebutt was not to be repeated.

"Komrade, let's not get distracted. Amerika isn't Iran or Panama. Despite its high standard of health care, each year, heroin kills 5.4 in every 100,000 Y-Ds. That's over 15,000 Doods per year. So you can imagine the death rate in countries, such as Iran, with third world health care environments. As for the so-called drug company panacea — methadone. The so-called cure is merely less deadly. You don't die in one day. You remain a social parasite, year after year. Finally, you die. With heroin proper, you die sooner. Either way, the life of an addict is foreshortened, during which he's a social deadweight."

Palachnin scowled. But, Basil ploughed on.

"And, do Amerikans and Europeans admit to the truth of 'The Heroin Holocaust' they have created? Oh, no. No damn way. All they ever yap on about is how Ragheads hate Israel, Iran is a global threat and all the other Zionist agenda cluck-a-Doodling. Why do you think Al Jazeera, an Arab version of England's BBC, cannot get a license to broadcast in the Jewnited States?"

"The Zio-Nazis, of course."

Basil slammed his shot glass on the desk — "Exactly. Al Jazeera doesn't strut Y-D's Zio-Nazi cock-a-Doodle goose step. Consider a classic example — the asbestos dust generated and breathed in by thousands in the hours after the collapse of the World Trade Center. Potusson ordered the EPA to quash any leak of this reality.[2] Website reports were China'd in hours, scientists got 're-assigned'

---

1 Pig's cunt (Rus).
2 See multiple US Inspector General and Congressional Hearings on the coverup of asbestos poisoning.

and EPA equipment was turned away. Ever since Al Guido's dioxin attack in New York made woppery NBC *Today Show* reality, Y-Ds everywhere are waking up to how real-life toxic dust doesn't vanish into nowhere like sarin gas and how their dinosaur cities are nothing more than gas chambers waiting to be filled with 'jihadi' dusts. The best locations are those with heavy foot traffic — subway systems, shopping malls, stadiums or office spaces polluted with cheap and easy to create toxins like dioxin or asbestos dust. You breathe — you die. Be it one week or one decade, you die. And, toxic dust is cheap — dirt cheap."

"Cheap? How cheap?"

Basil froze, pondered and resumed.

"Ogrom, let's not go there. Trust me, it's so cheap and so easy, you'll piss your boots. Focus on the big picture. Dioxin is just another manifestation of the program US-NATO use to terrorize the world with starvation enforced slave-made heroin and then 'Blame it on Kabul' as a so-called Noriega-style '*mea non culpa*'[1] exit strategy. A laughable pretense made possible because superpower hypocrites own the big, fat, scary A-Bomb — TV's Doomsday weapon."

The military man in Palachnin stifled a laugh.

"Call me a 'Soviet-Silovik', but even I know Dioxinomics makes nukes a joke."

And, Basil followed through.

"Just as Dioxinomics makes a joke of all that overpriced city real estate. Like a tobacco farmer saying his acres are more valuable than a wheat farmer's. Or a poppy farmer in Drughistan saying his acres are more valuable than an acre in Moscow or New York. The science of Dioxinomics states that one acre of land is worth no more than the cost to pollute it. Nukes make cities expensive. Dioxin, the complete opposite. And, as for amassing pollutants, it's easier than robbing a bank. For example, asbestos insulates all the steam and hot water piping around all our cities. Remove the sheet-metal cladding and you have as much asbestos as you can cart off. Insecticides are readily bought or stolen in bulk. Ask any wheat, tobacco or poppy farmer. Even a brainless twit can pulverize asbestos or even fiberglass and mix it with an organic toxin and surreptitiously pollute an enclosed, densely populated area. Unlike explosives, pollutants never fizzle. Nor does pollutant deployment require some crazy suicidal mentality. If city-slickers breathe in only a fraction of the dust, be it one time or multiple times, within days or weeks they will chart a new future — irreversible demise filled with chronic disability. Dioxinomic Bzombies."

Without thinking it over, Palachnin responded on reflex.

"Obviously, we must ban all hazardous substances."

Basil chuckled tactfully.

"What about oil? My dear Marshal, forget about the Arab countries, Bushkin would have a fit if you're suggesting we seal off all Russia's oil wells. Would you have us put armed guards around them too? Not to mention all those PCB transformers on the electric grid?"

Palachnin flashed Basil a puzzled look.

"Ogrom, benzene constitutes between 3% to 6% of crude oil. And, bi-phenols another 0.5%. Every 100,000 tonne tanker load of crude oil carries into each

1 Not My Fault (Latin).

country a minimum of 3,000 tonnes of benzene or one million three kilogram urns of dioxin precursor if you prefer to think of it that way. Most benzene ends up in a variety of plastics. The most prevalent is polystyrene."

"You're telling me that packing peanuts are a source of dioxin?"

"Bear in mind that cleaving the benzene group from the polyethylene backbone is an additional step. The big joke is that dioxin is easier to cook-up than TNT, a nitrate of benzene.[1] Consider picric acid, trinitrophenol, TNT's sister explosive, extensively used in World War I. Instead of using nitric acid to make picric acid, rather chlorinate phenol to produce trichlorophenol[2] from which dioxin is readily derived as a diether, using a variant of the Ullman Ether Synthesis reaction.[3] Furthermore, a pollutant doesn't have to be pure or perfect. Amateur explosives often fizzle. The outcome? A scary zero but a big, fat zero, nonetheless. But, psychologically or physiologically, a pollutant never fizzles. *Never.* Not even amateur crap. Not even a bag of flour."

Basil froze. *Pollutant* — the word triggered a memory, but what. It was that voice hovering in taunt, as clear as a layer of tobacco in a smoke-filled saloon in the dead of winter. It presented itself, yet presented nothing of itself. It was beginning to needle Basil to the point of apoplectic distraction — *Was it the second urn? What was that damn message!*

Seeing anxiety in Basil's face, Palachnin leant forward.

"Basil, my friend, are you alright?"

Basil felt embarrassed.

"Excuse me, I was thinking of Nata … I mean Miss Bogomolski."

Palachnin smiled knowingly. Their romance was an open secret. In a voice as warm as a grandfather to a pining grandson, Palachnin made reply.

"You miss her already."

Basil grimaced to squint back an unwelcome heaviness in his eyes.

"Yes, Ogrom. The moment I stepped into the transport at Chkalovsky Aerodrome. You know we have the most extraordinary connection. This whole wop mess is a vast tragedy. Pollution — there's a more spiritual element to it. I just can't find the words."

And, Basil fell eerily silent. When it was clear to Palachnin that he needed to get his komrade's focus back on task, the elder Soviet's graveled voice sprang to life — "Basil, I guess your point about 'fizzle' is that woppery prefers to turn people into cot cases with amateur toxins rather than kill people with pharmaceutical ones? The goal — cripple not kill. A weapon of spastic as well as Dioxinomic devastation rather than merely destruction."

It worked.

"Definitely, Ogrom. Think about the word 'woppery.' Humans …"

And, the more Basil discussed the matter, the more Marshal Palachnin understood that everything Tim Delancy[4] had ever written about military

---

1 TNT - Tri-Nitro-Toluene, nitrated methyl-benzene. An explosive.
2 2,4,5 Trichlorophenol leads to 2,3,7,8 Tetrachloro-dibenzo-para-dioxin.
3 See first chapter, *The Chemical Synthesis of Pollutants*, in *Dioxinomics: The Myth of Superpower in the Age of Dioxin*. First Volume in the *Dioxinomics*® Series.
4 The Delancy Group, a billion dollar US defense company. Tom's domain is the creation of literature validating the appropriateness of the vast sums America spends on 'securing the planet.'

hegemony was a 'Captain A-Bomb' fantasy based on toy soldiering paradigms using fairytale war conventions. And, it became clear to the Supreme Kommander that the great invitation-only Western-era tradition of 'champagne and black-tie' warrior-style garden parties formally waged in the 'open arena battlefields' of third world countries by a few privileged nations with embedded TV coverage was coming to a close.

Dioxinomics made it so.

The October Revolution

It was the eighth minute of the eleventh hour of the twenty-fifth day of October. The door to Undead Chamber No. 2 shuddered open with a rusty, submarine-hatchway squeal. Russian Vice-President Chainikov wasted no time stepping across the threshold. He ordered his guard to seal the door from the outside. Chainikov marched behind his guest, would-be-Tsar Sergio Romanov, and bent over his right shoulder. Before whispering into the man's ear, Chainikov placed his hand over his mouth to conceal the movement of his lips.

"Recognize my voice, wop?"

On camera, Romanov appeared to nod.

"We had a deal. Yet you brought that crap into the motherland and unleashed it on your own people, not our enemies."

On camera, Romanov shook his head. It was unmistakable.

"I guess you and your 'Project Glaudio' goons have watched too much wop television about war to annihilate Russia, the so-called Evil Empire?"

Romanov shook his head vehemently.

Chainikov gave a lengthy description of what the rest of the detainee's life was going to be like. Nothing audible — all in whisper. The man writhed in protest, his faced puffed red with a desire to cry out. Whatever was spoken, went on for a solid minute and a half. Chainikov checked his watch now and then. Suddenly, he stood at military attention. Movement was minimal. Like a father bonding with his young son, he stroked the Romanov's bald scalp periodically as if they stood together in a crowd on a windy day watching the parade through Red Square that celebrated the October Revolution.

This went on for three silent minutes before Chainikov unbuttoned his suit and rifled his hand through his trouser pocket. The fidgeting stopped. He took a stride to the right and brought a polished Tokarev TT-33 level with Romanov's temple. He barked a final farewell. A blast and the head jerked hard left. A right eyeball dangled from its socket. And, from a crater of puckered skin — blood and gore — drizzled raw and slow.

Brave New Peace Dividend

Given the weekend to size up his best moves for maintaining world peace and with Dioxinomic disturbances now becoming routine as woppery goose-stepped across the globe, President Bushkin decided to make Chainikov's actions public. Director-General Karl Besstrashnikov would handle the details. And, to this end, the president's ten-minute call was winding up.

"Yes, Karl. The Doodles must get raw video, raw audio, and a man from their embassy needs to take a DNA sample directly from the cadaver before we toss it to *Ol'Munchkin* at the Moscow Aquarium." He squelched a chuckle — "Next, item. I've green-lighted 'Operation Y-D Born.' Submarine incursion. 'Bethlehem' in northern Alaska. We'll kidnap a local doktor and priest for the day. They'll certify Bogomolski's child is a native born Amerikan. Start hammering out the details."

A light flashed red above the president's private-access elevator.

"Karl, another meeting beckons. Hear from you later. *Poka.*"

Bushkin sprang from his chair and opened his office door.

"Evgenia. Tea service, please."

His secretary passed him a sterling silver tray — coffee and a platter laden with Nigras shortbread. Two call-back notes lay wedged between the sugar bowl and cream decanter. One from the Prime Minister of Britain, regarding a dioxin attack on Wembley Stadium. The other from the Emperor of Japan requesting access to Miss Bogomolski for the treatment of heroin addicts.

"Thank you, Ev. No interruptions, except Alpha-One."

Bushkin guided the door closed with the outer-rim of his gloss-black, medallion-cap Santonis,[1] set the service on his desk bureau, hit the [ACCESS GRANTED] button, and welcomed Doctor Chernikrov into his office.

Bushkin gestured towards a chair to his left.

"Alexei, sit, please. Your coffee, black — right?"

"Yes, sir. *Chernie, pajalsta.*"[2]

"So proceed, doktor. No, hold on. First, Bin Laden. Has Miss Bogomolski been able to reverse or stabilize things?"

And, Bushkin tucked into preparing their refreshments.

"Sir, Doktor Mozhgovich is in a better position to explain, but the diagnosis is Bin Laden's brain has degenerated passed the point of no return."

"Are you sure it's not torture from sleep-deprivation or waterboard hypoxia?"

"MRI scans confirm spongiform encephalitis. Mad cow, sir. Whole regions in both his hemispheres are nothing but plaque-filled burls. Torture would only accelerate the damage. I doubt the CIA would want that."

"Unless they wanted to mask—" Bushkin stopped abruptly — "OK. Doktor, let's get down to the business of Miss Bogomolski's pregnancy."

"Sir, here's my written report. It's lengthy and technical, but I'll cover the gist in our Q&A. Later, you can—"

---

1 Courtesy of Italian P.M. Aurelio Calamari.
2 Black, please. (Rus).

Bushkin chipped in — "Remember, 'Eyes-Only.' To be clear. Director-General Besstrashnikov and everyone below him has no authority to know anything you and I know, or are about to discuss. It's you. It's me. *Ponyol*?"[1]

"*Absolutna*, sir. But, what about Basil and Natalia?"

"Did you clear up the ultra-sound discrepancy with Miss Bogomolski?"

"After a second ultrasound, she accepted my explanation about a faulty machine duplicating another patient's uterine video. Trust is restored."

"Good. Bogomolski carrying quads remains secret until I decide otherwise."

"Sir, until delivery we'll need to keep Major Gratski on call. I used her as the source of the single-fetus ultrasound switcheroo. My only choice at the time. Please ensure the Director-General keeps her in Moscow."

"Can't you issue a medical order of detention?"

"Already have. But, the Major is protesting to the Director-General."

"Ah. Consider it done, Doktor."

Bushkin passed Chernikrov his coffee and returned to his chair. He savoured one sip of coffee then asked — "The CVS[2] results. Is paternity still in debate?"

"The boy is Basil's, except for the additional pair of chromosomes. As you may know, all humans have 23 chromosome pairs, or specifically women do, and men have 22 pairs and a single X and a single Y-chromosome. Sir, all humans have 46 chromosomes. Only apes have 48."

"Just like the boy," and Bushkin glared at the doctor.

"Yes. Sir. Just like a gorilla — 48."

"So, why isn't this aneuploidy?"

"The boy has the usual 46 plus an additional homologous pair of alien chromosomes. A Y-chromosome assay confirms Basil is his father. The alien chromosome pair are being tested and genotyped as we speak."

Bushkin held the hot coffee directly under his nose.

"Assure me, doktor," he murmured while casting a fretful eye.

"Sir, there's been no error."

"World's stupidest question — No horns or cloven feet?"

Doctor Chernikrov laughed out of camaraderie.

"Don't blame you. No, sir."

"I see."

Bushkin took two sips while pondering the matter.

"And, the three girls?" he asked.

"Sir, all three are normal, except they're monoamniotic[3] triplets. DNA tests confirm two girls are identical twins. The third, a fraternal twin. But, here's the mystery. Basil is not the father of any of the girls. Just the boy."

Bushkin squeezed out a smile, but the look was more one of moral discomfort — "Well, it seems like Miss Bogomolski was intimate with Mr. Mitchell. Let's just say they kissed and made up, and leave it at that."

"I, too, assumed the obvious. But, tests, say *nyet*."

Bushkin furrowed his brows.

---

1 *Ponyol* - Understood. *Absolutna* - Absolutely (Rus)
2 Corionic Villus Sampling. Extracting and testing genetic material from inside the womb.
3 Triplets sharing a single amniotic sack.

"Obviously these girls have … Hold on, do they have the same father?"

"Excuse me. Yes. A common father, sir."

Bushkin rocked back in his chair and exhaled in dismay — "A slut pregnant from a sperm cocktail. That's abnormal but not unnatural. This definitely stays secret, doktor. After General Novimirov's divorce from his wife Galina, he went into a deep depression. I had him training Veronikas[1] to rejuvenate his spirits. I won't have him devastated by a woman he's devoted to who's little better than—"

Doctor Chernikrov interjected — "Sir! Natalia Bogomolski's no slut."

"Science says otherwise." Bushkin softened his tone — "Doktor, it's personal. Basil is one of my closest and dearest friends. And, our world's descent into Satanic chaos requires our nation to crown a hero, and moreover a heroine. A woman cut from a Vatican endorsed prophecy is what Russia has in Bogomolski. A Living Saint to Children, everywhere. And, I won't short-change our nation, the whole Christian world, or God Almighty based merely on med-science jibber-jabber about sperm cocktails and sluts run amok."

Bushkin picked up a Nigras Ladyfinger and waved it.

"Bogomolski's a Russian Orthodox Virgin Mary — end of story."

"So the father—" Chernikrov began.

Bushkin hammered back.

"Doktor! Unless you can confirm it's Jesus of Nazareth or Dan Brown, the identity of the three girls' father is academic. So, no more digging. As for Basil and Miss Bogomolski, they can never know any of this."

"So aborting the girls—"

Bushkin chopped in.

"Absolutely not. Unless I decide the boy dies, nothing puts him at risk. After caesarean delivery under anesthetic, the girls will disappear into decent homes."

Chernikrov felt greatly unburdened — "Understood, sir. But, I'd like to run tests for special genetic abilities on all four. Is that off the table, too?"

"Proceed, as we discussed in our last meeting. Just take proper medical precautions. Since Miss Bogomolski has these powers, let's hope it's coded itself into the genetics of all four of these little angels. That's another reason to separate them. If the boy is God's peace dividend to mankind, as the Patriarch has been speculating in private, I don't want them living together as one big tempting target for the forces of Satan."

And, during the remaining hour, they discussed the medical contingencies for transporting a heavily pregant Bogomolski by submarine to Alaska in June of 2006. Next, they dissected her psychological condition, including her lapses into altered personality because Bushkin wished to aid the Patriarch, whose many global initiatives included seeking secular support for awarding Miss Bogomolski the Nobel Peace Prize. To the statesman in Bushkin, the 'Holy Trinity's Resurrection' into the world presented many scenarios for instituting a brave new-world-order with a brave new peace dividend for all mankind.

Especially, Russia — The New Jerusalem.

---

1 Russia's Amateur Spy Corps. In honor of Veronika Lewintsova, captured by 'Capitalist Pigs' in 1998.

In the Oval Office, Lester Coverdale made brisk reply.

"Mr. President, DNA confirms it was Sergio Romanov."

"And the audio and video?" Weissbrot asked icily.

"Clean duplicates. Not a trace of tampering. There was nothing to lip-read. Basically, five minutes of room noise before the audio at the end. Just '*Da svidaniya svinya*' — Good-bye pig. Then the shot to Romanov's head."

Weissbrot reclined into the folds of his chair, still as stone. Bushkin had been away from Moscow with this Bogomolski woman, the decontamination scientist he'd met at the Kremlin dinner and now flaunted in the Russian press as the 'Princess of Peace.' While Bushkin was reviewing his troops, Russia's so-called Living Saint had been healing heroin addicts in Russian-occupied Central Asia as well as many brought in by transports from Afghanistan and Iran.

How opportune that Chainikov, a Soviet-era die-hard, was the acting president at the time and had written himself a presidential pardon. Officially, the Russians maintained the execution was not authorized. But, that could be a ploy. To help dispel ill will, the Russians had sent CIA clean-cut digital audio and videotape replicas. Or so they claimed. And, how convenient it was that the mystery man, the so-called Grand Duke claimant to the Throne of the Tsar, and who had reputedly contacted the terrorist responsible for dumping the second urn of dioxin on the NBC *Today Show* set, was now a corpse.

Lester read his boss' mind.

"You're thinking *Mallory Wilson* — right?"

Weissbrot didn't know whether to laugh or cry. He blinked his eyes, tensed his lips, blinked again and merely nodded.

"We're doing our best, Norman. Russia's unified like never before. Rebuilding deep independent contacts remains a huge uphill battle. Assuming he's alive, it's clear our best informant, 'Squirrel,' sees his country in a whole new light. The Soviet-era is history. The 'Mallory Wilson Affair' has cashed out all the dividends from that period. I doubt we'll hear from 'Squirrel' again."

Weissbrot gazed plaintively at his Vice-President-nominate. No one, anywhere on Earth, was pretending that the Romanov legacy had come to a close. If Carter, his predecessor, had been a Negro president, within weeks of coming into office, the perversity of Afghanistan and its *Children-of-a-Lesser-Darkness* might well have ended amicably. And, perhaps, even resulted in a Nobel Peace Prize for a US president. *Dream-on Barbie-World*, he thought.

No sooner had Afghan opium plantations started burning then starving, rag-tag poppy-ninnies in their thousands clamored for food and liberation. Like heroin-whores in the West, many poppy-ninnies were strung out themselves. Outrage from all over the planet finally registered with the disbelieving citizens of America and Europe, at least those citizens not immersed in the drugo'sphere of glamor addictions imported from militarily-occupied, third-world countries.

Even his attempt to stem the tide of ill will had resulted in a storm of derision from right-wing pundits. Pure politics of pandering, screamed the hawks of not-my-kid, neo-con blue-blood rectitude: Appointing Ms. Amanda Lincoln, a great-great-great-grand daughter of Abraham Lincoln, as the US representative in Afghanistan with the United Nations Human Rights Commission's 'Project Emancipation.' What hokey internationalism was that, they taunted. In the twenty-first century, the word *slavery* had about as much meaning as the word *torture*, *bribery* or *Dioxinomics*. All of it — fictional hogwash.

Iranian addicts were worse than scum, they cried, because four hours after President Bushkin disclosed 'Operation WOPPERY' to the world, Iran joined the campaign and marched forty thousand infantry troops thirty kilometers inside Iran's thinly defended eastern border with Afghanistan to establish its own zero-slave, zero-opium liberation-zone. The saber rattling came to a head two weeks later when all the heroin in the supply chain had vanished. Squirming in withdrawal like skinned adders, Iranian addicts were ready to don bomb vests and cross into Iraq to end their suffering. So, Iran threatened to export refined uranium to generate funds for treating addicts. That was when Bushkin unveiled to the world the 'Princess of Peace,' the Living Saint of Children, Miss Natalia Bogomolski, and her addiction curing powers and offered the Iranians her aid.

But, in the Western press, hoots of scorn for Iran and Russia only grew louder. Pro-Nazi wonks even started promoting outright 'Heroin Holocaust' denial and obscurantism after the President of Iran denounced Crusaders for refusing to grow opium in the open on America's verdant fields of green. 'Captain A-Bomb' despised using American labor that paid American wages because the Zio-Nazis behind Satan's 'Heroin Holocaust' could reap piles of political and economic capital through the false-flag occupation of Muslim lands and the reinstitution of starvation enforced slavery.

Any sober Muslim need only open his eyes.

How is the Allah Psychosis any different from the Money Psychosis, Weissbrot thought. In a word — Dioxinomics. Only Allah remains standing. And worse, one feeds the other. To prepare his nation for the Dioxinomic future, Weissbrot activated the draft. He figured all Americans deserved sobriety and full employment.

Weissbrot stared down pensively at his desk blotter. He'd already laid to one side a shrill letter from the televangelist, Rob Paterson, atop a similarly shrill letter from Pope Benetoni III. Both men claimed that the Second Prophecy of Fatima about '*Russia spreading its evil over the world*' was still in the process of unfolding. While the Pope laid into Patriarch Mudretski's efforts to secure the Nobel Peace Prize for Russia's 'Princess of Peace,' Paterson invoked 'Satanic Deception.' Dismissing the Vatican's penchant for hagiolatry, he asserted the woman was in reality the 'Whore of Babylon,' as foretold in the Book of Revelation. And, 'Where there's whore, spawn will follow,' came his admonishment.

And, the Pope and Paterson weren't the only ones. Intelligence scuttlebutt held that, tiring of their 'Counter-Defense against Woppery' catch-cry, the Russians were retooling their national security and religious relations agenda to embrace a new millennium meme — 'War on Satan.' *What newsflash comes next*, he thought, *Russia claims their 'Living Saint' cures homosexuality. Oh, wouldn't Paterson, the Vatican and the LGBT mob go ape-shit about that.*

He looked aside for a moment at the waste paper bin. A gift from his dead wife when he'd made captain. It was adorned with a nautical chart of the world.

Rubbish bin, half-empty or half-full? he thought.

To distract himself from all the *what-ifs* the world was facing, including the mass rendition reports coming out of Italy, Weissbrot picked up his platinum-nibbed fountain pen and refocused on matters closer to home. Lying atop a scallop-cut, gilt-edged card inviting the president to lay the cornerstone of the future Liberty Plaza at the World Trade Center redevelopment site was a forlorn piece of White House stationary. Like the not-a-whisper news media, Weissbrot well knew how twenty-two US veterans committed suicide each day, 660 every month, over 8,000 per year — fifteen times greater than the civilian rate of suicide.

But, before him lay the specter of assassination.

He huffed upon the ink on the letter he'd signed. His condolences were addressed to Miranda in Tucson, Arizona — an elegant lady now widowed of her husband, General Fidel Noriega, an old buddy at CINCPAC during his rear-admiral days at Pearl Harbor. A solitary US military issue, Teflon-jacketed sniper's bullet drilled through his friend's head. It could be passed off as suicide, but he knew better. Noreiga wasn't the only target. Five days earlier, he had approved an expanded Secret Service detail for ex-President Potusson because intelligence satellite chatter picked up several nations were covertly gearing up to indict Potusson for drug and war crime offenses. Only now in the depth of his heart, coming as it did on the heels of his friend's murder, did Weissbrot begin wondering whether the leaders of the great powers of the world would ever claw back some modicum of civility.

'Operation Bushkin' seemed humanity's only hope at restoring moral-heartedness to a world besotted with settling scores.

Anarchy was on the ascent.

Superpower was a myth.

Dioxinomics made it so.

The Epic Continues — A New Beginning or a New Doom ?

The Family Novimirov®
Love is a Battlefield
and the

Dioxinomics® Series

www.ingramcontent.com/pod-product-compliance
Lightning Source LLC
Chambersburg PA
CBHW080821250626

47160CB00008B/2821